FORBIDDEN

13

FORBIDDEN LEGACY - BOOK ONE

Erin Richards

Midnight Muse
PUBLISHING

FORBIDDEN THIRTEEN
Erin Richards

Print ISBN: 978-1943800070
Digital ISBN: 978-1943800087

Cover Designer: Fiona Jayde Media
Editor: Kimberly Cannon

Books by Erin Richards

Psychic Justice Series
Chasing Shadows, Book 1
Twilight Rising, Book 2
Stealing Twilight, Book 3
Seducing Darkness, Book 4

Forbidden Legacy Series
Forbidden Thirteen, Book 1

Standalone Books
Wicked Paradise

Young Adult
Vigilante Nights
Dragonfly Nightmare
Bittersweet Wreckage

To Mom, my first fan of "THIRTEEN."
Your ten-year wait is over (at least it wasn't 13. LOL)!
Thanks for letting me "borrow" Cody & Cleo.

FORBIDDEN

13

ONE

It figures my natural bad luck and a blind date on Friday the 13th dumped me in the emergency room. I should've shied away from the creepy combination of cursed luck and locked myself in a closet. Lucky for me, I was okay. Unlucky for my date, Michael, he'd suffered an allergic reaction after eating Mexican cornbread. Talk about bonehead move. *I mean, hello, he has a corn allergy.* What part of Mexican *corn*bread had he missed in that little tip? To top that off, the inept artist had left his epinephrine shot at home. Zoe, my soon-to-be ex-best-friend, swore her cousin was available and smart. No wonder he was single. *No sense in pleading the fifth on smart.* Just another craptastic date on a merry-go-round of losers.

A guilty sigh pushed out of me as I stepped onto the elevator. I punched the fourteen button and the doors whooshed shut. The fact that Michael had ordered dinner number thirteen and the thirteen sombreros hanging from the ceiling had everything to do with him landing in the hospital. My stomach became a tight fist of unease.

Too many thirteens together equaled crapstorm in my life. Cursed at birth, I'd entered the world on Friday, January thirteen, at one thirteen in the afternoon. Or in military terms, thirteen thirteen. The bad luck number affected everything around me. I controlled some of it if I caught it in time, and fate took a spin on the rest.

Had Michael become an unwitting victim in my jinxed life or what? I certainly hadn't known he had a corn allergy until after his face nearly exploded. Honestly, I barely paid attention to what he was ordering while he ogled my chest and babbled on about how he'd love to paint me in the nude for an art class project. *As if.* Knowing it was Friday the 13th, I should've paid more attention once I'd counted the sombreros due to my insane need to count everything to avoid the number thirteen. Or my not-so-insane need to use my telekinesis to thwart the inevitable bad luck. Or I could've persuaded him to order dish number seven, but he was so freaking obnoxious, he'd left my brain practicing its freedom to terminate the date.

I sucked in my bottom lip. It was just too risky for others to be near me. I mistrusted my ability to control the bad luck side of my telekinesis, and I didn't know where my so-called freaky *gift* stemmed from. I wasn't sure if I had been born with telekinesis or if it'd developed over time. My abilities hadn't shown up until I'd turned seven years old.

Thank my lucky stars I'd never gotten caught. I mean, seriously, if the government honed in on my abilities, they'd lock me up like Hannibal Lecter, pink mask and all. For the most part, practicing any kind of extra-sensory perception and magic, whether innate or externally created, was illegal. People were scared of ESP abilities and magic, a deeply rooted fear from over three hundred years ago, when Earth was overrun with sorcerers and fairies who'd done the nasty and created a race of powerful fairy-sorcerers. Eventually, the governments eradicated them all and enacted permanent worldwide laws and heavy sanctions on magical use after the Abolishment. Yet, they never defined "extrasensory perception" as magic. That spooked me, so I lived way under the radar.

The elevator stopped on my floor, and I slipped between the doors before they opened all the way. I slid my card key into the security slot and pressed my thumb to the bio-reader. Automatic entry lights flickered on, lighting my way inside the dark condo on top of the Stargazer Casino, San Jose's newest residential-entertainment complex. The top floor of the residential tower was really the thirteenth floor, but marked fourteen. *Like people can't count.*

I kicked my pink pumps off and dumped my jacket on the antique chair in the foyer. My purse clunked on the marble console, the strap leaving tracks in a film of dust. I jiggled the potpourri bowl until a wimpy bouquet of cloves and cinnamon drifted to my nose. Housework hadn't risen to the top of my To-Do list yet.

"Here, kitty, kitty, kitty." I yanked my phone from my front pants pocket and hopped the two steps down to the living room. The floor-to-ceiling windows overlooked the glittery amber dots of downtown's lights. Winds had swept away the clouds, and a soothing star-blazing night greeted me, a far cry from the doom and gloom of my date.

"Cody, Cleo." My two Himalayans *always* skittered away from the havoc they wreaked the second they heard my voice. "Where are you?"

Creepy crawlies teased the nape of my neck. I slanted a glance down the two empty hallways. My right pinkie twitched. *Oh, hell.* If the crawlies advanced to a pinkie twitch, it was bad. Alarm dipped in and squeezed my heart.

Slipping my hand inside the small drawer of the end table, I gripped my stun gun. I tapped in casino security on my cell phone without punching the send button. The wall clock tick-tocking from the dining room eclipsed the sound of my uneven breathing in the quiet-as-a-church space. Not even a mouse stirred.

"Where are you ding-a-ling cats?" My voice trilled unnaturally. "You better not be leaving stinky presents in my new ficus."

Three halls broke off from the living room. The wide hall led to the foyer, and two narrower halls led left to the kitchen and right to the bedrooms. I tiptoed down the right hallway. The recessed lights automatically winked on. At the first door—the hall bathroom—a whiff of cheap Old Spice cologne assaulted me, reminding me of the casino blackjack dealer who marinated in it. My heart thudded in my ears, and I about hightailed it toward the front door. Gossamer threads of something foreign fluttered in my head. As a telekinetic, I sensed ESP, and I oddly absorbed the intangible energy of other beings through my aura, but never to the point where it invaded my mind. I'd never even sensed a telepath tickle my telekinetic sensors, and I sure as shit didn't think an intruder was reading my mind.

I gripped my focusizer, a pendant encompassing the number thirteen. It helped me delve into deep telekinesis and concentrate my energy. Something just clicked in my brain whenever the dang number was present in any way, shape or form. Focusing also allowed me to deflect bad luck...when I knew in advance I needed to deflect. The enameled leaves on the vine and rose lucky charm dug into the flesh of my fingers, comforting and scary at once.

When I crossed the threshold of the wide open bathroom door, the automatic light flashed on. Stun gun held outward, I shoved aside the purple shower curtain. Empty. My heart pounded against my ribs. No rest for the terrified, I still had a bedroom and an office to check. Hating to expose my back to the hallway, I spun to face the door. Where were my useless fraidy cats? I should've gotten the drooling Rottweiler who ate kitties for snacks.

A crash echoed in the office next door, followed by two twelve-pound thuds on the hardwood floor. I nearly stunned myself as the furballs slid down the slick hardwood in their headlong rush toward the living room.

Feathers wavered in and out of my telekinetic receptors. Puzzled, I concentrated on the foreign invasion, but my thoughts muddled. More gossamer wings flapped in the corners of my mind, working toward the middle to totally unhinge me. *What the freaking hell?*

My phone rang. Startled, I hurled it into the air and it clattered onto the hallway floor. Lunging out of the bathroom, I stooped to snag it. The second I cleared the doorway, strong hands gripped my upper arms from behind.

A banshee scream erupted up my throat. Kicking backward, my bare feet connected with steel beam thighs. I thrashed side-to-side, hoping to break his death grip as his hands slid down my arms. My heart drummed so hard I thought it would pop out of my ribcage. I lost my grip on the stun gun and it spun across the hardwood to kiss my phone.

"Hold steady," my attacker growled. He cinched both my wrists in long, lethal fingers.

Pain seared my shoulders as he yanked my arms behind my butt. He grabbed my short hair and snapped my neck back. Needles scored my scalp.

"Take whatever you want," I gasped out. His weird ESP hit my brain in a puzzling jumble, and my telekinetic brain waves floundered beneath it. It was as if he was sending commands from his head to mine. I didn't care for his terrifying mind commands, not one bit.

He chuckled, his skanky breath hot on my neck. "That's the plan."

The stench of male sweat and *very* Old Spice filtered into my nose. "Okay." I stalled to collect myself. "Lock me in the bathroom and do your thing."

Sausage fingers tightened around my wrists. My shoulder muscles burned. I muffled a gasp, refusing to dignify the attack with proof of my pain and terror.

"My *thing* is with you, Aria Walker." The brute released my hair. Coarse fingers grazed the nape of my neck before sliding beneath my blouse to grip my bare shoulder.

"What are you?" I had to know what caused the tangle inside my brain.

He chuckled arrogantly. "Never met a Scrambler?"

I sucked in my stomach. "Scrambler" was slang for a strong telepath who had the ability to jumble and temporarily kill psychic abilities. A powerful Scrambler could even permanently destroy a person's ESP, leaving behind a shell of emptiness. Some used to have the mental ability to coerce, but they hadn't existed in centuries. Anyone with an inkling of ESP knew what a Scrambler was. The last sorcerers to permanently eradicate magic from the world used Scramblers to do the government's dirty work.

No wonder I'd dropped my guard. The slimeball had messed with my head.

An arctic blast of shock iced my flesh. My innate electromagnetic energies swelled, steadying my growing terror. Energy surged, melting the ice, filling me with warm, heady power. My aura barriers vaulted in place to protect myself from the intense energy seething for liberation. A familiar, alluring darkness mushroomed inside my head. A flame ignited, a pinpoint of white-hot light, growing brighter, blazing hotter. I envisioned slipping into the Scrambler's mind, forcing my command upon him. *Sleep*, I willed fiercely, drawing upon the light, oozing my will and my brain waves into the heat. *Sleep, lights out, asshat.* My bioelectric energy field—my aura—surrounded us, raining a paralysis on the guy.

Spears of energy pierced my shroud, numbing my flesh where it made contact. Mutually increasing horror threw us off kilter against the bombe chest in the hall. *Holy crap.* I'd never felt my aura touch me in anger.

The dude's fingers dropped away. The sound of ripping cloth split the charged air as he thumped to the floor. Jagged silky edges tickled my bare arm as feeling quickly returned to me. Sidestepping the heaped intruder, I scooped up my stun gun and smartphone in trembling hands.

Goose bumps broke out along my bare arm. Regardless, I scouted out my condo to ensure no accomplices waited in the fringes. My defiled haven turned up empty and my shoulders sagged in relief. What did the guy want with me? Surely, my secret telekinesis was still *my* secret. The Scrambler hadn't had enough time to screw up my head. So what had caused my aura to expand to the point that I actually felt the normally intangible energy?

I tiptoed back to the hallway and scrutinized the body. The man's bald head, trim brown beard, and mustache didn't ring my familiar bells. Criminals were sure well-dressed, or he was wearing his charcoal, pin-stripe suit for a funeral. I hoped it wasn't for my funeral. "Not much of a Scrambler, are you?" I kicked his thigh. "Maybe you're a wannabe." Maybe I was a Scrambler. *Holy mother of illegal magic.*

The quaking in my hands fled across my entire body. Backing out of arm's length in case he awakened, I called casino security. City cops didn't show their faces on California casino property without an in-house security request first. New laws for an era of overpopulation and legalized stupidity. In a shaky voice, I informed the officer that I'd apprehended a burglar. The grumpy security man of the hour wasn't too jazzed to hear about a breach in their high-tech system, but assured me he'd dispatch a man stat.

Minutes later, the doorbell gonged. On wobbly legs, I managed to jog to the front door. A badge flashed through the peephole. I disarmed the alarm, opened the door. My breath left me in a rush. "You guys are quick."

I looked up and up into the handsome, arrogant face of a broad, muscular guy as he slipped his wallet into his jeans pocket. He appeared twenty-one, same age as me. Shoulder-length black hair framed sun-kissed skin that took poker face to a glacial extreme. Then he cracked.

Concern flashed across his somber expression, and his gaze drank me in before his gray-flecked, blue eyes flicked over me, assessing, discounting. The hair of his right eyebrow was a strange shade lighter than his left, emphasizing his disregard.

"R.L. Walker," he said as if I had a sticky note with the answer pasted on my brow. He hauled a gun out of a shoulder holster and shoved past me, nearly knocking me against the wall.

His aura tangled around mine in a way I'd never experienced. Harmless, it seemed to seek relief, leaving a tingly sensation over my exposed skin. I froze, held my breath.

The strange sensation dissipated as quickly as it hit. Maybe the Scrambler *had* screwed me up. "Geez, what'd I do, interrupt your snooze fest?" I scurried down the hall behind him.

"Stay here." Without waiting for an invite, his long legs hiked over the downed intruder as though stepping over a twelve-pound cat.

Speaking of which…my two felonious felines proceeded to sniff Old Spice. Arms crossed to keep myself from wilting into a puddle of terror, I waited in the living room. After he swept the entire condo, Security Goon barreled out of my bedroom. I checked out his snug jeans, black boots, black T-shirt, and black leather jacket. A cliché in the making? Did he wear black skivvies too? All the security guards wore plainclothes at the Stargazer, so his appearance wasn't unusual.

He fingered the Scrambler's neck pulse. "Did you call the cops?"

"No." I rolled my eyes. "Isn't that *your* job?" My cats dared to rub against Rent-a-Cop. I tried shooing the furry traitors away with gentle toe jabs, but they wouldn't spare me a morsel of their time. What was up with that? My cats hated the male species.

Suspicion erased his blank expression. "Who *did* you call?"

"You." I hugged my arms tighter to my chest. "Aren't you a casino watchdog?"

Straightening, his eyes bored into my face. "Did you call them?" He stuck his gun into his shoulder holster, a good sign he didn't plan to use me for target practice.

Bowing my head, I pooled my sketchy mental resources and knotted a knockout spell in slow motion—a fancy way of saying I'd spring an electric emanation on his mind that'd send him to Snoozeville. Why hadn't I examined his badge closer? I swallowed my renewed turmoil and glimpsed the stun gun where I'd dumped it on the chest across the hall, next to Fake Cop. Did I have enough mental energy left to protect myself?

My gaze flitted from his chest to his face. "Who are you?"

"He's dead. Call security off."

As my dwindling brain waves dissipated, my "knockout spell" unraveled as fast as it knitted together. I wagged my head, dispelling my mental sludge. "Not until you tell me who the hell you are and what you're doing here."

He tapped his foot on the floor. "Ronan Riley. I'm bagging your ass to keep it alive."

"Alive?" My eyelashes twitched up a breeze.

He snatched up my cell, stabbed redial, and handed it to me. "Call them off."

"Or what?" I tugged my torn blouse over my lacy pink bra.

Ronan pointed at the intruder. "Or you'll face murder charges, if you live long enough."

Those icy eyes pierced me, bright and beautiful against his winter tan. Energy rolled off him, and I shivered from a sensation of familiarity, almost like a connection. Heat flared low in my middle, startling me with confusing inappropriateness.

"Right. The sleazebag may be out cold—" I bent over the Scrambler. Ronan jerked my hand down and pressed my fingers to the man's lifeless pulse. The phone clicked on at the other end and I stuttered as my brain malfunctioned, "Aria Walker from P14. Ummm...false alarm on the burglar. Safe word, *Triskelion.* Just my boyfriend playing bonehead games." I waited for dismissal, then shoved the phone in my jeans pocket.

Through slit eyes, I studied Ronan's dark Viking build compared to my fair, petite stature. As night and day as women and men. Renewed warmth flushed my neck. I twisted my hands and scanned the unconscious intruder. Ronan's words registered. "He's only knocked out, right?" I whispered.

He landed his assessing glare on me. "Did you feel his pulse? You have no clue, do you? He's *dead.*"

"No. No." My knees buckled. I'd have kissed the floor if Ronan hadn't swept me into his arms.

He carried me into the living room, dumped me on the couch, and backed away as if I'd sprouted dragon wings and spewed fire. "Water?"

"No. Thanks." I stuck my head between my knees, fighting the nausea inching up from my stomach.

"Your first kill?" Ronan's deep voice penetrated my chaotic thoughts.

"First...kill?" I closed my eyes. I couldn't even kill an ant. Bug spray didn't count. How could I have done that? Was that what had happened? *Oh, God. No.* The room spun.

"I know who you are, R.L. Walker." Arrogant impatience layered his voice.

"Obviously not, since my name's Aria." I screwed a lid on my raging horror. I had to deal with the...situation. I had to deal with Ronan. Hoping the nausea stayed buried, I lifted my head.

No one ever called me R.L. except my... *Holy shit, Batman.* He'd called me that twice. I gaped at Ronan the barbarian. "How do you know me?"

He hunched down to my level. "I knew your father for a minute. He called you R.L., short for Aria Elle." Empathy spooled off him in waves.

I longed for someone to fix this mess, to tell me what to do. Instead, I focused on his words. He *knew* my father? That rat-bastard who'd split from my life when I was six? The man who vanished into thin air, leaving his family behind.

Ronan stood to his full height. "We'll talk about him...and other things later." His hard voice held no sympathy. "Right now, we need to haul ass."

Numb, I rose from the couch. He cupped my elbow, steadied me. His touch baffling and uncomfortable, I cast him off and clutched my throat. "What did you mean by first kill?"

"I caused my first bad luck kill when I was fourteen. On a Friday the thirteenth."

TWO

Another telekinetic plagued by bad luck? I twisted around to face Ronan. His grim face halted my inquisition. Small disappointment pricked my heart in learning I was no longer one of a kind, but a warm rush of excitement quickly eclipsed it. My earlier intuition at a connection between us was right on the money. Had a door opened in the life of my aimlessness? The door hidden from me as I searched for my true place? Everyone had died and/or left me too soon, leaving much unsaid and undone, enhancing my bumble into a world in which I never felt connected.

Over the last few years, I'd searched high and low for others like me, hoping I'd blunder upon hidden talents, since magic was illegal to practice. It's not like people walked around flaunting their abilities and risked arrest. My strange abilities weren't documented anywhere and spoon-bending, book-flying show-and-tell tricks were all I'd ever shown Zoe, my most trustworthy confidant. Although there hadn't been a forbidden magic death penalty case in decades, I certainly wasn't going to become a freak-frenzy for the media and law enforcement.

Fearing the unknown, the New Urban World government, known as NUW, established twenty odd years ago, continued the antiquated laws against magic. If anyone exhibited magical ability above a certain kindergarten level—gifting of gemstones for their positive energy properties and palm, tarot card, and crystal ball readings—they were put on the government's Paranormal Science Practitioners list, otherwise known as PSPs or just plain paranormals. It was like going on the terrorist watch or the FBI's most wanted lists. Once on the PSP list, you couldn't pop a squat without calling someone first. Big Brother at its finest.

Ronan and I regarded each other silently until he spun on his heels. "I'll dump the body." He snatched the Scrambler's gun, jammed the weapon into his coat pocket. "Pack a bag for several days."

"Excuse me." Slack-jawed again, I stared at his back. "Why?" I needed answers before I obeyed a stranger, connection or not, dead man notwithstanding.

Ronan ceased fumbling with the body and rose to look down on me from his towering height. "You've been outed, and you're wanted by...people who'll go to any extreme to bag your ass and lock you up forever." He thrummed his fingers against his thigh, nudged the dead psychic with a booted foot. "He works for them, and a shitload of bounty hunters aren't far behind."

My mind reeled as I wrapped it around this eye-opener. Who wanted a lucky charm maker, college art student so badly? Rubbing my ear, I gawked at Ronan. "Why me?"

"They know you have the powers of an ancient sorcerer."

I waved my hand in front of my face and uttered a short relieved laugh. "I'm not...no one—" My heart plummeted toward my stomach. "What're you talking about? Sorcerers died off with the dinosaurs."

He scrubbed his hand over his face, giving me a look eager to melt skin. "Can you manipulate mind, matter, and other kinds of energy? Are you affected by strange things, bad luck, good luck?"

Face growing hot, I plucked at a loose thread on my new fashionista blouse. "How did *you* know?"

"Your father ratted you out to my fucking father," Ronan spat out. "We're both wanted." He grabbed my bare arm in a vise grip. "Now shift your ass in gear." He propelled me in the direction of my bedroom, giving a final prod on my lower back. "Pack or not. Either way, you're coming with me."

"Bastard," I muttered. My *ass* still in park, I turned. "Why the hell would my father tell lies about me? He doesn't know anything about me. You're freaking delusional." I snorted. "Why're you here and why're we both wanted? And who elected *you* puppet-master?" Hands on my hips, I glowered at him so hard my face practically pinched into place.

"Look, we don't have time for this. I'll explain it later. I won't hurt you, but if *they* snag you, you're screwed. You'll wish you were dead. The man they work for will do a helluva lot worse than kill you." He kicked at the downed intruder. His impenetrable facemask descended again. "Move it or I'll drag you out."

Apprehension gnawed at my usual confidence. Under the strain of an emotional kaleidoscope, I trudged toward my bedroom, snagging my stun gun off the bombe chest. I knew what being outed meant. Stranger or not, Ronan was right. I had to run. I couldn't risk getting caught by the authorities, or anyone for that matter.

I stopped in my bedroom doorway, faced him. He watched me, his brooding face easier to read than earlier. "Where are we going?"

"Safe house near Los Gatos."

The ritzy, high-rent town bordering San Jose sat along the nearby foothills, close enough to escape into the familiar if I needed to. "Safe for whom? You or me?"

"Both."

"You'll tell me everything?" My stubby fingers latched on to the door molding, needing to touch something normal. He nodded. "What about…how did…do you know what I did to him?" I waved a shaky hand at the Scrambler.

"Take two minutes to pack a few things. We'll talk later." He returned to hiding the dead man as if he taught body snatching for fun.

Thoughtful, I zoomed into flight mode.

My father had gone Benedict Arnold on me in the worst way, and I wasn't going to take it sitting on my rear, losing my freedom, or my life.

I secured the alarm behind me. Ronan carried my two overstuffed bags of jumbled clothes and whatnot. I left out bowls of water and dry cat food—enough for two weeks if the furballs didn't stuff themselves the first day and kick off from bloat—and both litter boxes filled for Cody and Cleo.

Ronan hadn't divulged what he'd done with the Scrambler's body. Honestly, I preferred to remain clueless about that aspect of my night from hell. I wasn't sure how to deal with my first accidental kill, so I buried it, knowing it would haunt me forever.

His voice butted into my thoughts. "Where's your car?" We stepped onto the elevator and he jabbed the first level casino button.

I studied the earthtone granite tiles. The reek of pot-laced cigarette smoke lingered, and I scrunched my nose to avoid inhaling it. "Where's *your* car?" The elevator dove to the first floor casino level.

He sneered. "I'm driving on a run-flat."

My head snapped up. "That was *you*? You were tailing me earlier?" I'd sensed someone following me from the hospital after making sure dipshit Michael was okay. At least until we passed Thirteenth Street and he'd popped a tire.

That perpetual scowl froze on Ronan's face. His sour lemon features didn't detract from his rugged handsomeness. He appeared menacing, a bar bouncer you'd evade at first until you got a tip-off at what lay underneath. Right now, frustration with a hint of fear played along the chiseled planes of his tan face.

The elevator dinged, the doors slid open, and I walked through the opening, staring at the slate tile floor. I pointed toward the door at the opposite end of the hallway. "My car's in the resident garage."

"We're not taking your car. Too obvious."

"I thought—"

"Try not to think. It's not working for you right now."

Slowing, I gave his backside a dirty look. "Screw you, Ronan Riley." I wavered at the first row of dollar slots. He kept on walking with a silent, lethal grace that had part of me dying to give chase. His nice firm ass was so worth it.

Rainbow lights sprayed the casino. Spinning wheels, videos, and bells created a symphony of noise. I spun out of Ronan's sight, jogged to my favorite machine. As usual, the thirteen-thirteen machine was unoccupied. I squeezed between two older women with identical brunette dye-jobs wearing polyester pantsuits differing from blue to purple floral working the flanking slots. Ugh, I hoped that wasn't me in thirty years. I didn't do floral well.

I dug a Player's card out of my rear pocket and stuck it into the card slot. The fifty-credit balance registered. Anonymous and transferable cash-in-a-card after an automatic flat-rate tax hit on any winnings. Usually I waved my smartphone at the machine, but I didn't want this transaction traceable. As I punched the triple play button, Ronan grabbed my wrist, dwarfing half my lower arm in his hand.

"What are you doing?" He mashed his teeth.

Red, white, and blue sevens stopped on my machine's winning line. The woman to the right squealed. Digital bells clanged. Lights above the bank of dollar slots blinked in rapid succession, glints of red bouncing off the chrome and plastics.

"Lookie, sweetheart, I won!" I said in my best Southern belle twang. I eased my wrist from his grasp, jumped up and down, clapping.

Ronan's mouth gaped like a hungry tax man. "You just won twenty grand."

The two women gushed over the jackpot I'd risked my luck to win. Seriously, it was the biggest jackpot I'd ever won. I merely expected to win a thousand credits for emergencies. I never let myself win larger jackpots. I did maintain some morals and personal rules when manipulating my telekinesis.

Ronan plucked the card out of the machine and stuck it in my back pocket. His fingers lingered a few seconds too long before he whisked his hand away. I couldn't halt the bizarre desire trickling into my veins. *Add to To-Do list: therapy.*

"Time to go, babe," he drawled, matching my phony accent. He leaned down and whispered, "Move it" nastily in my ear, grabbed my hand and hefted my bags over his shoulder.

His long-legged stride forced me to skip to keep pace. "Slow down! I didn't drink my EnerRizer this morning." I knew I'd regret not replacing my supply of rise and shine instant energy in a bottle.

"Shut. It." Ronan's stride revved up as we traversed the midnight Friday casino crowd.

I dropped my voice to a whisper. "Hey, cut the 'tude. I can't go on the run without cash. How much cash do you have shoved up your ass for this jaunt to Insanity?"

We flew by the entrance to the Licensed Escort wing designated by a swish of ruby lips across an ebony door. Wildly popular, Licensed Escorts were NUW's legalized slant on prostitution. I tended to avoid that part of the entertainment complex. Ronan did a double take, slowing, his head spinning like the *Exorcist* girl.

"What's wrong?" My right pinkie spasmed. "What the what?" I muttered under my breath. Couldn't I skid through the night without more bad luck dumped on me?

"We've been tagged by another bounty hunter." Ronan released my hand and slipped on a pair of black leather gloves he'd snared from a mysterious pocket in his jacket's interior. "If you have gloves, put them on."

"Hell. Lo. It's *California*." I narrowed my eyes at his worn gloves. "You came prepared for a crime spree? Are you a prophet or just a kidnapper?"

Ronan shouldered me behind a jungle of fake trees and bushes toward a tropical paradise. "Can you get us out of here?"

"What? You're asking me to *think*?" Sarcasm dripped venom from my tongue. "I thought you knew what you were doing."

I had much to learn from Ronan, and it pained me to admit that I was growing to like him. *Don't ask my love-struck eyes.* His aura gave off an energy that frolicked nicely with mine. Normally, when I absorbed energy, it was barely perceptible, rarely identifiable. Even though it enhanced my aura, I'd never *felt* other people's auras. Mine was always too dominant. His aura I definitely felt, warm and prickly at once. Fear also prevented me from trying anything stupid on him. I might be blonde with three-quarters of an art degree, but I wasn't dumb.

"*You* know the casino." He glowered at me.

I peered through the fake jungle and spotted *the* man. "Slim guy, navy suit recalled by the '50s? Dirty blond? Just came out of the escort wing." Rubbing his bulging crotch. I screwed up my face.

Ronan grunted something akin to a yes. He hovered behind me, peering through the fake branches I'd spread to form a peephole. "Is there an exit behind the waterfall?"

"Probably, but—" I paused. We'd end up on the frontline of a chase. "Lure him closer. Let's knock him out." I watched the bounty hunter in an aisle of electronic bingo machines. He spun in a slow circle, scanning the thinning casino crowd.

"Like you did to the guy upstairs?"

"Yes." I almost missed the incredulous scorn lacing Ronan's voice. The impact of his words smacked me upside the head. "I didn't mean to kill him." I blanched, forcing the memory aside. Dropping the fern branches, I pivoted on my heels. Ronan stepped back, probably afraid I'd whack him too. "I meant *knock* him out."

"Won't work." Ronan investigated the granite boulders bordering a garden of soaring pampas grass, dense enough to hide in for days. The phony sea breeze fluttered a palm frond at my head. I smacked at it, snagged my foot on a silken vine, knocking down a red parrot. It thumped on Ronan's foot and he booted the bird toward the wafting pampas grass, where it landed with a loud thwack.

I gave him a tight-lipped smile. "Why won't it work? I can control it." In dismay, I peered at the upside down bird.

Ronan stepped behind the waterfall. Crouching, I inched toward him into a utility room off a corridor leading to the rear of the building.

"I'm doing it," I said, hands on my hips.

He scrutinized my face, but I masked it, stealing a cue from him.

"Two telekinetic sorcerers negate one another when together."

I rolled my eyes. "I think not. Didn't I just win twenty grand? Way I see it, if you really are a sorcerer, you didn't negate me. You probably boosted my energy." Okay, I exaggerated since I wasn't absorbing his energy at all even though I felt his aura, but the idea seemed plausible in this new universe of the weird.

Ronan groaned, indecision painting his face as if he struggled with bad information about this negation thing. Suddenly the air wavered around him, streaming into a thin opalescent rope. The rope shot toward the parrot, and the bird rose a foot off the floor, then plopped back down. "You negate me." His eyes had gone dark. "I tried to shoot the bird into the waterfall."

"I'm special, aren't I?" A smirk might have been overkill so he received my beauty contestant smile.

"Yeah, something like that." Ronan curled his arm around my waist, plastering me to his side. His hard body pressed against mine, and I shivered with that puzzling familiar awareness.

I inhaled his exotic spice on leather, filled my lungs with the intoxicating cologne. His aura stirred around mine, creating a cocoon effect. My heart pulsed in the most bewildering way I'd ever experienced. *Cripes, I don't need my hormones to rampage.* "Umm...dude...what're you doing?"

"He's nearing," he said, his mouth close to my ear. "Pretend we're hooking up."

My aura swelled and panic smashed my warm tinglies into smithereens.

"Calm it, Aria." Ronan's arm tightened on my waist. The heat of his chest pressed into my cheek. "You'll off him if negation doesn't affect you. It's probably why you killed the other guy, if you absorb energy to boost your own." His breath wafted my hair against my temple. "Give me your stun gun."

All I'd experienced in the last hour scared the bejeezus out of me. More than anything, I wanted freedom to discover who and what I was without mercenaries tailing

me.

Ronan began patting me down. He brushed the sides of my breasts, my nipples stiffened, jutting through my thin cotton T-shirt.

"Did you earn a cop badge in the last two minutes?" Face flushed, I pulled the gun out of my jacket pocket before he caused further harm to my rebellious hormonal system.

He snatched it and released me. "Stand behind me."

"You have a plan?" I scooted behind him.

His body obscured my view of everything except his back, broad shoulders, and amazing firm and round ass. "Go along with me." Ronan hid the weapon in his coat pocket.

Faux foliage shifted, rustled. Leisure Suit Larry had breached our hideout. My heart thudded against my chest.

I heard a nasally voice. "What's up, kid?"

"Murph," Ronan greeted, an edge of iron to his tone.

"You found her." Murph rubbed his hands together.

"I'm taking her back." Ronan shifted from one foot to the other, his spine arrow straight.

Say what? Aural energy escaped me, cracked heads with Ronan's energy. Tangled telekinetic energy pulsed around us, smacking of electrical wires twisting in a windstorm.

"Come on, man," Murph whined. "You don't need the five mil bounty."

My mouth mimicked a flycatcher. I quickly smacked it shut. Who'd have ever thunk lowly telekinetic Aria Elle Walker was worth five million dollars? Dead or alive?

Murph took two steps closer. Stale smoke clung to his clothes. My nose crinkled, and I longed to bury my face in Ronan's back, but I fought the urge to touch the potential traitor, kidnapper, and hormone charmer.

"Stand down, Murph." Ronan pulled his hand from his pocket and eased it toward his hidden shoulder holster.

"She's my take."

"Let's split the dough. No one'd be the wiser."

Would I have to knock them both out? "Hey, Murph?" I called from behind Ronan. "Guess what?"

"Shut it, bitch," Ronan warned.

I gnashed my mouth. He better be acting, or else I'd give his ass the smackdown to Australia. I needed a few more minutes to absorb energy from around me to recharge my brain waves. Not sure what Ronan was up to, I wanted my own escape route. "Murph? How bad do you want the bounty?" I scooted to the left, remaining halfway shielded behind Ronan.

Murph halted in the doorway of the utility room. The tinkling waterfall's splashes drowned our voices in the casino beyond. Grinning, he stroked his chin, displaying a gappy set of tobacco-stained teeth. A weapon hung loosely in his other hand. "Darlin', if you only knew. Now you gonna come with me willingly?"

The heat of his gaze felt like slimy hands on my boobs. I angled my head, eyeing him critically. "Do I look stupid?"

"Dial it down." Ronan stepped in front of me again. I moved along with him, my sight glued on Murph.

The unmistakable cocking of a gun hammer clicked. The gun engulfed in Murph's hand moved into position, aimed at Ronan's head. A muffled shot exploded in the air. It was barely long enough.

Relying upon my focusizer, I invoked my telekinesis, sending out an electrical vibration. Breathing in deeply, I focused on the path of the bullet. It zoomed above our heads, so close the hairs rose on the top of my scalp. A ceiling tile popped behind me after I deflected the bullet's course. My aura lashed out and connected with the energy Murph emitted. He slumped to his knees, arms dangling at his sides. A wet stain darkened the front of his pants as his bladder released.

In one swift movement, Ronan aimed and shot Murph

point-blank between the eyes. Even with a silencer, the shot boomed in my ears. Blood oozed out the center of Murph's forehead, dripped down his hawk nose.

The heavy thump of his body on the glossy, red cement floor obscured the hiss of tropical white noise and the screaming in my head. My legs became seaweed, dumping me on the floor near Murph. I stretched forward and yakked my quesadilla dinner into a bucket in the corner. My stomach heaved until I expelled the entire ghastly night.

"Stay hidden." Ronan shoved my stun gun in my curled hand.

The barbarian of Hidden Bodies 'R' Us went to town without sparing me a second thought. By the time my clarity resurfaced, he'd stashed Murph's body in the fake fauna and kneeled beside me.

"Leave me alone," I said, voice hoarse and throat scratchy. I tried to invoke my power again, but it sank into a teaspoon of acid in my aching stomach. The energy I'd expended that night had shut down the intangible doors to my ESP. A tingle of electricity fluttered my hair. I just wanted to go upstairs, drag myself into bed with my kitties, and sleep the nightmare off. A blasted tear slipped down my cheek and that pissed me off the most. I slapped at the offensive droplet, smacking sense into myself. Before I could stop him, Ronan picked me up and hoisted me over his shoulder as if I were another sack of dead bones he needed to hide.

"Put me down!" The diminishing splashes of the waterfall drenched my croaky voice as he tramped down the hall toward the rear of the casino. My travel bags, slung over his other shoulder, banged against my skull. Using the last of my strength, I bolstered my arm to muscle the bags from hitting my already rattled head. His shoulder dug into my empty stomach, and my gut ached with every step. "Come on! I can walk."

"If I drop you, will you turn it off?"

"If you ask me nicely, I'll zip it, turncoat."

"Please?" he asked with considerable trouble. "We don't have time to screw around and you're going to draw attention."

Blood coagulated in my head, fogged my fried brain. I hated being upside down staring at the shiny, red floor. "I'll behave." That word hurt to say.

Double steel doors barred us. Ronan wrested me off his shoulder, his hands encircling my waist as he set me on my feet. Surprisingly, he straightened my skewed jacket, and then stripped off his gloves to work the security lock on the service door. Well, one second of gentlemanliness didn't make up for a night of murder, mayhem, and mystifying magic.

I fished mints out of my purse. Blood drained from my head, easing my encroaching headache. I contemplated my next move. Stun and run? Go along with him? I studied a crack zigzagging the length of the cement hallway. The red river zigged to Murph and zagged to the sane, safe life destroyed in one measly hour.

I couldn't go back. If Ronan told the truth, there'd be more Murphs, and the cops would lock me up tighter than a nun's chastity belt. With a decisive squint, I watched the silent hulk's hand enclose the electronic lock. He exhaled a couple of times and the lock clicked. The security light flashed green, and he shoved the door open wide.

"How'd you do that if I negate you?" I accused wanly.

Sweat glistened on his pasty forehead. "Cheap lock. I managed."

So there was a way around the negation, or he lied. I probed his features for any clue I could steal. Shallow lines of pain around his eyes aged his face, my only clue. I trudged past him out the door. We found ourselves by the delivery docks. Not a soul in sight, not even a bat. Chilly air flowed around me, dispelling the bloody stench from my nostrils.

Ronan motioned for me to follow him to a crevice between two loading docks. Shadowy lights illuminated the deserted area. Even in the dim lighting, I saw the pained tolerance on his face. "Get it out."

I blinked rapidly. "Get what out?"

"Your rant."

I braced my weary body against the exterior wall. What could I say? Murdering people squarely shoved me outside my element, even if the victims included skeevy bounty hunters. "Thanks, I guess." My stun gun grew arctic against my palm.

"Aria. Murph was a hired enforcer with a mile long rap sheet. He would've taken a few days with you...before collecting his bounty." His jet lashes swept down, up. "Five million. Do you get it now?"

Revulsion rolled through my middle as his innuendo sank deep. I clutched my jacket tight around me and said the only thing I could think to say, "You don't want the money?" My teeth chattered.

He grasped my upper arms. "It's not about the money."

I jerked out of his hold. "Then why do you care about me? Why do you want me?"

His fists clenched at his sides. "I need your help to take down my father."

THREE

As much as I wanted to believe otherwise, I didn't exactly live a ho-hum life, especially due to my father's desertion at age six and my mother's death at thirteen. *Yeah, unlucky thirteen strikes again.* My grandmother raised me afterwards until she died after a bizarre topple off a ladder last fall. A few other traumas I'd rather pretend were fiction, and all involving the number thirteen.

I'd always known I possessed paranormal talents that defied description. Now people wanted me for them. One part of me wanted to knit a red carpet with my toes for the recognition and potentially finding my true purpose in life, something to kill the emptiness inside me. The chicken part of me didn't want the exploitation—or to die for it. Dying just didn't appeal to me. Ronan appeared to have information I wanted and needed. I refused to ignore that. Obviously, it wasn't safe to stay at home, and as much as I hated to admit it, I needed his help to get out in one piece. And he'd let me keep my stun gun.

Ronan and I left the shadows skirting the casino complex. My feet dragged and I was thankful he carried my bags.

"Where's tenant parking?" He slowed his long-legged stride.

My heart galloped from the exertion of keeping pace. "I thought you didn't want to take my car?"

"We're not." Ronan plucked a small tool kit out of his pocket.

"We're stealing a car?" I sucked in air. "I don't steal—" Ronan placed his palm over my mouth and my heart plummeted into my stomach. I bit him and his skin tasted salty...and chocolaty.

He yanked his hand away. "You little—"

I forced winter's fury into my glower, prodded his hard chest with my fist. Forget the evil eye. "Don't ever put your hand over my mouth." I punctuated each word with a finger jab to his shoulder. "Got it?"

His mouth hung open and he rubbed my reddening bite marks.

Shaking like a mad leaf in a gale, I spun on my heels and marched toward the parking garage. I wiped his taste off my mouth with the back of my hand as I approached the black-as-death Mustang I'd bought with Granny's life insurance money. Mom loved Mustangs and had driven one at my age. She was with me whenever I drove the hot rod. But I didn't trust Ronan with it. Maybe *borrowing* a car wasn't such a bad idea. *Oh, sweet hell's minions, get your pitchforks ready.* I'd have a lot to atone for if I ever made it home alive.

Ronan's booted footsteps pounded a few paces behind me. Before I knew it, he'd picked the lock on the driver's door to an older dusty Cadillac. The sport model was parked in the thirteenth spot from the end. *Wonderful.*

"I have another vehicle waiting," said Ronan the barbarian. "We just need to clear out of the area."

Aggravated heat warmed my chilled cheeks, and I whirled to face him. "No fingerprints."

He slipped on his black gloves. "That's why I brought gloves." A hint of a smile curved into a devastating grin. His smile set off the slate specks in his eyes, sparkling from the fluorescent bulbs directly over his head.

What prompted that irresistible grin? My pulse raced circles around my hormones.

"We cool?" he asked as I neared the passenger side of the car.

"As a cucumber." *Rolling in the desert.*

I used the bottom of my jacket to open the door. Careful not to touch anything, I slid into the passenger seat. Leather bolsters wrapped around me, the leather cracked and rough. Rose-scented perfume lingered in the car, masking the scent of *eau de smelly ashtray and locker room carpet.* I banged my elbow on a half-empty water bottle in the cup holder, knocking it toward the driver's floorboard. As I made a grab for it, Ronan's hand tangled with mine. Electricity buzzed through his glove and I jerked back.

Wiped out beyond reason, I pressed the recline button, scratching the strange tingling away. The seat eased back softly and I wanted to snooze the night away. I'd placed my life in the hands of a total stranger, but resistance seemed as pointless as my date with Dipstick Michael. One hand resting on the stun gun at my waist, I huddled in my seat. If Ronan so much as looked at me cross-eyed, I'd find a way to jinx his luck.

Our swiped car jolted to a stop, flinging me out of a nightmare featuring the dead intruder chasing my cats on *Survivor* island, immunity up for grabs. I bolted upright, practically braining myself on the roof. Aural energy trickled from me and dissolved like tissue paper in a bonfire. I hadn't meant to fall asleep, which proved my telekinetic reserves had sunk to the level of ground squirrels. My brain ruled my body, and I needed time to recuperate, or there'd be a war of wills between my head and body. I wasn't quite sure who'd win.

Ronan strung his arm across the center console to brace me in the seat. "Sorry. Mutt ran in front of the car." He parked in the circular driveway of a secluded mansion nestled within a shadowy forest of Douglas firs, oaks, and redwoods. Little starlight penetrated the canopy of towering trees. The headlights and a single porch bulb illuminated the fir strewn, pea gravel driveway. *Did the butler forget to buy lightbulbs?*

A black lab puppy trotted into the headlight beams, tail wagging sixty miles a minute. I did a double-take, my eyes narrowing as I inspected the dog. Strange psychic energy flashed into my center of power, stemming from the dog. I sensed an old soul inhabiting the pup's body. Exhaustion bogged my mind, and I shook off the weird sensations. Dogs weren't my thing, or I would own a salivating Rottweiler.

I tightened my grip on my stun gun. "I thought we were switching cars. Where are we?"

Ronan killed the engine and shifted to face me. "Adam's place in the foothills. He'll return the car, grab our other ride."

Anxiety circled my chest. "Who's Adam? Is he like us? Do you trust him?" A fiery focus of energy coiled in the pit of my empty stomach. "Whose puppy is that? He friendly?"

Ronan stretched out a hand, thought better of it when my eyes prepared to launch fireworks. "When you bit me earlier...did someone try to shut you up?"

"What's it to you? I ask a lot of questions, so call your lawyer." *Ronan Riley, meet Aria's tangent.* "Why do you think you can forcibly shut me up without any consequences?"

My last question stopped the words about to trip from

his open cavern mouth. He closed it, a veil descending over his expression.

He tapped the dash. He must've been a drummer in a past life, or even in this life. Heck, I knew nothing about him. Gaze fixated on the shadowed house, Ronan ceased his finger solo. "There's a lot you need to know. You're gonna need to trust me. If you can't..." His wide shoulders rose and fell, the leather seat squeaking in protest.

My defiance melted in the wake of my fatigue and curiosity. I suffered his words grudgingly. "I'm listening."

He scratched his jaw. "If I were you, I don't know why I'd trust me. I understand why you didn't come willingly." He rasped his hand over his stubbly cheek, appeared to battle with a desire to extend a gesture. "You're just like your father described—feisty, stubborn, cute as hell."

"Cute is a six-year-old bouncing in the driveway on Friday the thirteenth, waving to Daddy as he drove off to get cookie dough ice cream." I crossed my arms over my stomach, cramming down the angry grief I despised.

A dense silence enveloped us until Ronan whispered, "I'm sorry, Aria."

"He lied to me. Deserted me and my mother, left us destitute, broke my freaking heart." My tears had dried up for my father long ago, and I'd only cried twice since the day he'd left. At that moment, divulging the deepest dregs of my life, I almost ended the drought.

I ground my back teeth. *No!* I refused to surrender so easily. Not after learning of his betrayal. Fury wiped the sorrow from my heart so painfully my breath hitched. I pressed my fingers to my mouth. The timing of our conversation sucked. I wanted to be two hundred percent lucid when Ronan gave me the goods on my father, and why a five-million-dollar bounty hung over my Goldielocks. And how did my father know about my telekinesis?

I touched the back of his hand. "If you hurt, betray, or lie to me, I'll hex you six feet under." I hadn't figured out how to hex someone, but I was working on it. Of course, I only had to wait for my *unluck* to handle it for me.

"I figured that was the lay of the land." He massaged the spot I touched as if he wanted to buy the slightest bit of contact he could afford. "I had no clue I was rescuing a killer." His lips ruffled up at the corners.

My bitterness skated out on my laugh. "Yesterday, I couldn't kill a pesky fly. Look at me now. One dude in the hospital, a dead man or two. What's next? Am I a secret killing machine? Thirteen curses and I'm dead?"

Ronan dipped his head. "If you only knew," he murmured clear enough for me to catch his drift.

I swallowed the egg-sized lump in my throat, cracked open the door. "Is the dog friendly?"

"Yes." He unfolded his large, sinewy body from the front seat. Gravel crunched loudly beneath his boots in the still night.

Easing into the pitch-black night, I gingerly planted my boots on the ground. Unafraid of dogs, I just didn't want to step in any little presents that might stink up my shoes. The tail-whipping lab loped over to me and waited on its haunches. It seemed too well behaved for a puppy. Threads of energy wafted off the pup and skimmed through my aura like slivers of cool, luminous moonlight. The dog's energy flitted around me similar to an unshielded psychic. It was cozy, exploratory, a light sifting of the hair on my arms, my special brand of psychic sensitivity. I'd only experienced that sensation from a human. Unease slipped over me as if I hovered in the stargate to the Twilight Zone.

"Let her sniff your hand," a male voice crackled from the porch. "She won't hurt you."

Silhouetted in the doorway, within the shadows of the porch light, stood another tall hunk. The mysterious Adam, I presumed. The puppy swung its tail, swishing pine needles on the ground. My sight adjusted to the dark and I reached toward the black pup. Cats were my specialty, but the puppy was adorable. Both guys watched me as though I had an initiation to pass. Love*ly*.

The puppy stretched its neck, sniffed my hand, its nose cold and wet. Goose bumps fled across my arms as my aura crashed into another band of energy. I patted the dog on its soft head, my fingers tingling against its silky fur. Kneeling on a bed of dry leaves, I looped my arms around the pup's neck. She smelled of firs and spring meadows. The lab licked my cheek, its tongue sloppy wet. A freeze swept through purgatory as cat lover Aria bonded with a dog.

"Hi, baby." It wriggled in ecstasy. I kissed her nose and stood up. The pup gave a croaky bark.

The guy looming in the doorway moved toward us into the shelter of darkness from the surrounding forest. "Her name's Infinity. Fin for short."

His low, melodious voice drove chills down my spine that quickly warmed and flooded me with... Heaven forbid, I squirmed. Suffice it to say, his voice skimmed my bare skin, simulating a lover's hands, vibrating in parts of me that had no right to vibrate to a voice.

Even with a baseball cap low over his brow, I saw his eyes glow like an animal's at the end of a flashlight. The violet orbs mesmerized me, and the glow bathed me in the unimaginable. Heat dripped into parts of me that had suffered a cold front for a long season. My mind challenged my body's response to him, tried to dampen my smitten hormones. I'd never burned for another in such a sexual manner. Invasive and welcome, the sensations both excited and frightened me.

I managed to close off my mind to his coercion and conquered whatever mesmerism he nailed me with. His violet eyes changed from emerald to teal to azure before the glow petered out. The stranger didn't possess an evil or harmful nature from what I sensed. He touched my arm but I withdrew a step, bumping into Ronan. I hoped Ronan would jump in if his friend meant to harm me. Of course, he could've led me into a trap as I skipped along on a suicide mission. One thing for sure, Adam possessed a strange breed of ESP I was certain wasn't documented anywhere. I'd stumbled upon the motherlode of criminal activity that night.

Fin leaned against my leg, lending me comfort only an ally offered. And I needed all the allies my love could buy. "What's going on?" I finally asked. A breeze breathed across my shoulders, shifting the tips of my hair. Trees stirred in the wind, and papery dry needles showered us in more death. The air carried the scent of Christmas trees rounding the bend toward Easter lilies.

The pup sidled toward Adam, looked over its shoulder, and waited for me to follow.

"Let's go inside," Ronan said. "It's been a hellish night."

"I'll bet." Adam's voice crackled again, no longer sinking inside my soul, lacking the layers that first skimmed my flesh. He extended his hand, this time with no pretenses. "Adam Freshfields." His cultured voice and manner along with the McMansion fit the life of the privileged.

Wary, I hesitated to touch him. However, my inflamed body screamed at me to take more than his hand. To its indignation, I ignored my fickle body and allowed my faltering mind to shift the gears. His fragmented aura joined Ronan's aura still teasing mine.

Fin gave another one of her short affable yaps, which I took as approval. I'd have to sleep with one eye open if my cats ever found out I accepted affirmation from a dog.

I inhaled deeply and grasped Adam's hand. "Aria Elle Walker."

"I know." His tone held a smile the darkness hid.

He led me through the dark, his aura wrapped around mine, merging within it and Ronan's aura surrounding me. Since when could an aura meld with someone, let alone two people? I derived aural energy from other people, but I just absorbed it like oxygen. I never felt it because my aura always dominated. What was happening to me?

An owl hoot splintered the night's tranquility, and I tripped on the first porch step. The screech of a bird of prey grated across the back of my neck as Adam caught me against him. I wished I could fly off into the night and ease the horror crimping my intestines.

Ronan stopped in the doorway. "You've only touched the tip of the iceberg tonight."

Mechanically, my fingers tightened on Adam's hand. "I kinda figured that out all by my little self." My cheerful tone fell flat even to my ears.

Ronan nodded, pinched-lipped as ever. "Things will get worse."

"Before they get better?" *You're just full of ominous clichés, aren't you?* "I get it."

Adam squeezed my hand, released it. "What he's trying to tell you," he interjected, "is that my appearance may unnerve you."

"You've already mesmerized me with multihued glowing eyes." I tapped an index finger on my chin. "What's one more link on the chain of weird?"

A random thread of Adam's aura spilled outwards and dissolved on the brick porch, as if his aura was dying bit by bit. "Look at me, Aria. Here or in full light."

Brushing my shoulder against Ronan's chest, I forced him inside the woodland mansion. Fin raced to her bed beside a stone fireplace. A fire snapped and popped, spitting crimson and amber flames, its heat luring me closer. Adam voice-commanded the ceiling light to turn on, adding near daylight brilliance to the great room.

A triangular gouge in the polished hardwood floor drew my dread. Without squandering the last iota of endorphins this bizarre night had instilled in me, I faced Adam.

My gaze traveled his length, feet upwards. Loose khakis encased muscular thighs, slim hips, and a rumpled long sleeve dress shirt clung to an oddly familiar rippling abdomen and broad chest. Then I saw the skin of his hands. My smile died. A gray-violet cast tinted his skin. *Dude, the sun shines in California, even in winter. Rent a tan.*

The faint odor of fruitwood smoke irritated my nostrils and I tweaked my nose with a knuckle. I pressed my other hand against the hard knot forming in my stomach as my gaze honed in on his face.

He looked like Ronan's identical twin, after a dip in a pool of bleach. And so much more.

My fried eyes blurred. "I've had enough of today." Without waiting for an invite, I staggered toward a soft chenille couch in the center of the room.

FOUR

I awoke in a humongous bed, a heavy jewel-tone comforter knotted around me. Sunlight filtered through angled blind slats on one wall, which I gathered opened to a view of the woods and the muted creek gurgling and splashing nearby. I slanted a bleary glance at the clock. Already noon, I'd slept the morning away as if my problems didn't include extinct sorcerer twins and a psychic pooch. Oh, yeah, count the Scrambler's murder in my condo and Murph in his time-capsule suit. *Oh, God.* A groan slipped out and I rubbed my temples as the events of last night flooded my foggy brain.

After I'd crashed on the couch, Adam Freshfields guided me halfway-to-dead to the master bedroom, the only bedroom with a lock on the door. He'd chucked a couple of logs on the toasty fire in the bedroom and locked the door on his way out—not locking me in, but locking them out at my insistence.

Who was Adam Freshfields? Why did he look so like Ronan—if you looked past the corpse pallor—but have a different last name? Ronan had called Adam his *friend*, not brother.

Wary, I brushed my fingers over my stun gun under the pillow, glad it was still part of my arsenal. Shock shivered down to my toes as the realization sank in that I'd allowed myself to sleep in a house with two strangers. I slept deeply too, which begged me to believe my gut instincts that they had no nefarious plans to hurt me. Adam and Ronan's auras tangoed so sweetly with mine, as if we were three parts of a whole. I never sensed a threat. In fact, the warmth of their protection and want wafted over me. Not wanted because of my strange abilities, but desired as part of a threesome. "Yeah, did I just think threesome?" I muttered. I'd never experienced that rash of aural warmth from anyone, not even my beloved mother and grandmother.

Refreshed energy vibrated along the sleepy nerve endings in my brain. My telekinetic receptors were working overtime to connect to Ronan and Adam in that strange way I'd experienced last night.

The air outside the covers was frigid, the fire stone-cold ash. I stretched out my legs, plucking the covers to my chin. My clothes lay in a heap on an overstuffed armchair by the windows. My travel bags sat between closed double doors and a carved mahogany dresser that matched the nightstands and four-poster bed. Seascape paintings in settings from dawn's hazy light to star-spangled midnight's ink covered the taupe walls. All painted by the same artist—someone I'd love to bribe. My condo had yards of wall space desperately begging for splashes of color. I might be a digital art student at San Jose State University, but wall art wasn't exactly my specialty.

Rubbing my icicle arms, I worked the circulation from wrist to elbow, mentally preparing for the nightmare beyond the doors.

High-pitched yapping joined scratching paws on the

door, alerting me to Fin's presence. My head began to ache anew. Morbid thoughts of the dead men rose to the forefront of my mind. Focusing on Ronan, Adam, or Fin was far easier to process, even though they were all related, all a circuit on the same memory board. Fin whined and scratched again, forcing me to tackle the here and now.

Adam shushed her from behind the door. "Leave off, girl."

"It's okay." Stun gun wrapped in my fingers and teeth chattering, I shoved off the comforter and ran to unlock the door. Without breaking stride, I dashed back to the bed and snuggled under the covers. "She can come in."

"You don't know what you're asking," Adam said in that curious flat monotone. "She hogs the bed."

The dimple my body made in the gargantuan bed earned my head wobble. "Let 'er rip." I piled up the pillows and leaned against the headboard.

Fin scrambled on the hardwood, sliding to the rug at the foot of the bed, landing with all four legs skewed like a newborn foal learning to stand. She—I refused to call Fin *it*—passed me a dog's equivalent look of acute embarrassment. More human expressions than...well...Ronan flashed across the dog's mug. Taking stock of her dignity, the pup leapt onto the bed. Barely palpable now, Fin's weirdo energy felt more like an old comforting friend.

Adam remained in the doorway, and I hesitated to confront him either verbally or visually. You know what they say about *De Nile* being a river. With my mind buried in my surroundings, I pretended my life hadn't flipped topsy-turvy, nor did I reside in the home of the lighter half of twin sorcerers who impersonated a human-sized, wingless fairy. The quick glimpse I'd stolen of Adam after I'd arrived had tattooed itself on my brain. I had a credible hunch he wasn't dressed up for Halloween.

Fin's earthy energy raised the hairs on my arms into a

gentle sway. I'd never heard of psychic pets. Hell, with all the newfangled PSPs popping up, it wouldn't surprise me if all living beings on Earth had paranormal ability. No wonder the NUW government kept beefing up PSP law enforcement with their newly minted Paranormal Vice Division, PVD for short.

Fin snuggled against me, and I rubbed my cheek over her silky fur. Static waved her hair against my skin. "What's your story, little missy?"

Adam padded into the room, his weight sinking onto the edge of the bed. Scooting farther away, I feared looking at his face, scared to acknowledge my odd attraction to him. Afraid to confess I sensed a similar bond to Adam as I did to Ronan, despite the mesmerism stunt he'd pulled on me in the front yard. I scratched and rubbed my temple, trying to smooth out my confusion. As if they were two halves of a whole, I *felt* Ronan in Adam and vice versa. Worst of all, I feared the story, whether truthful or not, Adam and Ronan had yet to dump on me.

"Aria, look at me." Adam's low voice crept along my twitchy nerves.

My empty stomach clenched. Fin slobbered on my cheek, and I made a dodgeball play of slowly wiping my face on my shoulder.

Ronan sauntered in. "Room for one more?" he teased, a far cry from last night's barbarian attitude. The tension in the room fractured.

The moment of reckoning had sprung. What was a girl to do when two gorgeous men wanted to leap into bed with her? I couldn't be luckier sitting in a field of four-leaf clovers, not a number thirteen in sight.

Ronan set two steaming mugs of coffee on the accent table between the chairs. He opened the blinds and dappled sunlight brightened the room. His butt took up residence on one of the empty armchairs by the windows.

The scent of caffeine ambrosia drifted to me and my

stomach purred. How'd he know caramel mocha was my downfall? I hooked my stun gun on my thong for lack of a better hiding place. Still hedging, I flung off the covers. Fin lay splayed on the comforter, as if waiting for a bowl of popcorn and the main feature to start. I swung my legs over the edge, wintry air hitting my bare skin. "If you're trying to freeze me into an Otter Pop, you're doing a stellar job."

"Sorry," Adam replied, his voice devoid of emotion. "I need cool air."

Out of the corner of my eye, I watched him walk to the closet and pluck something off a hanger. I bucked up my resolve and jumped off the bed.

He froze, a gray sweatshirt dripping from his fingers. One second his skin glowed and his eyes shone brilliantly. Then it was if gray mist swallowed his vibrancy. That radiance had clued me in on his fae nature last night. No human ever gave off such innate, ethereal beauty. The fae had always fascinated me when I'd learned fairies and sorcerers were the last and strongest magical beings to roam Earth forever ago. Until now, it seemed.

I reached for the sweatshirt, my hand brushing against Adam's hand. My crackling aura mingled with his the way it tangled with Ronan's last night. Yet, he lacked something in his energy field, empty boxes that should be full. Parts of his body shimmered in and out of focus as if he fought with Satan to remain topside.

"Whoa," I exhaled the word, fought my hand from its hormone overload and touching his solid, but faint right arm. "You're disappearing."

"I'm still here," he said. "It's some bizarre cloaking spell I tried that won't stop trying to work."

I tugged on the sweatshirt. Warm and smelling of fabric softener, it hung to my knees. I rolled the sleeves up to my wrists. Slowly, I raised a hand toward Adam's face. "May I?" I didn't know what compelled me, but my hands had to feel what my eyes were witnessing.

"Sure." He smiled, shrugged.

Not a muscle budged as I stroked his cheek, traced the outline of his bones. His magical energy encouraged me to explore every inch of his muscular body. *Did I just think that?* Like I'd ever get the chance for a further arctic exploration. For now, I'd start with his face.

No hint of stubble marred his baby butt smooth chin. He had high cheekbones, a blade nose, and square jaw, mimicking Ronan's facial features. I traced my thumb over his dry full lips, the color of putty. My thumb dipped into the crevice to the left of his mouth that stretched to a dimple when he smiled. A dimple lacking on Ronan. His gray eyes were flat, the pupils a shade darker than the irises, fringed by translucent lashes. His eyebrows matched his hair, which changed from clear to lavender and gray to white. I couldn't tell if the color was changing or if all those colors tinted his hair.

His thick shoulder-length mane lacked sheen as if coated with powder, negatively setting off the wet-cement cast to his skin. If Adam weren't kicking it in front of me, I'd swear death had called. Yet, he was very much alive. Our mingled auras could testify to that in a court of law.

He smelled of pine and meadow, edging the scant scent of smoke from the room. Every time part of him wavered in and out of sight, the crisp and fresh scent strengthened. Beautiful to me in so many ways I couldn't explain, he was Ronan without the color of health and life.

I hugged my arms to my chest. His energy stroked my aura, leaving me in breathless confusion. Adam tucked an errant lock of hair behind his ear, and my gaze rested on his one ill-formed pointy ear. It looked as if Fin had nibbled on it at one time. His other ear was normal.

"I take it you're not a Vulcan?"

He smiled in a boyishly shy way, his dimple coaxing a spark of vibrancy to his features. "*Star Trek* fan?"

"More of a *Star Wars* fan." I had a gazillion questions.

Corralling my thoughts, I studied a moonlit seascape painting on the wall to his right. Completely non-confrontational, his magical energy—on him it could be called nothing less than magic—screamed for my attention.

Ronan watched as if waiting for us to jump each other and do the nasty in front of him like we were trying out for a porno flick. All we needed was popcorn, Milk Duds, and soda. I sensed no threat from Ronan either, even in the electricity that always seemed to bristle beneath his tanned skin. It was as if he also felt the strange aural bond and wanted to see where it tugged all three of us.

"What ESP do you have?" I sifted my fingers through kinks in my bedhead.

He patted down a lock of swaying hair floating toward me. "I've never had ESP...before this happened." He wanded his hand up and down in front of his delectable body. "Now...I'm not sure what abilities I have."

I tilted my head. "Mesmerism?"

He winked and his smile spread to a captivating grin in response to the coil of energy I accidentally released. I about dissolved into a puddle. I hunched into the sweatshirt, hiding my body's betrayal.

"Okay, so we're done with the show part of show and tell." I forced a glance over my shoulder at somber Ronan. "Let's get on with the telling part."

Adam's aura fell flat, knocking the air out of me. I staggered, my eyes threatening to shoot nails at his lack of finesse in dealing with our intertwined energies. His form solidified as if humanity won that particular battle, the war still up for grabs.

He gripped my shoulders, steadying me. "Sorry. You okay?"

I eased away with a conciliatory smile. "Warn a girl, will ya?" My aura recoiled, leaving me bereft, as if someone had stolen a cherished keepsake out of my hands and flung it into the fireplace.

Adam's throat bobbed. "I'm still learning...still getting used to—" He dug his hands in his front pants pockets, shot a glance at Ronan.

I pulled the sleeves of the sweatshirt over my freezing fingers. "What are you, twenty-one, two?" With a tween's lack of control over extreme energy. His and Ronan's auras, and mine for that matter, were beyond calculation if we could meld together. Fascination zoomed through me.

Ronan rose from his chair, a cup of coffee in one hand. "Twenty-one, same as me, you. We think he may also be descended from the fae," he paused for emphasis, "and immortal. He may have a long time to grow into his powers."

"Blood of one of the Forbidden," Adam said hesitantly, gauging my response.

My hand slinked southward to rest on my stun gun. Shit was getting real. Hazily, I recalled my paranormal history class from high school. The powers-that-be at the time of the Abolishment had called anyone with magic the Forbidden. The Forbidden included witches, fairies, and sorcerers. All magical races had been extinct for centuries. If Adam was fae, then Ronan probably was too. If Ronan and I had the same telekinesis, was I part fairy or just...what? A sorcerer? The hollowness inside me tingled as if my body was ready to accept my true self. Or was I overreaching into the land of delusion?

Laugher erupted, a crazed sound I tried to push down. I pinwheeled my arms wildly. "I'm being punked right? Where's the camera?" Hot anger bubbled up my chest, and my blood pressure shot to stroke zone.

Adam sank onto the bed, his sadness riding the air. He balled his ashen hands into fists on top of the comforter.

Time to schedule my brain surgery. My self-loathing became a palpable anchor in my aura. "Oh, God." I pressed my fingers on my eyelids. "I'm sorry."

"You've got nothing to be sorry about," Ronan replied

softly. "It's my fault Adam's the way he is." He handed me a cup of coffee, the warmth barely penetrating my icy fingers.

Adam laughed roughly. "He'd love to believe he's all that powerful."

I sipped the coffee, savoring the caramel on my tongue, rinsing away the acid of epic confusion. "You promised to tell me everything." I had to exert mental pressure to prevent my energy from leaking out to party with Ronan's aura. I usually didn't have to fight to keep tabs on the stuff. It was normally instinctive. Yet, I'd never experienced anyone who oozed energy like Ronan and Adam.

"Clean up and we'll eat." Ronan finger-combed his damp hair, triggering a waft of citrus shampoo.

"I'll warm the kitchen for you even if I have to strip to stand the heat." Adam rose, tugged his wavering hair over his pointy ear.

A hot and cold shiver raced up my back at the idea of a naked Adam. He shared Ronan's bodybuilder physique, but with skin tone that'd send the unwary into a mental freakout.

"Okay." My stomach rumbled in loud agreement, and I mentally slapped it to and fro for intruding in the conversation.

They left the room and I locked the door behind them. Fin hopped off the bed, her toenails clacking on the hardwood floor behind me. I spun around. "A little privacy, huh?" I stooped and ruffled the fur on her neck, her cow eyes going round and sorrowful.

"Okay," I said with fake exasperation. Dog voyeurism was the least of my problems. "Come in and keep to yourself."

The pup stretched out in front of the tub, stared at a tiny splotch of crystalized tree sap on the slate floor, her mug averted. Okay, maybe she did get human-speak.

I turned on the tub water, squirted in lavender bubble bath I found under the sink. Swishing the water around, I dug deep into the box in my mind labeled NUW History 101. Unfortunately, the Ancient History 101 box had gotten lost somewhere while my mind tried to comprehend my ridiculous reality. History had never been my favorite subject.

A sigh escaped me as I sank into hot, bubbly heaven in the sumptuous jetted tub. Heat turned my muscles into mush. I drew forth the boring history lesson to satisfy that niggling doubt. There was a reason why the world had originally abolished the Forbidden, and it'd cropped up again during the change to the NUW reign.

Twenty-two years ago, the world experienced a cluster of harmless earthquakes on every fault line known to man and then some. It took years for the geologists to yank their heads out of their respective butts and cough up some fib no one believed that a series of new ley lines—invisible lines of earth energies—had exploded from the tremblers. Supposedly, the "lines" spat out a ton of harmless energy, triggering latent ESP in people who hadn't otherwise exhibited paranormal abilities. More and more cases of psychic sightings kept the police and governments busier than a queen bee serving her horny swarm. Most other scientists didn't believe it and still searched for answers to this day.

Scientists and paranormal fanatics went berserk and had warned the governments what would happen if they didn't slap shackles on the newly minted PSPs. They'd reminded the governments that pre-Abolishment days would seem like cake compared to the magical threats to the enormous 21st century population. They'd demonstrated mock horror scenarios of what would happen if PSPs were given free rein to use their increasing abilities at the drop of fly spit. It scared PSPs into hiding, even when the government couldn't prove telepathy, telekinesis, or the like was Forbidden magic.

"Congratulations on the birth of the New Urban

World." I sighed as the history emptied out of my brain, leaving more questions than answers.

After what seemed like hours of pure pampering in the luxurious marble bathroom, I left it, refreshed and invigorated. I donned my favorite jeans with a hipster topping black and pink sweater. My stun gun accessorized a belt loop. Black riding boots topped off my ensemble of comfort. Maybe unicorns existed in this fantasyland and the boots might come in handy.

Fin and I stepped into a cozy reading loft overlooking the great room. I didn't even remember passing through it last night. Male voices rose up from the first floor beyond the swirly wrought iron railing. I trudged down the hardwood stairs. The thirteenth step emitted a squeak loud enough to awaken the rest of the Forbidden.

Ronan peeked around an arched doorway. "She's alive." The darker color of his left eyebrow lent him a natural mocking expression.

"Funny, ha fricking ha." A ghost of a smile passed my lips as I strode under the archway into the kitchen.

Adam waved his arm at the expansive table centered in the dining area. Afternoon sun streamed through the kitchen windows and set off a faint shimmer around him, transforming his skin tone to opalescent.

Burying my head deep, I pressed on my severely deprived stomach. Pancakes, sausage, toasted English muffins, and juice met my bulging stare. Adam might make a lucky lady very happy one day. I sat in the chair he pulled out. With a flourish, he set an empty plate in front of me and unfolded a cloth napkin on my lap.

French doors and floor-to-ceiling windows filled two dining room walls. Puppy nose prints smudged the bottom panes on the doors. The room overlooked a stunning redwood and conifer forest beyond a clearing of wintergreen bushes and a meandering creek. Maybe I'd get the chance to shoot pictures on my smartphone. I never knew what jewelry design a client might request. Flora and fauna were prominent in my enamel charms, the job that put food on my table while I finished college. I touched my handmade pendant, the small rose and the bigger rose growing out of a heart represented Mom and me.

Fin trotted into view along a bed of battered purple pansies bordering the circular driveway. She lifted her leg and oh so delicately watered them.

I heaped a bit of everything on my plate, smothering it with butter, jellies, and syrup. "Your dog's got serious gender issues." The smorgasbord beat the fruity protein smoothies I usually sucked down for my morning energy boost.

Adam chuckled. "Don't let her hear you say that."

A moment later, the swing of a doggy door creaked in the kitchen, and toenails clicked on the hardwood floors into the dining room. My new best friend sat on her haunches beside me.

As I grabbed the salt shaker, I accidentally rolled two sausage links onto the floor. Fin attacked them like a starved wolf in winter. I tested the holes in the shaker and the lid fell off, spilling a mound of salt on my palm. *Crap on toast.* I tossed a pinch over my left shoulder, hoping to ward off bad luck.

Adam handed me an empty plate to dump the salt on. "Sorry about that." Eyebrows fused into a V on the bridge of his nose, he examined the shaker.

Stifling a smile, I looked at my watch. Thirteen after the hour. Enough said. Slowly, I cut my pancake into bites, waiting for the guys to start eating. Call me paranoid about eating meals prepared by paranormals. As soon as I saw them shovel food into their mouths, I inhaled two sausages, and drowned it with orange-pineapple juice. I pointed my fork at Ronan.

He clanked his coffee mug on the wood tabletop. "Suppose you want answers."

Part of me did. The other part was halfway out the door. I studied Adam's ethereal features and knew in my heart that whatever set off the hunt for me was linked to his...issues. I grew clammy just thinking about an unknown future and the things Ronan knew about my father and me. It was bad enough my life seemed to revolve around Ronan and Adam. Our auras had converged the moment I entered the dining room and continued to play hide and seek around us.

The bond with Adam and Ronan reached into every crevice of my aura. It was one bond with two similar halves, not two bonds, which freaked me out. How could two people have an identical aura? Or maybe Ronan's aura overpowered Adam's and I only sensed the one. If they weren't twins, what were they? Cloning experiment gone haywire?

Thoughtful, I bit into a strawberry jam slathered English muffin and chewed. Swallowing roughly, I addressed Ronan, "Start at the beginning. How you knew my father. What he did and why. Who your father is and why you want to stop him. Why everyone is hunting me. Why you and I..." I skimmed Adam's face, tried to gauge his knowledge of secret clubhouse things.

"Why you and Ronan have weird telekinetic powers?" Adam wiped his mouth on a napkin.

The question lingered in the air for a moment. "Right. Are there more of us? Why does Adam look like a half-human fairy corpse?" I gave him an apologetic look. "Sorry, no offense."

He chuckled, short and grim. "Like I don't already know it."

Ronan and Adam exchanged a sly meaningful look. I hated being in the dark. Honestly, I wasn't a control freak or anything, but if something affected me, I needed to know about it.

"You want to know why the three of us are magically connected," Ronan added in a gloomy voice geared to plant the fear of Hades in me.

And magically delicious. I licked syrup off my bottom lip. "Damn straight." Spearing a sausage link on the serving plate, I left my fork sticking in the air.

Adam's back tensed against the chair, his hair spiraling around him like smoke tendrils. Ronan muttered, his tangible aura causing my hair to flutter and crackle as though I'd stuck my finger in a light socket. I leaned back, my arms folded across my chest for the reality show of fairy tales.

Ronan's fork clanked on his plate as he angled his chair to view me better. "Ever heard of a company called Dominion Research?" I shook my head. "My father's pride and joy." His nostrils flared in disgust.

Ronan's aura suddenly erupted, jealously driving Adam's energy off me. The tiny electrical zaps didn't hurt much, but they bothered the heck out of me. I clenched my focusizer. Using my telekinesis, I slugged Ronan's energy and coaxed Adam back into the ménage. I'd never done that before, but it worked. Relief coasted down my shoulders and relaxed the taut muscles in my arms.

Ronan wiped the nape of his neck. "What'd you do?"

"Your aura threatened." I shrugged. "I deflected."

Ronan looked bewildered. "No, I didn't."

My exasperation lashed out in a cool aural wave. "You projected stinging energy all around me."

Adam plucked a lock of hair off his eyebrow. "I felt it too. You shoved my aura away from Aria." His hand disappeared for a blink as it morphed into his swaying hair.

Ronan leaned forward, his jaw thrust out. "I don't feel Aria. I'm deliberately containing my spastic telekinetic energy. When she's near, I have a tougher time controlling what little ability I have left."

Obviously, you have no control. I pinned my sight on Adam. "You felt him, right? You feel me?"

Adam nodded, swatting at the lock of hair that swung over his eye again.

"I feel both of you, sort of." I clicked my frosty pink nails on the table, looked pointedly at Ronan. "Who can you feel?"

"No one." Sweat dotted his forehead. "I'm not projecting anything outward." He shoved his chair back and stood as stiff as the redwoods outside. Caustic electricity bristled off him.

Then I guess your power's slipping out your oh so fine ass. Suspicion flickered through my head. I channeled more energy to fight off his thorny aura, pulling the Aria Special off my belt loop. Nothing I did halted his intangible attack. It overpowered Adam's aura again. "Are you sensitive to other ESPs?" A bead of nervous perspiration trickled between my breasts.

"No, just a plain telekinetic, like you."

Proof is in the chocolate pudding. My agitation escalated as well as the heat up my neck. Thank my lucky charm I wasn't absorbing his creepy energy or Adam's tainted magic, for that matter, despite the bond we shared. Or was I and I just didn't feel it?

As Ronan's irritation swelled, it felt like he was dragging his feet in the desert, touching every inch of me.

FIVE

The hot prickles multiplied, causing me to sag in my chair. "Ronan, you're not holding anything back. I feel your energy attacking me." I scratched my neck and flicked on my stun gun. An idea bloomed. "Go outside for a sec." I pulled myself upright, dipped a napkin in my ice water, and patted my face.

Ronan scowled his way out the French doors. The farther he moved away, the more he lugged his irksome aural energy off me.

Cool relief trickled through my fiery body. "Better." I threw Adam a smug look. "You?"

A puzzled smile curved his lips, brightening his dull violet eyes. "It's just you and me, babe" he teased.

My heart hitched. The last thing I needed was an immortal, sick fairy-whatever in my life. *Can we say oxymoron?*

I waved Ronan back, and he entered the kitchen. Tingles swept up my neck and I scratched them away as more gave chase. "I don't get it. Your telekinesis didn't go psycho on me last night." I cut Ronan a sly look.

Adam went outside and nothing changed. I motioned for him to return. My pulse quickened in response to Ronan's intangible attack.

Ronan gestured toward the living room. "See if you can deal with me from there."

I nodded. "Adam can hang here." Adam's energy wasn't strong, but it hinted of happiness and luck, overshadowed by something that mimicked a layer of soot. His paranormal makeup was seriously flawed. I hoped it was reversible. I'd go bonkers if I lost my telekinesis, flawed or not, illegal or not.

Ronan paced in front of the picture window looking out onto the front yard where a large black SUV with ebony-tinted windows had replaced the Cadillac.

Ronan's barbs finally ebbed. Log one more item in my Book of Bizarre to muse upon later. "It feels better. What'd you do?"

Tolerance masked his confusion. "Nothing." He sat at the table again and pushed his breakfast plate aside. "Tell me if it gets bad again."

"Count on it." I tapped my fingernails on the tabletop. "You returned the Caddy to the casino?" I asked Adam as I hooked my stun gun on my belt loop.

"They'll never know it was missing."

I flicked a couple of crumbs off the polished wood table. Fin chased after them, toenails clacking, and she skid underneath the table. "Tell me how you know my father." Ronan earned my solemn stare. In order to concentrate on the rest of his tale, I needed to check my father off the list.

A prickle of Ronan's energy mixing with Adam's and mine tingled around me, but it appeared to be our new norm. Fortunately, my pinkie hadn't balked before Ronan's aura attacked me. The normal sensations I experienced before a bad luck occurrence were second nature, but the pinkie twitch *always* alerted me to danger...and also granted me time to turn it around by focusing on my telekinesis. With enough notice, I could raise my telekinesis to thwart unlucky thirteen's threats.

Adam began clearing the table, flatware clanging against pottery, making a racket only a male could make in the kitchen. Steam rose from water splashing in the sink, adding to the feverish sheen on his mottled face. Ronan crossed his arms over his broad chest, his biceps bulging. I licked my lips, squirmed in my chair. Damn, I loved muscular arms. His were double divine.

"Your father was Patrick Walker from Cork, Ireland?"

"Did you think I doubted you?"

He shrugged. "He and my father were college buds. They attended Dublin City University together."

"What's your father's name?"

"Richard Riley." Ronan's gaze pierced my face for a sign of recognition.

The name meant diddlysquat. I didn't know who my father had befriended in adulthood, let alone his youth. Another chain of missing clues of my real identity. "Go on." I stretched out my legs, crossing my ankles, the nonchalant act belying my inner turmoil.

"About all I know. I was hoping you knew more. I think they were doing research together. There's bad blood between them. I know that from the way your father threatened mine, hoping to score a big payoff and walk away."

Adam clattered pots and pans into the dishwasher, the noise echoing up to the twelve-foot ceiling. The air grew unsettled and Ronan's energy turned tickly. An awkward introspective hush reigned. Even Adam's movements quieted.

Light flickered in my brain and a truth dawned sunshine bright.

I snatched my legs back, straightening my spine against the chair. "So your father is after me because my rat snake father gave him a dose of his own medicine?"

"Not exactly." A growl rumbled in Ronan's throat. His booted foot hitting the hardwood floor resembled a clap of thunder, adding an ominous air to the story.

Adam returned to his seat, anticipation schooling his features. Our three auras tangoed wildly. My skin smarted, on guard from further attack.

I picked at the cuticles on my right index finger, a nasty habit I usually reserved for boredom or indecision. Guess that didn't apply any longer. "What then?"

Uncertainty squeezed that part of my heart my parents—even my father—still owned. I tried to look away, but Ronan's troubled eyes revealed an indecision that seemed to torment him, and I couldn't break contact for fear he'd disappear and I'd never know. "What?" I fought down the scream in my voice. *Just kill me now.*

"Your dad came crawling to my father last year, couple million in debt. He said my dad owed him."

My stomach contracted. I held up a hand to preempt the torture I sensed coming, but Ronan took sharing as caring to heart. I'd asked for it.

"Your father threatened to expose him, me, and my abilities to the authorities if my father didn't pay up. My father broke him down and Patrick gave him the info he wanted to find you. Your dad walked away with four million." His voice lowered. "Then my father had him killed. He thought Patrick too big a risk to his plans. He knew too much."

I wanted to cover my ears, but sat on my hands to prevent them from exercising their independence from my brain.

"The dead man in your condo pulled the trigger." He paused, as if waiting for a fencepost to speak. "And here you are."

Abandoned *and* betrayed? And I didn't even know why Dad had left us all those years ago. I dropped my head between my knees, battling sudden dizziness. Ronan thrust a glass of water at me, knocking it against my hand. I held the cool glass to my cheek.

"He's a screwed up bastard, Aria. He'll do anything to get what he wants."

"Your slimy father or mine?" I patted my eyes dry with a napkin, lifted my head.

"Mine."

Adam shot me a sympathetic look, but I didn't get all warm and fuzzy about offing the enforcer in my condo, even though he was collateral damage that probably deserved to die.

Ronan leaned forward and picked at a scab on his palm. "My father was livid. I don't know all the details of what happened between him and your dad. But that's when he cranked up his efforts to locate you, supposedly with the intel your dad dropped on him."

The remains of my heart splintered under the weight of too much knowledge. I threw up my hands. "What does your father want from me so badly that he'd pay my father a fortune, then bury him six feet under?" I asked the only question I might find an answer to from the dark and light twins in the room. "I'm a measly telekinetic. He didn't even know it!"

Adam contemplated the dishes stacked on the counter, tapping his fingers on the tabletop. "You aren't simply a telekinetic."

Welcome to Tongue-tied City. "Excuse me?" My disdain not only leaked into my words, it painted the sneer of all sneers on my face.

Ronan shrugged his hands. "People with extrasensory perception became stronger after the earthquake event twenty-two years ago. Kids born with ESP within a year of the quakes are the strongest according to my dad's extensive research. Not only can you and I manipulate mind, matter, and energy from our telekinetic ability, we're pulling energy from everyone, everything around us, which enhances our telekinesis and gives us this abnormal ability to manipulate *all* the energy from external sources, people, the earth, and not just from our own brain wave energy. Makes our abilities stronger." He paused and stared at my face as if waiting for the fencepost to burst into flames. "Like the ancient sorcerers. Like the Forbidden Thirteen." His voice lowered to a stage whisper. Fin nosed Ronan's arm, as if providing solace, and he gently pushed the dog away, rejecting her as if he didn't want to infect her with his delusions. "Although I think you can manipulate a lot more energy than me." He tipped his head, popped his neck joint. "Right now, I can barely bend a hair with or without you negating me."

Was he kidding? Could he really manipulate earth energy in addition to people energy? Could I? I thought I had only been harvesting aural energy from people. Did we really have the blood of ancient sorcerers? Surely, the sheriff of Cuckoo Town's on the hunt for him, right?

"What do you mean the Forbidden *Thirteen?*" A cold sweat slicked the nape of my neck. "Magic was eradicated. The Forbidden were banished. So what? I'm just a lousy telekinetic. If you tell anyone, I'm going to kill you. I won't go to jail for this shit you're spewing and loading the blame on me." Their silence told me otherwise. *Oh, wait.* "Your father's looking for anyone with magic to test to find your mystical Thirteen because he wants to freaking rule the world or something?" And if he tested me, I was doomed.

"Bingo. Give the lady a stuffed dog," Adam said. Fin snuffled and choked up a hairball, stared at it as if willing it to speak.

As Ronan's bright and shiny truth dawned, with increasing difficulty, I swallowed, my hands holding onto my stomach as if to keep Riley Senior away from me. "What the living hell on Earth does he need us for? What's he planning?"

"He needs *us* to properly open a gateway he found—the Rift—to the Realm of the Void to let the banished magic of the Forbidden return to Earth." Hunched over, Ronan rested his forearms on his thighs. "My dad thinks *you* and I together can open the Rift properly using our telekinesis to manipulate the energy keeping it closed. Once open, the Rift should function normally, the way it did way back when, allowing the banished magic to return to Earth. He wants to locate the descendants of the original Forbidden Thirteen, to control the returning magic...to control them."

A hiccupping laugh slipped out and I slapped a hand over my mouth. Forcing a few calming breaths, I still had to smother a giggle. The Realm of the Void was a plane of nothingness between Earth and the Afterlife, which most people didn't believe in. Those that believed in it thought it was a place that existed in space, accessible through a space "portal." Stargate, *anyone?* There were obscure references to it in old history books as being a plane of existence where ancient magic originally stemmed from...and was banished to. Again, most people just thought it all a big hoax and that the Forbidden simply died off.

Vaguely, I heard Ronan say, "She's speechless."

Adam replied, "At least she's not mad at you."

"She thinks we're cracked."

"Do you blame her?"

"Are you guys off your meds?" Eyes slivered, I glared at them. Fin propped her paws on my knee and planted a sloppy lick on my chin. "Forbidden Thirteen, Rifts, Realm of the Void, and fairies. What's next?" I grunted unladylike. "Zombies and vampires?"

"Demons too," Ronan added.

"Possibly. Who knows?" Adam's eyebrows quirked up, his hair shivering as he shrugged. "Doppelgängers?"

I played the game. "Werewolves and shapeshifters?"

"Definitely."

Slack-jawed, my mind spun. Could they be any more mental?

"Flies are swarming." Ronan flicked his hand in the air.

I quickly shut my mouth. "You guys aren't tripping off the reservation?"

Both chuckled, their laughter stilted and somber, trying to find a skosh of humor in their horror. Ronan tipped his chair on its two back legs. *Jerkwads.* They had me going. I tightened my arms over my midriff as though to keep the mythical creatures from encroaching on Riley Senior's primo bounty.

"You're not kidding about the Rift, are you? Why do I get the distinct impression you're gonna tell me something about these Rifts I don't want to hear?"

Adam sobered from their little joke meant to ease my dread. "The Rifts were the *doorways* the government forced the thirteen most powerful sorcerers to use so they could cull any magical beings left on Earth and abolish magic. They sent all the sorcerers and fae, the last magical beings, into the Realm of the Void through the Rifts. Up to that time, Rifts always existed and allowed magic to flow between Earth and the Void, enhancing the powers of the fae and sorcerers on Earth. When the government figured out the Rifts were truly portals, they concocted their plan to get rid of magic once and for all. They had the sorcerers destroy all the Rifts, until there was one left. One final exit."

I must have snoozed through paranormal history in high school. At that moment, Charlotte the spider was spinning nonsense in my skull, twisting all that I knew and all my zillion questions into a tangled web of horror.

"The Forbidden Thirteen, the strongest sorcerers alive, created doppelgängers in their likenesses in secret from a heavy mix of fae-sorcery magic, alchemy, changing blood and DNA, using the fae as their guinea pigs. The true identities of the original Thirteen weren't a secret and they were able to use their fae doppelgängers to take their place in the Abolishment, sending them through the last Rift and permanently closing the gateway, while they stayed safe in their havens on Earth. A suicide mission," Adam explained.

"Sounds like Frankenstein's lab to me," I muttered, trying to absorb their fantastical tale.

"The Thirteen faked out the government and went into hiding," Ronan added. "It's not documented for public consumption."

"You and Ronan are direct descendants of the Forbidden Thirteen sorcerers," Adam chipped in slowly, gauging my capacity not to go on a berserker killing spree.

I massaged my scalp, spurring my brain cells to perk up. "How do you know all this if it's not documented?" I squinted at Ronan.

"My father has part of a secret book called the *Illuminaria,* where it's all detailed. But he's missing a chunk of the book. One of the Forbidden sorcerers wrote it in secret to record their history, magic, and the eradication, but over time, the book got split up and separated, until others began to piece it back together. It's still not complete."

I starting picking at the cuticle on my thumb, absorbing their maddening tale. "What else is in this mystical book?"

"It's not mystical. Ronan's seen parts of it in his father's safe." Adam's hair sifted over the tabletop toward my hand.

"Everything about how to open and close the Rifts, how to control the Forbidden either physically or by using their blood in alchemy is in the book. Basically, how to rule the world either with magic or alchemy." Ronan scrubbed his face.

My heart stopped. "Where are the missing pages of the book?"

Ronan locked eyes with mine. "Good question. My dad has enough of it to be lethal. He thinks your original

Thirteen ancestor wrote the history, spells and alchemic potions, dismantled the book and hid the pieces."

Holy crap on a crappy cracker. The shit was rising to my eyeballs. Ronan and Adam's magic cascaded over me, a tingly meld of good and bad aural energy, filling my hollowness with both of them.

The muffled song of my phone blaring the latest alternative rock scattered our co-mingled energy. Our auras settled where they belonged, leaving me empty. I'd so forgotten the outside world that the ringing crashed me back into my sane and safe humdrum existence. *Cripes, was that only yesterday?*

I followed the tune into the living room where I'd abandoned my purse on the couch in my arrival trance. I rummaged inside my undisturbed purse for my smartphone, punched it on.

"Aria! Where are you? You okay? I've been calling you for forever." Zoe lobbed the words at me, her sultry tone turning shrill with worry.

"Calm down. I'm okay." A stack of leather-bound books resting on the end table drew my attention. I smoothed my finger over the embossed, worn leather of the top tome, *Ancient History of the Magical World.*

Ronan advanced, his stance fidgety, fingers extending and curling. I rested my hand on my stun gun, swearing to surgically attach the thing to my palm. He pressed into my side, his lips close to my ear, warm breath caressing my neck. Something weird and welcome tugged on my lower region, almost forcing me closer to him.

"Don't say a word," he whispered.

I backed away, seizing my own degree of personal space. My butt nudged the books, and the top three clunked to the floor, the first one opening to chapter thirteen, *The Forbidden.* I toed the book shut, hiding evidence of Ronan and Adam's heritage and the dread rising inside me.

Zoe continued to bitch me out. "Your condo's trashed..."

Her voice faded off.

My stomach lurched. Ronan mouthed something at me, his arms straining the sleeves of his T-shirt. Adam tucked his fists into his pants pockets, a muscle in his square jaw throbbing.

I concentrated on Zoe rather than the two hulking whack jobbers from ancient sorcery town. "What are you talking about? Where are you?"

"In your condo. You didn't show up for coffee and I got worried," she said in her classic mile-a-minute fashion. "Girl, you need to hire a brain 'cause your place smacks of a white trash hovel."

Panic jabbed my heart. I looked frantically at Ronan. My left pinkie kinked. *Ah, criminy.*

"Hang on a sec." I swiped the mute button, thankful Zoe hadn't invoked video to see the terror I couldn't wipe off my face even with a bar of my favorite Belgian chocolate. "My condo's been trashed. My best friend's there."

"Shit," Ronan muttered, a stony mask of distrust clouding his features. "More of my dad's henchmen."

His aura showered me in sparks, and the cell phone slipped from my fingers. "Get. Away," I managed to expel between clenched teeth, scratching at the fire licking my arms.

Without wasting a frown, Ronan exited stage left, slamming the front door behind his evil energy.

The stinging abated, and I snatched the phone off the Oriental floral rug. "I'd tell her to get out, but she'll grill me," I beseeched Adam before punching off the mute. "You still there?"

"Where are you?" Zoe demanded.

"At a friend's."

"Seriously?" The curiosity in her voice killed her initial surprise. "Wait. You don't have any other friends."

The new BFF ad was going viral tomorrow. "You're a few jokes shy of a stand-up routine."

A snarky giggle erupted over the phone. "You have got to scoop me on what went down with Michael last night."

Adam clamped his palm over the receiver. "Ask her to meet you someplace just to get her out of there."

An idea flowered. We normally met at the mall's digital media store & coffee shop every weekend. So sue me for being a book whore. Of course, we worship coffee and shopping for all things girlie. I engaged speakerphone, suggested we meet in half an hour. About to hang up, I heard familiar door chimes in the background.

"Hey, someone's at your door." Zoe's footsteps click-clacked across the tile floor, a haunting din in my ears.

My heart clogged my throat. "Don't answer it," I shouted.

"What's the big frickin' deal? Hang tight."

"Zoe!" I stamped my foot. A faint male voice mumbled something.

"Aria's not home," she replied.

"Will she return soon?" asked the man with an unrecognizable Scottish accent.

My heart thumped in my ears. My left pinkie twitched again.

Caution trickled into Zoe's voice. "Who's asking?"

"Family friend."

"I think not," she taunted. "I know all her friends."

I heard a sharp click, and then a thud hit the wall. Zoe's cry erupted from the phone, setting off a mini riot in my ribcage. Furniture banged to the floor. Glass or porcelain smashed and tinkled onto the travertine tiles. Mom's favorite vase?

"Aria Walker?" a man growled into the phone, then snarled in an explosion of rage.

The crack of a palm on skin and Zoe crying out thundered through my senses. I'd give up my puny life for Zoe. Not until I offed the person who hurt her, though.

"Aria Walker?" The man's Scottish burr thickened. "I

know it's you. Your number's on your friend's caller ID."

Adam and I locked eyes. He plucked the phone out of my hand. "Who the hell is this?" His formerly cultured, monotone voice mimicked arctic Ronan way too much.

"Where's the psychic?"

Ready for an onslaught of negative energy, I ran to the front door and motioned for Ronan to return from where he waited beneath a scraggly oak at the far side of the front yard. His long-legged stride swallowed the distance in a blink.

I returned to Adam's side. Hearing Zoe struggle and the man yell at her on speakerphone sent my adrenaline surging. My hand flew to my mouth and I stifled a savage cry.

"Riley?" The Scottish brute panted as if battling a tribe of Amazonians. "If you give up the Walker psychic, this one lives."

Ronan snatched the phone from Adam. "Who the hell is this?" Steel encased his icy voice, and I shivered at the lethal protectiveness he exuded.

"I think you know."

"Ian?" Ronan punched his fist into the entryway's stone wall.

More laughter erupted from the phone, quickly chased by a struggle and another loud slap on skin. "You little bitch!" he shouted. "I'll kill you if you don't buck up."

"Ronan, do something!" Fear vibrated through me.

Ronan held up a hand. "She's an innocent, Ian. Let her go."

"Not from where I'm standing. Not until I get what I want," Ian taunted. "Stay in touch." He laughed. The phone clicked off.

I raced to the end table and reached for Adam's cell. Before I picked it up, he grabbed it from beneath my hand.

"No cops." Adam pocketed the phone.

I spun on him, hands on my hips. "It's time for real

cops, not co-eds playing cops and *kidnappers*," I said the last with a sneer directed at Ronan.

"My father has eyes and ears everywhere. The minute you call the cops and give up your location, he'll have his minions on your lily-white ass in five minutes." Ronan blanched, scrubbing his head with both hands.

SIX

Slinging my purse over my shoulder, I dashed to the entryway, tripped over a rug, and caught myself on the stacked stone wall. "We'll finish our convo on our rescue mission." Acting as if I didn't almost just bash my brains in, I squeezed past Ronan in the doorway.

He grabbed my upper arm before I clawed through the screen. "Hold on."

I tried to shake him loose, but his grip was lethal. "Do you want another murder on your rap sheet?" I flung open the screen door, slamming it against a bench on the wraparound porch. A basketball hit an open box of dog treats and tipped crunchy nuggets into a tinkling lily pond. Sighing, I muttered, "Adam, I fed your fish."

Ronan loosened his grip without releasing me, his face a roadwork of granite. "Ian won't hurt Zoe. He needs leverage."

"Screw leverage. Let's go." I pushed ineffectively against the mountain of testosterone. Willing my drumming heart to chill, I drew in deep, even breaths.

A muscle stood out in a ridge along Ronan's jaw. "He won't hurt her."

I wrenched my arm again. Losing my footing, I staggered into the doorjamb, banged my funny bone against the stone wall, and caught my balance on the coat rack. Stars exploded in my vision. The sleeve tore on a defenseless windbreaker and the ripping grated on my ears. Dread surpassed my anger as I rubbed my throbbing elbow. "Okay, I get it. We're wasting time." Normally, with this kind of lame luck, I'd go back to bed and save the world from me. Not at the expense of Zoe, though.

Adam flew down the stairs, lugging my suitcases with him. "Ronan, grab our bags."

I hadn't noticed the two black overnight bags dumped in the foyer beside a planter until Ronan reached for them. "Where are we going?"

"San Jose, then Seattle."

My eyebrows hiked up to my hairline. "You had that planned? I'm sure glad I got the text message."

Ronan pushed out a weary sigh. "Did you think we were going to sit on our asses and tell campfire stories?" With stiff, jerky movements, he snatched up the two bags.

"Bite me, Ronan." At least campfire stories wouldn't strain his brain. I stomped down the three steps to land hard in the gravel. A jarring pain shot up my leg to my hip. If boredom set in, we could play connect the dots on my bruised body. Ignoring the new throb, I climbed into the SUV's front passenger seat.

"You wouldn't learn shit if we weren't stuck in this mess together." Ronan pitched the two bags into the cargo space.

Adam threw my bags on top and the hatch thumped shut. He climbed into the driver's seat and cranked the engine. Ronan folded his hulk into the back seat behind me, Fin settling next to him.

"You'd be sitting in a magic-deadened cell in Seattle if

Ronan hadn't snatched you." Adam maneuvered the black beast off the tree-shaded property.

"Whatever." I held my palm up over the center console. "Give me my phone."

"I'm already calling Ian," Ronan snapped.

"Who's this Ian ass-wipe? Why the hell are we going to Seattle?" I didn't need to ask why my condo was ransacked after Ronan's declaration about the *book*. The hunters were up shit's murky creek without a paddle searching my condo.

"He's not answering."

I stewed, trying to wrap my mind around the idea of anyone wanting me so badly. "I'm waiting." I barely got the calm words past my clenched jaw. No sense in pissing off my two new boyfriends, again. I'd laugh at the absurdity if my circumstances weren't in the crapper. I twisted around and fixed Ronan with a laser stare.

Adam jetted onto the highway and sped up to change lanes around a snail-powered van. Adam and Ronan exchanged a conspiratorial look in the rearview mirror. Ronan dragged his hand over his face, swearing and muttering to his other self.

"We should be on our way to Seattle to snatch the *Illuminaria* and take down my father, instead of wasting time on his shitstorms here." Rubbing his twitching cheek didn't help his chronic condition. "Ian O'Rourke's one of my father's most trusted bounty hunters, same as Murph. He must've been looking for the *Illuminaria* too. Only a couple trackers were given that task."

"At the time of the quake cluster, a Rift that no one seemed to know about, except Ronan's father, opened up at Washington Park in Seattle," Adam explained. "Ley lines exploded all over Earth and caused the Rift to fracture and spew out magic. That's about the time we were all conceived. This Rift's far from the last original Rift in Ireland."

"Whoa." My mouth hung open. "How does Ronan's

father know it's an actual Rift?"

"Everything about the Rifts is in the *Illuminaria*. He has gadgets that detect paranormal activity, and the park has the highest concentration of any place in the world. It all added up to what's in the book."

I didn't care for the rippling in my stomach, stemming more from rolling turns on a stuffed stomach than their word bombs. The implications of Riley Senior's bounty hunters tailing me had yet to reach a Category 10 Crapstorm. The seatbelt law didn't stop me from settling in a more comfortable position facing the back seat. However, I did need to keep my balance as Adam slung us around hairpin turns on the woodsy, tree-shrouded highway that separated San Jose and the Santa Cruz beaches.

"How many bounty hunters did your dad sic on me?" I asked. Ronan shrugged. "You don't know? I thought you knew everything." My sneer didn't quite reach my voice.

Ronan whipped out my phone and hit redial. A few non-responsive seconds later, he slammed the phone on the seat.

Adam took another sharp curve, and I grabbed the console. I dug into my purse for my tin of mints, popping a couple in my mouth.

He cranked up the air conditioner. "Settle back and face forward. You'll feel better."

So perceptive, Adam really might make a great prince to a nice fairy princess. After a season in the tanning booth and a bottle of Miss Clairol, though.

"Zoe!" I bolted upright, smacking my knee on the bottom of the dash. A river of pain coursed down my leg bones. Another dot to connect. "She's a telepath. I don't want him testing her. He'll want to keep her for his nefarious shits and grins." I massaged my knee. "Give me the phone." I practically knotted into a pretzel to apprehend my cell from the backseat thief.

"Dad won't kill her, or want to keep her." Ronan

switched the phone to his left hand, farther from my reach. "At least not until he snags you."

"Oh, that's comforting." Tears leaked from my eyes. Damn, not the tears. Until last night, I'd only ever cried when Mom and Granny had died. Oh, yeah, and when my rat snake father slithered out of my life. I yanked down the visor. My eyes had more lines in them than a fault line map of California.

Adam popped the glove box open to reveal a cache of napkins. I snatched a handful and blotted my face dry, wadding them in my fist. The drone of the beefy engine choked out the expansive silence. Breathing slowly, I counted to ten. I needed to get a grip, and fast. Traffic slowed to a crawl as we neared downtown San Jose, granting my emotions a reprieve.

Facing forward, I leaned my head on the headrest. "Isn't your father hunting Adam too? Aren't you twins, brothers, or cousins that the magic affected differently?"

"Not brothers. No relation." The skin of Adam's knuckles stretched white. If he paled any further, he'd be three days dead. "Only you two know I exist in this sickly form. Until six months ago I was a normal guy. No magic, no fairy look, just a regular human male."

My heart dived into my unwelcoming stomach. Not twins? "Then..." Aria Elle Walker was at a loss for words. Stop the world from revolving. *Oh, holy hell.* "You're doppelgängers. Like the beings sorcerers created from the fae back in the day."

Adam nodded. "We don't know how it's possible. We took blood tests and our DNA doesn't match. You've heard the theory that everyone has a double somewhere? Some were created by magic and alchemy by the sorcerers. Our bloodlines have carried the magic down through the ages."

"Sure," I replied, never believing in that old myth. Until that moment.

"They're few and far between," Adam continued. "They

aren't always lookalikes, sometimes having similar physical or physiological characteristics. They may have complimentary attributes, or opposite attributes."

"Like what?" Moisture formed on my flushed face.

Ronan gripped the back of my seat. "One might be cruel, the other kind."

"Or one might possess magic ruled by his psyche, his innate telekinesis," Adam added, "and the other, magic pulled from earth energies. But there's a bond between them."

"But the sorcerer-created doppelgängers were eradicated and booted through the Rift," I nearly accused, their story getting weirder and weirder by the minute.

As the vehicle flew down the freeway off-ramp, I grabbed the door handle to keep from sliding off the leather seat. Slowing, he merged into the late afternoon downtown traffic.

Adam gave Ronan one of their boys' club peeps in the rearview mirror.

"So we thought," Ronan interjected in his grumpy voice. "There's nothing about them in the *Illuminaria*. At least not in the part my father has. It only talks about the banished ones. We kinda believe the original Thirteen just didn't stop their alchemy when everyone was abolished. Or fae-doppelgänger magic is spewing out of the crumbling Rift."

"Or I'm an anomaly." Adam chuckled wryly.

My head ached. "What would Ronan's father do if he knew about Adam?"

"We'd all be in cages locked up tighter than Hannibal Lecter." Adam's low voice spread horror through my system.

A terrible sense of his bitterness hit me. Traffic snarled ahead. Adam braked hard and we screeched to a standstill. I braced my hands against the dash, preventing further bodily damage. The heat of his ailing body seared my skin.

As fast as Adam's bitterness erupted, a barbed thread of suspicion worked its way inside my gut. I drew a deep breath, forbade myself to get sick. Like my stomach ever obeyed my brain.

"Are you sure Richie Riley doesn't know?" I raised my eyebrows at Adam, refusing to look at the source of mistrust behind me. "Maybe Ronan's drawing you out into the open and they're hunting you and me?" Hopefully it wasn't true, because I needed someone to believe in besides an extinct fairy-sorcerer doppelgänger.

In a flurry of motion, Ronan lunged forward and flicked the latch on my door. The door flew open and my scream followed it. I scooted halfway on top of the center console, shaking with a mix of fear and disgust. My uncontrollable energy stabbed at Ronan, but it flared blind and shattered against his defective aura. Fire ants seemed to chomp on me as he lashed a barrage of tainted energy at me that did nothing but scrape my skin.

"Hey! Did you snort stupid dust?" I punched his arm.

"Get out. You're on your own." A dangerous cruelty laced his words.

Adam swerved to the curb amid the blare of a piercing horn behind us. The impact of him hitting the brakes swung the door closed with a bang that vibrated in my eardrums. Ronan hopped out and opened the front door, steam practically spiraling from his blotchy red neck.

"Knock it off, man." Adam thrust the gearshift in park.

I jumped out on wobbly legs. Ronan's fury drizzled over my skin in an eruption of molten nails. I prepared to go hillbilly apeshit on him.

"I'm done with you. Go back to the zoo," I snarled, triggering raised heads from the group of people waiting at a bullet train transport stop. My hand quaked as I thrust it toward him. "Give me my phone. I'll rescue Zoe on my own."

"Get in the car." Exasperation dripped from Adam's voice. He skirted the front of the SUV, held out his hand to

me.

Ronan crammed into the front seat, closing us out of his teensy world. The assault on every pore of my skin downshifted to a tolerable level.

Drained physically, emotionally, and mentally, too much had happened in the last day to upset my boring, secure world. Ronan's attitude and magic problems were collateral damage I could live without. The man robbed me of my wits. At least I hadn't spent half my life napping in front of an ion shield the way he had. I could get my wits back. Him, not so much.

I shuffled my boots through faded mulch in the planter between the street and sidewalk, kicking the smirking yellow head off an early dandelion. Not knowing what to do, I grabbed Adam's outstretched hand. He tugged me into his arms, and his warm hands stroked my back. I laid my cheek against his chest. Heaven help me, but that damn aural connection placed Adam squarely into über-friendly territory. His chest hitched beneath my cheek, and the tightness in his hard body pressed against mine, sharing Ronan's sinfully muscular body. Two doppel-peas in a pod.

"Ronan has one nice personality, but not for a human." I sniffed.

Adam swept a strand of hair off my eyelashes. "His father killed his mother a year ago," he said somberly. "Murph from your casino altercation executed Riley's orders. Ronan recently found out. He's dead serious when he says he wants his father destroyed."

My spine stiffened. I craned my neck to look up at Adam's downturned face. His baseball cap shadowed his unnatural complexion, granting him a semblance of color. "Seriously?"

"Riley will destroy yours and Ronan's life if he captures you, or any of us."

Ronan glowered at us. I eased out of Adam's arms, unsure why I felt the need to separate, but a naked vulnerability in Ronan's eyes gave me a cracked mirror into his soul. At that moment, his soul called to me even though he'd thrust me away.

"Hey." Adam thumbed up my chin. "We need you. *I* need you. I think you can help me return to normal or figure out what my new normal is."

I smiled wanly. "Did you guys think I fell for that protecting the damsel in distress act?"

Adam chuckled. "Not really."

Silent, we climbed into the vehicle. Ronan ignored us, his arms crossed defiantly over his chest, dark gaze fixated out the passenger door window. Thankfully, his aura had returned to the grid. Adam maneuvered back into traffic, avoiding a near miss with a traffic cop behind us.

Timidly, I placed my hand on Ronan's shoulder. He tensed. "I'm sorry. You didn't deserve my smackdown." I squeezed his shoulder, dropped my hand. "I need answers. I think both of you need me." I snorted. "Well, you get my drift."

Ronan cleared his throat. "I have no clue why my power's attacking you. It's pissing me off that I'm hurting you."

My cell rang, and I nearly peed my pants. I retrieved it off the backseat floor where it'd dropped during Ronan's conniption. I held the phone out to him. He hesitated to take it, but I nudged it onto his palm, my way of acceptance.

He jabbed it on. "Riley," he barked, listened for a moment. "Ian, what gives?"

Adam sailed into the parking garage at the Stargazer and headed for the public lot behind the residential tower. San Jose was littered with entertainment centers and most included residential towers due to overpopulation. It was a normal way of life. *Was*, being the operative word.

A long pause ensued. "Whatever." Ronan clicked off, pocketed my phone. "Ian's taking Zoe to the old Santa Clara University chapel for the exchange." Ronan and Adam traded another one of their doppelgänger-knows-all looks. "We have three hours," he added.

I massaged my temples. *I'd like to buy a clue or two hundred.*

Rebuilt on the original site of Mission Santa Clara, the chapel was one of the Franciscans-built California missions. A public place open for self-guided tours to anyone. What kind of moron move was that?

"Why there and why so long?" I asked as Adam parked in the first empty slot he found in the back.

"You said Zoe's a telepath? What exactly can she do?" Ronan not so subtly deflected my question.

The dashboard clock flashed thirteen after the hour. I dampened my tangible wave of irritation. The clock reset to twelve and stopped.

"Can we agree on one thing?" I didn't wait for a rhetorical answer to my rhetorical question. "You need to stop putting me on ignore. You have a boatload of information I need."

Adam sniggered. "She's got your number. I want her around, if for nothing other than to help me figure out why I'm stuck in this half-human, half-dead fae body."

I decided to move things along the path of full disclosure. "Zoe can read most unblocked minds." She was going to trade me in for a new BFF if she found out I spilled her secret. "What happened six months ago to change Adam?"

Grooves creased Adam's pasty forehead. "Six months ago, Ronan's dad tried to get him to open the Rift with a ritual from the book using Ronan's telekinesis and his blood. Instead, Ronan screwed up the spell and now tainted magic is leaking into our world, which started my decline. At first, I began gaining abilities. A cloaking spell, mesmerism, powers the ancient fae wielded. The more I gained, the more it began to affect how I looked and felt, and then my fae powers started to decline."

"Now Dad thinks he needs at least two sorcerers to open the Rift, set it right, and stop the taint from spilling out." Ronan gave me a pointed look. "Apparently, those pages are missing from the book."

I drummed my fingers on my purse, trying to contain my excitement. My mind lingered on Adam rather than the implicit idea that I may have access to the other parts of the book. *Yeah, right.* I swallowed hard, pushing down my encroaching unease. "Do I have a doppelgänger too?"

"No one knows." Adam grinned at me.

"Hell help us if there's another you," Ronan muttered. Fin jumped onto the front seat with Ronan, snuggling into his side.

I shot him a scathing look. Hiding a grin, Ronan scratched Fin behind her ears. She licked his hand as if he were a fat, juicy steak. Guess I was a skinny, dry hamburger.

A warm jolt of jealousy rose up. I ignored the fluttering in my stomach. For some stupid reason, I wanted to be snuggled up to Ronan, licking his hand while he kissed and fondled my ears...or some other body part. I gulped. "Then Adam's part fairy and part sorcerer, one of the final dominant Forbidden?"

Adam sifted his fingers through his flowing hair. "If I *was* fae or a sorcerer, I didn't know it. After Ronan screwed with the Rift, I started changing." He waved his hand over himself. "We have a link, but Ronan's got all the magic. I got nothing now except what I pull from him. He's the sorcerer and I appear to be fae, whatever that means."

"And you're doppelgängers just like the beings the Thirteen devised back in the evil dark ages. Ronan's a descendant of a Forbidden sorcerer and Adam's a descendant of a fae-based doppelgänger, created by sorcerers and from fae who didn't go through the Rift." As I said the words, I knew they didn't make sense, but my head accepted them. What else could it be? It made sense if our ancestors were so über evil and industrious. *Hail to the original Forbidden Thirteen. Sneaky bastards.*

Holy convoluted hell in a handbasket. My right eye twitched up the dust. "But the magic link is a good thing. You found each other, however that occurred." I lifted an eyebrow indicating the time was right for further sharing on that score.

"If you can call that a good thing." That errant muscle throbbed in Ronan's left jaw. "We aren't sure how the doppelgänger bond works. It's screwing with us both. We don't know what magic leaked from the Rift, whether good or bad, and who else it affected. The history of the Forbidden Thirteen is documented in the *Illuminaria*, but it was written deliberately vague about the secret doppelgängers or any fae-sorcerer doppelgänger bonds. My dad's been researching the Forbidden, sorcery, and Rifts for over thirty years and he still doesn't have half a clue."

"Why do you think we're descendants of sorcerers?" I turned to look at Ronan. "ESP is not sorcery. It's not magic based."

"It was a closely guarded secret among the Forbidden Thirteen. They had sorcery type powers *and* psychic abilities." Ronan cursed under his breath, seeming to hate his lot in life. "The Thirteen closed the Rift, went into hiding, and supposedly their magic winked out throughout the ages of their descendants."

Until the Earthquake Cluster-Muck—the year we were all conceived. Chocolate-charged adrenaline streamed through my veins.

"If we *open*" —I did air quotes— "the Rift all the way, if that's even possible, will the magical population explode?" I held my breath.

Adam blanched paler than pale. "Probably. Energy will explode on Earth and those with a seed of magic or ESP, whether they know it or not, will flourish."

"Or more residual tainted magic will leak out. Like

now." Ronan scratched a throbbing muscle in his jaw. "It's not exactly written in blood."

"Can a doppelgänger coexist with his sorcerer counterpart?" Unease expanded like a wet sponge in my gut.

"We don't know the full gist of the bond," Ronan said.

"It's all new to us," Adam reiterated.

I dared not think of the implications. Should we try to close the Seattle Rift even if we could? Traveling through a vacuum sucking up a clue every hundred miles scared me.

The windshield had fogged and Adam cracked the windows. Sweat beaded his flushed face, and he untangled locks of hair wrapping around his wrist like sinuous seaweed. Our auras tangled and I forced a calming vine toward him. "Why did humans back then chase off the fae and sorcerers?"

"Chase off?" Ronan's hand froze on Fin's head. "Our human ancestors murdered them."

"To rid Earth of everything humans feared and couldn't control." Adam rolled up his sleeves, exposing his faintly shimmering forearms. "Magic upset the balance humans wanted to maintain. They worried sorcery would eventually annihilate humans. Humans of that era were afraid of otherworldly beings and thought there was a regular door to the Realm of the Void and that more and more magic would smother the earth." A lock of his livewire hair shifted, slid down his arm, and fell onto the steering column.

Ronan grunted. "The idiots back then hadn't comprehended that the Rift gateway might not outlast time, or crumble and unleash twisted magic." He fixed me with a pointed look. "Twenty-two years is a long time to leak tainted magic and who knows what into the world." Ronan's parting shot served up a side order of lunacy. "According to ancient and modern laws, all three of us are walking felons."

SEVEN

Before my brain could digest that rusty nail in my coffin, I spied a tall woman approaching the SUV, her lustrous black hair raining down her back. Decked in black from her neck to her heels, she wore glossy, spike-heeled boots I'd sell my cats to own. Her porn queen chest filled out a skintight turtleneck sweater. Raspberry lipstick with matching fake claws completed the panther in heels.

Adam and Ronan swiveled to check her out. The early thirty-something Queen of Darkness parked her stilettos a few feet from the front passenger door. Her beckoning eyes twinkled so brilliantly under the fluorescent lights, her eyes appeared to shoot sparkling emerald icicles.

"You guys know her?"

Ronan drew his gun, his caustic aural energy spearing the air. "Melisande Aguire, my father's right hand and number one tracker." Without moving his sight off her, he pulled a silencer from his coat pocket.

The woman teased her tongue over her bottom lip,

causing Ronan's faltering energy to shift to sexual anticipation. I don't know how I knew that, but I did and wished bleach ran through my blood to wash the sensation away. The witchy bitch probed the cab in his general direction, hunger brightening her eyes into emerald jewels.

"Ronan?" I gripped my necklace. "You've hooked-up with her, haven't you?"

"Shit, Aria." He fumbled, dropping the silencer on the floorboard.

"If you've had a relationship, it makes a helluva difference how this goes down." I nudged Fin's front paws off my leg before I knocked her over in my frustration. "She obviously knows how to push your buttons. Is she a Forbidden sorcerer too?"

Ronan slammed the glove box shut. "No. She used me, played me against my father." His scowl deepened, his voice rasped. "She has some freakass coercion ESP, almost telekinetic, but she's not Forbidden. Last I heard my father was doing her."

Where's that ear bleach when you need it? "Can you knock her out if it comes down to it?"

With careful deliberation, he flicked the safety off his gun, cocked the hammer. Answer enough.

"Well, alrighty then." I dusted his shoulder with my palm. "It's crunch time." When I snagged a spare moment to think, I might detest myself from the murderous hell I'd landed in. "Is she capable of enthralling me?"

"Anyone." His emotionless voice spooked me stiff. "It's easier if a prior relationship exists. She can leverage off what she knows of you, your weaknesses." He punched the dash, a dull thud in the aura storm brewing. "Asshole father. He figured out I came after you, and he knows what she can do to me. He wants to make sure I return *and* bring back the prize."

Aka, moi. The five-million-dollar prize of three centuries.

"Obviously he knows you're working against him now."
I fiddled with my stun gun's safety catch, restraining the
urge to blast her down a notch. Ronan gave a too sharp
emphatic shake of his head. A warning went off in my
brain. He held more secrets than Dominion Research's
closet vault of Forbidden Thirteen trade secrets.

Adam turned up the air conditioner. "Let's find out
what she knows."

Sweat dripped down Ronan's temples. The acrid smell
of his turmoil filled the interior, his tension scraping the
edges of my aura.

"I can't go out there."

"Avoid her eyes, man. She can't be that good." Adam
dipped his head in case she was able to see through the
dark window tint, even though it appeared impenetrable.

Ronan landed a mad dog look on Adam. "She is *that*
good, especially when my telekinesis is screwed up."

"Geez, do I have to bang down the double-D witch
myself?" I made as if to open the door.

Ronan lunged between the center console and pinned
me against the back seat, practically knocking the wind out
of me. Poor Fin got shoved to the floor where she yelped and
scrambled to steady her legs.

"Ronan, I know you're in there." Melisande's low, sultry
contralto carried on a current of air inside the cab. "I take it
you have the psychic? Let's have a little talk before you do
anything with her." She smoothed her hand down her
pancake flat stomach. *Skinny, sparkly bitch.*

"Don't be a total moron. I wasn't getting out," I
whispered fiercely and shouldered Ronan's hands off me.

A vein pulsed in his neck. "Get down behind the seat
before she looks through the windshield. Don't look into her
eyes." A palette of dread, anger, and bewilderment mottled
his face.

"Okay. Okay." I wiped a rivulet of sweat off his face
before it plopped onto my pants. My fingers lingered on his

cheek. His sick aura kicked into gear at my touch, but it wasn't the stinging sensation of before. This trail of power sought aid from mine. The scared, sensual mix warming my center of power startled me. I snatched my hand back, my lashes twitching rapidly. Surely, I must have misinterpreted the sensation. Ronan attracted to me? *Put the crazy back in your cuckoo clock, Aria Elle.*

Melisande poured herself over the front fender in a seductive pose. She scrutinized her smooth, flawless face in a compact mirror and patted powder on her button nose, slowly sweeping her tongue over her collagen plump lips.

"Aria?" Ronan croaked out.

"Whatever. Um...you can back off. I'm not going anywhere." Except down a deep, dark hole. No hole in sight, I dipped behind the headrest. "Oh!" An idea flowered, the thought cooling my untimely passion.

Excitement fluttered in my chest. "I can trip Ronan's brain to resist her when he steps out. Then I'll stun her brain to sleep," I said in a loud whisper. They ogled me as if I'd fallen into a vat of crazy. "What? It'll work. We'll figure out what to do after she conks out."

"Won't work." Ronan wiped the sweat off his forehead. "You can't split off your telekinesis to resist her and knock her out at the same time."

"Get real." My scoffing became an evil grin. "Who do you think's been dumping ice on your prick *and* preventing the witch from skipping to the front of the SUV? At the same time, I might add." By absorbing extra energy from around me, I can use my telekinetic receptors to hinder someone else's actions and also knock another out. Without absorbing the energy, I was pretty limited to one action. *Holy hell! Was I a descendant of a Forbidden sorcerer or what?*

Scarlet embarrassment painted Ronan's face. "You can invoke two telekinetic spells at once?" He squirmed in his seat.

I gave a start in surprise. "Can't you?"

"No." Swiping a hand across the back of his neck, he asked hesitantly, "How many can you?"

I thought back to a bullying incident when I was ten. Those three brats deserved my smackdown for taunting my best friend just because she was a little on the hefty side. I speedily chased the disturbing episode away for a snow day in hell. It was the first time my telekinesis had split off into three targets. "Three, maybe. I might need to connect to your aura for an extra boost of energy." If my unluck didn't plunk a jinx on my luck, that is. Even with Ronan and Adam's tainted aura thrown into the mix, I shouldn't have a problem with two spells. I hoped. I nibbled on the inside of my mouth. *Hell, I'll just pull energy off the Queen of Darkness.* "Or I'll just stun her." I patted my pocket with my trusty stun gun.

Defiance tightened Ronan's square jaw. "You negate me. I have no power with you around. What little I have is nearly dead."

My eyes prepared to roll before I put the skids on them. "I can still use your faulty aura to pull energy from, or even hers. Leave the rest to me."

"Ronan, come out to play." Melisande's purring voice seemed to filter from the speakers. "If you've got the psychic in there, I can help you with her. First, I want to chat."

Ronan's psyche responded to her false allure, his desire palpable in the air around us.

"Dude, rein in your horses." I slapped another dampener on his mind. "She's too old for you."

"Uh, yeah, thanks." His voice mimicked the crackling of a pre-pubescent teen. He not so furtively adjusted the crotch of his pants.

"Can we get on with this? Remember my *kidnapped* friend, Zoe?" My pitch intensified with my irritability.

"It'll have to work." Adam reclined his seat and faced the driver's door.

"Aria, get on the floor. I don't want her locking eyes with either of you," Ronan barked out in a loud whisper.

The moment I dropped down, Fin planted a soppy slurp on my chin, her energy filling me with warm and fuzzies. I patted her and peeked around the seat to glue my sight on Melisande, avoiding her weird, overly bright eyes. Time to get it on before she licked the collagen out of her lips.

Adam merged his aura with mine, expanding our natural fusion, leaving the mix warm and inviting. I hardly noticed his taint as my cleansing aura stole the limelight from him. He almost didn't have to worry about hiding from the witchy bitch since his entire body wavered in and out of visibility. Guess his body couldn't choose a side: human or fae, life...or death. I gulped down a lump of air lodged in my throat.

Ronan opened the door and Melisande's over-sexed enchantment collided with our combined forces. A gasp escaped her, and I suppressed an urge to gloat.

Ronan left the door slightly ajar, standing just outside it. "What the hell are you doing here, Mel?"

"Ronan, love." She tried to sprinkle holes of bitchcraft magic in our aural shield. We hung tough, and I intangibly spackled the holes as fast as she created them. "Richard doesn't want you involved in the capture of the Walker girl. You were to remain at the compound. Now it's my duty to take you in with the girl. If you got her, that is. But maybe we can make a deal?"

"What else does he know?" Hostility poured from Ronan's tone. Yet fear, in a mix of sweat, spice, and leather wafted off him. *Come on. Man up, man.*

Melisande's ESP strained against ours. "You resist me." A raspy laugh followed. "I taught you too well of my charms."

"Cut the crap. Why're you really here?"

"For you. What else?" Another gag-me laugh. "Do you think I'd stoop so low as to play bounty hunter for some idiotic psychic?"

I bristled and readied a knockout spell. *Keep talking, witch hag. Maybe you'll say something intelligent.*

"Aria," Adam cautioned. "Not yet."

Cramps were tightening my calves as I squatted on the floor, peeking out a corner of the back window.

"Give me a fucking break. You're Dad's number one hit man. Did you tell him I was here?"

"I considered calling him after detecting your bio-footprint in the girl's condo."

She stepped closer to Ronan, her spiky heels clicking on the tarmac. Her nearness fenced in our combined auras, but she couldn't penetrate the shield even if the proctologist freed her magic.

"I'm giving you a break." She uttered an uneasy, silvery laugh.

"What's your deal, Mel?"

"I'm on your side. Don't be so hostile."

"Prove it. What hand can you play in this game?" he asked. "You're holding shit without Richard Riley backing your ass."

"We can be a force, you and I." She paused, held out her arm, her black bag sliding off her shoulder to her wrist. "Take my tablet out."

"Why? What's on it?" Wariness laced his words.

"What proof will sway you to my side?" she taunted him.

"The *Illuminaria*." I celebrated Ronan's sneering voice.

Our merger began breaking, and I faltered, allowing holes to form. "We need to speed it up," I whispered.

Adam held up a finger. One minute to Catwoman blastoff.

"Then I guess we just sealed the deal." Melisande's husky voice crawled evil over my scalp, lifting the hairs by the roots. "I want you, Ronan. You're the power force, not your father. He's a useless old man relying on his son. You and I could destroy him, take over his mission. Check the tablet. Your idiot father scanned the translation into electronic format."

"And encrypted it to hell."

"And I broke his encryption," her voice slid to a conspiratorial hush.

Stunned, I peeked over the headrest. Melisande caressed his arm with one hand, her other stuck inside her purse. She kept flicking her eyes toward the driver's seat. I strengthened my spell, helping Ronan cope easier. Adam nodded, giving me the signal.

My left pinkie twitched, then my right. *A little late for that, you think?* I concentrated on wielding two separate threads of energy. Just as I was about to toss my mental knockout spell at her, a gunshot shattered the air, booming through my chest as if the bullet struck me. From the shadows of the garage to the right, a second shot chased the first.

Melisande screamed a shallow gurgling noise. A shot knocked Ronan against the fender. Grunting, he clutched his left shoulder. Strangled screams rolled up my throat. Fin's mournful howling joined the din. The blast punched our aura, moved over me in a red haze, shooting fiery arrows into my cramped leg muscles. I rose from my elevated crouch and latched onto Adam's shoulder. He said something, but I didn't understand him, all my senses riveted on the scene outside. Terror seized my heart, left my aura quivering around me.

A dark stain spread across the upper sleeve of Ronan's black T-shirt. Melisande tottered on her spike heels, and I saw the point of impact, a gelatinous mass on the side of her head, soaking her long, midnight hair. I gagged and quickly looked down. She fell toward Ronan, her limp form slithering down his arm to the ground in a blot of ink. The last of her nine lives streamed down the side of her head into a darkening puddle where her black-clad body and the tarmac morphed into one.

Pain speared my head and my knockout spell went wild. My thread of energy sped toward the source of danger hiding in the shadows. Uncontrollable brain waves leached out of me, leaving me shuddering from the force. A gargled yell echoed in the garage and a body thudded onto a car near us. The memory of last night's deathblow resurfaced, and I shielded my mind, cutting off my telekinetic waves.

I scrambled over the back seat to the door on the right, dropping my stunner and bumping Fin onto the floorboards. My heart seemed to stop beating. Gasping, I flung open the door and launched off the seat. My right foot landed on Melisande's open hand. Her rings crunched into the asphalt, the sound of bones creaking renewing the turmoil in my full stomach. I hopped to the right, wanting to dunk my foot in that mystical bleach to rinse the feel of her death away.

Ronan leaned against the fender, holding his wounded arm tight to his side. Blood drained from his face, pain mirrored in his eyes. All thoughts and emotions escaped me. Only one thing mattered. I stepped over Melisande's prone body toward the man who'd saved me last night. The *one* who mattered.

"Get in the car." Adam jogged toward us, surveying the area for shooters.

I clasped Ronan in my arms, anchored down by his weight. Lines etched his forehead, his eyes glazed over.

"You okay?" I struggled against his weight, not taking stock of the weird ache in my chest.

"Yeah," he ground out. "Get me into the seat." Before we moved a step, he bent double and pulled the black purse off Melisande's arm.

I helped him into the vehicle. Adam hefted Melisande up and carried her like a giant sack of cat litter between two other hulking SUVs.

"The bullet didn't penetrate." Ronan gritted his teeth,

hoisted his legs onto the floorboard.

Warm blood soaked his sleeve. The coppery tang filled my nostrils, invoking gruesome memories of last night. Gently, I probed his bloodied arm, patting it with a stack of napkins he'd handed me from the glove box. I breathed in deep to steady my frantic heart.

I assessed the damage, gently plucking the T-shirt from his skin. As it rasped over the open wound, Ronan mumbled a string of blue curses. He had an ugly gash and it needed stitches. Even though the bullet only grazed him, it had to hurt like a mother. I offered him a bleak smile, until I looked at my rusty-red, tacky fingers holding pressure to stem the flow of blood. My smile disappeared.

Ronan placed his hand over mine. "You're alright in a crisis."

Another one of those jolts of warmth weakened my knees. Before I could make fairy heads or dragon tails of what it meant, Adam raced back to the SUV.

"We're on the move." He shoved the doors shut, then bolted to the driver's side.

Ronan twisted into the front seat, his hand replacing mine on his wound. I climbed in, left with no choice but to straddle his legs. *I had doctoring to do, didn't I?*

I'd barely seated myself on Ronan's lap, our faces inches apart, when Adam slammed the vehicle in reverse. Ronan's arm encircled my waist to keep me from knocking myself comatose against the dash. I managed to press on the wad of napkins without causing him a world of hurt.

"Where's Melisande?" Ronan shifted to give my knees better purchase, one knee between his legs, the other on the side of the seat. Any other time and a girl could love that.

The tires squealed out of the garage as Adam sped deeper into the rear of the casino complex. "Dead. Sorry, man."

Ronan's aura spiked, settled. "Who shot at us?"

"Guy wore a Celtic sword pendant. Probably one of your

father's bounty hunters."

The knot in my stomach reformed. I touched Adam's arm. "Did you kill him?"

He kept his focus forward, his mouth compressed. "Didn't need to."

The knot unraveled into a pool of acid. "He's dead?"

Adam nodded. Ronan gently squeezed my waist, more solace than support.

"My energy went wild. I didn't mean to do it." My free hand spasmed and I pressed it to my gut. What the hell was I?

I focused on the immediate situation before I ran screaming for the loony bin. What had Melisande done to incur such murderous intent not just from Ronan but from her peers, if you could call bounty hunters peers? "Ronan, what did she do to you?"

"Turned my father against me, caused—" Ronan grabbed the armrest.

Adam bounced over a speed bump. My head grazed the headliner and I lost my balance. Ronan yelped as I fell against him. I eased back, one hand anchored on his steely thigh. "Sorry. You okay?" My morbid curiosity couldn't wait for a response. I needed answers before I lost it. "She caused what?"

Ronan's eyes shot blue flames of pain. "She talked my father into making me try to open the Rift before we understood what would happen or got our hands on the rest of the book. I screwed it up. It's her fault the screwed up magic is causing Adam…" He lowered his head.

I stuck two fingers under his chin, forcing his gaze to mine. "To what?" Deeply rooted pain hazed his eyes, more pain than the flesh wound deserved.

"To die," Adam said with a detached air. "I don't just look like a cadaver. I *am* dying."

EIGHT

The info bombs Ronan and Adam kept dropping on me created more questions than answers. I hated it. Too many people were dying, and I loathed that even more. If my mother was alive, I'd want to ream her a new one for withholding dangerous and secret family history from me. No wonder I'd always sensed I never really belonged in this world, no matter how hard I tried to lead a normal life, have friends, go to college, make a few bucks on the side. I wanted to scream, cry, rail at everything I didn't know about myself and how Ronan and Adam knew it all...or not enough.

The SUV bounced in a pothole, knocking my head on the roof. Ronan cried out and I gripped the seatback to hold steady. We had time to head to my condo before we rescued Zoe. Ronan's arm needed attention and it gave us a chance to canvass my home for clues.

Adam explained what he meant about dying. When Ronan screwed up the Rift, the bad magic leaking through the portal had caused serious damage to Adam's developing powers, destroying him from the inside out. The doppel-hunks believed the taint would eventually cause his body to shut down unless someone figured out how to stopper the magic or allow it to flow unfettered by opening the Rift completely.

Funny thing, Riley Senior believed that *someone* might be me, not that he knew Adam existed. Yet, Ronan dubbed my telekinesis clumsy and erratic and not much better than his when he was at peak condition. *You think? Hello, unlucky thirteen.* Of course, I neglected to mention that I'd hatched in the middle of a triangle of earthquake fault lines surrounding the San Francisco Bay Area. The more fault lines, the more ley line energy the earth held or emitted. Probably the reason why energy and I had an easy time hooking up. Since California had more fault lines than the number of guests at a pre-Abolishment sorcerer reunion, I wasn't totally convinced I possessed the abilities the doppel-geniuses expected, or if the faulty Rift caused my bad luck episodes. Nor was I sure I didn't. A parking lot puddle had more depth than I did after that conversation.

We entered the foyer of my condo and I reengaged the alarm. Reality stared me in the face and nausea bloomed in my stomach. A very messy and intrusive reality. I needed an infusion of antacids.

"No forced entry. They bypassed the security system." Ronan jabbed buttons on the touch pad, examining it as if he expected clues to pop out in crime scene bags.

Perps had tossed everything in their hunt for the blasted book of Forbidden life and death. I kicked a chunk of dried potpourri on the tile floor, slipped on a twig, and fell against Ronan who grunted out an oath to the horned one down under. Adam caught me before my butt kissed the marble tiles.

I gained my balance, not so much a calm stomach. "Thanks." I smiled apologetically at Ronan who backed away from the storm of Aria. "I'll snag the first aid kit." I bolted toward the hall bathroom, dodging the scattered litter of normal life. The life I no longer fit. Or ever had.

Bile stung my throat. I rushed into my purple haven and propped my elbows on the counter. Inane sludge filled my head, forcing the bad stuff into a crowded corner. By the time the dry heaves settled in, I was sitting on the cool tile floor.

A few minutes later, Adam entered. Hunkering down, he handed me an open can of ginger ale. "It'll make you feel better."

"Thanks." Our fingers touched as I took the can. A dash of his soothing energy flushed my self-pitying down the toilet. I sipped the calming soda, bubbles popping in the back of my throat.

Adam stroked my hair. My scalp tingled beneath his warm touch, and liquid fire fizzed along the rim of our auras, reenergizing me. Oddly, I felt as if I'd known him forever, even though it was the beastly Ronan also stirring my senses into a tizzy. The idea of Adam's potential, impending death tortured my soul. Why hadn't I realized earlier how off the network of the living he was? With gun-toting bounty hunters on my tail, it became increasingly difficult to concentrate on everything happening around me. I vowed to try harder for all our sakes.

I squeezed the can until soda splashed out the top. "Does it get easier?"

"What?"

"The killing."

Empathy filled his eyes. "I've never killed anyone."

"Oh." I wiped the soda off my hand onto my pants. Should I be happy or frustrated his resume didn't include assassin? "I guess I should ask Ronan. He graduated from Murder 101."

Adam helped me stand, released me gently. "It's not so bad."

I peered at his reflection in the mirror and lifted a

shoulder.

"Dying," he said, edging closer until my shoulder blades touched his chest.

Warmth trickled into my southern federation. Damn it. My hormones needed a major time-out. Cruel reality knocked any stupid romantic notions out of my head. I backed away. Facing him, I gripped his shoulders. "Swearing by all that is fairy and holy, Aria Elle Walker will not allow you to die."

He grinned slowly, so freaking gorgeous. Despite his gray pallor, dull eyes, and brittle-looking hair, that is. "If anyone can save me, it'll be you."

A loud bang on the door tweaked the nerves in my neck into a twitch storm. "Time's running," Ronan said in a raw tone.

I spun away and grabbed a towel. "I'm not normally a weak-kneed drama queen. Really."

"Hey." Adam caught my arm. "Neither Ronan nor I think any less of you."

"I'll think less of her if she doesn't get her ass out here."

I yanked open the door and bestowed a scathing glare on Ronan. "It's not every day you kill two—"

Faint smile kicking up his lips, he held his gunshot arm to his chest.

Remorse tripped me up. Had the idiot store issued a recall on me yet? "Sorry, I spaced out." I rubbed my settling stomach.

He brushed past Adam on his way into the bathroom. "Feel better?"

"Yeah, thanks." I motioned for him to sit on the closed toilet seat.

He unhooked his gun harness, set it on the counter, and called out as Adam walked away, "Scour the bedrooms. I can't tell if anything's missing." He lowered his voice. "You have a computer?"

"Laptop in my office, tablet in my bedroom."

"Gone. What's on them?"

"Homework, business and customer files, zeros and ones." I frowned at his bloody, torn T-shirt. "Strip it."

He arched his eyebrows but he ripped off the ruined shirt.

Desire rose as I drooled over his to-die-for shoulders, muscled chest, and the washboard abs tapering to slim hips. *Oh. My. God.* His natural tan didn't help my bulging, lusting eyes either. Fortunately, Ronan wasn't paying me an iota of attention while he rummaged in the vanity drawers, gathering first aid supplies as he discovered them in my haphazard glory.

I swiped the fresh coat of perspiration off my upper lip and stared at his gun to stop from totally making a fool of myself.

Perched on the rim of the bathtub, I soaked a rag in antiseptic cleanser. I dabbed the cotton cloth over Ronan's raw gash, generating a wince. "It's pretty deep."

"Wrap it. We don't have time for a Med-Hub stop."

Easy to find, Med-Hubs were scattered around the city. They were just small emergency clinics open 24/7 and catered to anyone with a name. I supposed he didn't want to cough up his name if his father was the all mighty Wizard of the Emerald City.

Frowning, I cleansed the wound and eased the towel up his arm toward the hollow between his neck and shoulder. I wiped the smoking hot tattoo twining his bicep. Green ivy and barbed wire twisted around his arm, dripping drops of red tattoo blood. Each twisted knot on the barbwire formed a swirling number thirteen. Did Ronan also need a focusizer? A strange inner excitement trembled down my limp legs.

I brushed his hair aside, revealing crusty red inflammation bordering two small scabs on his neck. "Who's been gnawing on you? I think it's infected." I touched the cloth to the wounds. He flinched and clenched his hands.

"Sleeping with vampires?"

He flicked my hand away. "Leave it." Tension stood out on his shoulders in knots.

I gripped his square jaw, forcing him to meet my gaze. His smooth-shaven skin blistered beneath my touch. "If we're in this together, no more dodging." My thumb rubbed over a tiny white scar beneath his lower lip.

Ronan exhaled his annoyance. "My dad stuck me with a monitoring chip to track everything my body did. If I lost an eyelash, the monitor picked it up."

My hand faltered, the cloth fell to the floor. "Bastard." I grabbed the antibiotic cream, squeezed the tube so hard a glop of cream shot out and landed on Ronan's chest. Heat zoomed to my face. As much as I was dying to lay my bare hands on him, I had to hold my hand back as it warred with my hormones...and the doppelgänger aura meld thingy screwing up my head.

Ronan slid his fingers through the creamy glob and wiped it on the twin wounds. "I agreed to it for my dad's experiments."

"Did you have a leak in your think tank or something?" I pushed his hand away and finished slathering the cream on his scabs.

"He also snuck in a tracking chip. I dug them both out before I left Seattle."

"I suppose he's the type who can sell black widows to women with arachnophobia too." I slung the tube on the vanity. It skittered across the slick granite and bounced behind the toilet. "Your father's a piece of work," I spat out. Doing my best with an angry air blanketing us, I bandaged his arm.

Ronan guzzled the rest of my soda and tossed the can into the trashcan. "It doesn't get better, but it becomes easier to shift focus and detach."

"What?" I taped the last of the gauze in place.

"The killing."

I shoved the medical supplies into a pile on the counter, my fist crushing a helpless tube of cortisone. "Was your first bad luck kill an accident too?"

"That was the first of two times I lost control of my telekinesis after a ton of energy hit me from external sources."

"How?"

He shrugged. "I lost focus."

It didn't compute. I hadn't lost focus last night. "This won't be the last for me, will it?"

He took my hand, wrapping it in the heat of his. Our auras vibrated around us before his taint flared up and killed the meld. "Our powers are mixing in creepy ways I'm sure no one gets. I doubt anyone ever factored in Adam. Who knows how the Rift magic will affect us." He squeezed my fingers. "Or any other doppelgängers and other sorcerers in the world."

I knelt between his knees. Our eyes locked, and the certainty in his gaze would have shot me out of orbit if I weren't already docked for repairs. Reaching his bad arm forward, he feathered his fingers down my cheek. His thumb slid over my lips and he tamped down another wince.

Butterflies fluttered along the back of my neck. I shifted my attention to his arm and eased away lest my traitorous body betray my head beyond the point of no return. "Adam's...dying because his powers are tainted and erratic, and you've lost most of yours. You both can't exist without sharing your powers until the Rift is fixed." One way or another. "That's why you can't control it and why it keeps attacking me."

"I guess that's the doppelgänger effect. Who knows?" Surprise sparkled in his eyes, slid to his mouth. "You're smarter than you look."

"We're like bats twisting upside down in the sunshine." I swatted his knee and rose to my feet. "Let's go. First we save Zoe. Then we stop your father's nefarious plans."

I helped him slip into the clean T-shirt he'd brought, sticking a finger through a weak seam under the left arm, ripping it. His brow went all wrinkly, but he wore the shirt anyway.

In the living room, I surveyed the sea of disaster with a sharp poke of dismay. So we had a few wrenches chucked into the saving-our-butts goal. Ronan hooked his thumb in a belt loop to stabilize his arm. One-handed, he uprighted an easy chair as if it weighed nothing.

"I've never seen any book like this *Illuminaria* your sperm donor thinks I have. My tablet's encrypted so they're up crap creek without a plunger." My customer data included communications and drawings. I kept my personal charm designs in encrypted files. Fortunately, I backed up to two clouds. One can never be too paranoid.

My diatribe drew winged eyebrows on Ronan's sallow face. "What're you hiding?"

I heated from his scrutiny and shoved up my sweater sleeves. "I make enameled charms and keep my designs private, that's all."

"Do you sell the charms?"

I shuffled through a life's worth of decorative odds and souvenir ends to the corner of the living room. My collection of dragon statues in the curio cabinet appeared to have survived the destruction. I closed my eyes for a few seconds, then set the colorful creatures to rights on the glass shelves. Most of the dragons had been gifts from my mother and grandmother, and my favorite pink and purple one formed the logo of my company.

Thank My Lucky Charms. I couldn't very well name my business *Lucky Thirteen*, huh? "I sell pieces to local jewelry shops, craft shows, and on my web store. My main business is in custom pieces pursuant to customer specifications." Hail to my new mission statement. 'Bout time I nailed it down. *Note to thieves: update Aria's website.*

Ronan seemed to chew on my words as he reset the

chairs around the dining table. The perps had slashed the burgundy and gold chair cushions, the stuffing hanging down the sides like sopping clouds. I watched him punch the innards into place, his hands searching inside the cushions a little too long for my tastes. Annoyance flickered through me.

Racking my brain, I stalked from one end of the room to the other. Hiding the rage and terror clawing at me, I rubbed a gouge along the corner of the mahogany end table where it had banged the edge of the steps. The table was one of the few things I'd kept of my mother's. I gripped the edge until my knuckles whitened and Ronan gently pried my hands away. Combing for additional evidence, I hid the rage and terror clawing at me. "Your father really thinks my mom and her ancestors hid parts of the book?" Both our gazes slid to Melisande's tablet sitting on the sofa.

"He spent years searching for the *Illuminaria*, ancient texts, and journals of the Thirteen sorcerers. He has sketchy evidence that your ancestor wrote the book," Ronan replied. "Your mother's the descendant. Did you train together?"

Reluctantly, I threw the pillow clutched to my chest onto the couch, met his trademarked Cro-Magnon stare. "Get real. She hardly knew the extent of my abilities." Regret slipped over me.

Dawn's light bloomed inside my mind, illuminating a rocky trail to a forgotten memory. I sank down on the frayed couch, shoving wads of stuffing through the zippered cushion. The dead strolled across my spine in lopsided gaits, sending shivers up and down my backside. "She always pounded into me that if I possessed unusual paranormal abilities I should keep it zipped, even to my grandmother." Mom totally knew about me if she was a descendant. I slapped my hand over my mouth. It was all a ruse. *Why, Mom?*

Adam finished his clue gathering in the bedrooms and

joined us. "Did she leave anything behind?" He stopped in front of the windows overlooking the wintergreen hillsides. Wistfulness flared in his eyes, and his hair swayed as if air drifted through the strands. He scratched his pointy ear, snagging a thatch of hair off his scalp. "Journal, books, letters?" he added as if nothing were amiss, shoving the wadded hairball in his pocket.

A pang of alarm chased off the perennial cobwebs in my head. How much longer did Adam have to live?

"Nothing like that." A wayward thought cut through the lingering head fuzz. Years ago, I used to see her hunched over her desk, researching and writing during every spare moment. I couldn't put my pinkie on it, though. Whenever I had asked, she'd said she was writing a book. I never dug deeper.

"What—" Interest increased the unnatural sparkle in Ronan's eyes.

I waved my hand, scrunching my face. "I remember Mom writing a novel in a notebook when she usually used a laptop." I ransacked my memory to the day I had plowed through her paperwork, recalling all the useless drivel I'd shredded. My face fell, as well as my anticipation, into a puddle of frustration.

Sudden horror clamped that infernal claw around my heart. *Duh, blonde alert.* I pushed off the sofa and cut across the room to the hallway. I wheeled toward Adam. "Did you see my cats?"

"Hiding under your bed."

Relief snipped a knot in my neck. "I'll check on them, and then we should take off."

I coaxed Cody and Cleo out from underneath my bed. My purple swirl comforter hung in tatters off one side of the skewed mattress, and Cody had polyfill wrapped around her neck. Seething, I snatched the stuffing away and flung it into the trashcan. I wanted to fling the bastard who'd done this off my balcony with a wad of polyfill shoved up his ass.

Hugging each cat, I kissed their furry heads, and they snuggled on the bed. Cody swatted at the key ring stuck in my waistband and I knew they'd be okay. As I turned to walk away, that wayward thought decked me and I skidded to a halt. I yanked the keys out of my waistband, flicking the three keys until the small brass key to Mom's old trunk where she'd stored mementos from her past stopped me cold. I always kept the key close to me, to remind me that Mom had a life before me. A haunting memory from my childhood filled my head. *Oh, holy mother of the craptastic.*

I closed my bedroom door. Her steamer trunk with the padded bench on top rested at the foot of my bed, the lid lifted open, cards, costume jewelry, and mementos scattered across the littered floor. I reached into the bottom and moved some ancient T-shirts around until I found the hidden catch and pried a nail file underneath the false bottom. I lifted the hidden panel only Mom and I had known about. Two packets of papers encased in thick envelopes lay on the layer between the two bottoms. Dickhead Riley's men should stick to picking fleas out of each other's hair. Bounty and treasure hunting certainly wasn't their *forte.*

I walked into my bathroom and locked the door. Avoiding my ravaged face in the mirror, I opened the thicker and larger envelope, my hands shaking. Older than dirt vellum paper with a slight dusty, musty smell met my gaze. A strange language covered the pages with drawings, maps, symbols, and what looked to be recipes. My heart palpitated. I'd just hit the motherlode of my missing life in the lost pages of the book that held the keys to the Forbidden magical world. The *Illuminaria.* Carefully, I shoved the packets flat on the bottom of a zippered tote bag and stuffed a few of Mom's T-shirts around them. Mind spinning into a vortex of excitement and dread, I rejoined my new wingmen.

NINE

Ronan and Adam were swiping through Melisande's tablet at the dining room table. I set the alarm on my cell, plunked my bag by my side, and they moved the tablet closer to me. Typed manuscript pages with diagrams, maps, and symbols, eerily similar to the pages I just saw, flashed on the screen. Ronan scrolled past so much text, potions, spells, and what appeared recipes and diagrams my head spun.

"She really did have a translation? I thought she was yanking your chain." I gripped Ronan's wrist to slow his scrolling.

"Enough to be lethal," he replied. "Not all of it, though."

"Hold up!" Adam exclaimed, stopping Ronan's finger from swiping to the next page. The new page on the screen bore a decorative flourish at the top and a number eight chapter header. He read aloud, "'Note: A cataclysmic earthen energy-based event could trigger a failure in the magic securing the Rifts and allow Forbidden magic to flow over the earth once again, triggering latent magic in descendants of the fae or sorcerers who may have escaped the Abolishment or those not counted among the Forbidden, those who may have an inkling of magic in their blood without knowledge of such. However, such an event is unlikely, and without the formidable magic of at least a pair of Forbidden sorcerers, the doorways to the Realm of the Void should remain secure.'" Adam scrolled to the next page. "That's the Earthquake Cluster event."

"It says *two* sorcerers. Why would your dumbass father have you open the Rift alone? It's like he deliberately had you screw it up." I continued reading over Ronan's right arm, then stopped, a dawning revulsion pinching my heart. "Wait a freaking freakshow minute. He knew what he was doing without the need of two kickass sorcerers! Was he really using your blood with his alchemy, Ronan? Or did he have the blood of another Forbidden? Whose blood?"

Adam and Ronan ogled me, the truth drawing down the horror on their faces.

The tablet fell out of Ronan's hand, clattered onto the table. "He siphoned enough blood out of me to supply a blood bank. I always assumed it was my blood he used in his potion." The pallor of his face gave truth to his father's blood-thieving activities.

I rubbed the vein in the crook of my left arm. "Did my father give him my mother's blood?" Had my father stolen her blood when he left, put it on ice, and sold it to Riley all those years later? Or my blood?

Ronan lifted his eyes to my face. "I...I don't know." He rubbed his head, his confusion seeming to drain him. "My father's brilliant. There's no way he'd attempt to open the Rift with just my telekinesis and alchemy based on my blood."

"Then he used someone else's blood in his alchemy," Adam said. "Someone not quite strong enough. Not as strong as Aria or you."

"My mother. Who else? Maybe he's had her blood since

they all knew each other in college." I drummed the table so hard, my fingers ached. "Has he captured any other descendants?"

"Not that I know of. He pretty much has focused his biggest attention on you. And me. Not that he wasn't searching for others."

"Because we're the strongest? But not our mothers?"

"Appears so."

Well, screw me screaming and the other Forbidden descendants born of the Earthquake Cluster-Fuck-it-to-Riley's Hell.

I leaned over Ronan's arm and continued reading aloud, "'If one Forbidden sorcerer uses strong sorcery to attempt to open a Rift, he may incur cracks in the original magic and cause faulty magic to leak out over Earth. This magic may be unpredictable and may cause death to the sorcerer who attempted the opening...and possibly to others—'" I clutched my hand to my throat. "Your father tried to kill you."

"That's another reason I want him dead." Ronan shoved out of his chair so hard, the chair toppled over backward and clattered to the floor.

My alarm chirped, sending me slipping halfway off my seat, dropping a crumb of reality back into our numb minds.

With the few minutes we had to spare and my ravaged stomach aching the whole time over Zoe's plight, we rejoined Fin snoozing in the SUV.

"Didn't you bring enough clothes in your other *ten* suitcases?" Ronan grimaced at the stuffed tote bag at my feet in the back seat.

I gave him a black look. "I need something a little lighter."

Ronan grunted. "You do know it gets cold in Seattle, right? And it's February?"

Even though I lied, I ignored the man who seemed to know nothing about women and fashion. Bypassing the latest chapter in our manifesto *de* lunacy, I asked, "With all the bounty hunters on my tail, why would your father send Melisande? Didn't he trust the others to bring both me and *you* back?" I refused to admit that Ronan might be working on his dad's side until I saw more proof. Breaking into Melisande's tablet went a long way, though. Hell on high, I needed someone to believe in. May as well be the barbarian.

Ronan tugged a red smartphone out of his pocket. "We'll find out."

My mouth rounded in my newest flycatcher parody. "Were you a pickpocket in a former life?"

The SUV's beefy rumble drowned out the lull in the cab. Ronan grunted like a caveman playing with a box of matches from the front seat. He scrolled through Melisande's smartphone trying to decode her passwords. In vain, by the one-syllable grunts he spewed forth.

Finally, I waded into the silence, fear for Zoe paralyzing my thoughts. "What's your plan?"

"Ian usually works alone, but I wouldn't count on it. Sometimes my dad's men team up." Ronan stuffed the phone into his jacket pocket. "Adam will cover us in the wings. I'll negotiate with Ian. You'll stay with me."

Clutching my purse to my stomach, I studied the side of Ronan's head, liking the way his dark locks layered in a windblown tousle.

"Do I knock them out all at once or one at a time?" I asked almost too eagerly, as if knocking out people was the norm.

Ronan checked his gun again. Was I that boring or was he that anal? He lifted his head. "They'll have bio-energy detectors and deadeners. They'll sense and kill your magic."

My eyes rolled back into my head slot machine style. "If we have the same ability, don't you know how to toss out brain waves to shield from bio-energy tools? I can get by a 6000D." The 6000D was the newest detector/deadener used at airports, government, and military sites. Supposedly, no

ESP bypassed one without detection. Deadeners killed innate energy and dampened aural energy. Sometimes the tools were so strong and people so weak, the electrical waves they emitted knocked people out. Did I mention that NUW equaled paranoid? For some weird reason, I oozed by any detector undetected.

Ronan rubbed his jaw. "With full strength, I can bolster my aura to shield my brain waves from the older models, but they might detect Adam if he's channeling my energy. You'll have to drop any block you can erect to invoke your telekinesis."

I fluttered my hand in the air. "I hate to short out your memory board, but you forget I can do more than one telekinetic spell at a time."

"Shit." Ronan slowly ran a finger on the inside of his leather shoulder harness. It seemed weird hanging out with guys parading guns as fashion accessories. At least I wasn't in the 'hoods of Oakland.

Adam lowered his sunglasses and regarded me in the rearview mirror. "Hope we're never on your bad side." He turned the SUV down a side street of older businesses, a less traveled route toward the university.

My grin broadened, but my nervous, cold heart didn't enjoy the rash of selfish pride. I huddled into my jacket. "Sooo we locate Ian, you give the signal, I knock him out and anyone else working with him. We snatch Zoe, then bounce to smack down on Richie Senior and fix the Rift."

A puppet string seemed to yank Ronan's spine arrow straight. Adam hissed out his breath and tossed his sunglasses on the dash. Even Fin scooted away, regarding me with her doggy eyes as if I was a pariah from the Void.

My grin faltered. Ronan's aura attacked me in waves of pins and needles perforating my skin. Not that it did much good, my aura ascended to defend against his lack of control.

I observed his flinty profile and Adam's deer-in-headlights reflection in the mirror. "What?" I rubbed my neck, struggled to deflect Ronan's tainted energy. The prickles intensified. By Ronan's reddening sourpuss cast, he struggled with it too. Fin growled and the hackles mounted on her neck.

"Stop the car." Ronan reached for the door handle.

Adam swerved out of traffic into the parking lot of a skyscraping residential building. Ronan flung open the door and jogged away before the vehicle stopped rolling.

The barbs on my skin eased. A strong blast of cinnamon-vanilla wafted from the vents. I took shallow breaths, using the air freshener to focus on my diminishing pain.

"Better?"

"Yeah, but it's getting more intense each time."

"The Rift's screwing with his power."

I massaged my temples, wishing I could rub out the woodpeckers pecking for dinner in my head. "Is it affecting me because I'm supposedly one of the Thirteen?"

"Your guess is as good as mine." Adam squeezed my knee, his fingers feverishly hot.

"Wonderful." I traced the prominent blue veins on his opaque hand, stark against my dark jeans. "Why'd you two freak out?"

"Our meld of magic whipped up a static funnel. Weird."

"Oh. I didn't feel anything." Weird was my middle name, and changing the subject was quickly becoming my game. "So there's got to be a reason why Ian came to the U."

Ronan paced the half-empty parking lot, one hand fisted at his side, the other fingering the scabs on his neck. Thirteen parking spaces separated us, enough distance for now.

Adam glanced at his watch. "Riley has the university on a dead zone list. It makes it the perfect place for a paranormal ambush."

"What the heck's a dead zone?" My stomach caved in

waiting for the answer.

"Dead zones naturally kill magic. Best guess is that it's due to dead ley lines and the earth or people can't emit energy."

Son of a dead zone bitch.

The SUV's engine spluttered, shuddered, and croaked. I picked at a ragged cuticle, flipped the fringe on my retro suede jacket. Color me cursed. Adam clicked the engine button off and on, receiving a metallic grinding for his effort. He punched his finger on the screen of the diagnostic computer, scrutinized the readouts.

A breeze whipped a sheet of paper at the side of Ronan's head. He grabbed at it, trod into a puddle of freshly dumped coffee. Curses chased after the paper and he stomped his boot on a patch of grass. Poor guy. *Hexes come and go when you play with me.*

The engine rumbled into a smooth purr. Adam cast me a quizzical look, and I gave him a thumbs-up. At least I had a positive attitude about my unfortunate destructive tendencies.

Thankfully, my skin had quit poking me to death. I rolled down the window and beckoned to Ronan. Quiet and tolerant as a mute mummy, he clambered into the front seat. Adam drove into traffic, his fingers dancing across the computer. I fidgeted in my seat, the creaking leather grating on my last happy nerve. My heart rate sped up the closer to the university we traveled.

Ronan interrupted my troubled thoughts. "Sorry 'bout that."

Without thinking, I combed my fingers through his silky hair, caressing his cool neck, leaving a trail of gooseflesh that traveled up my arm and warmed a jagged path to my heart. Why tall, dark, and barbarian of all people? It wasn't as if Ronan was attracted to me, but something existed between us. When his aura wasn't trying to off me, it was calming, akin to a soul deep tie. A connection I wanted to test drive around for a while. There might even be Belgian chocolate at the finish line...or Adam. *Another note to self: zap my brain cells when I get home.*

"Again, what's our plan?" Before my hands did something stupid, I switched to ruffling Fin's short fur. She nudged my hand for me to scratch behind her ears.

Too much going on and I was getting lost in thought. A scary place, I might add. I had so much to learn before I went off half-cocked on my own. Zoe was my first priority.

Ronan stared forward at the thickening traffic. At the rate we traveled, Zoe would be a vengeful ghost by the time we got to the university chapel. *First haunting: Aria Elle Walker.*

"Count on multiple trackers and we go with Aria's plan." Ronan sounded like he was biting off words and spiting them out. "If the university's not in a dead zone, can you spread out your aural block? My jacked-up magic may not slip by detectors."

Inwardly, I gloated. "Probably." Linking our auras was the only way to do it. "Adam too?" My good aura and Ronan's residual power should be strong enough to tackle Adam's taint.

"Why'd I know you were going to say that?" Through glittery silver-flecked eyes, he tossed me a sideways calculating look. Fin's tail whisked up a breeze. "How many can you knock out while shielding us?"

"With the way my power's been acting, a few within ten to twenty feet."

"How close do we have to be?"

"Maybe two to three yards."

"How exactly do you knock them out?" Adam swerved to avoid a driving-impaired lane changer. He slapped his palm on the horn, letting it blast for a few seconds, the loud honk drowning out the indecision wailing in my brain.

I nibbled on my lower lip, tempted to chomp on a

fingernail, and smoothed the fir on Fin's neck. Did I have a rent-to-own deal with Satan, or what?

Adam busted out laughing. "After all this, you distrust me?" His laughter held such warmth, I felt like an idiot savant for holding back.

I didn't trust Adam any less than I trusted Ronan. My secret telekinesis had been such a private part of my whole life. Now I had two strangers with whom to entrust my most precious secret. One already knew what it meant to be a freak of nature. Both were sinking into my soul with an awakening that left me reeling. I resisted the urge to dip my fingers into Ronan's soft, thick hair again.

Adam flicked on his right blinker. "If it bothers you that much—"

"No. You've exposed your whole being to me when you didn't have to. I respect that."

"You'll kill us if we tell anyone?" Ronan chuckled.

He laughed! Did a blizzard blast hell last night?

"That's the deal." If they betrayed me, I could always drizzle them with curses for the rest of their lives. Eventually, I'd figure out how.

The mere thought of how my telekinetic energy had morphed and expanded last night sent my brain spinning. I tried to bury the thought, but it kept rising faster than a hungry zombie. Could I control my power better? What if I failed? What if it had happened because of Ronan's proximity?

As casually as I could manage, I said, "It's an instantaneous telekinetic hypnotism. I mind bend them into a deep sleep. I can't explain it. I just think someone asleep and he is. Lights out, Snoozeville. Ya know, brain wave to brain wave." An odd tense vibration shifted the aura bubble around us. "Well, it's not like I've done it a lot." I wiped my sweaty palms on my pants. "Not counting the two, you know the ones I accidentally, not on purpose...killed." I almost choked on the word and it left me reluctant to ever use my abilities. If my life was threatened again, I'd have to focus harder to restrain my power to prevent a deathblow.

To think they feared *me*, tiny Aria Elle Walker. Didn't Ronan's telekinetic talents work the same way? I'd tax his brain about it later. Hopefully, it wouldn't hurt much.

"Um, guys, what's the deal if it's a dead zone?"

"You still got your zapper?" Ronan pulled out his gun and did his anal check again. "What do you feel? Do you still have your magic?"

It still seemed weird calling my ESP "magic." It scared me, because it solidified the fact that not only was my telekinesis illegal, *I* was a criminal. The government may not have originally written the laws to distinctively forbid ESP as Forbidden magic, but they would now if they knew about us.

I patted my hip for my stun gun hanging on a belt loop. *Magic* rumbled inside me, ready for action. I tossed out a feeler of aural energy and Ronan's hair stood erect as if the roof was full of static electricity. "Yep. I work."

Adam laughed and Ronan smoothed down his hair, shaking his head and grumbling to his other selves.

Adam parked behind the university's multi-purpose court. A sterling moon slivered the northern sky, granting little illumination. An amethyst sky gobbled the tail of the sun and twilight's first stars glittered. An occasional student and security droid wandered the near-deserted campus.

We had thirty minutes to cruise the grounds and move into lynch mob position. It appeared safe for Adam to go one way, Ronan and I another. We decided to split up to keep Adam from being detected if Ronan and I were followed. Adam's screwed aura would send bio-energy tools through the nearest stargate, shifting any focus off him. Enough people milled around the campus to clue Ian and potential crew into thinking they were picking up random paranormal footprints.

Ronan and I moved within the shadows of the buildings. We dashed from one structure to another, ducking behind bushes, trees, and garbage cans, evading as much security camera detection, human and droid contact as possible.

The narrow silhouette of a one-story building hid us as an under eaves camera made its sweep. Unused to this cloak and dagger routine, my heart raced. February's humidity seeped through my clothes. I rubbed my hands together, now wishing for those elusive gloves.

Tightness rolled down Ronan's back as he leaned into me. "They're not motion activated," he murmured. He took my hand and we resumed the mission impossible.

Adrenaline blazed through me, a rampant wildfire I hadn't experienced since...ever. I had a difficult time deciphering whether it stemmed from danger or something even more sinister, such as desire. *Whatever.* I bottled up my spineless jelly senses to focus on the meet and greet.

The whirl of a droid's wheels hissed behind us. Ronan towed me between two brick buildings. As the security droid rolled closer, my heart began to drum a rock solo. A cool breeze kicked up, swaying tree branches in a frenzied dance. It swept the spike of warmth out of me and my teeth chattered anew. I had a hard time concentrating on keeping my electromagnetic energy on an even keel.

The droid skated past us intent on an abandoned backpack dumped on a bench ten yards away bordering a lawn area. Its monotone voice called in a report, and the click of a camera eye filled the quiet night with a sense of normalcy. *Oops.* A ditzy blonde cell must've escaped, since normal had pulled a one-eighty on me.

"You still have magic?" Ronan asked.

"Yes. Guess it's not a dead zone."

Ronan went all frowny. "What little magic I had is dead. I can't feel anything here."

"Maybe your pops was wrong. He's not the Master of

Wikipedia, is he?"

Ronan hooted. "He wishes."

"Hey." I fisted my hand in my pocket until my arm hurt. "What did you feel at the Rift?"

Once we escaped the droid's sensory range, we continued on our way. Automatic landscape lights flashed on, providing more illumination than we wanted. We passed an overflowing garbage compactor, and the stench of rotting bananas barraged my nose. *Thanks, but I already popped my daily dose of potassium.*

"When I went to the park the first time with my father, I felt like I was being eaten alive from the inside out."

I eased closer to Ronan's side, shivering from his download as much from the night in wintry Iceland. All of a sudden, he wrapped his arm around me, tugging us behind a palm tree. Dry papery fronds rasped together. Two college-aged guys skulked by, gazes darting left to right, silent, treacherous. My heart began that incessant pounding again. I leaned into Ronan, my power boiling to the surface. A low throb in my jaw radiated to my temples.

"There it is," the taller of the two guys said and streaked toward the droid rifling through the backpack on the bench.

I kept tabs on my power, despite the false alarm. It cost me a dull headache whenever I forcibly focused too often on holding in brain waves that tried to escape. Or when unlucky thirteen wanted to walk all over me.

Ronan dipped his head and whispered in my ear, "That was further proof the Rift was already leaking from the earthquakes. Magic existed before I'd done a thing."

A breeze carried the smell of dampness and mold, adding the flavor of distaste to Ronan's tale. I froze in the elongated shadow of a three-story building. Despite the temperature, my palms sweated. "What would you feel if the Rift was fully open?"

"According to the *Illuminaria*, intense energy. More

extreme than the energy the three of us whip up together." The silver moon highlighted the flecks of charcoal in Ronan's eyes brighter than the stars twinkling in the indigo sky. "When my father forced me to invoke the spell to open it, magic wrenched on me, trickled into me. It belonged inside me in every sense." He cupped a hand around my neck and the heat of his fingers lingered in a wash of pained pleasure. "Like thousands of bodies and minds had invaded me and wanted to hijack my body."

When I absorbed energy from around me, I hardly noticed it any longer. It totally belonged inside me or as part of my aura. I pressed my neck into his hand. Revulsion kicked off a rave in my stomach, but I forced it into a tea party. "Now?"

He bent his head to my ear again, his warm breath fanning my lobe. "Since I met you, the feelings have caved. I feel alive again, like I've found salvation."

Tremors traveled up from the hollow of my back, and I realized it was Ronan's arm trembling around my waist. The weight of his gaze weakened my knees. Shock struck me and my heart lurched madly. A slender, delicate thread formed between us and I sensed his vulnerability. I clutched his leather jacket in my freezing fists. The warmth of his body offered me no comfort as our auras spun in an unpleasant mix of dread and sorrow.

He gathered me closer. "You want to open the Rift now, Aria?" he whispered, his voice soft, dangerous.

TEN

I registered Ronan's words, losing the ability to breathe for a moment. Did I want to toy with the Rift in any way, shape or form? Was the energy there different from what I already attracted and absorbed? Would I be able to fight off my unluck the way I can when I know it's coming? *Can I trade this assignment for the one behind door number 7?*

We rounded a bend and the church rolled into view, dark and ominous under a slash of pale moonlight. According to Ian, the tower doors would be unlocked, the church undergoing remodeling. We cased the perimeter. No foreign magic intruded upon my senses outside my aura shield. "Aura shield" was just my snazzy tag for jumbling my energy and the energy I absorbed from around me into a force field of indeterminate energy, or magic I guess. Usually, I blocked my telekinetic footprint if other ESPs sniffed around me as if I was a catnip-scented mouse to a fat cat. This happened more often than I cared to admit. So much for the Abolishment. So much for a fake dead zone too. My magic was doing a little smirking inside me, wanting to go bat-shit crazy on kidnapper Ian.

A window halfway up the tower reflected a wedge of moonlight, liquid illumination dripping into the tower and chasing away the bogeyman shadows to reveal the menacing double doors. I flicked the safety on and off my stun gun with one hand, clasped the other around my lucky charm. The electricity buzzing within me couldn't dial down my erratic heartbeat. My muscles tensed as I prepared for bounty hunters to attack.

Ronan drew me into the undulating shadows of winter-bare trees. "Do you feel energy from anyone else? I still don't sense a thing." He sent out a jagged feeler of energy that sputtered at our feet.

"Just your faulty aura," I whispered, wishing I could bolster him with my powers.

He slicked his hair off his forehead, winced as he hugged his bad arm to his side. "Am I hurting you?"

"No." My fingernails dug trenches in my palm. I loosened my clench around my pendant. "If this is a dead zone, I'd know it by now." A white owl ruffled a palm tree and screeched off into the night. I nearly lurched out of my thong.

The grunting of an injured man carried to us from inside the bell tower. Obviously, he wasn't trying to hide the racket. Ronan hefted his gun and motioned me out of the way. I drew my stun gun and hopped safely behind him. Stupid wasn't my middle name. He was bigger and badder than me. I mentally readied a knockout spell for blastoff. The Aria Special was just for bad luck backup.

The grunting evolved into drawn out groans. The cool, prickly air carried a soft thumping, like someone dragging a sack of body parts across gravestones.

Ronan motioned for me to hang back while he snuck around the tower. My heart pulsed into turbo mode. It wasn't every day I became embroiled in a high stakes illegal paranormal revolution. *Like you hadn't already been hit with a cluestick.*

I peeked around the adobe wall. Ronan's silhouette disappeared through the doors. A bird whistle rang to my left, and Adam's aura grazed my cheeks like sandpaper. Suddenly, his firm chest pressed against my back, boosting my armor a smidge. I knew I shouldn't need it, but, he*ll*o, my comfort zone was far, far away.

"Coast is clear, security and a few kids. What's going on?" He spoke low in my ear.

A gargled yell echoed inside the bell tower followed by a thud against the interior walls. The clatter of metal scraping a wall resonated through my skull and prodded us into action. Adam lunged for the door. I ran fast on his heels, clamping a restraint on my seething power. My pounding head screamed for release. With Ronan and Adam's intoxicating, rabid energy assaulting me, it was increasingly difficult to control my own. I didn't usually live by the saying, "payback's a bitch," but kidnapper Ian would live to regret that night.

Adam kicked the right side door open, an ebony gun a startling clash against his ashen hand. I scuttled to the closed side of the thick wooden doors.

"Damn it, Riley." Ian's husky Scottish burr tipped off his identity. "Leave off the force."

I shoved past Adam into the square tower, my gaze zipping around the cluttered room. No redheaded firebrand met my frantic search among the construction debris. Ronan rested his booted foot on a burly man's hip. Sporting thick chestnut hair, he looked in his early twenties. The dude flopped on his side on a spattered painter's tarp. How much of the red splotches were blood versus paint? A wet stain darkened the left shoulder of Ian's gray T-shirt. Blood flowed from his right thigh, staining his jeans a deep purple. Gunshots, I presumed. Both must have missed major arteries or organs since Mr. Scottish looked more alert than a whore on a crack diet.

"Where's Zoe, you piece of shit?" I primed my stunner. "If you've hurt her, I'm gonna zap the life out of you."

"Gone." Ian began hacking up a lung. A crimson flush stole across the pain crinkling his handsome, whiskered face.

So help me thirteen, I wanted to yank those crinkles into ditches until I got answers. With all the frosty hatred I was able to muster on my face, I took a step toward him.

Ronan held out his hand. "Hold off." His gaze impaled me with a warning.

He had one lousy minute before I got my spin at the Highlander prick.

Ronan shifted his boot off Ian's hip. "Start talking and maybe we'll call an ambulance."

An expression of part evil and mostly pain consumed Ian's feeble grin. Blood loss changed his skin to vampire white. An ambulance might be too late for him the longer we delayed medical treatment. I think he knew it by the look eating the arrogant satisfaction in his eyes. Still I didn't trust him and wanted him tied up.

"Do you want a swift death or a crawling, tortuous one?" I nudged my foot into the blooming stain on his leg.

He roared bloody murder and grabbed my boot. His waning strength propelled me off balance, twirling me onto a sawhorse. Before I could say, "Hells bells," I was tumbling to the floor. My head crashed into an aluminum ladder and my left hand struck a saw blade. The blade serrated my palm as my hand slid to the canvas covering the floor. Pain blazed up my arm and unconsciousness flirted with my mind.

Shouts and scuffles ensued. My aching back and thudding head beat me into submission. The four bells towering above me multiplied into a dozen. I closed my eyes to stop the spinning and ringing, the nauseating sinking of despair as fate tossed another bad luck wrench into my village square. If I died, who'd save Zoe?

Adam's face floated above me. "Aria." Concern pebbled his voice. "Where does it hurt?"

I opened my mouth to speak but my throat had gone Sahara dry. A tear slipped down my cheek. I didn't think I was crying. Maybe my head was numb and leaking.

Adam's hands tightened on my shoulders. "Talk to me, Blondie."

I cracked open my eyes. "Blondie?" That cut past the desert in my throat. Zoe was the only one who had the nerve to call me Blondie. A tiny cheerleading squad tossed pompoms in the pit of my stomach. A lock of his translucent hair curled around my mess of short tresses. "You're one to talk." His relief trembled against me in his exhaled breath. Air wavered, and Adam's aura surrounded me in warm and fuzzies, chased by flakes of cold taint.

I didn't much care for this artificial reality if it was going to hurt so badly. "Other than a concussion, a sliced palm, and a twisted ankle, I'm okay." I rolled onto my side, patted my hair into place.

Adam gently pulled me into a hug, cradling me against his six-pack abs beer companies would kill for. After they killed for Ronan's tanned six-pack. I buried my face against his shoulder, inhaling his citrusy, amber cologne. Our magic generated waves of energy, sweeping the fog out of my brain until one measly thought blew away the mist.

"Let me at that scumbag!" Woozy, I wrestled out of Adam's arms. He hoisted me up, balancing me on my feet. I waited for the dizziness to pass, steadying my legs. "Ian's contribution to the population problem has just been accepted."

Ronan found masking tape in the construction gear and tied Ian's wrists behind his back and taped his ankles. He trained his gun at the goon's head. Said goon slumped on his side, a parody of pleasure contorting his pallid face.

My inner cat wanted to scratch his pleasure into pain

so bad, I had to fight to keep my claws dangling at my sides. "Where's Zoe? Who did this to you? Why did you want to meet us here?"

Ian's mouth slackened and his eyes closed. He sagged onto his stomach, his body limp.

"No!" Outrage paralyzed me. Lightning strikes of luck filled my telekinetic receptors. Lucky for Ian, not me, as it ignited an excruciating fire in my battered body. I launched a wave of uplifting energy toward him. Air Drugs, one might call it. When I was twelve, I'd tried it on a neighbor's cat after a car hit it. I kept the cat alive while I borrowed my neighbor's motor scooter and zoomed to the vet who saved its eight other lives.

Ronan checked Ian's neck pulse. "He's alive."

Ian's eyelids fluttered up. "What'd you do to me?" His opaque gaze found a home on me.

"I can do more if you give it up." My grip grew moist on my stun gun. Antsy as all get out, I danced from foot to sore foot.

"I didn't hurt Zoe Marino. We have no need for her to die. I wanted you two, same as the other dozen trackers Riley sent." His ragged breathing stabilized. "I was told this was a dead zone and a good place to make the trade without incurring your magic."

Ronan cursed a blue streak under his breath. "Who took Zoe? Who told you this was a dead zone?"

Ian coughed, his body shaking hard. "Who do you think? We're all fighting for the money. Thought I'd found an alliance. Said she had something to show me here. Instead, she betrayed me, set this up, and sicced your father's dogs on me." Another racking cough rattled him perilously close to comaland.

"Who?" Ronan growled out.

"Melisande—"

Ronan's aura tickled mine, exploiting his hatred and fury toward the Botox hag. I gave Ian another boost of calming energy to keep him talking. It worked and didn't cost me much since I was already in two worlds of hurt.

Ronan rose, stuffing his gun in his shoulder holster. "Someone betrayed her too. She's dead."

"Where's Zoe?" I nudged my booted toes below the bloody trickle staining his pants. "Don't make me ask again."

Pain sunk the sides of Ian's mouth and he gnashed his teeth. "Stop," he cried. "I'm done with this shit. I didn't sign up to die. Let me live, I'll divert Riley away from you. I swear, man."

Danger gleamed in Ronan's eyes, and a smile twitched up the corners of his mouth. "Who the hell took Zoe and shot you up?"

"Micah Duprey." Ian's torso spasmed. The prick laughed as if his sanity was leaking out his new air holes.

Ronan growled and beat a fist into the adobe walls.

"Who's Micah?" I whispered over my shoulder.

"One of Riley's enforcers," Adam replied. "More than a bounty hunter. Riley's sparing no one to hunt you down."

Ronan's anguish smothered the air, bogged me down. Why was Ronan's father so formidable that he hired enforcers and bounty hunters? Fresh waves of pain stung my palm, and I raised my scraped hand to rub away my terror.

Ian coughed. "Here's a tip for you. Get out now, they're coming back for you, if they aren't already circling the wagons."

Adam grabbed my wrist from behind me. "He's right. We're wasting time."

Just as Adam said the words, my magic dwindled, as if an electronic deadener was approaching. And fast. "They're here."

I bolted and stumbled on the doorsill, falling face forward to the ground, catching myself on my hands and knees. White-hot pokers of fire burned my palms. More dots of pain to connect. Adam tripped over me and took a header into a planter of mulch nuggets. Ronan jerked me up, his chest against my back. He half carried, half pushed me toward the walled rose garden.

"Damn it, Aria. Watch what you're doing." As soon as we approached the gate, he released me.

Ire shot through me, becoming a normal emotion renting space in my body. "Thanks for the tweet." Knees now throbbing, I sprinted through the gate into the garden, leaving Ronan on the other side of the wall. A body thumped to the ground behind me in the dark. My heart scudded in my chest. "Ronan?" No response. I slipped my injured hand in my jacket pocket. Empty. Just once, I'd love to use my stun gun before I died.

Rose bushes provided a paltry waist-high shield. I couldn't even rely upon a cloud covering. The crescent moon and the sky of twinkling diamonds ratted me out. Power festered in me, but I feared using a knockout spell in case I hit Ronan. Not that it mattered because I think he was out cold.

"If you want to see Zoe Marino alive, I suggest you reveal yourself." A nasally voice breached the night from the other side of the wall where Ronan had disappeared.

I slipped along the adobe fence closer to the wrought iron gate. "Where is she?" I hid in the shadowy cover of the twelve-foot high wall.

"On her way to Seattle," he said, his stupidity vaccine working overtime.

Another presence drew nearer inside the garden. My alien body of perpetual mystery couldn't absorb blocked energy from anyone at that moment.

I hugged the wall and tried to think, but my head thundered from its collision with the ladder. "What'd you do to Ronan?"

"He can't help you. He's taking a siesta."

"Please." I snickered. "Like I need help from any tool." I

received a hyena bark in response.

Security lights illuminated the other approaching man. A glow reflected off a thin silver rectangular gadget looped around his bull-neck. Although I'd never attempted to manipulate a spell against a deadener, there was a first time for everything, especially with my new meld of doppelgänger power. Mentally, I pitched a net of energy. It scuttled back onto me, showering me in stinging ice. *Oh, hell, squared.*

The man behind the wall strolled under the archway. Both cavemen leveled high-tech guns on me. I was pretty positive the goons had orders to take me alive, so I didn't fret about dying. But I bet the guns held illegal bio-deadeners. Enough to conk me out and stuff me in an airplane cargo hold. Fingers of ice twisted around my heart. I sure wanted to know what church picnic Adam had crashed. "Richard Riley Dominion Research trackers, I presume?"

"Good guess," Neanderthal number two grunted out, his voice deep and raspy.

Did DR get these goons from the Caveman Zoo? He strolled within three feet of me, one man at each shoulder. Both had a deadener strung around his neck.

Baldy grinned at me. "You're cuter than your friend. I've always been partial to blondes. How 'bout you, Frankie?"

"Nah, I love 'em red." A hunk of hacked auburn hair hung from his fist.

I ground my teeth at the sight of Zoe's tangled hair and tossed another wave of bad luck at them. It bounced back and spit static at me. "If you hurt her, I'll pluck out every hair from your bodies one-by-one, then torch you alive."

"Big words from a little gal." Baldy advanced on me. "You willing to come with us, or do we have to haul you out of here?"

Frankie moved a smidge and light glinted off both

deaeners. Then a light-bulb moment whacked me. If I aimed a destructive wave of energy at one deadener, would the other counteract it and fry them both? It was worth a shot. Not like I had many options.

A mockingbird call from the dwarf palms by the bell tower split the thick air of evil. My aura swirled and I recognized Adam's crackling aura. Neither of my would-be captors appeared fazed by the noise.

The dark-haired man took another step closer. "Grab her, Milo, and let's get on the road."

"Wait!" I held up my hand, backing into a spikey rose bush. "I have a deal for you." I mushroomed that weak white flame in my brain and heat expanded as I imposed my will on it. I loosed an extra controlled barrage of energy, pushing against the dampeners, and flung it toward the two deadeners. Rose thorns pricked my butt but I needed the distance. I couldn't risk releasing too much energy in such close proximity if I jammed up the deadeners. No way was I killing anyone else, even if he was a walking argument for birth control.

The air screamed with the surge of energy. A bolt of electricity flickered between them, blinding me for a few seconds. The men roared and scrambled to thrust the sizzling deadeners off their chests. I ducked and skirted around them. Milo lunged and grabbed my legs, knocking us both to the ground. Air whooshed out of my lungs from the impact of my side slamming the damp grass. A mass of screeching nerves burned across my hips, down my legs. My body was so going to betray me and sign that ownership deal with Satan if I lived to see tomorrow.

Milo pinned me on my back, his hulk spread on top of me. "We gave you a choice," he spat in my face. I scrunched my nose, the reek of roadkill on his breath murdering my sense of smell. "Give me the syringe, Frankie."

Milo's crushing weight numbed my torso, and I rotated my head to face Frankie. He rolled and writhed on the ground near the gate, moaning and sputtering. A landscape light illuminated a patch of singed cloth on his chest.

"Hell, we'll do it my way." Milo's fingers dug into my upper arms. Laser pain stabbed my head.

I screamed. *No. No. No. Not another Scrambler.* I'd destroyed the deadeners that held back his ESP and he took full advantage. Stars exploded in my vision and I once again flirted with oblivion. Flickers of lightning zigzagged in my skull, snipping my energy receptors. I vaguely heard Milo chuckling, yet the rumble of his laughter jiggled along the length of me. Confusion muddled my mind and I was unable to draw upon my telekinesis. I gripped my focusizer, but it was cold and silent. I couldn't even lift my knee to knock Milo's family jewels into his throat.

Suddenly, the sound of a blunt object hitting flesh stilled the behemoth on top of me. The magic infiltrating my head cut off, and as quickly as the explosive pain invaded my skull, it vanished. The slumbering weight rolled off me and Adam pulled me to my feet.

"I'm gonna kill that bastard," I managed to say through gritted teeth, balanced against his side.

Strength coursed into my muscles and I wheeled around. Baldy had toppled on top of the other in a mound of twitching cavemen, out like nightlights at sunrise. Or dead. I wasn't about to stick around to ascertain which. I'd had enough of that night.

Between my tortured body and dragging a semi-conscious Ronan, Adam and I lumbered to the SUV without another clash from the Neanderthal Asylum. We decided to follow Zoe to Seattle ASAP. The crapfest had dinged Level Ten.

Adam called in an anonymous report of gunfire at the mission church and a plea to send an ambulance, and then we sped toward the airport, barely staying legal. I shoved my rescued stun gun in my pocket and splayed my fingers against my thumping head, needing a diversion to talk me off the ledge. Ronan flopped in the back seat, Fin sliming his face while he groaned and twitched. He assured us they'd only shot him with a bio-energy stun dart, but I still worried. However, from the grumbling overflowing his mouth, his He-Man pride hurt more than his body.

I leaned between the front seats and studied the half-comatose barbarian, his cloudy eyes open, blinking rapidly. Lines pulled at his mouth, etched the skin around his eyes. The pooch nuzzled me, wagging her tail in his face.

Cursing, he swatted at Fin's rear. "Something you need to know." He rolled onto his side. "They shot me with an ESP energy depressant my father's team developed for the government to throw them off his real shit. Normal doses don't work on me so they doubled up. It kills my magical bandwidth for hours. Not that I have any magic to kill right now. Thanks to the Rift. And you."

Another evil eye had Ronan scowling at me. I laughed. "Have you been diagnosed? Your scowls don't work on me."

"Your rabid eye doesn't work on me either." He prodded his head, groaned. "Damn it. DR knows how strong you are now."

I straightened the fringe on my jacket. "Your father also knows for sure that we're together."

"Get me something to eat. It'll absorb the drug burning in my gut. Chocolate peanuts in the glove box."

Chocolate! Why didn't he give it up earlier? I rooted out a full bag of double-dipped, chocolate peanuts. One at a time, I fed them to him, sharing with Adam, tossing several into my mouth. Even the beggar Fin got a peanut after I bit off the chocolate. I was hungry enough to scarf down a fat, juicy burger and a bushel of fries, but the peanuts calmed the tempest brewing in my stomach. My thoughts wandered down Foodville, and I didn't notice Ronan nibbling on my fingers until he sucked the tip of my forefinger into his mouth.

The most intense flare of desire boiled the chocolate in

my belly and left me craving...Ronan. I wrenched my hand away as if scorched.

"Feed me."

I stuck two peanuts between his lips, threw him the half-empty bag, and shrank into my seat in acute misery. The lines between no-man's land and reality city had blurred, and I needed to stop my southern federation from shipping out invitations. *Holy cow. Ronan?*

Silence bombarded us until we approached the airport. The SUV lurched to a stop at the light, and Ronan pushed his fists on the center console to steady his dead weight.

Adam swung the vehicle into the San Jose Jet Center and parked in the loading zone. Tongue-tied, I stared. The only kind of jet that flew in and out of the Jet Center was a private one. I'd never been on a private jet! That was more exciting than dwelling on a wrecked Rift, a psycho kidnapper and all-around evildoer. I sorely needed a break from my new hell in a nice private jet with my two doppel-hunks.

"Adam will fill you in some more on the plane." Ronan opened the back door. Fin leapfrogged over his lap to the ground.

"Why can't you?" I slid off the seat and held his arm while he steadied his legs.

"I'm flying commercial. I can't spend two hours on a plane with you."

A normal woman could be offended by that remark. "You can't go by yourself. You're not well. Your shoulder needs attention." I twisted my fingers on his jacket. An iron mass crushed my shoulders. Fear that I'd never see him again worked to destroy my confidence. "I'll be okay."

"Aria." He exhaled my name. Flares erupted in my awakening southern region. "I can't risk hurting you." He fisted his hand around mine. "I'll sleep it off on the plane. You'll be safe with Adam. The jet's secure, not traceable to us." He handed his gun to Adam for safe keeping. "I'll use

Adam's identity."

"What about you? Your power's shot even without the depressant."

"I'm not exactly useless without it." The corners of his mouth twitched.

Overhead lights altered his unfathomable eyes into molten silver pools. "Can you take another private jet?" The heat of his gaze seared me.

"We don't have time to kill." Caressing my chin, he slid his hand around my neck, teasing the hair at my nape.

I shivered from his touch and pressed into his hand. "Be careful," I implored. "Please?"

He leaned forward, brushed his mouth across my forehead, and gently pried my fingers off his jacket. "Count on it."

I watched him drive away, taking a part of me with him. It was more than just our entwined aura. Turning to Adam, I realized another part of me was eyeing me critically.

ELEVEN

Super-soft leather seats wrapped plushy comfort around my battered body. Fin rolled onto a doggy bed in a strapped-down pet carrier. Adam returned from the cockpit and took my crusty hand in his. I peered at the first aid kit on his lap. "Dr. Freshfields?"

A smile lit his sickly face, his dimple an abyss of heaven. He oh-so-tenderly cleaned my cut. The attention gave me a chance to memorize his face. I loved his boyishly charming smile that twinkled in his ever-changing eyes. Despite his pasty coloring, the shifting washed-out hair, and his one pointy ear, he'd retained his smooth skin and model bone structure. His beauty extended far deeper than skin level. With our aural bond, it was easy for me to envision his true self beyond the cadaver coloring. Of course, I only had to look at Ronan to recognize the darker side missing from Adam. If only the fairies would sprinkle light and happy dust on Mr. Grumpy.

"What do you do for a living? Is this your bird?" The antibacterial solution stung, and I forced my bellyaching body to suck it up.

"I'm a VP in my family's import, export business, Freshfields International. The plane belongs to the corp."

My brows hiked into my hairline. "That Freshfields?" It hadn't registered earlier that I was tag-teaming with a member of one of the richest families in California. He sure didn't appear the corporate VP rolling in a gazillion dollars. Not that I'd ever dated any white-collar corporate types at my age. I usually attracted tall, cheap, and dumb. "And so young?"

"Surprised?" His humble laugh feathered across my skin.

My hand flinched from the prickly aural energy—guess I should break down and just start calling it *magic*—his touch triggered. "Should I curtsy when I address you?"

"A simple kiss will suffice." Adam laid my doctored hand on the pillowy armrest. He tossed his baseball cap on the seat in front of us, his opalescent hair flowing free. It had grown several inches since yesterday despite the locks that continued to fall out. The electrified tresses swayed in a nonexistent breeze, reaching for me and fluttering in the energy my aura kicked up.

The plane taxied down the runway, but my gaze remained unwavering on Adam. The bird ascended, thrusting us against the seats. He leaned into me and his mouth claimed mine in a brief, heart-skipping kiss. Soft and firm, his lips tasted faintly of spearmint. His aura pooled warmly around mine. Fingers on my mouth, I quickly drew apart. My pulse skittered and his touch melted me into the seat. His violet eyes glistened with an unknown promise, leaving my mouth blazing. This was so wrong when I had feelings for both Adam and Ronan and my heart was working overtime trying to figure it out. I eased away as much as the seatbelt allowed.

"Did...did you feel that?" he rasped out.

"Definitely weird." Several degrees of guilt sprinkled

cold water on our mingled auras. Ronan's frowny face sprang to mind, not that he truly ever left it.

Two men, one Aria. What was a girl to do? I twisted my clasped hand, rubbed my temples, spurring my last two brain cells to work in harmony for a change.

He straightened in his seat, shaking from my frosty aural blast. "I've never felt...I think the Rift—" He hesitated. "Our auras are intertwined," he blurted out. "At the house I felt your aura around me, not inside me. Ronan and I are connected that way. I never knew it until he told me what I was sensing."

Dazed, I nodded, feeling the hollowness inside my core, a missing piece. It might be Adam's tainted magic causing the emptiness, or not. Even though I sensed a smidge of Ronan within Adam's aura, part of him was absent from the equation. *Can I freak out now?* Doppelgänger magic? Two halves of a whole? What kind of magic did the Rift spit out? Fairy dust love potions?

"Aria?" Anxiety stamped his face. "I'm sorry." He squeezed my knee.

What if we didn't make it to the Rift in time and I lost both of them to the tainted magic? *Whoa, what?* I didn't even *have* both of them to lose. I'd met them less than forty-eight freaking hours ago. Who was playing such a sick joke on me? I needed an instant lobotomy to stop the chaos in my brain.

Even though I so desperately wanted both doppelgängers in my life, a tiny part of me didn't. I didn't want them only to lose them. I had serious abandonment issues. Every morning I called Zoe to make sure she was kicking and hadn't toppled me off her BFF pedestal. At least with the doppel-twins, I needn't worry about my wacky telekinesis chasing them away. Scared spitless, I didn't know who I was, let alone who wanted me. Or who I wanted.

I picked at a spot of caked blood on my jeans. "We need

to focus on the Rift, healing you and Ronan."

Adam hunched over, probing his pointy ear as if he felt it growing. "Tell me one thing."

"Sure." I leaned into him, tilted my face toward the need in his eyes. My heart spooled.

"How do you feel about Ronan?" His jaw tensed. He lowered his hand and a lock of hair stuck to his fingers. Flicking his wrist, he scowled as the lock of hair fluttered to the floor.

Heat rushed up my neck. "I feel the same...I feel...Ronan in your aura. It's confusing." No illusions would mar my relationships—whatever they evolved into—with Ronan and Adam. *Note to self: find a doppel-magic cluestick, and fast.*

The plane leveled to cruising altitude and Adam unbuckled our seatbelts. His warm hand lingered on my thigh, gently drawing thirteens on my pant leg. "Ronan and I speculated about this over a bottle of Irish whiskey when we discovered we were doppelgängers and began sensing each other's energy and aura. We wondered what would happen if one of us found a woman whose magic merged with one of ours, what she'd feel. We knew it was a possibility since ancient sorcerers and their doppelgängers were connected the same way. We wondered what it would do to the other. And we laughed it off." He snorted, his derision all but palpable in the air. "I'm not laughing now."

"I'm sorry," I whispered to the vast, bleak clouds I felt from the occasional bump of turbulence in our dark haven in the sky. After a moment of tense silence, I asked, "How did you really determine you two were doppelgängers?"

"Like we said earlier, it's a big guess based on Forbidden Thirteen history." Adam touched my shoulder, but the blinking beacon of hope on the wing captured my bleary gaze. "We'll work it out." He yawned with loud exaggeration. "Hungry?"

"Starving!" A shaky sigh of relief chased my reply. One

more thing to add to that mental journal of items to dwell on later. Soon I wouldn't have capacity left, and I'd have to start checking things off that list, reformat my brain's hard drive, or proceed with that lobotomy.

We ate a gourmet dinner of fresh garden salad, steak, garlic mashed potatoes, and sourdough bread slathered in butter. By the time I pushed away the empty dessert plate, I felt ready to pop out extinct fairies.

The creamy taste of cheesecake lingered on my tongue. Ibuprofen appetizers lessened the brunt of my aches and pains, and I wilted into my pillowy seat, the faint roar of the engines lulling me toward Snoozeville. My mind relived the heady heat of Adam's kiss even as I found his nearness both puzzling and exciting. Yet, the memory of Ronan's tan face and his full, firm lips pressed against my forehead refused to grant me quarter.

The flight attendant cleared away our dinner dregs. Adam dimmed the lights and romantic starlight twinkled in the black abyss. The flight attendant carried in mugs of coffee on a tray, and the scent of caramel mocha nearly launched my pulse into the next galaxy.

"How'd you become a VP at such a young age?" I sipped my ambrosia.

Shadows hazed Adam's eyes for a second. "My father died last year from an aneurysm. I was next in line when my mom became CEO."

"I'm so sorry." I smoothed my hand over his knee. "Which parent do your fae genes stem from? Is anyone else affected?" I whispered discretely.

"It's a mystery." He smiled ruefully. "As far as I know it's just me. My mother hasn't seen me recently since she's been in Ireland opening up a new factory."

Steam wafted from my coffee. "Aren't you curious?" I gently blew into my cup. "Maybe she knows...things."

"She was adopted. So was I. Plus, she wouldn't know a fairy from a dragonfly. I've tried to track down my real parents, but the trail is deader than dead. Almost as if I didn't exist, as if I just popped out of the Rift after the quakes."

My eyes bugged out. Could it be true? Had other sorcerers, fae, or doppelgängers oozed through the gateway from the Realm of the Void? Were they roaming the world trying to figure out what's wrong with them and who they are?

"Who or what else skipped through the Void and is playing in our sandbox?"

"No telling." Leaning forward, he sized me up with an intent look. "You know, if we figure it out, we may close the Rift, secure it again. I'm hoping Melisande's tablet has new info Ronan's never seen."

Shock cooled the warmth of the coffee sliding down my throat. I straightened my spine, planted my feet on the floor. "Don't you start popping circuits too. Shouldn't we open the Rift, let the pure magic out and deal with the consequences later? Isn't that the only way to heal you two? What happens if we close the Rift, even if it's possible? Will you disappear...or worse?" I swallowed hard. We hadn't really discussed goals beyond stopping Ronan's sperm donor and rescuing Zoe. "Why wouldn't we want sorcery restored and usurp the Abolishment laws enacted by pea-brained humans?"

"It's dangerous. We don't know what will happen when the Rift opens and Forbidden magic is fully unleashed. We have no clue what will come out. Plus, it's illegal to practice magic."

"NUW won't have a choice but to lift the Abolishment and change the laws against magic." Excitement started my foot tapping. "It'd be wicked cool living next door to fairies and sorcerers." I set my empty cup aside.

He gawked at me as though I'd opened a demon gate, sprouted horns and a scaly tail. "Not if Ronan's father has his way and nabs all the Thirteen sorcerers for his world domination goal. They're supposedly the strongest, or will be, of their descendants. Residual magic's been building and regenerating throughout the years, probably more so since the quakes. What happens if others have the same ideas once magic escalates? We're talking world chaos."

"Then we go back to the incubation box. It's best to toss out the dumb laws, anyway." I gave an annoyed sniff. Silent, he pinched the bridge of his nose. "FYI...Ronan's rubbing off on you." He might have a teensy, tiny point, but I wasn't ready to play the acceptance card. "With magic unleashed, groups such as Dominion Research won't have a donut's chance in a police station."

His pale eyebrows drew together in a V at the bridge of his nose. "Who'll control the Forbidden from destroying the human race once magic becomes rampant again?"

"Okay." I swished my hand in the air. "We'll need ten boatloads of cash to buy all the clues." My thoughts resurfaced in morbid land. "What if the Rift continues to crumble naturally? It's already been fractured from the quakes and Ronan messing with it."

"We'll need to focus on that problem ASAP." A silken edge of warning rose in his lackluster voice. "That's even worse to imagine depending on how fast the tainted magic has already infected the world."

"God, Adam." I thrust forward and threw my arms around his neck. His strong arms embraced me in comfort, regardless of the unnatural heat of his body temperature. "I wish I could heal you." I buried my face against his shoulder. "And Ronan." *You can't walk in with a short shelf life and leave me to tackle this on my own.*

He caressed my hair. "I know, Blondie." The air conditioner kicked on. Despite my layers, I shuddered. Adam needed the cool temp to alleviate his perpetual fever, to provide him a skosh of relief from the faulty magic burning him from the inside out.

I settled back into my seat, needing distance from his

aura wrapping me in the feel of him. "How did you and Ronan find each other at the Rift?"

He took a swig of coffee and set the mug aside. "I was on a business trip in Seattle when Ronan went back to the Rift after his first attempt to open it with his father. He tried to close it on his own. I had the bizarre idea to go hiking in Washington Park. My fairy connection to the earth—or to Ronan—was working, I guess." He shrugged. "Not that I knew it at the time. But strange energy drew me to the Rift where I found Ronan, his heart barely beating. I thought he was dying." His legs tensed. "He was out of it, babbling weird things."

The jet flew into a patch of clouds, rocking us side-to-side. I grabbed the armrests as Adam steadied our mugs. As swiftly as the plane escaped the roiling clouds, his mood soared and starlight swept a tender curve to his mouth.

"What strange things?" I eased up on the armrests before they absorbed my hands.

"Stuff about my life. Things no one should know. Later, I had visions about Ronan's life. Anyway, we found no link to prove we might be related other than our research on doppelgängers." He raised his hands, dropped them.

"Do you still have visions?"

"No, but our auras are intertwined now. At first, we were able to draw energy from each other. Not anymore." He propped his feet on the edge of my seat. "Hey, tell me how your telekinesis works."

My telekinesis had always been difficult to define, something I'd taken for granted since I always believed I was alone with the ability. Now I knew the mother ship had opened its hatch.

"You know, telekinesis, the ability of the mind and body to manipulate matter, time, space, or energy. My abilities have soared radically since I was a teenager." I wasn't ready to cough up how much energy I absorbed to enhance my innate energy. Such a secret might keep me alive longer. I held my pendant, rubbed the enameled pattern. "The unexplainable part is how the number thirteen affects me. It basically causes bad luck when I'm not paying attention, sometimes sneaks up on me. When I sense it, which is when my aura starts to tingle around me, my head aches or my pinkies twitch, I can usually stop the bad luck from hitting me by counterattacking it with my telekinesis. I use my necklace as a focusizer. It acts as a conduit of aural energy. Whenever the number thirteen's around me randomly, it usually precipitates a bad luck event."

"But you wear a number thirteen on you." His eyebrows lifted up.

"Its base metal is copper beneath the enamel. Copper's a bridge for energy, or magic. It provides protection and is a conductor that draws away negative energy." I fluttered my hand, sketched numbers on the outside of my coffee cup. Adam rubbed his leg against mine provocatively. My mind drew a blank, all thoughts flying out into the ether.

"Go on." He chuckled, stopping his flirtation.

I blinked rapidly, dispelling the fluttering in my lower abdomen. "That's it. What else is there?" Every sore muscle in my body stretched painfully tight. "What did Ronan tell you?"

"He's telekinetic. Like you, it's natural, inborn. Things happen around Ronan when the number's present. Since he's a descendant of a Thirteen sorcerer, he's been trained from the *Illuminaria* to use his internal energy, brain waves, to manipulate elements, people, and events. He's regained some of the magic his sorcerer ancestor possessed. He tattooed the number on his arm, creating a focal point to negate bad luck, similar to your pendant."

I frowned. "But then how does his tattoo negate bad luck? There's no copper in it."

"Exactly. He hasn't relied on it since he was fourteen, and mostly has control over his power, enough to thwart his bad luck. You probably never needed your necklace with the kind of power you have."

I scoffed. "Seriously? I get hit with bad luck every day. How else do you think I'm still alive if I don't drive it away?"

"Did you ever think your necklace might be drawing it to you?"

"Hell to the no way. I lived nearly sixteen years without it. My unluck was ten times worse before."

"It's all in your head, and now it's all in your strength and control of your telekinesis, the older you grow." Adam reached forward and uncurled my fingers from around my pendant. "Take it off."

Did a stupid ghost possess him the last time I blinked? A Baja sandstorm seized my mouth. "What?" I scrunched against the sidewall, but he wouldn't relinquish his hold on my chain. "No. I can't do anything without it. Bad luck will kill me." The lie rolled of my tongue. I don't know why I said it, why I was hiding my abilities, my last bastion of normalcy.

"Please, Aria. I want you to try something."

"You think I don't know what I can and can't do?" I retorted. Without a focusizer, I got lost within my own head. It wasn't a pretty picture. I hated not having control. My abilities were growing and it frightened the crap out of me, especially since my aura wasn't entirely mine. I always wondered if all the energy I absorbed might have a lasting detrimental effect on me. Or land me in jail.

Adam pushed up from his seat and grasped the armrests, pinning me between his steely arms. "Everything's different now."

"Any connection between your reality and mine is purely coincidental." I tossed my head and eyed him with flinty triumph. "The Rift crumbling doesn't affect me." After everything they'd told me, I knew it had. What else explained my soaring abilities?

"I think it did." Adam's voice dropped an octave. "As I

weaken, you grow stronger. I feel it in your aura."

I'd noticed a difference, but I chalked up my recent souped-up power to our eerie threesome bond. What he suggested was three sorcerers short of the Forbidden Thirteen. I shook my head vehemently. "I'm not stealing your magic. Don't put that on me. If anyone, Ronan's stealing it."

"I didn't say that." He crouched, his arms caging me in, blotchy aura cloaking me. "You're keeping our magic alive, feeding us through our shared bond." His opaque hair quivered over his shoulders, a drifting mantle of snow.

"You've snapped a bolt. Let me go." I elevated my feet on the seat to push against his confining arms. Fin trotted over and uttered a short, happy yip as if I held a steak bone...or her bestie, Ronan, had materialized on the plane.

"Do you think your abilities are normal for a telekinetic? *Think*, Aria. You and Ronan are deriving your powers from the leaking Rift—from what's left of the Forbidden, from magic that shouldn't exist."

I shook my head so hard brain cells packed their bags and hopped on a cloud. "Get real. I've had these abilities all my life." The lies continued to snowball off my icy tongue.

"We both know that's not entirely true. You were born with the blood of a Thirteen sorcerer. As the magic leaks out of the Rift, you channel it and unleash it through your own breed of telekinesis." He drew closer, his heat flickering around me.

For the trifecta of my scorn, I gave him my evil eye, a glare, and a scowl. "Did you sneak a bottle of tequila in the galley?" I asked feebly, knowing the truth was staring me in the face. I couldn't escape it. Adam and Ronan knew too much.

"Some of the abilities you possess are unheard of. They're powers only a Thirteen sorcerer exhibited, as far as sketchy ancient texts explain."

"I'm not a fairy or sorcerer or whatever else existed in

ancient Whack Job Town." My aura rose defensively, suppressing my roadmap of body aches. I raised my hand to grip my necklace. Adam beat me to it, yanked the chain off my neck, and hurled it toward the galley in one dumbass move.

I skidded off the runway. Hands on Adam's shoulders, I shoved him flying backward to land against the couch across the aisle. Air held him down, and I sprang toward him.

Eyes glowing, he attempted a crappy mesmerism stunt to compel me to freeze. He exuded the illusion of freedom, rising from the couch, but I hacked through his newly minted illusion powers as if he were an ESP wannabe. Wind swirled his hair into knots as fast as his livewire hair untangled the snarls.

The violet glow in his eyes winked out and empathy tightened his lips. Air held him immobile. "You just proved my point," he said softly.

"Shut. Up."

His aura had gone to ground, ripping a piece of my soul out of me. Heat swept over me, despite the cabin's frigidness, stabbing some sense into me. What had I done? What had I become? An unholy panic buckled my knees. My aura fizzled to nothing in the wake of my meltdown. Adam hauled me into his arms, and I buried my face against his chest. His aura bent around me, then shifted back to mingle with mine.

I grabbed a handful of his polo shirt. "Why me? I'm not a plain old telekinetic, am I?" *I'm not Aria Walker, little ole college student, am I?*

He grazed his hand up and down my back. "You're growing, changing. You've probably been able to do that for a long time."

I stiffened, recalling the first time I'd noticed odd sensations and occurrences when my emotions dove overboard and I couldn't redirect the energy. The day Mom died.

He swept tendrils of limp hair off my cheek. "You've noticed, haven't you?"

"I thought thirteen was jinxing my luck."

"Ronan noticed his ESP footprint shift last year too."

"Ronan's changes are a train wreck."

His hand stilled in the hollow of my back. "We thought you'd feel the same." He laughed, a grim humorless noise. "Instead, you're changing for the better."

"Better?" I grazed my chin along the contours of his pecs. "I thought my Catwoman superpowers arose from our aura meld. Maybe my doppelgänger is still in the Void." It seemed weird saying that. "Do you think?"

"That would be my guess, if one existed. Somehow the tainted magic isn't affecting you."

"Prepare for descent." The pilot's booming voice through the speakers nearly sent me leaping to the ceiling. A perfect excuse to put distance between us.

Adam tracked down my broken chain. The flight attendant cleaned up and headed to the galley. I slunk to my seat and strapped in. Fin hopped into her carrier and curled up for another pup-nap. Lucky bum.

Adam handed me my chain and pendant. "Forgive me? I'll replace it."

In dismay, I inspected the broken chain, hating that he'd resorted to brute tactics. It made me wary of him, despite my head and heart begging to trust him. What new secrets had my brain bribed my heart with?

I jammed the charm in my jeans front pocket and tossed the chain at him. He caught it easily. "So you won't forget."

"I won't forget to replace it." He clicked the seat buckle, the snap a loud definitive sound.

I gave him The Look. "That's not what I meant."

Adam's face hardened as if I'd slapped him. "It's a damn chain. I needed to prove a point."

Stripping off my personal belongings mirrored Ronan smothering my mouth outside the casino. The last two people to smother my will were permanently napping six feet under. Not by my hand, mind you, but dead nevertheless. I'd always thought my bad luck caused their deaths so long ago. They deserved punishment, but not death. I recoiled, and hastily sank the Gruesome Twosome into my mind's dungeon.

"Points are for ice picks." The plane dipped into the clouds, wobbled up and down. My ears popped as we sliced through the dense, roiling shroud. Waves of multi-hued lights below illuminated the huge city, jewels in a sea of the black unknown.

Fin whimpered in her sleep, probably dreaming of the big dogs pounding their will into her pretty little body. The plane began its final descent, and I braced myself against the seat for landing. A wintry hand grazed my heart.

Adam's soft voice pierced my frenzied thoughts. "Something good did come out of the Rift." His fingers brushed my thigh and I flinched.

"You, probably. What else?" I could tell he wanted to touch me but feared my reaction. Even I feared me.

"Fin."

I met the challenge in his stony, alien eyes. "What do you mean?"

"Fin came through the Rift. She hasn't grown an inch in six months."

TWELVE

The silent heat of epic astonishment severed the wintry grip on my heart. I contemplated Fin's soulful eyes, the thin web of energy wafting off her.

"You're not surprised?" Adam asked.

"I thought only magic cruised through the Rift." I unbuckled my seatbelt before the plane hit the ground. *Arrest me for being a rule breaker.*

He shrugged his hands. "We found Fin sitting on the ground in the Rift opening after Ronan screwed it up the second time. You have to admit she's not normal."

Point taken. We needed faster microprocessors in our brains to process Forbidden info overload. Or some Einstein cells.

The jet's wheels bounced on the tarmac. The pull of the brakes sucked me forward, and I clutched the armrest, grasping at reality again. I was raring to rescue Zoe. I even missed Ronan, although I couldn't fathom how he'd gotten under my skin so quickly, Thirteen connection and doppelgänger bond notwithstanding. He had and I did.

Enough said.

I rose, rubbing away the sharp pain in my lower back. Fin molded her small body against my leg, leaving black fur on my pant leg. When the furballs at home got a load of this, I was so dead.

"Hey, Fin, what's up with you?" The mystery amplified the thumping in my head amid my brain's sluggish return to work. "What time is Ronan's plane landing?" I picked up my purse and the tote bag, felt for Mom's envelopes.

Adam gathered our bags from the inside storage bin. "We have an hour's lead. He's setting up a telecon with his father. We do nothing until he gets to the hotel."

Dying to drop an unlucky bomb on *Dickard* Riley, the idea of the telecon appealed to my sense of safety. Worrying for Zoe contributed to the persistent ball of fire in my gut. Ronan assured me his father wouldn't hurt Zoe, not if he needed leverage to snag me—us. I believed in that *modus operandi*. Better choices weren't flinging cue cards my way. Calling the police played big-time in my backup plans. Zoe could handle herself. Not that she was a slut, but she knew how to use her voluptuous body for the good of mankind. And she loved a challenge, especially when it gave her fodder for her next paranormal psychology research paper. I could almost see her fingers flying over her keyboard already. Ronan's warning rang in my head, dispelling the vision. We were breaking laws just breathing.

A driver waited with a sweet black limo at the bottom of the airstairs. "Aria Walker, meet Jon Morrison," Adam said. The older brother next-door, auburn-haired driver threw me a winning smile. Tall and built like a tank, Jon filled out a black suit nicely. A flock of blackbirds—thirteen birds to be exact—squawked overhead. A white bird bomb smacked Jon's shoulder. *Oops.* The frown on his face was worth the unexpected bad luck I didn't even try to foil. I stifled a grin as he wriggled out of his jacket without smearing the gooey glop.

Adam took my arm and steered me to the limo, shaking his head. "You make him nervous."

I clutched my chest and in my best Indian chief voice said, "Me? Little Aria make big, beefy man nervous?"

"Chill, Aria." Adam pressed his hand in the small of my back. "Get in."

"Yes, *Ronan*." Barbarian dust was definitely sticking to Adam.

I sank into the lap of Luxury—with a capital *L*—again, deciding I could get used to Adam's lifestyle. Men from rich families didn't impress me any more than men without the dough. However, hot ticket items like private jets and limos worked for me when I had friends to rescue, doppelgängers to save, and Rifts to conquer. I might be blonde, but this cookie had a full load of chips. I planned to use every one of them.

Adam's thigh pressed against mine. Like we didn't have an acre of space to spread out in. "Jon's been on my mom's payroll for three years. He and his brother, Jax, are the best in security." He blushed. "I think my mom's hot on them." He nodded toward the smoky glass partition. "I'd rather certain matters remain between you, me, and Ronan." His hand landed on my knee as if he'd been touching me since the Abolishment.

Awkward warmth infused me. I tried to ignore his friendliness by rearranging the inside of my purse, which took all of five seconds. Too friendly too fast, and it twisted and turned inside my chest. Didn't fairies love to get all touchy feely with people? *That's all it is, right?* Add another item to my expanding research list.

"I'd miss you if you weren't near me," Adam said in a pebbly voice.

I flicked the vent toward me. Sixty degrees and it wasn't cool enough sitting so close to him, hearing the flirtations spewing from his too-sexy-for-mortal mouth.

I shifted in my seat, placing distance between my deaf

hormones and his natural and unnatural fairy charisma. "A girl could take that comment several ways."

He rested his head against the seatback. "You kill my pain."

What the what? Sympathy fogged my judgment, and I fitted my palm flat against his chest. "Does it ease when we're touching?"

"God, yes." He walked his fingertips from my knee up my thigh, stopping before traveling out of bounds. "It's a slow burn in my blood, bones, muscles, eating away at my skin. When you're near, I feel your aura inside me, around me like a cool breeze in a heat wave. When we're touching, the burn's almost gone."

"In true romance fiction, I'm a balm to your senses?" I snuggled into the curve of his side. I knew he wasn't playing me because his fever subsided whenever I touched him. I had mistakenly thought it was his aura making room for mine. "Why didn't you cop to this before?"

He swung his arm across my shoulders. "I didn't want to scare you off or cause you to think I was hitting on you. We just met yesterday." He dragged his fingers through his undulating hair, silky strands that kept intertwining with my shorter locks.

"Is the proximity to the Rift making it worse?"

He nodded. "Ronan will feel it too. I don't think we have much time."

"Which means Ronan and I probably can't be on the same sphere." The words hung in the air as if visible. Weird doppelgänger effect?

"His magic's making your faulty developing power worse and vice versa?" The limo drove beneath the *porte-cochere* at the entrance to the Rainbird Corporate Suites.

"That's our guess, although I'm not sure I'm adversely affecting him as much as the tainted Rift magic." Adam climbed out of the limo behind Fin. Fin always had to be in first place. Must be a dog thing. My cats would still be lounging on the seats, giving me the stink eye for subjecting them to the rain. I took Adam's outstretched hand, his sick magic tugging on my aura, seeking relief.

Nippy, damp air clung to the Seattle night. Billowing steel clouds blocked the night sky, threatening to unload at any moment. My heartbeat sped up. I cast a glimpse at the solid cover over the drive-through and my anxiety subsided. Did the sun and stars ever shine in Seattle, the Emerald City of perpetual gloom?

Adam flipped his hood up and stuffed his baseball cap on, hiding half his face. We entered the lobby and rushed toward the bank of private elevators. I expected no less, so my eyes only bulged slightly in surprise. Jon engaged the elevator lock.

Off to the left, I spied a petite figure determinedly striding toward us, a navy snowcap tugged down to her eyebrows. Matching gloves covered her hands and her chin dipped into a navy and white stripped scarf. I suspected her berry lipstick and tan foundation hid her cadaver look. I literally felt her tainted magic burn into me. *Hello, I'm not the Fairy Godmother!*

Adam stepped into the elevator, tugging me along. Nervous wrinkles broke out around his eyes, and sweat beaded his forehead. Jon sprang in front of us, a gun ominously engulfed in one large hand hidden behind his back.

The young woman stopped a few feet from the elevator. A wisp of pale blonde hair flapped from underneath her snowcap. The strand sprang out like a corkscrew and she tucked it back under the cap. Angst assaulted my aura in a blaze of red, leaving me jittery.

"Please, I must speak with you." Her gaze darted around the sparsely populated lobby before resting on my face.

Adam moved in front of me, abreast of Jon.

I skirted him and nudged the tower of Jon, without

much success I might add. "Let her in."

"Jon, scan her." Adam stepped back. "Touch her," he whispered in my ear.

I nodded, my mind already one step ahead of the bodyguard brigade. Although, I didn't need to touch her to know she could be Adam's fairy princess. If she was a fairy doppelgänger, that meant she was linked to a Thirteen sorcerer or at least another Forbidden or some other creature from that era. The more I experienced each hour, the more I believed Adam was truly a descendant of one of the created Forbidden Thirteen suicide doppelgängers. I don't know how I knew this, but the idea refused to die. Yet, I didn't think that meant he'd strolled out of the Rift after the quake rave twenty-one years ago.

"I'm not armed." Her gaze continued to bounce, never resting on one spot long. "I...I sensed you across the room. I suspect we have a similar problem." She traded level stares with Adam, then pierced me with a look of deep longing. *Whoa, girl, I'd like testosterone with my order.*

Arms wide, feet spread, she gave in to the paranoia and allowed Jon to scan his handheld device over her from head to toe. Once my security detail permitted her onto the elevator, she leaned against me, gratitude swimming in her eyes, her aura flaring weakly.

I touched her feverish cheek. "Who...what are you?"

Sobs convulsed her shoulders. "Sorry." She buried her face in her gloved hands.

The elevator rocketed toward the top floor. Adam looked like he wanted to dive into the elevator shaft to get away from her. I didn't pick up evil vibes off her, just deader than a doornail vibes. At least Adam possessed some life within our linked auras, skewed though it was. With her, you'd think an archeological crew had just dug her pruney body out of the pyramids.

She wiped her eyes. "I'm just a normal girl. I don't know what's happening to me." Renewed tears welled in her puke-green eyes.

The elevator dinged and the doors slid open. We followed Jon into the depths of the penthouse floor. A chance peep at the crystal chandelier in the hallway had me ducking. The light fixture swayed as if a fan had suddenly blown on it. I deflected attention by grabbing the fairy girl's hand. Three of the thirteen bulbs popped dead in my wake. No one mentioned it. Lucky me, unlucky hotel.

"Who are you?" she asked, her hand pressed to her heart as if I possessed all the fairy bells and witchy whistles. "Do you know what's happening to us?"

Adam's hand tensed on my back, cutting short my urge to run screaming for the nearest loony bin for telekinetic-sorcerers off their meds. "Sort of."

Jon deactivated the alarm at the suite door. After dumping our bags inside, he split to retrieve my not-so-better third from the airport.

The penthouse's opulence was lost on me. I was too busy studying the newest freak to join the Court of Delusion. I tossed my purse on the earthtone granite counter between the living room and kitchenette. Wishing I could ward off the taint, I zipped my jacket to my chin.

Adam slipped off her cap, releasing her luminous hair. He yanked off his hood and baseball cap. Flinching, she stared at his one pointy ear.

Pretty in a country chic way, her translucent hair swayed like a wheat field around her shoulders. She was the same age as us with a few extra pounds and a rounded face that put her in cute territory. Her tainted magic stole the color out of her green eyes, leaving them dull and cloudy.

"Who are you?" Adam literally radiated suspicion. "How did you find us?" He stripped to a T-shirt, and then jacked down the thermostat. "Sorry, but I'm burning up."

I waved it off, but refrained from discarding my layers. A polar bear would freeze in the room at the current temperature.

"Kiera Kendrick." She released my hand. Our bizarre connection sank into the dense rug and my aura practically sighed with relief. "I was visiting my aunt who's here on business, and I sensed you as I was leaving." Her gaze shifted to Adam.

He edged closer, his arm brushing mine, seeking relief. I smelled his unease overriding the subtle floral perfume Kiera wore. "Are there others like you?" I asked.

Tears created muddy tracks down her cheeks. "Not that I know of."

"Have you seen anyone who looks similar to you?" I held my breath. "Were you adopted?"

"Why do you think that?" Her back drew straight and her expression stilled. "I mean, how did you know I was adopted? I'm not a twin if that's what you're thinking."

"You're sure?" I wasn't ready to spill the doppelgänger secret. Let her think I meant a twin.

Kiera averted her eyes, sweeping them across the paisley carpet. "I was left in Washington Park by my birth mother." She shrugged. "Alone."

The freak flags flew full mast. I plunked down onto the plushy armchair behind me. I didn't want anyone touching me, draining my spirit and energy. I wanted Ronan here so bad. Hell should freeze over after that wish. But I wanted his aura, sick as it was, fusing with mine. It made me feel safer, less hollow. I wanted to ensure he was okay. I wanted him to make Kiera go away.

The fairy wannabe in question flicked her hand in Adam's direction, anger sparking in her faded eyes. "There's something going on in the park, at the stone circle. Something drew me there a month ago. It was magical, for lack of a better term, as if all those fictional things you read about stone circles being portals to fantasy worlds is true. Ever since then, I've been getting worse, like him, with washed out skin tone, hair growing inches a day and falling out. A constant bonfire burns inside me."

Rocking forward, I dropped my face into my hands. "Fuck. A. Duck." Fin dashed over and gave me a sloppy, wet doggy lick. Absently, I scratched her ears, needing to distract my hands before they adopted a life of their own.

"Excuse me." I shot up, punched redial on my phone on the way to the bathroom. I sat on the closed toilet lid and waited for Ronan to answer. No such luck. My frustration careened off the rails as I whisper-yelled to his voicemail, "You need to get your ass to the hotel ASAP. Something's happened, and I'm ready to off your dickhead father myself."

No sense in not putting the bathroom to use. I cleaned up and stole a long look at myself in the beveled mirror. Dark craters had formed beneath my eyes. My hair imitated a victim of a tornado. In the mirror's reflection, I spied the jetted tub behind me and wanted to sink my thrashed body in hot, bubbly champagne with a hose connected to my mouth. Then I wanted to sleep for days, hoping I'd wake at home to a nightmare my overactive mind had conjured up in a snit of boredom. "Aria Walker, come on down. You've just won the grand prize for The Best Sucktacular Life."

A soft knock hit the door. "Aria, you okay?" Adam asked.

I propped my forehead against the door. "No."

"Kiera's not going anywhere."

No shit, Sherlock. "Give me a sec." I wet a washcloth, landed another hungry look on the tub, and left the dazzling marble sanctuary.

Adam stood over Kiera, her impromptu watchdog. I experienced a slew of emotions too twisted to separate, except for a maddening trace of stupid jealousy. Grayish rivulets striped Kiera's foundation, giving her a zebra complexion. Add the streaks of mascara and she had a silent shout out to a makeup-artist. I handed her the wet cloth.

She took it, her feverish fingers resting on mine longer than necessary, burning into my skin. "Thank you." Her eyes shimmered. "Adam said your name's Aria."

"Yes." I dug my fists into my front pockets. "What else did he say?" I asked with a dagger-launching look at him that set off the drums beating in my head. A dull ache plagued my leg and ankle. My hand merely throbbed. Time to party down with a bottle of painkillers.

"Nothing." Adam approached. "Sit. You look ready to crash. Need anything?"

I sank into the overstuffed couch, pressing into the lush comfort, easing the weight off my lower body. "Pain killers and a bottle of water, pretty please."

Adam left the room smiling.

Kiera perched on the edge of the chair. "Why does your touch ease my pain?"

She hadn't given me anything to dislike about her, but I remained wary. "I have no idea." I was so not letting every fairy in the world feel me up. "Do you sense Adam's *magic*?"

"Just a prickle of energy from him, nothing more. Your magic I definitely feel. It's drifting off you like a strong perfume." She patted the washcloth over her streaky face.

"Wonderful," I grumbled.

"Is it really magic?" She cast her gaze at her feet shuffling on the floor, as if afraid to hear the truth.

"Just exaggerated aural energy." A half-lie's not really a lie, right?

Adam brought me ibuprofen and water. "Thanks." I downed the tablets with half the bottle of cold reality. He sat, drawing me into the crook of his arm. As he rubbed my neck beneath my jacket, his pain diminished and his temperature normalized. The only fairy I wanted touching me was already wrapped around me.

"Have you seen a doctor?" Adam asked.

"Yes. I've been having weird symptoms for a month,

since I went to the stone circle." Kiera picked lint off her black pants. "Doctors have no clue. Best guess is the flu."

Tension twinged my aching back muscles. "Have a lot of people seen you this...sickly?"

She set the wet washcloth on the burgundy and gold paisley rug by her feet. "Not many. I attend an online college so it's easy for me to stay out of sight. My aunt was ready to call the CDC."

"Have you been to a scientific or paranormal research facility of any kind?" Adam tugged on his ear, his anxiety pressing on my aura.

"My boyfriend, Scott Walton, contacted a local place called Dominion Research and even spoke to the CEO, Richard Riley. They make those ESP detector devices and research paranormal phenomena."

Arctic air swept over me, crashing into Adam's fiery aura, alternatively freezing and boiling my blood.

He whispered in my ear, "Don't say a word."

I fixed him an iceberg-melting glare. "Go on," I urged Kiera with a heartening smile I didn't feel.

"I have an appointment on Tuesday." She reached toward Adam and quickly withdrew as if afraid she'd grow a ragged pointy ear too. "You should join me."

Anger tensed him against me. "Did they ask you to stay?"

"Sure. They agreed to pay my expenses while studying me. I didn't give them my full name or anything because I was afraid they'd turn me over to the cops. I mean, I'm not illegal or anything," she quickly added. "But I feel something growing in me." Renewed tears flowed down her cheeks.

"All that and a bag of stale chips." Rubbing my bruised head, I had no doubts Riley planned to imprison her.

Adam's finger dipped beneath my three layers to my bare shoulder, pressing a warning into my skin. "I think you should stay away from them. We believe their motives may be detrimental to you. We can help you, but we need to connect with others first. Give me your contact info."

Her face brightened, and she extracted a red smartphone from her Barbie-sized purse. "I'll send it to you."

Adam opened a link and she sent the information to his phone. At least she was malleable, cooperative, and seemed to trust us. Hurray for another link on the clueless chain of clues.

I angled my head against his steady shoulder. The world rear-ended my thoughts: Zoe, Ronan, Adam, Dominion Research, Rifts, *Illuminaria*, and fairies. *Welcome to my new world of truth and lies. We have nutcase cookies filled with crap chips.*

"Ronan should be here," I murmured, sinking into the deep velour couch. "Call him. He doesn't answer my calls."

Adam called and received the same voicemail of avoidance. The second he clicked off, his phone rang. He held the phone between our ears. I anticipated Ronan's voice, but thirteen gave no quarter. "Ronan wasn't on the flight," Jon's scratchy voice said. "I'll check other flights and report back."

My heart plunged into my stomach. I thrust off the couch, gave Kiera a brutal look. "Can you wait here while we talk in private?"

She cringed deeper into her chair. "Sure thing."

I handed her the remote for the flat screen. This time she hugged the chair arm and pasted herself to the seatback. Was I an ogre all of a sudden?

Adam followed me into the first of two master bedrooms. A burgundy and gold comforter with a thousand pillows adorned the king-sized bed. I salivated at the comfort begging my thrashed body to take it on a trip through the stars. I didn't give a hoot if there wasn't a pot of Belgian chocolate waiting at the end of the rainbow either.

"Calm down." He gripped my shoulders. "He'll be here."

"Do you think one of his father's trackers snagged him?" I picked at the gauze tied around my palm and probed Adam's pale, soulless eyes, trying to reach into his thoughts. "What if he's hurt or dead somewhere? What if he betrayed us? What if we've walked into a trap? Maybe Kiera's baiting us?" Every minutia incurred my distrust until otherwise proven innocent.

"Don't start doubting him. Not after everything we've been through." Adam glowered at me for the first time since we'd met. "Get your shit together and be a member of the team."

"What team?" I flung away from him. "The doppel-brutes who abducted me from my sane, boring life?" The hollow life I trudged through? Ronan already held my life in his hands. It didn't sit well and encouraged me to look for subliminal clues in ice cubes if I couldn't find them in my head.

A scream rose in my throat before I gulped it down. "It's my fault Zoe was snatched. I feel like I'm chasing a mirage." Not only did tears swamp my eyes, but sobs racked me. I must've soaked up energy from a hormone clinic. I hid my face against Adam's chest. He held me while I bawled like a two-year-old hosting a temper tantrum, party of one.

"Aria." Empathy and passion wore heavy on my name.

I linked my arms around his waist. Adam kissed the top of my head, tightening his arms even after I wiped my nose on his shirt. "Sorry," I mumbled.

His chuckle rumbled against my face. "I'd gladly wear your snot-rags if it means I get to hold you."

I sniffed hard. "Are you flirting with me?" My voice was croaky from anguish. Although desire wasn't far behind if that fire dipping into no man's land was my girlie parts revving up.

He chuckled. "Is it working?"

"Maybe." I wasn't ready to commit to squat, not when I

couldn't tell if my desire stemmed from Adam, his doppelgänger link to Ronan, or a fae glamour. Not when I felt the same desire for Ronan. *Hell to the no.* "Your pain better?"

"You have no idea."

He slid his hand beneath my multiple layers to massage my back, sending more warm swirling currents of need through me. *Oh, hell to the no squared.*

"Kiera feels it."

I fingered my eyes dry. "Damn if I'm gonna sleep naked with you two smothering me for the slightest touch."

A groan escaped Adam. "I was hoping I'd get you all to myself." Eyes glowing around the fringes, his hair curled and uncurled around his shoulders. I palmed his cheek. Pain in his eyes booted my good sense into the ether. If I could provide him with a scant few hours of relief, I'd do it. To hell with the consequences. I nodded.

He brushed my cheek with a crooked finger. "You can wear all the clothes you want."

"I may have to if you insist on sleeping in a morgue." I ran a hand over my forehead, shoving aside my hair, brushing aside my multifaceted reservations.

"I can keep you warm enough." A heart-stopping smile transformed his gray face.

The warmth between us made me want to curl up in bed with him that instant, draw his heat into me, assuage his pain. Logically, it had to be our aural bond, but I was beginning to feel something far greater, far scarier, far too twisted up with my feelings for Ronan.

THIRTEEN

A dam and I rejoined Kiera pacing a canal through the paisley ocean in the living room.

"It's late," she said, nervously dry-washing her hands. "Can we meet tomorrow?"

"We'll call you." Adam touched her arm. "Please don't talk to anyone at Dominion Research or tell anyone you met us."

I took her hand. She curled her fingers around mine, her body nearly dripping into a puddle of bliss. *What am I, fairy speed now?*

"You do know what's going on?" Hope dusted gold flakes into her dull peepers.

"Sort of." I hugged her and she clung to me, lost and alone in this new unknown.

Adam escorted her down to the lobby. The minute the door clicked shut, I located the address for Riley's Dominion Research on my smartphone. When Adam entered the suite, a Seattle street map was spitting out on the printer built into the suite's workstation. Just in case my GPS failed. Never could rely upon my luck.

"Don't even think about it," he growled out in true Ronan fashion.

I snatched the page from the printer, stuffed it in my jacket. "We need a backup plan."

"No plan includes going anywhere near Riley or his research facility." He spread his long legs in a he-man defensive stance that mimicked his darker half. "They'll sense you before you're in sight of the gate."

"Who said anything about going through a gate?"

Adam stalked closer, like a pit bull licking his chops at a kitten. His eyes glowed violet, skin darkening to the color of Seattle rain clouds. Reaching for me, he clamped his fingers onto my arm. "We're going to bed before we both drop from exhaustion."

Our auras tingled in a dizzying wash. The sensation of Ronan's aura was still achingly present and it was hard to separate the two. I fell against him, my nipples growing taut against his warm, solid chest. Aura drunk, I craned my neck back to look into the pain hazing his eyes. How could I refuse? For once, my head and body were in sync. First, I needed to scrub the day off my skin...before I did something I'd regret.

After soaking in jetted bliss, I felt sparkling clean and limber with some clarity restored. My signature scent— Zoe's birthday gift to me—in the bathwater filled the steamy room with a weave of freesia and vanilla. I washed my face with my disposable wipes, drying off quickly. I loathed the smothering, deadly feel of water on my face.

Unfortunately, my mind refused to wind down as thoughts of Ronan, both confusingly delicious and equally rotten, nagged me. Of course, agonizing over Zoe left a constant ache in my heart.

I heard Adam talking to Jon on the phone. By the time I slipped out of the bathroom, he was lounging on the bed, wearing a white T-shirt and gray shorts, not at all abashed at my seeing his deathbed glimmer. I knew what hid beneath that sickness so it didn't bother me. And I wanted the comfort of Adam's body draped around mine in my maelstrom of emotions and fear.

Not that I had designs on doing more than sleeping, I realized I hadn't slept with a man in over a year. Not since I'd dumped my boyfriend of two years once I'd found him coiled butt-naked around one of my lucky charm clients—a former friend now on mine and Zoe's shitlist—in my bed. It wasn't that I missed that intimacy much either. My unearthly bond to Adam was undeniable, and he drew me to him like a moth to a zapper, scary and liberating at once. How much of it was the bond versus reality? Or Ronan's other half? How hard would the zapper sting? Time to up my anti-crazy dosage of chocolate.

An admiring smile crinkled Adam's eyes. "There's another bed." Uncertainty erased his dimple.

"Leave it for Ronan." Suspicious, I scrunched my eyes. "He's coming, right?" I stood in my short satin robe outside the bathroom door, gripping my tote, Mom's envelopes stuffed securely inside.

"On his way." Adam held up his hand to forestall my scathing look, which didn't work, of course. "He has as much to lose as you."

Housekeeping would have to hose me off the walls if I didn't shut down for the night. Sighing, I stomped to the closet and snuck the envelopes inside the safe, realizing I hadn't thoroughly read the papers from Mom's chest. I'd peeked inside the packet again on the plane, enough to know I had some or all the missing parts to the *Illuminaria*. I wanted alone time to really dig into them without divulging my secret to Ronan or Adam. Yet. Other than going to the bathroom, I hadn't had a moment to myself. To escape my life just for a few hours, I dialed a seascape into the built-in sound machine. Waves lapped the shoreline and a foghorn blew in the distance.

I set my stun gun on the nightstand and stripped down to my fuchsia camisole with matching boy shorts. The glacial temperature sprouted gooseflesh on my arms, and my nipples beaded. Desire ignited in Adam's eyes, and a flush sailed up from my toes. I'd have worn long sleeves except I wanted him to have access to as much skin as I was willing to give. For healing purposes. Really.

He scooted to the middle of the bed and lifted the covers for me. I eased my sore body down, rolling on my side to face him, luxuriating in the sumptuous pillowtop mattress. Fin dashed into the room and bought a corner of the bed to worship me from afar, her gaze glued to me as if she were afraid I'd disappear. Funny pup.

"Are you sure you don't want to sleep in the other room?"

A shivery laugh escaped me. "No. Now warm me up, will ya?"

Adam's arms wrapped around me like vines seeking water and sun. His hard body against mine created fantastic tingles of heat scoring me. Linking my arms around his neck, I snuggled into him. Without a thought, I twined my legs around his, bypassing all real estate in between. The sandalwood smell and hard feel of his body stroked my senses, forcing me to inhale through my mouth to resist the temptation.

He smoothed his hands along the planes of my back, depositing a trail of heat. "Warmer?"

"Umm, yes." Our auras blended, one sifting in and out of the other. His hard tension eased as his pain fled, and the friction of our bodies burned away my last chills. We lay contentedly for several long moments, the soft pillowy mattress a boon to my tender, weary body.

Doubts meandered through my mind. "How's security here?" My thirteen pendant hung temporarily on a silver chain around my neck. I pressed it against Adam's T-shirt, hoping the good vibes kept my unluck at bay. Sleep was never a good place for me as I couldn't control my bad luck.

"Alarm's set. Gun's in the nightstand." He breathed in deeply. "You smell nice."

Heavenly spice wafted off him, but I wasn't about to admit it to raise his hopes. "Do you feel better?"

Adam slipped a forefinger beneath my chin, tipping my head back. We gazed into each other's eyes, his irises shifting from pale violet to indigo. My heart flip-flopped madly.

"I feel awesome."

I caught my breath, resting my cheek over his hammering heart. Waves crashing upon the beach and sea birds applauding filled the spaces between heartbeats.

"Aria," he said in that dusky, sultry way that sought an entrance to my heart.

I walked my fingers up his arm, magic quivering up my hand. "Why aren't you taken?"

Shivers of delight followed the touch of his hot hand stroking my back, his body a furnace beneath the covers. "I hadn't met you yet."

My knees weakened, and I tried to ignore the pleasant ache his words left in my limbs. "Right." I giggled to defray my muddled nervousness. "You don't even know me."

His eyes searched mine, reaching into my thoughts, possessing my soul. "Everything inside me tells me all I need to know."

I groaned into his chest. Every woman's fantasy in my clutches and I was torn into confetti whirling in a cyclone. The doppelgänger bond was going to bite me big time. *Holy hell, I'm so messed up.*

Locks of Adam's opalescent hair feathered my skin, seeking nourishment from my pure aura. I caressed his brittle tresses, giving what little healing I had to offer.

A heavy silence loomed between us. Fuzzy thoughts and feelings assailed me. What would change with Kiera on the scene? Where was her doppelgänger? Was her doppelgänger one of the Forbidden Thirteen? What could I offer Adam, Ronan, and any of the other sorcerers and doppelgängers that might pop up? What if I made their lives and the world worse?

Fear of the unknown nibbled away at my confidence. What if I couldn't sort out my feelings about the doppelgänger bond with Ronan and Adam? *Argh!* Someday, we'd look back on all this, laugh nervously, and change the subject. Yes, denial was my new best friend. I turned around in Adam's arms to avoid his uncanny allure.

"Goodnight, Blondie." Adam spooned around me.

I yawned. "Goodnight, fairy-sorcerer-doppelgänger king."

His biceps stiffened below my head. I let sleep tame my rampant thoughts.

"Why did you call me fairy king?" Adam's chest turned steely against my spine.

"Everything inside and outside me tells me all I need to know." I drifted off into the universe of the dead, a fallen lock of Adam's hair clasped in my fingers.

FOURTEEN

G roggy and barely awake, I luxuriated in the warm air whooshing over my face, noticed the emptiness of the bed where my fairy blanket had lain. Ronan's aura played fitfully with mine, his flawed energy shooting holes through it and scattering it around us. I rolled around in the mound of covers Adam must have layered upon me. As I clawed out of the cocoon, my bruised body screamed bloody murder and I stifled a whimper.

Ronan sat on the edge of the bed, watching me, a wry smile quirking up his lips.

Giving him my most disdainful glare, I lunged into his arms and he captured me in a fierce hug. Stiff and sore body be damned. "I should curse your luck on the spot if I wasn't so glad to see you. What happened to you? Are you okay?" I drew back on my knees and dog-eyed the rusty stain saturating his shirt. My heart skipped a beat. "Oh, Ronan!"

"Glad to see you too." He lightly traced the purpling bruise climbing my left arm, his touch leaving me tingling.

"Are *you* okay?"

I fingered the small bumps on the back of my head and winced. "I might live to get shot at again."

He drew away. "Where's Adam?"

I nodded my head at the closed bedroom door. "He's not out there?"

"No." His gaze roamed over me, then the bed, eyes burning first with lust, then jealousy. "You slept together?"

Surprise pinged my belly, but I impaled him with The Look. "What's it to you? You don't even like me."

He scowled. "I never said that."

"True." I picked at his bloodstained sleeve. He jerked away as though I carried a doppelgänger-destroying plague. "Quit being an ass. Let me doctor that."

I trounced into the bathroom for the first aid supplies from my cosmetics case. Never travel without them. Why risk even more bad luck? Quickly, I brushed my teeth and rinsed out my morning mouth.

When I returned to the bedroom, Ronan had already stripped off his Seattle Seahawks T-shirt and plunked down on the bed, holding a piece of hotel notepaper. I tried to ignore the fire climbing my neck at the sight of his rippling abdomen, thick biceps, and heavenly forearms. His sinful butt mashed my robe, and I couldn't cover my body's betrayal.

Yet the state of his shoulder easily quashed my lustful discomfort. He'd torn off his bandage and red rivulets blended into the wicked vines of his tricolored tattoo. I patted his wound with the wet cloth, applying pressure to staunch the bleeding. "How'd you tear it open?"

His biceps twitched. "Somehow, somewhere."

I pinched his forearm and when he tried to catch my wrist, I whisked my hand away. "What dimension is that on?" If he had another brain, it would be so freaking lonely.

"Adam left a note." He ignored me as usual. "He went into the office for a couple of hours before others arrived.

Jax is guarding the door."

My blood bubbled. "Jax?" I slathered antibacterial cream on his wound.

"Jon's brother." He set the note on the nightstand, threw a small tube of Med-Stitch on the bed.

I eased closer to examine the edges of the wound for infection. "Is Jax guarding me or holding me prisoner?"

"Probably both." Ronan tilted his head back to size me up. "What's up with that, Aria? What'd you do?" He averted his reddening face, coughed into his fist.

"What?" I picked dried blood off his arm.

His agitated aura stirred the air. I slanted a glance at his face, my boobs all but sticking in his mouth. Geez, the perfect subliminal turn-on for the poor barbarian. My own heat dialed up ten notches. Subtly, I shifted my chest out of his face. "Sorry, you're sitting on my robe."

"I'm not sorry." Ronan didn't make a move to free my cover-up.

I tried to ignore him, but touching him ignited sparks in my blood that left me jittery—in an unfamiliar desirable way. Easing to the side, I fingered a coating of Med-Stitch onto his wound. "Let it dry." I gathered the stained towels and rushed to the bathroom, needing the distance before my body betrayed me further. He followed, closing fast behind me, resting his hands on my shoulders. The towels fell in a heap on the vanity. We studied our reflections in the mirror. Light glinted off his glossy jet hair, startling against his tired face. The set of his chin suggested a renewed stubborn streak compelling me to rip into. "Where were you?"

"Taking care of business."

"What business?" My fists curled on the vanity.

"None of yours." He lowered his hands to his side, his mouth stretched tight.

I whirled around and poked my finger into his good shoulder. "Your business *is* my business. You dragged me into this mess."

Ronan walked away. "Damn. You sound like a girlfriend," he slung over his shoulder. He grabbed my robe off the bed and tossed it at me.

Purple satin puddled on my feet. My anger swirled around me and grappled with Ronan's weak aura. "It is my business because it affects me. Your life is my life now." I held up two crossed fingers. "In case you're too stupid or dead inside to notice, we're connected...our auras..." I flung out my arms in a dismissive move, bent to retrieve my robe. "I wouldn't be your girlfriend if you were hung like a stallion and had a zillion dollars." I straightened to my full height, my fists buried in satin.

Faster than I could blink, Ronan's hands spanned my waist and his mouth swooped down on mine. The second his lips touched mine, the heat in my body exploded, showering me in an inferno of lust. A groan escaped me as I melted into him, twining my arms around his neck. Our melded auras filled me with an incredible sensation of arousal and power. Tainted magic poured into me, and mine cleansed it, gave it substance. His mouth possessed mine in the most fantastically passionate kiss I'd ever experienced. I floated on a fluffy cloud of silver power, so much untapped energy between us, seething for freedom and exploration. Soft yet firm, his warm lips played over my parted lips, and his tongue tangoed sweetly with mine, the taste of him, chocolate and peanuts, filling my mouth. All my soft curves fit into the hardness of his body.

Then reality hit me, and I pushed away from him, my mouth burning from the hot as hell kiss. Ronan growled low in his throat. An array of emotions swam the liquid depths of his eyes, leaving bewilderment and speculation behind. *Ho. Lee. Doppelgängers.* Whoever said men were like potato chips and you can't have just one needed to live my life for a day.

"I'm not stupid. I sure as hell am not dead." His rough baritone thrummed through my feverish nerves, threatening to unseat me again. He gripped my waist, my satin camisole between us.

My mind froze in its swirling confusion and my mouth went on strike.

He skimmed his lips over mine. "I can't believe I'm saying this, but I missed you."

I blinked up at him, my heart finally catching up with its beat. "You did?" My voice wobbled.

Leaning his forehead against mine, he gazed into my eyes. "I don't trust easily, Aria."

I nodded in mutual agreement of my own trust issues and understanding what he'd suffered. That damn shock-o-meter churned out mad fairies in my stomach. Kissing two men? Even if I paid my mind with genius drugs, I couldn't reconcile the fact that they were two halves of a whole or which half I wanted as more than a friend.

"When you're not with me, a piece of me is missing." The baring of his soul made his voice uncertain, fearful. "You drive me through a minefield out of my damn mind." A slow hesitant grin tipped up the corners of his mouth. I wanted to dip my tongue into those corners. "And I still want you."

"So you do like me?" I teased, dying to dive into a tub of ice cubes.

Carefree and real, his rich, smooth laughter was a symphony to my ears. "I need sleep. Sit with me and we'll talk." Ronan moved toward the closed door, my eyes riveted on his firm rear that filled his jeans to perfection.

My heart revved into turbo mode. "Where you going?"

"It's bad enough I have to smell Adam on you, but I won't sleep where you two..." Crumbs of charcoal danger appeared in his eyes. He stalked out of the room.

I seized my robe off the floor and caught up to him. "Nothing happened. He needed relief from pain." I didn't need to explain myself. Did I? *Criminy, I'm going to hell in a pink Easter basket.*

Understanding softened his expression. He led the way into the other bedroom, an exact replica of the first one, except for the deep purple and gold bedding. Without hesitation, he stripped to his *black* boxer briefs. *I knew it!* Black to the core. Ronan took in the bed then landed a hopeful look on me.

I was definitely tripping to visit Lucifer when all was said and done. I slipped into my robe, belted it tight. The floor lamp by the door left the room in shadows, and I reached to turn it off.

"Leave it on."

"You need to sleep, not spend time looking at me."

"Who said anything about looking at you?" he grumbled half-heartedly. "I like light."

Despite my heart and head being ripped in two, I gave Ronan the same consideration I gave Adam. I would treat them as equals until one emerged the victor. Or none at all. *Damn my life to the Rift!* I needed Zoe. I wanted to cry at the weird injustice. Days ago, not a man on my radar. Now, I had to struggle to decipher the intentions of two hunks. How? *How do I accomplish that? It's bad enough I'm trying to figure out my role in the world of adults, the Forbidden, and now the world of men? Aria Elle's in there somewhere, right?*

I crossed the room and lay on top of the comforter, Ronan's arm a hard but welcome pillow. Our auras tangoed together as longing surged between us, but I hammered mine down before my heart trampled my head. I certainly hadn't felt that hungry energy spike in Adam's arms. Not that I hadn't been equally aroused. Heck, who wouldn't be in the arms of the doppel-hunks. It was just different. I'd have to develop a whole new language to describe how I felt.

Ronan settled on the pillows. I rested my head on his chest, his heart beating against my ear in sync with mine.

"I went to Melisande's hotel and snagged her computer. She always travels with a laptop and tablet. I couldn't let it fall into the wrong hands. We'll check it out later. Maybe she has more of the *Illuminaria*. Okay?" His fingers tangled in the hair at the nape of my neck.

A pleased sigh slipped out of me. The sharp tang of antiseptic tickling my nose eclipsed his spicy, woodsy cologne. "Sure, if you want," I answered with feigned nonchalance. *Yeah, baby! That witch is mine.* Ronan's chuckle rumbled in his chest against my ear. "We need to get our instruction guide away from your dad." Just from the few pages I now possessed, I knew that book was über dangerous in Riley's hands.

"I know. Dad wasn't very open with info, even to me. But Melisande worked me against him, and she had access to pretty much everything, except the full *Illuminaria*." He blew out a ragged breath. "Hell, I don't know. We need all of that damn manuscript."

His stomach earned a pat, and his skin twittered beneath my touch. "Zoe comes first. Speaking of—"

"We talk to my father at one."

I hugged him tight. We had six hours.

The heater clicked on and a soothing hiss of warmth filled the room. I lifted my face, drawing thirteens on his chest with my index finger and crossing them out before I invoked a rash of bad luck while we slept. *Sue me for being paranoid.*

"What?" His eyes went all dragon slit on me.

"We have more trouble."

"I know about Kiera Kendrick. Adam left messages." He knuckled his eyes. "Later. My head's killing me from that deadener."

I scooted up and placed a feathery kiss on his mouth, his nose, his forehead, finally dropping my head on his chest.

"Aria," he breathed out. "I do like you."

Twin doppelgänger arrows nicked my heart, spun my head into a flurry of epic confusion. Neither hit the bull's eye.

FIFTEEN

By the sounds of Ronan's even breathing, slumber claimed him in seconds. I stuffed a pillow in his arms and tiptoed from the room to take a quick bath. I turned on the tub tap, evil-eyeing the six showerheads. Showers made me super nervous, mainly because of that wetting the face thing that stems from the worst day of my life.

The night my mother died, I had gotten locked out of the house. I kept waiting for her to come home and she never did. Rain sleeted down, and I'd fallen asleep on the narrow covered porch. I'd awoken choking on water and couldn't catch my breath. Rain had pelted my face and I thought I was drowning. Then I'd lost control of my telekinesis and blasted out the windows on the front door, glass flying everywhere. Another Friday the 13th disaster. That night of death and torment never strayed far from my thoughts. My phobia had gotten so bad, Granny Elle had removed the showerhead in my shower and I removed it from my condo shower. Hence the reason why the multihead shower in the hotel tweaked me out.

Regardless, a half-hour later, clean and glistening, I inhaled a cranberry muffin and two cups of liquid fuel, then painted my face, moussed and dried my hair. I squeezed into a hipster-grazing purple sweater, slim jeans, and donned my black leather jacket. My clunky-heeled boots added two inches to my height. One last glance in the mirror told me I was as hot and ready for the outside world as I'd get with puffy eyes and a pasty face. Total waste of makeup, I might add. Although I twinged with every step I took, at least my outfit covered most of my war wounds.

The mystery pup waited for me by the door to the outside hallway. I hooked the leash on her silver-studded, leather collar. "Let's hit it, Finny."

A younger version of Jon dropped his jaw ogling me from his position outside the door. Potent psychic deadeners flattened my powers, and I eyed one hanging off his neck. Indignation surged hot in my veins. I really wanted to start thinking positive, but I knew it would be a wasted effort. Risking lockjaw, I ground my back teeth.

"Jax, I presume?" I held out my right hand. "Aria Walker."

He pumped my hand, his palm damp and hot.

"How many deadeners are you sporting? Are they for my benefit?" I grinned encouragingly, wiping my hand on my pants. After a few seconds of suppression and absorption of his aural energy, my energy staged a scathing comeback and my telekinetic brain waves surged for release. The night's rest had restored more than my normal cache of energy. The proximity to the Rift seemed to be working to my advantage. Or it was now spitting out a ton more energy. I buried the thought so deep I'd need a brain surgeon to dig it up later.

"No. They're...there to protect you. They're also detectors." Jax's mouth snapped shut and he got a grip on his puny brain down yonder.

My leg earned the ire of my slapping leash. *I'm so returning Adam to the Jerk Store.* Why did he feel the need to quash my powers? I wrapped my head around my reluctant brain waves and thrust outward, concentrating on the devices around his neck, one on each wrist and ankle. Five pops and Jax danced as if sand crabs nibbled on his feet. Using extreme caution, I forced him into semi-paralysis mode, enough to foil his chase for fifteen minutes.

"Gotta run. Nice meeting you." The poor sap reacted in slow motion to strip the devices off his prickly skin as he slid down the wall to the floor. Excitement kicked my pulse into fourth gear. My new power fuse was becoming easier to control and manipulate. The gloves were off!

I sprinted toward the stairs to catch an elevator on another floor. As soon as I opened the stairwell door, my right pinkie twitched. I looked at my watch, nine-thirteen. *Crap on a cracked cracker.*

A familiar presence wrenched on my aura. Kiera? Had she ratted us out?

Keeping my sight peeled around me, I unhooked Fin's leash. She remained near me, but I wanted her free to run in case I needed backup. Screw the hotel rules.

I held my stun gun as primed as my internal magic. Peering through the small window on the stairwell door, I met only empty stairs. Back muscles achingly rigid, I focused on the odd pressure in my heart of power. It felt like someone was sipping my magic out through a cocktail straw, tiny draws from the larger reservoir of my core. The sensation wafted in and out of my receptors. Such magic hadn't existed in the world before yesterday, and certainly not from Kiera. Was she suddenly gaining powers from her theoretical Thirteen sorcerer the way Adam did from Ronan?

I tiptoed toward the alcove housing the elevator. Fin trotted off to sniff at a chocolate peanut Ronan must've sacrificed. I stamped my foot, but she licked it up anyway. *I see where your priorities lay, Finny. Hope the chocolate doesn't kill you.* A second of worry sent me faltering until a gurgle worked up from Jax's throat.

He sprawled on his back down the hall, staring at the ceiling. No help for the wicked from him. My right pinkie twitched again, and a tug on my aura nearly sucked the air out of my lungs. The door swung open. Gasping, I spun around.

A drag on my aura slammed my heart into hyperdrive. A faintly glowing Kiera and her doppelgänger twin surged from the stairwell. Truth stared me down. *A Forbidden Thirteen sorcerer and her fairy doppelgänger, Kiera?* A viral bug in their webbed energy spun their auras in blurry, fragmented waves, slicing through mine, practically incapacitating me.

Breathing deeply in and out, I flung out a batch of sizzling energy to halt them in their tracks. Their taint hauled my blast every which way and the energy fizzled into the ozone. I tried again, but their caustic magic rendered mine useless. Dread streaked cold strokes up my spine. The supposed sorcerer doppelgänger tossed a brain wave of energy that aped a Scrambler.

"Stop it, Katrina!" Kiera turned on her lookalike. "She can help us."

"Maybe she did this to us," Katrina spat out. "She's pulling on my telekinetic receptors, same as you." Katrina shoved her fist in Kiera's shoulder.

"When did you two meet?" My curiosity got the better of the situation.

"Last night." Kiera scrubbed her hands together, veins visible in her translucent skin. "After I left here, she was at my house waiting for me. Dominion Research was there too. They brought her to me and said they could help us. They snatched her last week from her home in Las Vegas. After your reactions last night and hearing that they'd kidnapped her, we managed to escape before they nabbed me."

"And you came here to jeopardize *me*, the one person who can help you?" I pasted on my most fierce scowl and rabid eye. "Did they follow you?"

Kiera shook her head, eyes floating in a sea of apology as parts of her body wavered in and out of visibility as if she too suffered from a poorly executed cloaking spell. Katrina was the Ronan to her Adam, full of life and energy. Their auras tangoed with mine, copycatting the doppel-hunks' auras.

As if Kiera didn't just say they weren't followed, out of the stairwell behind them sprang a trio of cavemen. I recognized Milo from the university altercation. Riley's men tracked K-Squared straight to the hotel. *Holy, honking hell in the hotel hallway.*

"You idiots," I said through gritted teeth. "They stuck a tracking chip in Katrina!"

I raced toward the elevator, Kiera and Katrina hot on my heels. Fin snarled and nipped at the legs of the men. I slapped my palm on the elevator call button, fruitlessly pushing against the rabid paranormal attack the girls emitted. Even gripping my pendant, I couldn't focus on my power or deflect them. *What was I, flypaper for doppelgängers and their pursuers?*

"Come on!" I stabbed and stabbed the call button.

The men trapped me between the main corridor and the dead end elevator hallway. Two other men came up behind Double-K and locked their arms around the twits. The girls kicked and screamed until the men knocked them out with a needle in their necks, and they sagged to the floor in a synchronized wave. I crept to the end of the hall, butting against an ornate console table. A golden urn filled with fake flowers rocked on the marble top and toppled to the tile floor, breaking into a million splinters, cracking my barrier of fear. Bird of paradise flowers and tropical grasses thumped to the granite. *Good God, who hijacked lucky thirteen today?*

"Can I help you?" I shook ceramic dust off my boots one foot at a time.

Fin barked and trotted circles around the men. They kept toeing her away. Leaning more toward cute and cuddly, Fin wasn't much of a guard dog. I'd have to fix that later if we spent a lot of time together. *Only if my cats grant their divine approval, that is.* Yeah, my ass was in a whirl and my mind had revolted into the mundane of cats and dogs. *Focus, focus.* I nearly thumped the words into my head.

The largest man, a candidate for the newest weight loss craze, stepped toward me, crunching ceramic chunks into dust. His beefy hands flexed and curled. "Give it up, little girl. You won't get away from us this time. Put the weapon down." He smirked at Milo who reddened and advanced toward me as if he had something to prove. Like maybe increasing the size of his balls.

The elevator finally dinged its arrival. The doors slid open behind them, closed, and my escape hatch disappeared in a whoosh.

Arm wavering, I aimed my stun gun between Milo and Mr. Beefy. They sported deadeners even more high tech than what Jax wore. "Stay back." My stunner and my mouth were all I had until I figured out how to work with the deadeners. I was already visualizing the duct tape over my mouth.

I tossed a stab of air and watched it ruffle the fur on Fin's back. Head cocked sideways, the pup wagged her tail. Tension rolled out of my shoulders down my arms.

In a show of good faith, I held up my stun gun, then tucked it in my waistband. I hoped I shut the safety off. A zap down there could really confuse my already mystified hormones. I needed to stall Riley's mercenaries. My powers had begun to snip at their deadeners, subtle little attacks of energy primed to short them out. And I think I was drawing something from Kiera and Katrina, even though they were conked out.

"What do you want with me? I'm just a college girl visiting friends on winter break."

The men chuckled in stereo.

"Sure, and I'm the president of the fucking U.S. of A." Fat-ass moved toward me. His deadener crinkled through my telekinetic receptors, but my supposed destructive energy didn't dampen them further. It actually seemed to tickle them awake. "Roger, you and Chan take the other two out of here."

Oh, no! The two men picked up Kiera and Katrina, shrugged them over their shoulders, and headed toward the back staircase.

The elevator chimed, and the remaining cavemen twitched in their rain booties. Fin snarled, ears flattened back, teeth bared. Everyone spun toward the opening doors. Adam stalked out of the elevator with Jon, guns trained on Riley's three enforcers.

The disruption gave me a chance opening, and I mind-tossed a barrage of energy, zapping the three deadeners at once. Another headache-inducing arc sent the three men tumbling to the ground, writhing in pain. Adam and Jon sprang into motion to incapacitate the brutes.

I beelined it to the suite to snag Jax and Ronan. My feet dragged and fuzz filled my head. No way would I tempt fate and leave my meager haven alone again. Not until I had a solid plan to handle other sorcerers and fairies destined to flock to me.

The Rift, the whole shebang, was bigger than Ronan, Adam, or I ever imagined. Who else had the crumbling gate affected? Did they all have the ability to sense me? Who or *what* was I to them? A cold wash of goose bumps raced up my spine.

Stumbling, I rounded the bend and reenergized Jax's brain with a simple thought. Not quite sure how it worked, it was all the energy I managed to conjure. Jax crab-crawled away from me, distress scrunching his face. He struggled to sit up, and Adam skirted around me to help him.

"Five wasn't enough." Jax fingered the short-circuited deadener around his neck and looked behind him as if Adam were the sheriff of wicked Fairyland.

"So I see." Adam shot me an impatient frown.

I seethed and stomped into the suite, Adam close on my tail. Once behind closed doors, I blasted him a new one. "Who made you the master of me? I won't be imprisoned by you, or Ronan." I jerked my thumb toward the bedroom door.

His eyebrows quirked. "He's here?"

"You don't miss a trick, do ya? By the way, your fairy princess Kiera and her *sorcerer* showed up." His eyes bugged out. "Riley's men snatched them." I stalked to the empty bedroom. Fin snuck in before I slammed the door on Adam.

"Pack up, we're leaving before they return," he yelled through the door.

I sank to my knees on the plush carpet. "Why can't I feel your aura anymore?" I ruffled the silky fur around her ears. "Is the bad magic screwing with you too?"

She yipped twice in an acknowledgement that eerily represented a *yes and no.*

Determination got the better of me. I kissed her furry head, and then snagged Mom's papers out of the safe. It was time to face my heritage. To hell with sharing my treasure with my wardens, or packing. I eyed my belongings scattered around the room, knowing I needed to get my butt in gear before more of Riley's men popped up.

I stared at the envelopes so long they should've started talking to me. "Why did you hide these secrets, Mom," I whispered.

At times, I missed her so much I thought my heart might implode. After both Mom and then Granny Elle had passed, I resolved never to get close to anyone ever again. Zoe ultimately patched the hole and kept me from having an epic freakout about my cursed life. I certainly didn't know what to do about Adam and Ronan since I had no clue what direction my life traveled. I thought it'd be easy to toughen my heart with my crappy past and an unknown future. Not so easy now with the doppel-dudes softening it up.

Carefully, I emptied the packages. Most of the papers inside were so very old. I had no doubt they belonged to the *Illuminaria.* One by one, I looked at them, all crammed with writing in a foreign language. Half the sheets were newer and it appeared someone had translated the strange language into English. Was this what my mother had been working on all the time?

The pages contained the ritual to open the Rifts—the ritual Riley Senior was missing—along with the alchemic spells to go along with the sorcery-magic. Almost every ritual a Forbidden Thirteen sorcerer could do naturally with their inborn magic, someone could replicate with the right alchemic recipe and ingredients, ingredients that included blood of the Thirteen descendants. Richard Riley's ultimate goal. If he couldn't control the Thirteen naturally, he could do a helluva lot of damage with our blood. Worst of all, he could control all the Forbidden with the alchemic potions in the book. My body became a mass of gooseflesh as the implications imprinted my brain, an almost permanent condition of horrifically mysterious thoughts.

Once past the rituals and potions, the summary at the end of the *Illuminaria* stunned me more than anything else had in the last few days. My blood turned to ice.

I wasn't just one of the Forbidden Thirteen sorcerers. I was *the* last living descendant of the *thirteenth* sorcerer. What did that mean? With my blood alone, Riley could call all the living descendants of the Thirteen to him.

My heart clutched up. I continued reading the

enlightening and frightening text. The powerful sorcery that created one doppelgänger for each Forbidden Thirteen sorcerer, also ensured only one sorcerer was born in each generation of the thirteen families, even though multiple generations of sorcerers in each family could be alive at one time. How our bloodlines accomplished that was pretty random. If Mom was alive, either one of us could've been the thirteenth sorcerer, one being stronger than the other.

On and on the disturbing text flowed. The original thirteenth sorcerer—my supposed ancestor—had created the doppelgängers and the magic ensuring that sorcery survived throughout the ages even when most of the magic had been abolished. The magic may have waned for a time or became diluted throughout our bloodlines, but it remained in our blood. The thirteenth couldn't wield magic with a doppelgänger in the world with her. *Thank my lucky stars.* I didn't think the world could deal with another Aria. Only the thirteenth had a magical bond to the other twelve sorcerers, otherwise the other twelve were not bound to each other—unless the thirteenth bound all thirteen together. *Holy sorcerers on high hell.*

The pages spoke of the deliberate dilution of magic into odd and sometimes flawed ESP throughout generations to keep the Thirteen safe and undetected. Once brought together, they had the ability to invoke true and ancient sorcery. The pages included a magic spell and its alchemic ritual explaining how to accomplish the task. Only the thirteenth could invoke the final words to restore pure ancient magic to all thirteen. Only the thirteenth had the ability to pull magic from the other twelve and their doppelgängers once the sorcerer and doppelgänger pairs had bonded. It scared the bejeezus out of me.

There was much more in the few pages crammed front and back with magic, myth, prophecies, alchemy, and truth. None of this had to do with a Rift opening and pouring the abolished magic back into our world. I leafed through the pages until I found a frightening and obscure reference that wasn't so vague with what I'd already learned. "Eventually, a generation of Thirteen will be born that will restore the ancient powers of the original Thirteen. However, for all to be born of the same age, the old magic must be present on Earth to trigger the return and births." *Powerful scary magic hell*. How did the ancients accomplish this? Did they know a cluster of earthquakes could trigger the return of the magic, albeit tainted magic?

Stunned, my mind bended this proof in black and white as I opened a small envelope containing a note from Mom to me in case something happened to her and I discovered the book.

> *My dearest Aria Elle,*
>
> *I know you'll understand why I held this from you, and hope that you'll forgive me. I had to protect you from this at all costs, as I'm sure you'll come to realize. If you have this letter, then I assume I'm gone.*
>
> *I know the extent of your talents, as I was the same before you.*

Shock reverberated through me. Why hadn't she told me? I swiped my blurred eyes to read the familiar scrawl.

> *We belong to an extremely secret group. It has remained so secret throughout time that the members don't even know each other. The original members planned the secrecy at the group's inception. When the founding members entered into their final task on Earth, they did so with full knowledge of their lot in life.*
>
> *It's an inherent need in each of us to hide our particular talents from the world,*

including the members of our elite group. That's your cross to bear, as it was mine. I cannot divulge more in writing since it's dangerous, even with what I have written and what I have left behind. So much danger abounds that I cannot comprehend it, let alone write about it. You must remain wary at all costs.

However, you won't be alone in whatever you decide to accomplish. My seer's sight foresaw three good men in your future. They will protect you with their entire beings, as that's part of their task in life, as you will protect them. You will not be alone, and that soothes me more than anything. I'm sorry if that troubles you and compounds your life, but it is what it is.

Remember the danger and the secrecy at all costs. I love you and respect your decisions and choices. I'll always watch over you. Think of the good times we shared, the fantasies we traded, the exotic vacation we enjoyed before I passed on. Think of the realms we explored in our dreams and the one place we always came together.

Love you like the frosting on my cake! Mom.

Chilly air engulfed me, and I sat there for what seemed like hours, unable to turn the pages to read more of the translation. Finally, the absurdity of my life smacked good sense out of me and hysterical laughter bubbled up. I needed to laugh it off, because I really wanted to bury my head in a vat of Mom's decadent frosting. Who were the three men? Ronan and Adam? Who was the third? *Please, please, don't let one be Richard Riley.*

Vaguely, I heard a bang on the door, making my heart jump. I opened my mouth to tell him to take a hike, but my throat seized on the words. What if it was one of Riley's men? I struggled to get up, lost my balance on the bed, and knocked over the bell jar lamp. Despite the dense carpet, and probably because of my *unluck*, the lamp hit the bottom of the nightstand. The bulb popped and the porcelain cracked into pieces.

The bedroom door flew open with a splintered bang.

SIXTEEN

The doppel-jerks hulked in the doorway. I hopped off the bed, gently pulled the comforter over the precious and priceless papers. Ronan's aura assaulted me like a bulldozer of snow dumped over my shoulders.

"What?" My heart tumbled. Fin pranced in front of me, her tail whipping my legs. "I hope they don't kick you out for wrecking hotel property. Then where would you lock me up?" I trailed a scornful look from the guilty culprit's black boots to the scuffmarks on the white door.

They scoped out the room to ensure I wasn't the victim of an attempted *redrum* on their watch. *Note to self: Watch The Shining to make my life look like cake.* Adam returned from the bathroom with a wet washcloth and handed it to me. MAC Cosmetics could probably use me as a prime example of cheap makeup gone haywire.

"What's wrong?" he asked.

I wiped tear streaks off my face. "Nothing."

"Liar," Ronan said softly. They backed me into the corner.

Panic flitted through me and I spooled my energy for an attack. I felt like the trapped mouse Cody and Cleo batted around my patio last summer. I thrust away from the wall, forcing them back.

Greed sparkled in Ronan's eyes as he honed in on an empty clasp envelope lying on the bed. "Is that from your mom?" His eyes narrowed.

"Aren't you Mr. Nosey?" I shot back. "Appears as if I have something you might want."

"What the hell crawled up your ass?" Ronan dug his fingers through his slick hair. The clean, crisp scent of citrus shampoo infused the air. I breathed in deeply, basking in it like a love-struck ninny.

"She's mad at me for thinking of her safety," Adam quipped.

"For not trusting me." My eyes tried to fling switchblades, but I didn't possess that ability. Yet.

Ronan propped his good shoulder against the wall. "Why'd you leave earlier?"

Both nasty and nice answers sprang to mind. The kiss-ass angel on one shoulder quickly won the battle. "I wanted to scope out your father's compound, get a feel for it in person."

I swear on Granny's urn they both growled at me. What tripped me out the most was that their auras oozed fierce protectiveness. A frisson of heat incited a sexy dance low in my nether regions. *Attention: Aria Elle Walker has finally lost control of her body.*

"You're clueless." Ronan clenched his fists. He edged closer, hovering like a storm cloud of testosterone. His aura taint skated over my exposed skin. "Start packing. We need to get out of here. Now."

Adam plucked at a tendril of hair curling toward me. "Riley has deadeners all over his campus. He holds the patents on this shit." Fog seemed to obscure his right side for a second.

Our fused auras sizzled. I moved forward, pushed the doppel-wardens apart, and stomped to the other side of the room. "Well, I wasn't planning on waltzing up to the front door. We can disguise and shield ourselves like we did at the university. I can trip DR's cameras one by one." My determination was like the Rock of Gibraltar inside me. "I was only planning to scope out our opposition before we attack. Check out the deadeners. I wanted to see if I have enough power to knock them all out the way I did on Riley's cavemen at SCU."

Ronan's neutral expression evolved into a critical squint. Lines of concentration formed under Adam's eyes. A long beat of silence encouraged me to continue despite the thickening in my throat. "We can get bulletproof skin to avoid their bio-energy darts." Unease blasted that famous rock into molten pebbles in my stomach. I scratched at the nails teasing my neck. "It'll work. We just need to know where the deadeners, cameras, and sensors are. We have that info on Melisande's tablet, right?" Flames seared my insides and I bent double. Adam sprinted around the bed.

My knees gelled. Red pokers of agony stabbed my skin and muscles. Ronan's aura fed on me as if I was the only source of magical nutrient this side of the Rift. My spastic trembling caused me to lose all focus on my power, leaving me as powerless as spit. What new reality show purgatory had I landed in now?

"Son of a bitch." Ronan streaked out of the room.

"Blondie." Adam caught me before I crash-landed, and he laid me on the bed, avoiding my hidden paper treasures.

An inferno roared through me, decimating my power. "It hurts," I whimpered, crawling out of my head. My skin blazed as if demons were peeling me like an orange in H-Town. The rest of my aural energy dissolved, leaving me boneless and vacant. Clothes tightened around my roasting body, and I clutched Adam's hand in a wimpy clasp. "Clothes...get them...off."

He undressed me down to my bra and thong. Then he draped cool, wet towels over me. Nothing appeased my pain. No focusing on my telekinesis or my aura brought my magic back. It was the worst feeling I'd ever experienced. I'd lead a killing spree at DR to restore the energy that'd been my one and only companion throughout my life's upheavals. The one thing that I could always rely upon when nothing else remained constant.

Adam swept hair off my damp, boiling face. "What can I do?"

Another wave of serrated knives scraped beneath my skin, leaving me writhing on my side, panting in terror. Even with my eyes open, I saw nothing but a jagged darkness. Adam caressed my arms, whispering sweet somethings in my ear. I struggled to listen to his words, needing them to center me. My mind had frozen in limbo where all decisions and actions had gone the way of the dearly departed.

I bobbed in a sea of syrupy steam, so hot and wild it could only be tagged a firestorm. It cleared for a second, and I'd reach for that tantalizing pool of energy, then the mist hardened into lava, pushing me away. Everything inside me reached for my aura languishing outside my empty shell, refusing to come home. I screamed in frustration as it slipped from my grasp again and again. Adam's voice finally caught in my ears, and I concentrated on his words.

"Take my energy, Aria!" His fingers dug into my shoulders.

A shallow wave of familiar magic swept over me. It cooled my flesh, slowed my virtual skinning. The scent of spring meadows, summer roses, and cinnamon spices licked the air, flooded my nose, and saturated my tongue. With everything in my being, I drew on my shattered energy and doused the fire engulfing me. Magic rammed into me, jolting me against Adam. It was welcome relief to my near meltdown. My aura surrounded him, lending life to his sick body. He scooped me in his arms, cradling me against his chest, the wet towel between his hard body and my softer curves. Somehow, Adam's body filtered the taint and restored my power. Cleansed, vibrant magic seeped into me, driving out the tortuous pain.

He quaked against my length. "God, almighty. I felt your aural energy completely inside me." Adam kissed my head, his breath ragged. "What the hell was that?"

Achy and exhausted, electricity arced through me, rejuvenating my aural energy faster than ever as if every electromagnetic particle in the hotel filtered into me. Insane laughter boiled up. "Like I know?" I closed my eyes for a moment to calm my galloping heart. "In what fantasy-world hell are we role-playing?" Shivering, I stripped off the wet towels. Modesty was a moot point since he'd seen my goods.

"Wish I had answers for you." He gathered me closer, his clothes damp against my cooling skin.

I hauled the crisp sheet over us. "What did you feel?" Adam's magic settled in an acid puddle in my stomach.

"While your power shot through me, I felt awesome. My real powers surfaced, pure and vibrant, and my pain disappeared. Now, the pain's gone only because I'm touching you."

The last of our auras reverted to their rightful homes, except for a sharp spoonful of fairy taint sprinkling dry ice in my gut. I didn't know what else to call the icy stone. I drew my tongue over my lips, capturing the bizarre taste of fresh roses in my mouth. "Thank you."

His satisfied gaze caressed me. A new kind of heat zeroed in on me, creating sensations I hadn't experienced…well…since the last doppelgänger who'd held me in his arms.

"Anytime." He chuckled roughly, averting his flushed face.

Thank lucky thirteen I had a passion for sexy

underwear straight from a Victoria's Secret dresser. My sodden pink lacy bra and matching thong caused Adam no end of appraisal from the glint of wonder in his eyes. He helped me off the bed, steadying my rubbery legs. My lower back throbbed anew. I fingered the skin, feeling raised welts, my eyes bugging out.

"What's wrong?"

I craned my neck to scrutinize my back. "I'm not sure."

Adam looked behind me and made a small noise in his throat.

"What?" I scurried into the bathroom. *I'll take my straitjacket in petal pink.*

I peered at my backside in the floor-to-ceiling mirror. A raised tattoo scored the center of my lower back. Black and green, inflamed against my winter skin, a vague pattern of vines and thorns emerged.

My heart beat so fast I thought I was going to pass out. I leaned my elbows on the vanity, barely able to suck in more than puffs of air. Did Adam's tainted power cause this? Ten million ideas tumbled over each other in my head and none of them made a lick of sense. He hovered beside me, commanding me to breathe.

"What the hell?" Ronan's jealous voice splintered my tenuous foundation.

His aura waltzed over me, airy and pain-free. Adam backed away to give Ronan a view of my back. Straightening, I caught Ronan's wide-eyed shock in the mirror. He tenderly touched my lower back, never breaking contact with my gaze in the mirror. Adam retreated to the doorway. Ronan's fingers cooled and soothed the burning welt. Sniveling, I pressed my back against his hand.

"Why me? Who elected me mayor of Freak Town?"

"I wish I knew."

Turning, I touched his cheek, his skin cold beneath my fingertips. "What happens to you when your aura attacks me?"

"I lose more of what little energy I have left." He shrugged. "I don't absorb any more, it doesn't regenerate." He moved his hands to my hips and squeezed gently. "Like a piece of my soul is being ripped out when I feel your pain."

I froze, my mouth dropping open. "Why didn't you tell me? Do you feel my tattoo...thing?" I slivered my eyes. "What else do you feel?" That could be risky with my emotions battling for world domination inside me.

A slow smile spread his lips, crinkling the skin around his eyes. "You're feeling better."

"Tell me." I pinched his arm playfully, anything to sidetrack the butterflies tangoing in my stomach.

"A beautiful, hot-as-hell woman with far too many clothes on."

I smirked. "You have the right amount of clothes on."

"I meant you." A twinkle lit his eyes.

I glanced at Adam, already knowing his answer to the same question. "Fork over some answers," I said to Ronan, drawing away, needing to throttle that tangible bond that impelled me to sink into an embrace that included so much more than his hands on me. His darkened eyes had gone as wild as a wind-tossed sea on a moonless night.

Lost in his stormy eyes, it took a long moment to realize I was nearly naked. A flush traveled up from my toes, and I crossed my arms over my torso. My rebel body had totally invalidated my inherent mistrust of near strangers.

Reluctantly, he circled around me to examine my back. "When the pain hits you, it bounces on me then returns to you." He fingered the welts, skimmed his hand over my right butt cheek. To my consternation, my rear involuntarily tightened.

"Hand me the antibacterial ointment. It's my turn to play doctor." He kissed my shoulder, his lips warm and firm.

Adam left and returned with my robe. I forced my mind

off Ronan's unnaturally playful mood. A facet of him I planned to explore in-depth. As much as I enjoyed his flirtations and attempts to lighten the situation, we had no time for it.

Rescuing Zoe was no longer priority one. Many other people were suffering. I couldn't handle that any longer.

"We have to close the Rift *now*." Decision made, I lowered my stricken gaze in the mirror to Ronan's veiled reflection and Adam's accepting eyes. We couldn't risk opening it correctly until we got a handle on everything Forbidden.

"I know." The only words Ronan needed to say. Adam nodded his agreement.

SEVENTEEN

After I recovered from my newest short-circuit, we scrambled to pack. Once in the parking lot, the stink of wet asphalt caused more knots to form in my shoulders. Roiling charcoal clouds whispered a warning along my nerves. *Just kill me if I ever have to live in Seattle.*

I climbed into one of two midnight-blue SUVs from the Freshfields company fleet. Jon planned to chauffer Adam in one, and Jax got stuck carting Ronan and big, bad me in the other. *Suck it up, boys. Aria's here to stay.* If Ronan's aura went postal on me again, we'd deal with it. For the moment, our other options numbered zero.

Ronan and I planned to video link to his father while we randomly cruised the city. Even though we turned off our location settings and scrambled them by staying on the move, we didn't trust Richard Riley's ability to bypass the best in high-tech security. The guy was rolling in moola and subhuman gift basket ideas. Since Riley didn't know about Adam, we didn't want to risk him getting caught with us, hence the reason we split up. Ronan and I needed an easy way into DR's compound to obtain the ancient book of clues and to rescue Zoe, Kiera, and Katrina. Riley was going to offer us personal invites to nab his treasures. We just needed to stay one step ahead of him.

According to Ronan, years ago Riley had spent a fortune hiring treasure hunters to locate his portion of the *Illuminaria* buried in an Ireland crypt. My ancestor had purposely dismantled and hidden the *Illuminaria* around the world so no one person could lay sticky fingers on the entire text. Someone had previously found and buried the puzzle pieces Riley now possessed. Who'd shot Riley with a lucky shamrock? And did I possess the key to the kingdom of the Forbidden in the missing pages? My point being, the guy would have hell's minions safeguarding his treasures no matter the cost. Our game plan was eleven doppelgängers short of a sorcerer's dozen.

A lot depended on what went down at the Rift. If we left the Rift in its current state, Adam and Kiera were going to die soon, and possibly Ronan and Katrina. Maybe even me. Who knew? After the phone call with Dickhead Riley, we were going to the Rift to close it, then onward to rescue Zoe, the girls, and get the book out of Dickie's sticky fingers. There was no telling how much blood he'd siphoned out of Kiera and Katrina in hopes of creating his alchemic magic. With Ronan's and Katrina's blood—if she was indeed a sorcerer—could he open the Rift? We had to beat him to it and hope our magic took his down a notch and stuck.

Jax exited the parking garage, and Ronan pinned me with a wrinkly nervous frown from the right side of the back seat. "You'll follow my lead?" Half question, half command.

I peered at my haggard reflection in the smoky window separating us from Jax.

"Aria?" Ronan's voice lowered. "I've been around the block a few times with my father."

"Okay. I get it." I studied him from my limpet-on-a-door

position, unable to trust myself so near him. It was bad enough our auras partied around us. I couldn't afford the distraction or the torrent of indecision rushing through my body. How'd I blunder from a humdrum life of loser blind dates to two gorgeous hunks in my back pocket? Dumbfounded and lucky hardly defined it. That Wiki to describe my new empire was percolating way too slowly.

"What happens if we don't close the Rift correctly? Will we all die?" The brand on my back burned.

Unease painted Ronan's bland mask. "Let's wait and see."

My chin dropped. "Oh, nice. Thanks for the vote."

"I don't know." He punched the seat between us.

His cell jangled in the seatback pocket. A muscle stood out in a hard ridge in his neck. Snatching up the phone, he clicked on video and speaker. The call routed via Adam's line, and he remained on a three-way, muted conference. As planned, I kept out of view of the camera. Not that I didn't want to give Dickie a one-fingered salute.

"Son, it's a pleasure to speak with you again." Richard Riley's snarky sweet baritone was more refined than Ronan's and slightly nasally as if he suffered from a cold. One could only wish.

Ronan wasted no time. "Release Zoe Marino and I won't contact the PVD."

We didn't have plans to contact the federal Paranormal Vice Division, but the threat was real. We decided not to bargain for Kiera and Katrina, yet. We didn't want him figuring out how much we knew about the situation. I still hadn't said a word to Ronan or Adam about what I'd discovered in the missing *Illuminaria* pages. I needed to keep something in my back pocket in case I was walking into a trap of Ronan and Adam's making.

Riley chuckled. "We both know you won't do that. Not until you've obtained a few of my treasures." According to Ronan, his father's possessiveness was legendary. "Since you've squandered no time, I'll get to my point. I'll release the telepath when you return with Aria Walker."

"No deal." Ronan white-knuckled the phone.

"What happened to you, Ronan?" Riley's tone hinted at regret. "You used to worship the ground I *owned*. You believed in my mission. We've spent your entire life working toward this goal. Where did I make a wrong turn?"

I smoothed my hand over Ronan's knee, hoping to instill a calm vibe. Destroying Riley wasn't vicious enough for what he'd done to a crapload of people.

"Give Zoe up and I'll let you live."

My eyes widened. Would he really off his own father?

"Let me see Ms. Walker." Exasperation clipped Riley's words. "Her little friend wants an eyeful too."

Ronan flashed me on screen. I flipped Riley the bird, and Ronan shot me a tired look of frustration.

"Aria!"

I snuck a peek at Zoe's face filling the small screen. Her eyes shimmered with unshed tears, framed by long, tangled auburn hair. I latched onto the device to steady Ronan's hand. "Zoe, you okay?" Relief cooled the volcano dying to erupt inside me.

"A few bruises, but I'm kicking." She hiccupped, her shoulders heaved. Two of Riley's apemen removed her thrashing and snarling from the room.

Riley's mug reappeared. I glowered at him, but Ronan seized the controls.

"What's it going to be, Ronan?"

"I'll return to the compound. Aria and Zoe go free."

"You can do better." Riley laughed a silver-tongued, arrogant sound geared to charm the unwary. "You're not talking to the media or law enforcement. And we both know you don't have the balls to kill me."

Fury and hatred vibrated Ronan's taut body. Riley harbored major blind spots about his son. However, he was right about our inability to cry wolf or to wine and dine the media, which was just another death sentence. We had to gain access to DR's compound to swipe the *Illuminaria* and every iota of his research, and destroy his alchemic potions and blood. Then Riley bites it big time.

"Release Zoe. I'll return to the compound. You get three days with Aria, me present at all times."

"Growing fond of our Ms. Walker, are you?" Green-eyed egotism was rife in Riley's voice. "I want her for three years. By then, she'll beg me to let her stay, as will you."

I jerked against the seatback. "Bastard," I said under my breath. *The only begging I'll be doing is begging you to take a vacation on the bottom on the ocean, a block of cement your only friend.*

"One week," Ronan countered.

One *minute* was crazy risky. We'd located the compound's schematics, including security data and weak spots on Melisande's computer. DR had corrected the defects after Ronan's desertion, but Ronan knew of other weaknesses the latest schematics didn't reveal. We knew a way out. Out alive was another chapter. We just needed a way inside, and if we could do it by cooperating a smidge, so be it. Dicktard would never kill us, not if we pretended to go along with him.

Riley remained silent for light years. "Sorry to disappoint," he finally said. "I'm growing rather fond of Ms. Marino. She's an amazing telepath. Now that my darling Melisande has jumped ship—"

I slapped down the mute button. "He doesn't know the Queen of Darkness is dead?" Disbelief twitched my eyelids.

Ronan shrugged, yanked the phone from me, thumbing the mute off. "Here's the final deal, *Dad*." He sneered at the word. "You get one week with Aria. I stay indefinitely. When Aria's safely released, you'll receive a key to a safety deposit box that contains the lost *Illuminaria* pages." The prepared lie tripped off his tongue. "We want forty-eight hours before surrendering."

Riley's eyes did a praying mantis bug-out. "Now you're talking my language," he purred. "I'll give you twenty-four hours. Be at the gate at one tomorrow." The display darkened.

Ronan and I swapped nervous, satisfied glances. Ronan had predicted his father would give us twenty-four hours. We only needed a few hours. The phone rang again. Adam.

"I'll meet you at the Rift at seven thirty," he rambled off.

"I thought we were going together?" That had been our plan—before we'd sold our magic and bodies to Satan's pride and joy.

"We still shouldn't be seen together." Ronan jabbed the SUV's intercom and instructed Jax to drive to our new hotel.

We hadn't tapped all of Melisande's data, and we hoped it contained info even Riley didn't know she'd pirated. Adam would keep Melisande's gadgets and documents safe and be our failsafe on the outside if something went ass-end wrong at DR. That was, if we managed to close the Rift and he lived long enough.

Ronan curled his fingers through mine. Our magic link pacified my frazzled nerves and erected a thin barrier against Adam's nasty lingering taint from my recent magic flogging in the hotel. Ronan's aura amazingly soothed the incessant burn of my new eerie tattoo.

The privacy window rolled down. "We have a tail," Jax said.

Our fleeting harmony shattered. Ronan and I fixed our sights out the rear window. A late model silver sedan followed at a discreet distance. Two cavemen silhouettes filled the front seats, two hulked in the rear.

Pinkies twitched. The clock struck one thirteen. Too late to thwart my bad luck. *Love. Lee.* Could I give myself a crash course in ninja?

"Head away from the hotel." Ronan yanked his gun

from his shoulder harness.

Likewise, I tugged out my stun gun, primed it for distance on high. "Who is it?" I settled backward in my seat for an easier view out the rear.

A torrential rain began pounding the roof, drowning the sound of my heart's erratic rhythm in my ears. The rear wipers arced across the glass, unable to defeat the mini-monsoon.

Jax drove into a bleak commercial area peppered with manufacturing buildings. Occasional splashes of color decorated the stark facades. The SUV's engine chugged, rattled, bit the dust. I caught Jax's anxious expression in the rearview mirror. *You have got to be kidding me.*

Ronan locked his sight on the sedan. "What's wrong?"

Jax rolled the vehicle to the curb, stomping on the breaks as the tires bounced off the cement. "Gas gauge reads empty, but we had a full tank."

Ronan landed a glower on me. A bead of sweat dripped between my breasts. *Son of an unlucky thirteen bitch.*

Jax fiddled with the diagnostic computer. The silver car halted in front of the glass-fronted building a couple hundred feet behind us. Rain slashed the windows, making it hard to see through the murk.

Lightning sizzled across the sky in a blaze of white. A clap of thunder caused me to jerk against the door. Then I noticed Ronan's aura had disappeared. Our compelling, confusing meld of tingly power became a frozen black boulder within me. As if my arteries bled out, my energy slipped out and my aura dissolved. In less than a minute, I became a lifeless hollow, despite my blood, muscles, and flesh calling for the lilting melody to return.

Arctic floodgates swung open and panic crashed into me. "Ronan?" I clenched my weapon so hard the outer shell creaked.

He turned to me, his eyes flinty, calculating. One sweep took in my alarm. "We're in a dead zone." Concentration deepened his frown. He attempted to raise his paltry magic to no avail.

I loathed the soul-eating loss in my core. I zipped my jacket to my chin, insanely hoping the insignificant effort contained my last trickle of energy.

Ronan kept his sight peeled on the car. "More of my father's goons."

Jax slammed his fist against the computer monitor. "Piece of shit."

The silver menace behind us appeared no less threatening through the rain-slick window. What were they waiting for?

Ronan touched my arm. "Keep watch. I'm going to help Jax."

I nodded and pitched a rash of positive mental energy at the computer. It drizzled into a pin drop of emptiness.

Another boom of thunder without the precipitating crack of lightning rattled my bones. A glint of light inside the sedan caught my attention. "They're getting out." Something tight wound up in my stomach.

Four tall men in dark raincoats exited the car. One had a glistening bald head, and the others sported short, dark hair the rain instantly plastered to their skulls.

"We're not waiting," Ronan barked. "Jax, cover us. You're not an ESP and they won't hurt you." The back window latch popped open. "Out your side, Aria."

"I'm not worried. I've got an arsenal." Jax laughed maniacally. He crammed his beefy body past me and rolled into the cargo area. "Ready," he growled, one hand on the window to push it open, the other clutched around a handgun.

A hateful, familiar paralysis claimed me. Everything blurred and that flood of panic became a tsunami. I forced my fingers to maintain my grip on my stun gun. Ronan shouted at me, but I couldn't understand his words. All I saw was the rain sheeting the windows, smothering the world outside. Muscles throbbed in my temples, and I fought against the memories flashing in lightning strikes through my mind. Refusing to let the haunting episodes hit me, I pulled inane thoughts out of other pockets in my mind. *Cody and Cleo, bring chocolate to Mommy.*

"Aria!" Ronan shook my shoulders. "Get a grip!" He jiggled me again and his mottled face wavered into view.

I focused on that ruggedly beautiful face as fragile life crept back into me. "It's raining," I stuttered, numb from my scalp to the soles of my feet.

"We're sitting ducks and you're worried about rain?" He shoved past me and flipped the door latch. The freezing numbness remained, but my mind raced into action, delving past the morass of that horrible night eight years ago.

Ronan cupped my face. "Baby, what's wrong?" His thumb stroked my cheek, hot against my glacial skin. "You'll get your powers back once we're free of the dead zone. But we can't sit here."

"They're moving in," Jax said. "Hey, here." Something hit my shoulder and Ronan caught it. He jammed a baseball cap on my head, yanking the bill low over my face.

The muck in my befuddled brain sluiced apart and feeling mushroomed in my pits of dread. I took several deep breaths to still my heart and locked eyes with Ronan's perplexed gaze. "I'm okay." I hoped. Only part of me knew the rain wouldn't hurt me.

Ronan sprang into action. "Stay close."

I stole one last dismal look at the slashing rain suffocating the earth, then plunged into it. We lunged across a short span of slippery lawn to a large sign staking the home of *A Fantasy on Us, Inc.* Adults Toys. Illuminated, animated purple and black penis-shaped vibrators danced on the left side of the sign. Rain buffeted me, and I dipped my head, my chin practically touching my chest. The comical sign returned a raindrop of normalcy to my bizarre new world.

Lightning lit up the churning dark sky, sizzling into the heavens. It struck the emerald grass, a spotlight on center stage, blinding me with its dazzling performance. Thunder rumbled so loud it shook the ground. I stumbled and grabbed hold of Ronan's jacket to keep from slipping on the wet grass. Four more cracks answered in quick succession. Only that time it wasn't thunder.

I flicked on my stun gun. Rain dripped down my neck, and I shuddered from the dampness penetrating the collar of my sweater.

Ronan peeked around the end of the sign. "Make a run for the walkway between the two buildings."

We tore across the lawn to the buildings. Gunshots tracked us, but I knew empathically that murder wasn't their top priority, yet they had no such reservations about shooting deadeners. Call it my thirteen spidey sense. We dashed between the one-story buildings. An overhang connected the structures, offering a break from the tortuous downpour. Sprinting to the rear, we rounded the far right corner the same time two of Dickie's Douches reached the front.

My heart drummed against my chest, beating a way out. The building on the right housed four loading docks, locked steel bars across its doors. Ronan pointed to a narrow opening beneath one of the docks. We slipped through the three-foot-square doorway and scampered deeper into a crawlspace spanning the width of the loading platform. A mildew smell reminded me of dirty, wet socks in the laundry hamper. I scrunched my nose and crawled across pea gravel, praying I didn't cross paths with any creepy crawlies. A hairy spider spaz attack wouldn't be pretty.

Ronan scuttled around investigating. I hid behind a cement pillar, holding my fist to my mouth to stifle the rumbling sound of my breathing. Denim plastered my legs in a wet, heavy layer. Fortunately, my coat and leather boots were waterproof. I unzipped my jacket and wiped my face on my dry sweater.

The steel ramp above us softened the noise of the rain. Wind whistled and moaned a mournful, lonely sound between the gaps in the sheets of steel, the song of the dead zone, the weeping of emptiness inside me.

"Riley." A voice with a New England accent floated closer. "Daddy's looking for you, the girl too. Come out and we won't hurt you."

"We lost them. These detectors ain't picking up shit," a squeaky male voice intoned.

At least the dead zone had a positive benefit. I clasped my hands to keep from clapping.

A phone rang and one of Riley's goons answered, his voice too low to hear until he said, "Today's your lucky day. If you don't show up at the compound tomorrow, we'll be hot on your trail, sniffing your asses before you can say fart." Rainfall muted the group guffaw.

"Lucky bastards," New England groused loudly.

"Let's get outta this cloud piss." Muffled footsteps carried the voice away on a whistle of wind.

Diminishing sounds of rain engulfed us. Ronan slicked his saturated hair off his face. "Damn it. They have your magic footprint as well as mine. The SUV had impenetrable blocks on it and they picked us up before we hit the dead zone."

My mind whirled around the numbing air. Melisande must have coughed up the goods. The best PSP gadgets couldn't locate a body by their electromagnetic footprint; that was only possible by DNA and brain wave scanning. "Why would they give up on us so easily?" Something didn't ring right.

"I don't know. Dad's up to no good as usual. Probably trying to make it look like he trusts us, or spying on us."

We huddled beneath the dock for fifteen minutes before emerging under drizzling, thick clouds. Hiding in shadows, we worked our way toward the street, pausing in the corridor at the front of the building. The SUV had disappeared. Ronan tugged me into his side, surveying the street in both directions. Just as I yanked my phone from my pocket, a honk pierced the silence and the SUV raced up to the curb.

Jax drove us safely out of the dead zone. My power rushed out of hiding, filling me with the most incredible, delicious feeling of sweetness, desire, and heaven. I never wanted to return to a dead zone and miss the magic that had been a part of my life forever.

Shivers seized control of me and my teeth clattered. Miserable in my soaked clothes, I huddled against the door until Ronan pulled me into his arms, folding his own dampness around me. What cuckoo's nest had we flown into? I derailed the incident in my mind, squinted at his face, my insatiable need for information putting him in a full court press.

I drew invisible shapes on his thigh. "Do you have any brothers or sisters?" I began with the most innocent of questions.

A muscle flinched in his chest against my shoulder. "No."

"Are you dating anyone?"

His hand crushed my swirling finger on his leg. His whole body tensed cadaver stiff. "I have no life. Haven't you figured that out?" he said in the gruffest voice I'd ever heard. "Do we have to do this right now?"

I flexed my hand to escape his clutches. He held on, but relaxed his grip. "I'm scared," I admitted. "I need something to kill a few rogue brain cells."

Tension flowed out of his arms. "I know." He kissed my temple and his fingers butterfly-danced across my cheek. "My father pressured me into doing things that kept me from a normal life. Things I'm not proud of." His chest rose and fell heavily. "I never wanted to bring anyone into that life." The heat of his anger expanded around us.

I inhaled a humid whiff of his cologne, fed the tiny fairies forming a dance line in my tummy. Sensing the heat of his disgust, I changed the subject. "Are you sure I negate you? How bad is your magic failing?" His laugh rumbled in his chest. "Okay. I *know* hell just froze over."

"You still don't believe in the whole negation thing, do you?"

"Why should I when it doesn't affect me? I feel your aura." I dusted his thigh with the flat of my hand. "Try it. Pretty please?" I lifted my head off his chest, landing sparkling encouragement on his face.

Annoyance set into the straight line of his mouth. "Feeling my aura has nothing to do with it."

"Prove it." I scooted out of his arms, into my seat.

The air between us wavered for a second, and gloom rained on my happy aura parade. My eager anticipation fell into a black hole. "What'd you do?"

"I put your brain to sleep." The corners of his mouth ruffled. "Did it work?"

Unable to stop myself, I stuck my tongue out at him.

The mask fell over his features and he reached for me. "It's bad, Aria. Okay?"

As though his words destroyed another barrier between us, I wound my arms inside his jacket and clutched him to me.

EIGHTEEN

I rucked up my damp sweater and examined my back in the bathroom mirrors. The welts traveling south toward my butt crack stung and itched like the poison ivy I'd fallen into on a camping trip a few years ago. I swore never to go camping again. Nature and I didn't get along.

Ronan strode into the bathroom, wearing dry jeans and a T-shirt, toweling off his hair. Such was our newfangled relationship. He sucked in a sharp breath as he checked out my back.

He chucked the towel in the tub and grabbed the tube of cortisone off the counter. "Drop your pants."

"Yes, doctor." Careful not to scrape my raw skin, I undid my jeans and peeled the moist denim past my hips.

He crouched behind me and gently traced my new artwork.

"How bad?" I twisted to my side to see in the mirror.

"Stop wiggling." His fingers dug into my hips to hold me steady. "It's no worse, half-inch longer, if that." He slicked the ointment onto the blistering tattoo. His touch and the soothing medicine left my insides dribbling into a pool of happiness.

My palms flat on the marble vanity top, I studied my face in the mirror. I knew my name, but barely recognized the reflection. Pain dulled my usual sparkling teal irises. Seriously, people with paranormal abilities had an extra sparkle to their eyes. It's not overly noticeable except to the trained. My complexion had colored like death warmed over and then returned for a second helping.

"Why did you freeze in the SUV?" Ronan's question came out of the blue yonder and incited a mini panic attack in my chest as my heart tried to detach.

Breathe. Breathe. I didn't care to explain my unnatural rain phobia to Ronan and make him think even less of me. "I don't want to talk about it." I inspected a bullet-shaped glop of aqua toothpaste in the sink. So not a sign I cared to see after our day from hell.

Ronan's fingers ceased moving for the span of an eye blink before resuming their slow massage. "Better?"

"Mmmm." Eyes closed, I was drowning in his calming touch.

His lips brushed my skin above the brand, soft and sensuous on my back, sending a tingly jolt through my legs. He began kissing a scorching trail northward as he shoved my sweater higher, and I shivered from the impact of his soft caressing lips. A tainted barb pricked my skin, and my hip froze against the vanity. The sensation trickled into dancing butterflies, and an ecstatic moan slipped out. His flaming mouth and tongue continued to create amazing sensations on my skin.

"Ronan?" I pushed out the one breath that refused to budge.

"Hmm?" He spanned his hands over my hips and pivoted me around, his lips working magic on my stomach.

Desire streamed molten liquid through my blood, and I slumped against the vanity. My body might as well belong to someone else for all the restraint I had over it. "What if the bad magic returns? It affects us when your emotions flip out."

He raised his head, his eyes half-lidded chinks of charcoal. "Or when my doppelgänger's around."

I gasped. So much crud going on, I hadn't noticed. And speaking of doppelgänger, I pushed against him. "Stop, Ronan. I can't do this—" I wanted to cry, scream, and rage. He froze, a black scowl working across his face. And the bottom fell out of his seduction.

White-hot ice picks poked me. Fire scorched the brand on my back. His aura turned ugly and mine scurried away. It was that bit of Adam's leftover contamination from earlier that dominated us, as though Adam's tainted magic gloated in triumph.

"No!" Ronan slammed his fist into the marble wall.

"Go." I shoved at him. Sharpened nails replaced the wire brush scraping my skin. He shook his head, cupped my cheek. I kissed his palm. "I'll be okay." I fell back against the mirror.

Alarm raced across Ronan's hard expression, and he stalked out of the suite leaving the door jarring in its frame.

Thunder boomed in my head. Anger, dismay, and uncertainty all fought for the crown inside me. Guilt swept another blast of fire over my physical pain. I needed to figure out the weird doppelgänger connection to both Ronan and Adam. *Man, I'm totally embracing my crazy in a Defcon wake and bake.*

Groaning, I buried my face in my hands, suffering the receding pain. My life was too complicated for man troubles. I had too much to accomplish, too much to discover to allow a love triangle in the middle, or any boyfriend for that matter. If we didn't fix the Rift, none of it would matter. There wouldn't be a life for either Ronan or Adam. Nor me, because I couldn't imagine any existence without either of them.

Pinpricks continued a light assault on my skin. I rubbed my arms, soothing my ravaged flesh. My phone rang in the other room, and I darted to answer it, needing a break from myself. Relief traveled down my back as I clicked on video.

Distress knitted Ronan's eyebrows into unibrow territory. "I just want to see you," he said. "Hear you. Are you okay?"

"I'm good." I'd already told him what had happened during the last time his magic attacked, but I withheld the one oddity that made no sense. Neither Ronan nor Adam knew about the small piece of Adam's magic embedded in my core, so completely different than the magical energy I absorbed and assimilated into good energy. Although I had absorbed it the same way I absorb aural energy, it mimicked a fiery leaden ball of electricity, pulsing and ricocheting in my bloodstream.

Just when I was getting used to yesterday, along came today.

"We can't do this." I sat heavily on the couch, clutched my jacket over my chest.

"Obviously." His thick voice shook.

I hunched forward. "What I meant was...you and me."

Ronan flicked off the video. "Adam's not for you, Aria," he said with difficulty.

"That's not what I meant," I shot out. "Wait! What's that supposed to mean?" I bolted upright on the couch. "So you think I belong to *you*?" Indignation rallied my spirits and drove off the last of my pain. I envisioned his scowl and wanted to smack it off his arrogant face.

"Don't you feel it?" Emotion lay heavy in his voice. "I have, for every damn moment since I walked into your condo. I didn't ask for this. I hate it." He paused. "I want you so damn bad. It's killing me that Adam—"

My throat constricted. I clicked off the phone and studied the paisley pattern on the carpet, trying to wind my thoughts around my too-bizarre-for-words life. For the first time, my love life was as complicated as the maze of endless paisley.

The suite door opened and I smelled Ronan's cologne. The irritated flare of his sick aura grazed my naked flesh.

I scratched the last few tingles on my arm and said softly, "What I meant was that it's not the time to hook up until our lives are on solid footing."

Ronan didn't move from his rigid stance in front of the door. "Okay." Some of the anxiety fled his taut body as his shoulders slumped forward.

"I won't deny the connection I have with both you and Adam."

"I'm a Thirteen sorcerer, Aria." Triumph sparked in his eyes.

"And Adam's your doppelgänger."

"You'll have to make a choice."

Even though my emotions scurried all over the map, I shrugged nonchalantly. Slowly, I walked to him. Rising on my toes, I brushed a soft kiss over his mouth. "I need time, okay? We all need time. You have no idea how that doppelgänger bond affects me."

The thought of my boring, loveless life roared to the forefront of my mind. My inner fire glimmered, and then winked out. Lack of trust and fear of abandonment weren't terms in my new Wiki. How far I'd come in a couple of days. But I couldn't go back to that life ever again. The problem was I didn't know how to go beyond it.

NINETEEN

Foamy clouds splashed night's ink over twilight. Once again, rain slicked the streets and headlights bounced off puddles. Shivering, I adjusted the heater vents. Ronan maneuvered Seattle's busy streets toward Washington Park, the site of the Rift, along the shores of Lake Washington. Excitement railroaded my fear to connect with the mysterious source of ancient magic that seemed to grant me my identity. I wanted to find myself so badly. It was my life now and I needed to live inside it, for better or for worse.

The steps for closing the Rift revolved in my mind. At the hotel, while we'd waited for dusk, Ronan warned me what to expect from when he'd tried the ritual using a page from the *Illuminaria*. Apparently, only one Forbidden Thirteen was needed to close the Rift. *Go freaking figure.* I finally showed Ronan and Adam a few of the secret pages I possessed. They'd already guessed I carried the pages in the tote bag. My doom and gloom face had given me away.

We still didn't know what would happen to Adam or

other doppelgängers who may be alive. All Ronan remembered reading was that the sorcerer-created doppelgängers possessed no magic of their own and they shared their sorcerer's magic. To what extent remained a mystery. We had no legit clue where they came from since the twelve "created" doppelgängers had supposedly abolished themselves. Then we found an obscure passage in Mom's pages that the Forbidden sorcerers created the doppelgängers based on even older magic from a time when many magical beings roamed the earth. The *Illuminaria* detailed nothing about sorcerers and doppelgängers not being able to live together on Earth's side of the Rift. Apparently, way before the Abolishment both had lived on our side of the Rift before the doppelgängers replaced the sorcerers in the banishment.

On the other hand, everything we did could bite us in the ass and we'd all wind up dead. Releasing further forbidden magic caused a slew of illegal activity. I wanted the laws changed and I'd accept the gamble if it came down to it. I'd fight to end the government's long-term experiment in artificial stupidity. The world had no right to banish the Forbidden. What if there were other beings alive in the Void? The *Illuminaria* indicated that only sorcerers, fairies, and the twelve doppelgängers lived to the end of the Abolishment because they were the strongest to survive decades of culling by humans. What if they were wrong? Enough what ifs crammed my head to lay down tracks to the next century.

Before stashing the secret book in the hotel safe, I double-checked Mom's pages, and they divulged the ritual to open the Rift by both magic and alchemy, for the thirteenth sorcerer's eyes only. Only the thirteenth and one or more sorcerers could open the Rift together, which is why Ronan and his father had screwed it up. Ronan was adamant that he could close it alone, now that he'd seen a few of Mom's pages and Melisande's tablet. The steps made sense now, whereas they hadn't before. But I still had a hard time believing the closing ritual would work.

"What if we need all thirteen sorcerers to close it?" I flicked dog hair off my pants.

Ronan rattled his brain cells. "The *Illuminaria* didn't say anything about all thirteen."

I pressed him. "It didn't say anything at all, did it?"

"It said how to close it. It didn't say form a circle of thirteen freaks, dance, and throw a fucking party." He threw up his hands. "It's not like I ever got to read the whole thing. I had to take direction from my dad and the pages we have here don't say all thirteen either. What more do you want?"

"I want not to be playing with lives here," I yelled. Man, I needed to team up with Einstein to work the Rift.

I massaged away the slow tapping in my temples. Tense moments slipped by. Unable to handle the yawning silence any longer, I faced Ronan, stretching the seatbelt over my chest.

A slow flame of bitterness against Ronan's father ignited in my belly. "Your father didn't trust you much, did he?"

"Nope. He didn't even trust my mother." He gripped the steering wheel so hard, the vehicle jerked to the right. "Melisande came closer than anyone."

"Yet the hag betrayed him." I cut my hand through the air as if to slice off her gooey, dead head.

Ronan parked near an ill-lit path far from the park's mainstream entrances and visitor center. The rain had taken a breather, and I was eternally grateful for the jet-set priced ski jacket I'd picked up in the hotel boutique. Adam had left me a store credit, but I'd used my casino jackpot, not wanting to pimp myself out. Much.

Magical energy overwhelmed the air. It licked and nibbled my skin. For the most part, my aura protected me, but had no luck chasing the stalkerish magic away.

Ronan tugged a flashlight out of his backpack and handed it to me.

I flicked it on, the light bouncing off brown stick trees and winter limp foliage. "What's in the backpack?"

"Stuff."

I rolled my eyes at the scuttling clouds. Leading the way through a rickety ranger gate to the arboretum, he secured it behind us with a quiet snick. We trudged down an unmarked path cutting through the woods. An undeveloped, natural woodsy area shadowed one of the secondary trails, far enough away from the mainstream paths to ensure our solitude.

The air swirled, invisible fingers whispering over us, thick enough to touch. It glowed and dripped from the trees like bunches of moss. The farther from the park perimeter we walked the more the magic raided the air from my lungs. A mischievous evil saturated the sick magic trying to seep into me.

A tremor spooled up my torso and jumped over that thimble of taint inside my core. Was that what Adam sensed? It was bad enough I felt it around me and in the tiny piece of him lodged within me. *Thank you very much.*

"You feel it?" Ronan held aside a low hanging branch, allowing me to pass.

"Yes." I buried my pride and grabbed his free hand. Another bullet I failed to dodge.

He jerked out of my clasp and wrung his hand. Horror rounded his eyes as though I'd infected him with fairy slaying poison. The edge of the flashlight beam glittered in his frosty eyes. "You're full of tainted magic. You feel like Adam."

"What?" I hooked my hand in my front pocket.

"My aura can't even penetrate yours."

"It's around me, not *in* me."

He touched me again, wrenched his hand back. "It's there."

Was he insane? Or a mind reader? I hadn't felt or seen any external changes. "One tiny morsel of Adam's taint." Honesty would murder me one day, if the Rift granted me another sunrise. Of course, that wouldn't be in Seattle, since outer space had snatched the sun. I nibbled on my bottom lip. "It's only a smidge." I regaled him with my tale of torture.

"The magic latches onto fae-sorcerer DNA. You wouldn't have *his* magic in you unless you were—" He studied me as if I dangled the *Illuminaria* over his head.

"Get real. I thought we were sorcerers, not fae." Wait a hot minute! "What're you keeping from me? Are you saying we also have fae blood?"

I stepped on mushy pine needles and my foot slid out from under me. Catching my balance, I grabbed Ronan's arm and yanked him off-kilter. His good arm whipped the air, banging against a tree limb, raining dead pine needles in our hair. *Thirteen, where's the love?* I swatted off the needles.

Ronan shook his head like a wet Labrador. "I'm his doppelgänger, not fae," he lashed out in a surly tone. "We're bonded."

"Maybe we all have fae genes." I gave him an emphatic smile. We hadn't read all the pages from the *Illuminaria* yet. Just enough to get us through our task and ensure we wouldn't kill anyone. "Go." I pushed him forward and we stumbled along the craggy path. I clapped my hand over my mouth to throttle the rant waiting for one last credit to feed it. "Face it. We both could use a Scrambler right about now to stir up some history in our heads." An old branch snapped underfoot and the sharp crack split the jittery air, forcing us into silence.

The strong odor of wet dirt and dormant nature sharpened my senses. We walked for what seemed like miles before lumbering into a glade enclosed by trees and bushes. Overgrown and lush in winter's final chapter, it lured me closer. My light reflected off a narrow, babbling creek edging the oblong clearing. The air sizzled with magic, pure and tainted, more magic than I'd ever witnessed. So thick with it, the air whistled with every movement we made. The Rift taint had a death hold on part of the glade evidenced by the bleak, brown landscape at the far end of the clearing. Far bleaker than a Seattle winter warranted.

My magic mixed with the Rift's magic, pumped through every cell of my being. It swirled around us in a wash of warmth and barbs of glacial evil, becoming part of me, setting my stomach surging and contracting. I breathed deeply, the damp air congealing in my throat.

"Ronan?" I arced my flashlight in a circle.

He watched me a few yards away, a strange luminosity in his eyes that had nothing to do with the light. It was unnerving, cruel, and possessive.

"What?" He dumped his backpack on the ground.

Easing back, I brushed against a dried bush that crunched death's hold against my jeans. "Nothing." I swallowed roughly. Why bother telling him I wanted to swab out my guts with rubbing alcohol?

Approaching, he extended a tiny plastic bag out to me. "Chew one of these antacids. You took aspirin earlier, right?"

I popped two tablets in my mouth. "Yes." Perspiration dotted my forehead. "What happened at the Rift when Adam found you passed out?"

"The Rift was already messed up after my father's forced screwup. When Adam neared, the magic went wild, killing my power, knocking me out."

I chomped on my bottom lip, wincing at the coppery burst of blood. "What's to prevent it from happening again?"

"You. I wasn't strong enough since he was already drawing my magic. With you here, I can pull from you."

"Does the magic feel different?"

"Yeah, it's centered on you, not me." He took the bag from me, careful not to touch my hand.

Why me? I kicked at a clump of dead weeds. His evasiveness ticked me off. Man, I wished I possessed all of the ancient manuscript and the key to deciphering it. My thirteenth sense told me that Ronan knew more about it—and us—than he'd coughed up.

My stomach gurgled alarmingly and my knees weakened. I waved my flashlight around and found a boulder to sit on. Cold and hard against my rear, it enabled me to raise my knees and drop my head to relieve the magic snacking on my insides. After all, I had an illegal magic ritual to remain alive for. *I'll take my handcuffs in diamond-studded platinum.*

"Take your deadener off." Ronan's voice floated to me.

"I will when Adam gets here." I spun the gray band around my wrist, my elbows resting on my knees. Ronan had stolen a few of them when he'd left his father's compound. We wore them hoping to keep his father from detecting us. The deadener was only partially effective in the glade, if not downright useless. The antacids helped, and I lifted my head without feeling like I'd just woken up after a rave.

"You'll forget. Do it now."

"I won't forget." I lit him up, standing where I'd left him, scowling up a tornado. "What's got your briefs in a twist?" Nearby rustling foliage saved his reply. Adam's presence stirred the acid in my gut.

"Wow, the magic's changed. It's not so bad." A light bobbed toward me. "Must be you, Blondie." He sounded chipper while I was as irritable as a women's clinic full of PMSing girls.

"You think?" I vaulted up. "Let's get this fairy and unicorn show done with. Ronan needs a dose of sugar to sweeten his nasty."

"What's going on?" Adam wheeled on Ronan.

"Let's just do it." Ronan stalked to his backpack. "Take your damn deadener off, Aria."

I slipped the plastic band off my wrist and flung it at Ronan, hitting the back of his legs. He stuffed it in his backpack, mumbling and grunting to his various selves. Nothing changed in what I was feeling. The deadener appeared useless on me so near the Rift.

Mist dripped from the roiling clouds. "Brilliant." I zipped up my jacket and tucked the fur-edged hood around my head. As Adam moved closer, about to put his arm around me, I eased away. "I'm hot to touch, so you're forewarned."

"Blondie, you're hot, period." He grinned. "Why are you two—"

"Who knows?" I shivered more from the eerie magic raising the hairs on the nape of my neck than from the night air that had already frozen me into a Popsicle.

Ronan trudged toward us. He handed Adam a lancet to prick his finger and gave me a couple for later. "You have your cell?"

"It's in the backpack."

"If anything goes wrong and both of us are incapacitated, call my father. His number's in your phone."

Stone still, I landed a death-ray look on him. "Like hell. Did the warranty expire on your brain?" I bumped my breasts against Ronan's hard chest. External magic punched holes in our auras and he flinched.

Adam extended a placating hand toward me. "He's the only one who has the slightest chance of helping. You want to risk Zoe's life? Jon and Jax have instructions to alert the authorities with proof of Riley's illegal activities if he threatens or detains you."

"You guys planned this?" I stuck my hands in my coat pocket. "Thanks for keeping me in the loop. You're welcome, Aria. Glad you're part of the A-Team. Sure, no bleeping problem."

Unlucky thirteen reared its ugly-ass head. A droopy tree limb snapped next to us. I dodged to the side and it clattered to the ground between the doppel-jerks and me.

"You're out of control." Ronan flung the backpack on the ground.

"Thanks for the alert system warning." Stepping over the leafless branch, I rejoined them. "Let's get on with this so I can chase lab mice in a maze for the rest of my life."

Adam grasped my hand. At least the magic wasn't screwing with our connection. We followed Ronan toward the limpid creek, and stopped at a mini ring of boulders that mimicked Stonehenge. I swished my flashlight in the circle of boulders big enough for six to eight people to stand comfortably within. The narrow rocks ranged from three- to six-feet high.

My aura ascended as I absorbed energy from outside, sweet and full of zest. I erected an aural blockade to deflect the magic the way Ronan had instructed during our dry run. The air lifted my hair, tickled my skin. Ronan and Adam's energy twirled inside me as well. Richer, more intense power churned within the stones. Not dirtier energy, just more of it, period.

The external magic trickled through chinks in my shield. I strengthened it, but the magic was unrelenting.

"I can't block out all the magic," I whispered.

"It's okay. Neither can we." Adam squeezed my hand. "At least your pureness is tempering the wildness."

Ronan dusted the perimeter of the boulders with a mix of crushed yarrow to ground the energy and ward off evil, and jasmine to protect our auras. "She's not all that pure," he muttered sarcastically. I squeezed Adam's hand until his bones crunched. "Aria has your faulty magic clouding hers." Ronan stood to his full height and fixed Adam with a fierce look.

Adam dropped my hand, the glow of his eyes changing from light blue to violet. "What's he talking about?"

Well, crap. Since the whole world just got the text message, he might as well know how his magic latched onto me after Ronan's magic attacked me in the hotel room.

After I clued him in, he stroked my cheek. "Sorry. I had no idea that would happen."

"Not your fault. It is what it is." I knew it'd happened for a reason, though. By the end of the night, Ronan's magic might also be swimming inside me. *Let's ring the freakin' wedding bells if that happens.*

Ronan flung the empty plastic bag on the ground and handed another marked with red tape to each of us. The red tape identified the mix of angelica, thyme, and agrimonia herbs for healing, cleansing, and closing the Rift. He also handed me a paper bag of sea salt to break the circle or terminate the ritual, if necessary. My fingers twitched on the bag that held enough evidence to fry us for practicing illegal sorcery. Who knew the old geezers were the original source of herbal-based witchcraft? All the ingredients were easily bought from underground Wiccan vendors.

"Move over there." Ronan gestured at a copse of stick trees.

"I can't see from there."

"Your power's merging too much with the Rift." His shadow loomed, pressing over me as if to swallow me whole. "We discussed this."

"I know." I stretched to touch him, but he shied away. Dejection speared my heart.

Adam and I followed the small flashlight beam. On my thirteenth step, I tripped on a blasted rock and would've bit the muddy ground if Adam hadn't grabbed hold of me. I usually watched my thirteenth step, but my mind was too twisted at the moment. "Thanks."

"Hold my hand. I can see better at night with my fairy vision." I found his hand in the dark, my fingers rigid in his warm grasp. "We'll light him up so you can see."

I inhaled his meadow fresh scent rising from our

entwined auras, soaked in its familiarity. "I'm scared for you two."

Adam tucked me against his side. "It'll work this time. You make the difference. The magic feels cleaner, stronger."

"It's not cleaner to Ronan." I turned in his arms, leaned my back against his chest.

His chest hardened into a granite slab. "He wasn't complaining, though."

We aimed our lights at the stone ring. Ronan pricked his index finger and blood welled up, black as a starless night against his skin. Using a mix of rowan, willow, and mugwort, he created a twelve-point star around the thirteenth and final spot dead center in Mini-Stonehenge. The herbs helped protect against evil, increased psychic powers, and promoted success. Rowan herb originally came from the land of fairies. It kept diseased magic from haunting people or places. Perfect for our half-baked plan of no record.

Starting with the northern point, Ronan held his finger over the herbs and a droplet of blood fell. The rocks blocked most of my view, but the amber flash of fire was unmistakable. A finger of fog drifted above the tallest rocks and dissipated in the misty air.

A hot spike of electricity shot into me. Adam jolted against my hip. "Was that supposed to happen?"

"No," he said in a fierce whisper. "The cloud of magic should still be visible. We shouldn't have felt anything."

Ronan traversed the ring, dripping his life away in flashes of amber and gold fire that spiraled up in tiny puffs and disappeared. With each drop of blood, my magic intensified.

An intangible force tugged me toward the stones. Power singed my insides. Everything went red, and my lungs burned as if I'd swallowed boiling lava. I clutched my pendant, focusing on the charm to halt the loss of magic, to keep the bad luck away. My aura swirled above the stone circle in a halo of violet and pink. The unknown force tried to lure me closer to the circle. Adam tightened his hold on me. A roaring, whooshing noise filled my head.

"Aria." Adam sounded far, far away. "Pull it back!"

"I can't," I wailed, struggling in his arms. "Let me go." Pain seared my internal organs, a jagged blade cleaving me in two. Half of me filled with the tainted magic, the other with mine and Ronan's pure magic, emerging for the first time since I'd met him.

Spellbound, Ronan continued the ritual. His aura floated above him in shades of pale blue. A dead black spot contaminated the halo. Sheer terror stopped my heart. He shouldn't have the color of death in his aura. Holy fairy godmother, he was missing his other color.

Ugly, disgusting power evolved around Ronan as angry souls screamed in my head, taunting, daring. Invisible arms and wings wrapped around me, grasping at every inch of me, pinching, prodding. I screamed. The sound of my voice died in the seemingly endless stretch of ground to the stones. With the tainted crud seeping into me, my power spent itself cleansing and preventing it from harming me further.

Ronan cried out, a vicious, agonizing sound. He stumbled into the stones and struggled to stand. His pain and anguish burned my soul to ashes.

"We have to stop him," I cried, my heart in my throat. "It's not working. It'll kill him."

Adam's arms had already dropped away, the safety of his embrace having lost to the lure of the magic. "Go," he said softly and prodded my butt.

I lurched forward, propelled by my own feet and the intense, mysterious force compelling me. A tidal wave of realization crashed into me. I muscled against the compulsion, turned and held out my hand. "You're the missing color, the other half of his soul."

He shook his head slowly. "Not half, a third."

Wistfulness hung heavy in his tone, but he thrust forward and took my hand.

In that moment, as we stumbled to the stone circle, toward Ronan, I knew without a doubt how inextricably linked the three of us were. Our auras had blended as one from the first moment we all stood in Adam's driveway surrounded by the forest. Seeing the three halos of aural color above the stone circle, I knew it for real.

TWENTY

The hum of glorious power in the center of the stones encapsulated my world, pulsing in tune with my heart. Its jagged lure quivered over me, magnificent and devastating at once. Fierce adrenaline pumped into my cells that had never seen the sort. Hungry, grungy desire spiraled against my pure magic, trying to drill through it with its ancient taint, its ancient wonder. I fought it from conquering me completely with every ounce of physical and magical strength I possessed.

Magic choked the clearing, throbbing with a need for release, invisible walls pressing on me from all sides. The immense energy challenged me, dared me to take it. Double dared me to give it everything I had to give. A force of evil languished within the foreign power and I struggled against its magnetism. Earth and the Void seemed to fight for their right to open or close the Rift...or to possess me. Earth pushed back, whereas the Void flooded the glade with crackling, caustic magic.

Ronan's failing magic continued to damage the Rift,

adding to the taint surrounding us. He lacked the two vital ingredients that made him whole as a descendant of a Forbidden Thirteen—Adam, and in many respects, me. We made up the triad that could undo the damage and release the pure magic. Only the three of us could open the Rift, I knew that then. Ronan and I couldn't do it alone. He needed his doppelgänger. Had the Forbidden Thirteen known about this connection? Was this the cost they'd paid to trick the world?

I knew I was meant to do this, to be there, to re-activate this bygone world into the here and now. The urge flooded me, set my feet in motion. A cry escaped me, both terrified and excited. I hoped it wasn't too late to reverse the flawed closing spell. I bolted into the stone ring, startling Ronan. A ghostly light surrounded him, bounced off the stone pillars. Deliberately, I knocked my hip against him, shoving him away from the star he'd made on the ground. Drops of blood from his nicked finger missed the twelfth point. Adam curled his hand around Ronan's fingers, halting the blood from dripping onto the ground.

Awed, I spun in a circle and soaked up the glorious energy, fought the corrupt magic with everything in me. The magic in the Realm of the Void sought liberation, and it wouldn't allow the world to ignore it any longer. Why did we think we could lock the enchantment away again when it had tasted life after centuries of incarceration? How could Adam forego the untold power that promised to be his once cleansed and free? What price to the world would this freedom cost? Was there life in the Void, if it truly existed? Would we all live to see tomorrow?

Adam and Ronan tussled as Adam tried to get a dazed Ronan to understand what was happening. They ignored the urgency in the magic cloaking us until our intermingled auras seemed to knock sense into Ronan. Adam's minty aura joined Ronan's ring of blue, completing the circle. The ebony wedge in Ronan's aura disappeared. Three sundered

ERIN RICHARDS

auras gyrated wildly above us. The scent of heaven sprinkled the three rings, showering us with the intoxicating perfume of spring blossoms, summer flowers, autumn spices, and winter's holly.

A howling wind emerged in the circle, blowing the dried herbs away on a dazzling emerald current. Standing aside, I waved my arms to rush the wind and herbs along their journey. My presence tamed the air saturated with latent energy in its epicenter. My hair whipped about my head, snapping in the magic drenching us. The wind whispered between the stones in noisy voices discernible in sound, but indistinct in words. Without a doubt, I knew the voices belonged to ages of oppressed fae and sorcerers, the last known magical beings to walk our earth before the Abolishment.

Oddest of all, an ancient encyclopedia filled my head, waiting for me to decipher the knowledge it contained.

I plucked out the green-labeled plastic bag I'd hidden in my pocket earlier. Soft illumination lit Adam and Ronan's rapt faces, their bodies quaking in tandem with mine from the deluge of crackling magic. They followed my movements as though obeying my silent commands. Careful not to trample the center where I layered the herbs, they rebuilt the twelve points of the star.

I handed each a lancet, and one at a time, we dripped crimson life on the twelve points. After each drop of blood, fire flared, ending in a glittery cloud that ringed the perimeter of the stone circle. This time the magic held in the air around us. Unable to contain my joy, I laughed and shouted my triumph.

Holding back on the final point, I positioned myself in the center and raised my arms toward heaven. The Rift's energy anchored me to the spot, not that I wanted to move from the burgeoning heaven inside the stones. The aura halos spun above our heads, colors combining into a rainbow of mint, ice blue, and mauve. I'd never seen auras in living color!

As I lowered my arms, I brought my hands together. Contained in my cupped palms, the halos fused into a glowing ball of multihued moonlight. I became the thirteenth point, rooted to the earth. Centuries of magic centered me—heady power undulating in my core, streaming sweet pleasure through my blood, pumping excitement and relief into my heart—until the foreign magic consumed me. My telekinetic receptors invited in all the sorcery and fae magic streaming through the Rift.

Ronan closed the distance and covered my right hand with his left. Adam did the same with my left hand. We stood as one body, so close that the others felt the slightest breath taken by another. After a few seconds, our hearts beat as one.

All my senses blossomed with new life, and I drank in the magic's exhilarating sweetness, inhaled the unsullied air. Vitality usurped every fiber of my being, leaving me quivering as if I'd been reborn, the magic scrubbing clean twenty-one years of living. Melting sunlight and honey slicked my tongue, sweeter and smoother than the finest Belgian chocolate in the universe. I breathed in the intoxicating mixture of warm sunrises, hot afternoons, and cooling sunsets. Exaggerated sounds of grass growing, trees budding, and clouds gathering bombarded my head. An amazing sense of the earth's wholeness flooded me.

My hormones zoomed into a free-fall. For once, my head handed them the keys to the castle. Unutterably lost within the energy swamping me, my heart burst with love. Desire spiraled through me, rippling under my skin. It set off a craving for Ronan, for Adam, for the whole of their beings. For the completion of Adam's transformation to his fae-doppelgänger nature, for Ronan and me with the pure blood of ancient sorcerers coursing in our veins, and for the two of them, complete as one. What would become of our amazing triad when all was said and done? My rapture nudged that vague sliver of doubt to the wayside.

The Void's urgency crested in need, shooting gentle sparks into my core. "Ready?"

Brilliant silver flecks glistened in Ronan's eyes. He held his hand toward me, his lips thinning in anguish. The glowing ball of moonlight bounced to my left hand. I squeezed a drop of Ronan's blood onto the globe. It sizzled and a corona of energy radiated above our heads. My skin tingled as much from the ball as from Ronan's touch.

Adam grinned and I sensed his eagerness. His livewire hair danced in the electrified air, waiting for an infusion of life. I took his hand and squeezed his blood onto the sphere, layering it on top of Ronan's sizzling drop, the heat of his body coursing down the length of mine. The ball expanded, radiating pure brilliance, raw earthen and ether magic. I nodded at Ronan. He squeezed my finger for the final drop of the one life.

The luminescent globe exploded around us, blinding, blazing. Hands clasped, we formed a circle. Streamers of moonlit magic bathed the stone enclosure. I wanted to rip off my clothes and let the magic wash over my bare skin. I longed to tear off Ronan's clothes and finish what we'd started in the hotel. I yearned to comb my fingers through Adam's reformed hair, and gaze upon his newborn honeyed skin.

The sphere melded above us into another orb of light and power. It plunged into the middle of the star we'd made, exploding outward, blanketing us with magic. It bristled across my skin, rearranged me at the cellular level. Exquisite, energizing, strange magic replaced the old sluggish magic I'd known all my life. The final particles dispersed on a gentle balmy breeze. Ronan's power joined Adam's pure magic and tangoed evocatively with mine. Their exquisite magic became a part of me, providing me with hope that they'd always be a part of my life, in one form or another.

My tattoo sizzled like hot coals under my skin, expanding outward over my left kidney area. I longed for Ronan's cooling fingers and soothing lips to doctor it.

Pure magic poured into the clearing. We'd done it. We'd opened the Rift! We lived to shout it to the world. Okay, maybe we'd rethink shouting it to the world until we ensured we didn't wind up in an impenetrable dungeon.

Everything that'd happened in my life took me a step closer to the person I was meant to be. But as the sun had risen each day, I still hadn't known what I was, who I was. Then Ronan barged into my condo, and I had instinctively known *he'd* been missing from my life. *This is my place. He is my place.*

Adam glimmered with reinvigorated life, and his solid body took on a healthy coloring almost as tan as Ronan. An exhilarating mix of exhaustion and adrenaline melted my legs. Ronan caught me in his arms, and we clung to one another, lips pressed together hard in a fleeting kiss that ended way too soon. Not wanting Adam left out of our celebration, I reached for him, so fiercely longing to touch him in his renewed form.

But Adam had vanished.

"What the what?" Had the Void taken him? Panicked, I lifted my cheek off Ronan's chest to search for Adam only to find the shadowed outline of a trio of men behind Ronan. An air of menace radiated off them, sullying the beauty we had brought forth.

"Well done, son. You've unearthed the Forbidden Thirteen master." The unmistakable voice with a slight Irish brogue slivered terror through my heart. "And you've finally opened the Rift as I've wanted for so long. Kudos to both of you."

Shocked, I froze in Ronan's arms, searched his face in the dwindling light, but he veiled his features well, even to my expert eyes. Ronan dropped his arms and swung around.

A muffled shot cracked the night air, then a second and a third. The sharp bite of three darts hit my shoulder, stomach, and my right thigh. Power bombed my feet, leaving me an empty vessel of ordinary. Sounds of more shots filtered into my fuzzy mind sliding toward a hollow of nothingness. My weightless body tumbled to the ground in a heap of limbs and darkness.

TWENTY-ONE

My eyes battled the glue clamping them shut. Furious blinking attempted to clear the grit. I rubbed my fingers against my eyelids, and a prick of pain shot into the right side of my neck, forcing me to squeeze my eyes shut again. Soft breathing and a scuffle of shoes by my side encouraged my groggy brain cells to awaken. I blinked away my epic joy.

"Ronan? Thank god you're okay. Hey, what are you doing?" My hazy gaze landed on the nasty gun-like syringe in his familiar fingers...fingers I wanted holding mine, assuring me I was still kicking it. I ached from my desire to touch him to ensure he was okay. Aside from his previous bodily injuries, he looked absolutely perfect.

Hello, reality of mine. Hadn't his father shot him full of bio holes? Why wasn't he laid up? "Get that piece of Riley Senior crap away from me."

"It's a tracker. Don't fight it. Don't try to run either," he commanded in a voice gruffer than his usual McGrumpy self.

"Don't do this to me." My heart cricked. Weird wetness loosened the stickiness in my eyelids. I sure as hell wasn't leaking tears. Was I bleeding? "Ronan? What's going on?"

Absent a sound, Ronan ghosted and floated away on a soft white cloud. Maybe I was dreaming. No way would Ronan hurt me nor do his father's bidding of the illegal kind. *Nope. No how. Just a nightmare.*

My brain flirted with unconsciousness again, and I let it sweep me away on a storm cloud scuttling after Ronan and his fluffy white vehicle of confusion.

"Wake up that bleach blonde head of yours." A familiar raspy voice found a landing in my woozy mind.

Relief coursed the length of my leaden body stretched out on a plank-firm bed. "Zoe?" Fuzz coated my tongue and I had a horrible time dredging up moisture.

"About time you returned to the living."

Zoe's face swam above mine. An excavation crew seemed to dig in my skull for long lost brain cells. I squeezed my eyes shut against the brilliant ceiling lights and dragged the covers over my head. Thank lucky thirteen! She was alive. The last two days were all a fat, hairy nightmare.

Tossing gold bullion into a wishing well probably wouldn't wish away my delusions.

I thrust out my right hand from beneath the covers, feeling the bands cuffing my wrists. My blood pressure headed for DEFCON-10. Time to dial up and deal. Mustering lubrication in my throat, I spewed forth a torrent. "Tell me I just got back from my date with your brain-dead cousin, and you're here to dish the dirt. Cody and Cleo are slumped on my ankles after eating ten pounds of food, right?" I really wished it'd all been my worst nightmare.

Zoe pinched my arm. "Right. Here, kitties, come give Mommy a reality check." She tugged the covers off my face. "Did bleach frazzle your brains?"

"I don't bleach my hair." I made an attempt at outrage until tears skimmed down my cheeks, wetting the low thread count pillowcases. I think the bright lights caused my eyes to water. Seriously.

"Who are you and where's the real Aria?" Zoe's relieved voice shook me to my core. "Aria Elle Walker *never* cries."

"Shut up and hug me." Zoe climbed onto the bed and we hugged one of our nine lives out of each other. "I'm sorry to get you involved." I inhaled her cheap melon hairspray. "I'll get you out of this watermelon hell and back to your beauty salon lifestyle."

"I may have to shave my head to get rid of the drugstore smell." She sniffed.

Unflattering sky-blue fleece sweats covered her voluptuous body. You wouldn't normally catch her dead wearing fleece. Velour was more her style if forced to wear athletic clothes. And she detested blue. "Why did they let you in here with me?"

"You've been out of it since yesterday. The shit-for-brains were worried."

I glanced at my watch. Shock bulged out my eyes. Monday afternoon, and I scarcely felt as if I'd slept two winks. Fingering her jacket's hem, I grinned at her, barely able to contain my joy at finding her alive and well. "What's up with this? Slumming?"

"I could say the same about you, Blondie." Zoe flicked the covers off me, exposing an identical sweat suit in pink.

I smiled to conceal my terror. "At least they got the colors right," I teased, plucking at my sleeves to expose a deadener on each wrist. Pink *was* my color. My hair felt weird, heavy on my head. Locks fanned my shoulders, reaching lower than I'd ever seen it. Was I delusional?

Irritation darkened Zoe's smattering of freckles. "What's going on? Why does a paranormal research group who makes frickin' deadeners for the government want you so bad? Who wants you dead? Who's that hot piece of ass Ronan who carried you in?" She sank into the black vinyl and chrome bedside chair and leaned forward.

My eyebrows shot toward my hairline. I tried to sit up, but straps held my torso and ankles to the bed. "He carried me in?" I thought Riley had shot Ronan with the same triple dose of bio-poisons he'd shot into me. Had Ronan escaped the extra dose? Wariness centered heavy in my chest like an old wound that ached on a rainy day, which was every day in Seattle. The nightmare returned, and I fingered my neck, searching for the injection site. Nothing, not a stitch of pain. Had I dreamed him?

"Shoulder-length black hair, hot rugged looks—except for the freaky blank stare and frowny grimace. Muscles to die for. Held you like you were the last female on planet Earth."

The last female on Earth observation mitigated the edge of mistrust and anger creeping up my chest. Things still didn't play right in this bully versus innocent blonde girl playground fight.

A bang in the hallway sent us lurching in our cheap sweats. We exchanged nervous glances. Beeps dinged before the door slid inward. A stocky security guard sporting a Dominion Research logo on the chest pocket of his navy uniform, carried in a tray loaded with covered dishes. He had a bio-energy dart gun, a handgun, and a smartphone clipped to his utility belt. An earpiece stuck out of his right ear.

How'd they know I was awake and starving on the morgue's doorstep? A cursory glance of the blue and gray room revealed a camera eye in the flat panel display across the room. *Sneaky bastards.*

Security dude set the tray on a wheeled table near the

door. Zoe jumped up to investigate, swiping the covers off.

"Idiots. Aria doesn't eat ice cream." She shoved a bowl at Buzz-Cut. "On second thought, I'm still hungry." Snatching her hand back, she cupped the bowl in her palm.

Buzz-Cut pushed the cart to the side of the bed and retreated as silent as he'd arrived.

My eyes about popped out of my face. "Have you blown a gasket? He could have smoked your ass into a grave."

"Chill." Zoe licked her spoon and grinned. "They're afraid of you."

"I hate to burst your bubble, but I'm a bit tied up."

"Riley's men have been instructed to engage only under threat of life: theirs or ours. Or escape," she whispered, a hand cupped to one side of her mouth.

I whispered back, "How do you know?" I plucked the silver dome off a garden salad, snagged a small tomato, and popped it into my mouth. When I bit into it, a sugary burst of grapes and tomato masked the musty taste of fear coating my tongue.

She shoveled in another spoonful of vanilla ice cream, the sight of which sent the tomato somersaulting in my stomach. "Did that aneurysm hurt much?" she asked through a mouthful of goop.

Ding dong. Telepathy. Pocket lint clouded my mind as the depressant drugs wore off and energy dripped ever so slowly into my veins. In fact, incredible new power melted in exquisite harmony with my own. Food could definitely rally it along. I went to town on the salad, chunky beef soup, and chocolate milk.

Zoe licked her bowl clean and tossed it into the trash can with a clang. "Oh dear, did I miss the tray?" The spoon clinked against the bowl. "Spill it. This better be life threatening because I'll accept no less for being snatched and all." She tried her rendition of my evil eye, aping the Wicked Witch of the West instead. I wiped my chocolate milk mustache off with a linen napkin. Nice touch for a research institute, but they needed to read Martha Stewart's books on bedding etiquette. Martha had prison experience too. Every time my hand brushed the scratchy muslin sheets, I wanted to peel each thread apart and braid a noose for hanging Dickard Riley.

Zoe cast me a calculating look, her empathic brain spinning a million revolutions a second. *Oh, did I mention that she's also a secret empath?* By touch, she can feel emotions in addition to reading minds. It'd been tricky to keep my secrets from her since we'd first met in high school. Our ESP abilities were the reason why we'd hit it off so well. Now, I wondered if she might be a descendant of the Forbidden Thirteen. Turmoil sent my bowels churning.

"Does your ESP feel different?" I whispered.

"Same old."

I heaved out a sigh of relief.

"You're angry, feeling betrayed." Worry deepened tiny lines around her eyes. "What's going on? Did you succumb to my mind control and buy expensive makeup? What's in your hair?"

Mind control, my flat ass. "Huh?" I glided my fingers through my silkier and longer hair. I released Zoe's arm and swung the meal cart to the wall, having suddenly lost my appetite. "What's different?" Pulse accelerating, I patted my face and head.

"Your hair's way longer. Are you wearing extensions? Did you get highlights? You're, like, luminous."

My dinner sank to the pit of my stomach. Guess I wasn't delusional, at least on the hair front. Upon opening the Rift, I didn't think the magic had affected my shell. Whatever drugs and deadeners DR had pumped into me suppressed more than my magical energy so I didn't know what was normal or merely *new* normal. *It's been lovely, but I have to scream now.*

"What else?"

She shot a look at the flat screen then leaned forward

and whispered, "Your aura feels like it's not all yours."

"You can feel my aura? How many auras do you feel?" I continued to whisper in case the room was bugged.

She gloated. "I've always felt your aura. It's part of being an empath," she whispered close to my ear, touching my check. "I feel your aura and two similar, but indistinct ones."

Gripping her hand tight, I nearly shuddered in my bootie socks. "We need to get out of here."

"Why do they want you? Who's the hunk you're falling for? Why do you think he betrayed you?"

I sniffed. So much for flying under the radar. I couldn't hide it from myself let alone Zoe. I'd curse that barbarian Ronan if he betrayed me; double-cursed if he broke my heart in the process. *Whoa, wait? Ronan?* I knew in that moment that if I never saw Ronan again, I didn't think I'd survive life. Ronan had sunk so deeply into my soul, I'd need a bomb to blast him out.

The right side of my neck itched. I scratched it, trying to rub out my lame infatuation. "Dominion Research thinks I possess untapped ESP they want to study."

Disbelief rounded Zoe's eyes. "Why are they so delusional? I mean, how did they find you?"

Walls vaulted in my mind, and I lied like a dirty, wet rug. I hated blocking Zoe out, but sometimes it was necessary and *she'd* taught me the nifty trick. "I don't know." One of my ragged fingernails sacrificed itself for my dessert. "They sent Ronan after me. He set me up." I might be more accurate than I cared to admit. Clues weren't exactly hiding beneath the covers waiting to yell "surprise, dimwit." If Dickdouche was eavesdropping, he'd form his own opinions.

"Bizarre." Zoe hopped off the bed and began pacing. Her two-pairs-for-the-price-of-one sneakers were silent on the slate-gray commercial carpet that matched Ronan's eyes. "Do you have latent talents?"

I couldn't hide the guilty flush inching across my face.

"What've you hidden from me?" Zoe glowered from the foot of the bed, delicate hands on her perfectly proportioned hips.

"Please don't get upset." I held up a pacifying hand. "It's just more telekinesis." Ugh, a lie by omission wasn't really a lie, right? "It's developing and reacting to Ronan who has similar abilities. He dubs himself a descendant of an ancient sorcerer." I hated bending the truth I hardly understood myself. "What load of bull did they sell you?"

"Sorcerer?" Zoe's brow wrinkled and she wove her fingers through her long, tousled hair. It drove her batty if her flawlessness was less than perfect outside her apartment.

Tears welled again and I hated myself for them and their source. "Why didn't my mother ever tell me any of this?" I sniveled and wiped my nose on the scratchy pillowcase.

Zoe hugged me. "Oh, Aria. She died too soon, that's all. She didn't get a chance to tell you...whatever." She pulled away, clasping her fingers in mine. "How bad is it?"

"It's everything. It's me, my identity, my place in this world. Something was always missing and it wasn't just my dead mother and ditching father. Or Granny Elle. I never fully belonged and couldn't ever figure out why I never felt settled. Now I know why."

Zoe faked a horrified look, screwing up her mouth, aping the Wicked Witch of the West Coast. "You belong. You belong to me, Aria Elle Walker. I love you to death and back. Don't ever think otherwise." She gripped my hand so hard she may have broken a bone, and I yelped to get her to lighten up. "Sorry. But you know I'd marry you if..."

I quirked an eyebrow. "If you didn't love the male species and their equipment so much."

She laughed. "Well, there's that. But I was going to say I think *you* love the male species so much and one male in particular."

I shook my head so hard, I flung out my sorrow, and anger danced into its place. I deflected. "Apparently, I'm a descendant of an ancient sorcerer like Ronan. Mom was too, and she never said a freakin' word." The bed got the brunt of my fisted anger. "My father betrayed me to these assholes. Was I just a pawn in their lives? Something to bargain and barter with? Born to easily give away and abandon?"

Zoe smacked my arm hard, bitch-slapping sense into me. "Cut the crap. You know that's not what happened. Everyone loved you. What the hell's not to love, except this pity party you're having right now? You were born for greatness…apparently." She snickered. "It just took time for you to find your place. Looks like you've found it. So buck up little donkey's ass and get over it. Live this life you're supposed to live now. And love it…and him."

I could always count on Zoe to blast sense into me in her way…our way. Reaching for her, we hugged again. "I love you too, bitch. And I don't love him," I whispered in her ear.

"Liar." Before she drew away, she said, "They say you have a book that belongs to them. That you stole it."

"Jerkwads," I yelled at the flat panel in the corner. "Welcome to Kiss My Ass Avenue, at the corner of No Freakin' Way." I thumped my fist over my heart, and then had a sudden light bulb moment.

"Aria, why—"

"Forget the why. They're lying out their asses." I motioned her closer, my index finger across my lips. She rolled onto the bed and cuddled against me. "We need to get out of this pit. Follow my lead. Without snark," I said vehemently in her ear, knowing I was in for a bitch-out later. She nodded, a pensive mask pasted on her face. "Don't spaz if you see me do…strange telekinesis."

She unsuccessfully tried to suppress a snigger. "Like

what?"

"Scoot over and zip it." Her back faced the camera and she shielded me from Dickard's Eagle Eye. I stuck my arms under the covers. "I'm wasted." I faked a yawn and pulled the comforter to my chin, closing my eyes. "Drugs have whipped my ass."

The deadeners had worn off and my energy had returned for the most part. If the room contained blocks, they weren't working on me. I focused inward, reaching for the electromagnetic receptors in my head. The wrist and ankle gadgets sparked and hissed, broke in two pieces. Deadeners crumpled at the end of the thick bands holding me snug to the bed frame.

The torso band flicked against Zoe. "Oww." She rubbed her hip. "What'd you do?"

"I just killed the deadeners." We continued to whisper in case audio bugs swarmed the room.

Her eyes bulged unflatteringly out of her pretty little face but she kept her tongue.

I told Zoe my plan. It wasn't a great plan, but it bought us time and got us out of Little Dick's Prison. In true crime fashion, the ceiling hosted a commercial vent panel. If we stood on the bed, we could just reach it. No security goons guarded the doors. Just two advanced door locks blocked our exit. Riley's no-necks wouldn't be more than seconds behind once we escaped. The camera proved the biggest pickle.

"Aria, you need to eat more. I told Riley I'd get you to eat," Zoe said loudly, jumping to her feet. Playing her part, she strolled around the foot of the bed to the tray of lukewarm slop.

"Bite me." I stuck my middle finger in my mouth and gave the camera a nasty gagging look.

"You'll eat or I'll shovel it in." Acting the tyrant as though born to it, her voice dropped an octave. She held the full spoon to my lips.

I slid her a mad dog look. "That swill would kill a robotic pig." I flicked the spoon away, hitting her above her left breast, a target not too difficult to miss.

She dug her fingers in the bowl and threw a piece of beef at me, deliberately missing my head by a foot. I snatched up the bowl and Zoe grabbled for the tray. I flung the contents of the bowl at the camera eye, coating it and the monitor with congealing beef soup. Continuing to fake noises of a cafeteria food fight, we made a mound beneath the covers to make it resemble me. The fight ended, I stood behind the door, and we waited, hoping the soup hid our actions. We didn't have a lot to lose if our pathetic plan flopped.

"Go back to sleep," Zoe intoned, playing her Academy Award role. "Your bitchiness needs a break from reality." She patted the heap of pillows, turned the flat screen on, and perched on the end of the bed.

Only one set of footsteps echoed in the corridor. The guard peeked through the tiny door window, engaged the intercom. "Keep away from the door."

"Whatever." Zoe nonchalantly flipped him off and resumed watching the dinosaur of daytime soaps through clumps of oozing soup. All she needed was a box of chocolates and a cosmopolitan.

The locks snapped open. The goon bulked up the doorway, dart gun drawn, loaded down with useless deadeners. The deadeners pinched my powers, and I pressed my mind through the oppressive force. It felt akin to swimming from the bottom of the ocean and breaking through the water's surface, filling my lungs with clean, fresh air.

"Move to the bathroom." He waved his weapon at Zoe and spoke into his mouthpiece, "Walker's secure."

Zoe rose and backed farther into the small room. Just as the minion guard cleared the doorway, I pushed the door shut and pulled forth a slew of powers. Six deadeners popped. Minion's knees buckled and he lost his grip on the gun. It clattered to the floor and Zoe snagged it up.

I snarled in his ear. "Tell them the room's secure. No backup necessary."

Acrid fear mixed with musk cologne wafted off him, his shoulders strung tighter than a guitar on steroids.

"Do it!" I grabbed his wispy drab brown hair, snapped his neck back. "When I tap your earpiece that better be all you say. Got it?" I slammed my knee between his shoulder blades.

"Yeah," he grunted.

I fought to control my madness, the new power roaring to life, almost sinking me to my knees with its ferocity. I tapped his earpiece.

"No backup needed." He sounded slightly strangled. "Walker's out, Marino's secure. I'll clean the lens and report back."

I pressed his wireless off and patted his head. "Good guard dog." My new brew of magic boiled up, and I hurled an onslaught of energy into him. He made a choking sound, flopped forward, out like a stuffed puppy.

"*Move it*," I mouthed at Zoe, swishing my arm toward the ceiling.

Wanting to appear as if we'd escaped out the door, I touched the door locks, heat eviscerating them. They snicked apart, smoldering in a puff of smoke. I vaguely wondered which one of my new personalities had accomplished the feat. I slipped on the pair of hideous white sneakers we'd found in the empty closet and joined Zoe on the bed. She'd already pushed up the ceiling tile, and I helped her shove it inside the vent. We didn't have much time before Riley's goons caught on. But waiting for shit to happen wasn't in my playbook.

I boosted Zoe up, and then she helped hoist me into the air duct. I closed the vent hole behind me, we scuttled away from the grill, then stopped to reconnoiter in the tight duct.

Zoe grabbed my ankle, her hand trembling. "Did you kill him?"

"Doubt it." Not so sure myself, I didn't want her to dwell on it and detract her sanity from our getaway.

"What've you been hiding from me?" Accusation riddled her tone. "I guess I taught you how to block me too well." Even with a frown turning down her mouth, she still mirrored perfection.

"Later." I patted her hand. "What's in the rooms on each side of mine?"

"I was caged to the right. Same layout. To the left is another holding cell. They brought in a sickly blonde girl."

"Kiera Kendrick."

"You know her?"

"Met her yesterday. Did you see another girl who looked like her, but less sick?" On hands and knees, I slinked through the square tunnel on the left, elevating my feet to minimize the noise.

"No."

"Did your room have a window and camera?"

"Yes. Pervs."

I stopped at the screen over Kiera's room and peeked down at the tidy bed. Empty. Crawling onward, I wanted to find an unlocked room that Satan's big brother wasn't spying into. Zoe closed in on my heels, only the sounds of our breathing and shuffling audible. Cool air flowed through the duct and a long shiver rolled to my feet. The shiver stemmed more from apprehension than the temperature, because my heart was racing on the Indy 500 circuit. The next vent overlooked a supply room.

Familiar voices drifted to me from a few vents down the gray tube. The voices belonged to Ronan the traitor and Richard Riley, the murderer, kidnapper, all around evildoer. Eyes closed, I hunted for Ronan's aura, but couldn't thrust beyond my spreading patch of hyperenergy and the deadeners leaching beyond the room's perimeter.

I counted to ten, steadying the pitter-patter of my traitorous heart. "Stay here." I scooted down the duct, stopping shy of the screen above what appeared to be Riley's rich and expansive office. He lounged behind a humongous wood desk in a worn leather chair. Ronan sat across from him in a sumptuous Edwardian guest chair. A chair I might pilfer to replace the one smashed into firewood in my condo. Zoe slunk toward me and rested her chin on my leg. *Mental eye roll.*

The room's deadeners pinched me, but whatever magic I'd gained at the Rift roiled inside me, punching holes through Riley's rinky-dink technology. I glanced over my shoulder, finger to my lips to silence Zoe, then tossed out a tester wave of magic and sent her hair floating up from her scalp. The deadeners were dead to me.

Ronan smiled at his father, a steaming cup of coffee at arm's reach. The heavenly scent of caramel mocha drifted to the ceiling. *Un. Freaking. Believable.* My heart skipped a beat.

"What do you really want, Ronan?" Riley asked oily smooth, steepling his fingers under his chin.

"Freedom."

"You've always had your freedom."

"Only when you gave it to me." He paused. "You got Aria Walker, the Rift's open. The other sorcerers will come out of hiding now, drawn to the magic." Unidentified emotion thickened Ronan's voice. "You don't need me any longer."

"That's where you're wrong." Riley's smarmy tone dribbled candy canes. "You're as crucial to my project as Walker, either by cooperation or by making blood deposits. By the way, where's Melisande?"

"In San Jose."

"Dead?"

Another beat of silence elapsed. Did Ronan nod?

"She tried to betray you. She wanted me and her to

work together to take you down."

Hatred clamped onto my splintering heart. My hillbilly apeshit, Catwoman, ninja claws joined the power scrabbling for freedom inside me.

"Prove it." Did I hear the slightest sadness in Riley?

Rustling drifted up, followed by the metallic sliding of a zipper. I crept forward, peeked through the vent holes. Ronan handed him Melisande's laptop and red tablet. *We need the witch hag's devices!* I backed up, focused on controlling my breathing, which took a turn for the ugly. I nearly hyperventilated myself into a tizzy. Closing my eyes, I breathed deep and even.

"Tell me what you really want, Ronan."

Ronan mumbled and a shuffle drifted up. "Truth about my mother and her death." His voice coasted from the far side of the room. "I want freedom to come and go as I please. I want assurances that you won't hurt Aria, Kiera and Katrina, or any of the other fae or sorcerers you capture. I don't want further involvement in retrieval missions or other criminal activities."

"That's a long list. What do I get out of it?"

"My silence."

"I already own your silence. You have as much to lose as I do by going public."

"I doubt that."

"I'm waiting."

"Did you kill my mother?"

"The NUW government executed her for practicing forbidden spellcraft," he said as if giving a lecture to witch wannabes.

"That's not what I heard."

"You heard wrong."

"Give me everything I want, I'll go along with you, and you can have the keys to the kingdom."

"If I disagree?"

"If I'm late reporting to my team, they'll know who to

contact to shut you down."

"You'll go down with me."

"At least I'll be free of you and this hell."

"This hell, as you call it," Riley said with no small amount of disdain, "will make you a powerful and rich man. You and Walker will have all the control, all the limelight and power beyond imagine. The world needs you both. You'll restore order, balance, and purity. You'll own this world. You'll control the other Forbidden. They'll do what you want." He paused for emphasis. "What's so wrong with setting to rights what was done in ignorance and fear?"

Ronan snorted. "That's only part of your pipe dream."

I tried to sense Ronan's aura, but it didn't exist on any planet where I had free range.

"What could you possibly have that's worth so much to me?"

"The lost pages to the *Illuminaria* and their translation into English, all the magic and alchemy spells you're missing. Enough to give you everything you've always wanted. To dominate the Forbidden. To rule the world."

My heart shattered. My life exploded. Anger rejected the pain with a ferocity that nearly sent a torrent of bad luck throughout Riley's building.

TWENTY-TWO

*R*onan and his equipment are so dead! He had no clue how much danger the world was in if his father got his paws on the full text of the *Illuminaria*. And some of the spells in the *Illuminaria* could only be done by my magic or the magic of two sorcerers, not by my blood or the blood of another Thirteen. Which meant Riley had plans to keep us *both*. And our blood. I rubbed the bruise on the crook of my left arm. *Dumbass barbarian.* I had to get the entire book out of Riley's hands before he realized the extent of power he had with or without me. He could literally destroy the world.

Snarling louder than a tiger on the fringe, I pried up the vent and heaved it to the other side of the two-foot square hole. Since I was Richard Riley's ticket to the majors, I knew he wouldn't hurt more than one hair on my head. I swung my legs through the hole, aiming for the desk rather than risking my balance by jumping to the floor. I kicked his mug onto his laptop, cursing the fact that he kept his desk so tidy and his mug wasn't entirely full. My foot slipped and I knocked something else onto the floor where it landed with a quiet thump on the plush rug.

Riley scampered out of his chair. By the time I steadied my balance on the desktop, two guards leveled tranq guns on me. Ronan went all scowly, glowering at me, and a little something tried to die inside me. I jumped to the floor, backing against the windows overlooking a tree-lined grassy courtyard.

"Ms. Walker, it's a pleasure to finally meet you."

I wanted to slap his ingratiating smile off with fingers of thirteen curses.

"Screw. You." I swung on Ronan. "Give it to me." I held my hand toward him. He gripped one of Mom's envelopes. I battled to suppress my straining magic, making Dickard think his elementary science class deadeners were working on me.

"What're you doing?" Ronan clenched his teeth so hard that infernal muscle in his jaw ticked. As usual, his barbarian shell masked his emotions. That is, if he had any left to mask.

Riley's arrogance rolled out on a smooth laugh as he edged closer to Ronan. "You don't really think Ronan will do that, do you? He works for me. Always has."

Mammoth Guard number one looked from me to Riley, his dart gun aimed at my heart, a film of sweat on his forehead. A frisson of magical energy wafted off him, despite the room's strong deadeners wrapping around me like a steel straitjacket...with beautiful escape holes. He moved to my left as the other Rent-A-Guard pointed his gun at my belly.

"Stand down," Riley ordered. "The room's deadeners are active."

I hope that thought lets you sleep at night!

The sweaty, olive-skinned guard lowered his gun, his gaze flitting from me to Dickhead. I recognized the dilated look of the drugged in his foggy eyes. I drew in a soft breath, releasing it slowly as my mind chattered away at this mind-bender.

The weight of the disintegrating deadeners jabbed my shield, robbed my air. Breathing shallowly, I fought to ignore it. I reached for my pendant and noticed for the first time that it was gone. Had Ronan told his father how it helped me focus my telekinesis? Shock jolted my hip hard against the edge of the desk. Adam was right. I didn't need it.

I tossed a ripple of energy at a verdant hilly landscape painting to the left of the desk. The frame rattled against the wall. Both my pinkies twitched up a tempest. *Crap squared.*

Ronan's betrayal hurt so bad I wanted to wither into a sun-bleached grape. But not until I unleashed the Wrath of Aria and hexed him to a portal.

"Hand it over, Ronan," I said slowly, ominously.

Before he moved a muscle, his father clamped down on his arm. A medley of red splashed across Ronan's blank mask. My head, heart, and magic warned me not to let Dick Tator Riley get his tentacles on my heritage and the clout to royally screw the world. My half of the book also represented a lifeline to my mother and my ancestors. I'd fight to someone's death for them.

I lunged at Ronan, scrabbling for the envelope. Using my full strength, I plowed into them and aimed my knee at Riley's groin, bashing his thigh instead. I managed to bowl all of us to the floor. Riley grunted low in his throat and punched a bone-jarring fist into my hip. Lights dimmed as my abused body sucked up the red blaze of pain. Ronan never lost his hold on the envelope. My hand slapped against him, his flesh sparking on mine. Nothing close to our previous erratic aural problem, though. More like energy scouting for an alternative fuel source, finding it, and struggling to test it out.

Two guards closed in on us. The drugged guard touched

my hand. A zap of electricity zinged between us, and I jerked away, trying to crush my magic. Surprise quickened my pulse as I realized from his electromagnet pattern that he was another Scrambler. Where did Riley find all these illegal Scramblers?

Klepto Riley swore up a streak in a parody of Ronan and extricated himself from beneath me. I guess the wormy, rotten apple didn't fall far from the poisoned tree. He snagged a needle off the desk, the plunger no doubt filled with his special deadener cocktail.

I lay halfway on top of Ronan. The cold-blooded look of his jet-flecked eyes killed my stupid wish that he was playing his father. Ronan took advantage of my shock and flung the envelope at his father. Riley caught it midair, and Ronan lifted off the floor, hauling me against him.

"You just signed your death warrant," I said, deadly for his ears only, my rigid body quaking my rage and fear against his lethal hardness.

"I'm already dead," he grumbled.

"Not dead enough for me." In one swift movement, I spun around and kneed him. Lucky for him, I flinched and my knee slammed halfway into his thigh. I absorbed the jolt to my spine with a shudder. "Your ridiculous little opinion has been noted."

"Damn, Aria." His arms dropped away from me. He staggered, his foot slipping on the thick geometric-patterned rug.

I backed into an unoccupied corner of the room, listing against a Roman pedestal displaying an exquisite hand-enameled genie bottle. A plaque beneath it read: *To Ronan, may all your wishes come true. Love, Mom.*

Several more guards joined the party and even Zoe had crashed the Caveman Ball. One henchman strong-armed her, holding a scary-looking gun pointed at her temple.

Riley salivated over my mother's papers represented inside the envelope, a shit-eating grin on his face.

"Beautiful." He beamed at me. "Think how much fun the three of us will have together with access to Forbidden sorcery."

"Think how much fun you'll have dying." I matched him smile for smile.

Ronan tottered toward me, halting outside my personal bubble of space, as if he actually gave a damn about me. Something recognizable flickered in his wintry eyes, then dissipated into the pond scum he'd become.

"Take Ms. Marino out and kill her," Riley said as though ordering a pizza.

"No!" I lunged at him. Ronan and the guard shoved between us, pushing me back.

A strangled roar erupted out of Zoe as she writhed in the grasp of the guard holding her. Red-hot fury and fear obscured the freckles across her nose and cheeks.

Magic plowed through my brain mass, shoving it aside to open the gates to the molten flame, feeding on Riley's words. The pressure of the deadeners continued disintegrating in the turmoil. New energy derived from the Rift ballooned inside me, and I didn't think anything could keep it at bay for long. I merely needed to wait it out, but not while they offed my best friend.

I pinned Riley with a bitter look. "I'll do whatever you want. Just let her go."

Smug satisfaction burst like an elusive Seattle sunrise across his face. The deadener needle didn't leave his hand, as if it provided him with a boatload of protection.

Zoe struggled against her captor, kicking him in the shin. "Aria, no," she wailed.

Unable to face her, I kept my hatred focused on Riley. "Please, I want her released with an untraceable phone and car. Alone." Eventually, I'd find a way out of this hellhole. At least Zoe would be safe, and I'd get answers to the questions torching holes in my brain.

Riley didn't hesitate. "Done."

Muscles rippled along Ronan's powerful arms as he molded his bad arm against his side. "Take Zoe to her room, get her shit, then bring her back."

The Scrambler guard opened the door and Riley held up his hand. "One more thing." He turned toward Zoe. "You'll never see Ms. Walker alive if you talk to the police or anyone else for that matter. Clear the room." Riley addressed the guards, "Carlos, you and Harrison guard the door."

Pensive, Zoe studied my resolute face. Two other guards herded her out, and the door shut behind them with a definitive, life-altering click.

Chaos, panic, disorder. Check. My work here wasn't done by a long shot.

Ronan made a small choking sound. Again, I gleaned nothing from his blank slate or waxen body. *What gives?*

Magic roiled and tingled within me in new ways I'd learn to adapt. It surged and contracted, fighting the room's deadeners, wobbling me on my feet. I plopped on the couch before I crash-landed. Minutes crawled by as we all settled in the cement-thick tension.

Riley leered at me. "You are so much more than your father promised."

"That's because he didn't stick around long enough to make promises on my behalf." I clutched my arm. "Is the turncoat dead or alive?"

Mock sympathy stole Riley's joy. "He came to me in November, loan sharks biting the flab on his back. I helped him regain his feet in exchange for..." he paused and spread out his hands, "...information. He left a wealthy man."

Did I believe a word? Maybe Ronan had lied to me and his father told the truth. Dismayed, I scratched the stinging tattoo on my back, eyeing the syringe in Riley's hands. "You get off on sticking your little prick in people?"

Riley laughed, set the needle on his desk. "Ah, you don't care for my special deadener recipe?"

The double doors reopened. Zoe barreled in, wearing her designer jeans and a form-fitting black sweater underneath her faux leopard jacket. She clutched her purse in one hand and her purple smartphone in the other.

"You sure about this?" She rushed to me, saw my glum look, and halted.

"Your life means more to me than all the cats in the world." I smiled wanly at our private joke. "I'm staying to help with *research*. I have a lot to learn from them about what's going on in my head." I might make a chronic liar out of myself yet. I'd lie up a storm to keep her safe. "I'll be okay."

"What?" she screeched, stamping a spike-heeled boot, slivering her eyes. "What's going on? Talk to me, Blondie." Zoe ate the distance and dug her fake claws into my upper arm. "What can you possibly help them with?"

Ouch. That almost offended me, but Zoe didn't know much about the Forbidden Thirteen, or me, the thirteenth. It left *my* mind batty.

I composed my features before I popped a blood vessel. "I want to stay." Ronan shifted his feet, the tranq gun held ready in his hand. Lowering my voice, I said, "Riley knows things about my father and family I need to learn."

Her freckly skin glided into the pale. "You trust him?"

"I have no choice," I said loud enough for Riley to hear and gloat.

The guards steered Zoe past me. I threw her a grim, apologetic smile. Jagged silence stretched while we waited. The jeweled genie bottle in the corner drew my attention like a lighthouse to a life raft in a foggy sea. Focusing on it helped me control the rage slurping up my endorphins. I itched to hold it, but I wouldn't give Dick-Fuck the satisfaction of knowing I drooled over an art object he or Ronan owned.

A few minutes later, Riley's cell rang to prove that Zoe was free. Relief sagged my shoulders as she sped away alone in a spiffy Mercedes, with instructions to leave the car at the airport.

Riley squandered no time. "How did you open the Rift?"

I shrugged, trying to dial past the static my mind broadcasted. "What Rift?" *What the what?* Why was he asking that if he already knew opening the Rift required two sorcerers?

He tossed back his more salted and less peppered head and laughed. "I guess I'll have to read and find out?" He nodded at the large padded envelope Ronan held.

"Sure, whatev. Maybe your OCD will collide with the Milky Way too." One ace of an idea hid up my cheap fleece sleeve. I'd toss out snark to divert him till the crows came to rest on his roost.

"Ms. Walker, don't you wonder how you and Ronan opened the Rift together?"

The doppelgänger link! Had he not seen Adam at the Rift? Had Ronan told his father about his doppelgänger? My gaze darted from Ronan's vacant face to Riley. Older, leaner, and more distinguished than Ronan, Riley shared the same height and coloring. However, the similarities ended there. Azure colored his eyes in a rounder and softer face that betrayed his emotions, unlike his son.

"Maybe we had help?" Out of the corner of my eye, I saw Ronan's shoulders hitch.

"The only help we had was the ritual in the *Illuminaria* pages," Ronan answered indulgently, flicking his hand at the still-unopened envelope.

He had to be protecting Adam on whatever side of the Abolishment he played. I hoped to hell Adam was okay. I couldn't feel him inside me any longer either. The blasted room blocks or the drugs severed our bond, even though my powers had skipped past the deadeners. Or maybe opening the Rift had changed our triad bond. The thought might have left me sad if I wasn't in my current jam, or if Ronan hadn't sold me to Satan's top dog.

Hunger illuminated Riley's dull peepers. "Thirteen sorcerers. Classic number for magic. Ronan part fae and telekinetic. Only one Forbidden sorcerer and the thirteenth can open a Rift. Are you getting it now?"

Ronan part fae? Silence shut down the static in my mind. Blood drained from my face. "Are you saying I'm part fae too? Big deal I'm telekinetic. I can bend a spoon. Want to see?"

Riley smirked. "Let me tell you a little story." His smirk turned jubilant. "The thirteen Forbidden sorcerers closed the Rifts to the Realm of the Void, as I'm sure Ronan already told you. They conceived the methodology well before the government decided to kill them off. The Forbidden Thirteen had been around long before the governments found out about them. They showed the world how strong they were by killing off any other magic except fae magic and sorcery." I gasped, clutching my stomach. I side-eyed Ronan and watched him blanch. Riley continued as if he didn't just sign his death warrant in my head. "The Void and the Rifts existed well before the Abolishment laws were enacted. The Thirteen used the Rifts and the Void to destroy other magic. But they weren't strong enough to destroy the fae, so they bred with them until they became one powerful race." He lifted a sword letter opener off his desk and picked at his fingernail. "The Thirteen didn't want a sorcerer to unilaterally take it upon her or himself to close or open a Rift. So they created a secret master key, so to speak, one dominant sorcerer who had to work with at least one of the other Thirteen to open or close a Rift. Two who could manipulate all the earth's energies and magic, who would also stand the test of time and dilution. Ancient sorcerers were quite industrious. Their alchemy was incredibly formidable. I thought Ronan and the blood of another sorcerer could open the Rift." He shrugged. "I was wrong." Riley hesitated as if waiting for my mind to turn on.

I digested his stunning story. Whose blood? And did I truly stem from a vicious group of magic killing, half-fae sorcerers? Still unable to comprehend, I deflected. "I think you need to lie down and rest your brain. Those XCrack cigarettes you've been smoking aren't helping much." I certainly wasn't the freak *de jour* master key descendant. Maybe I needed to inhale a crack-laced cigarette to return to my previous life.

He barked out a laugh. "Your ignorance is precious. Mixed fae blood is in your DNA. As the Rift unleashes magic, it will trigger the dormant magic in your blood. The more magic in the world, the more power you'll obtain. In time, the other sorcerers will gain additional powers unheard of in this day and age."

What about the doppelgängers? He knew about them, but acted as if he didn't. I didn't want to tip him off, though. Full-fledged hysteria swirled and blustered in my chest. "I suppose you're the only one who knows this because you have half my *instruction* manual?"

Riley smiled from me to Ronan. "Not the only one."

Rising, I paced around the couch, clutching my throat. "You knew all of it?" I spun toward the defector who'd flipped my life into a hexed hell.

Avoiding my fiery gaze, Ronan tweaked his shirtsleeve and picked at his bandage. "I suspected."

"When?"

"When I grabbed Melisande's laptop from her hotel room. She had much more on her laptop, notes she'd pieced together." Color traveled up his neck. "Things I had heard and read took shape."

"Whose blood did you use?" I asked. My fingernails dug into my throat.

Riled waved a dismissive hand in the air. "That's not important now."

Their wary stares held me hostage. The nightmare had no end in sight. My gaze bounced around the room, begging to find purchase anywhere but on the son of a bastard and the bastard himself. A glint of light from one of the recessed bulbs landed on a matte black object on the floor sticking out from behind a desk leg, hidden in shadows from the desk skirt. Ideas sprayed my mind.

Riley, seeming to sense my panic, gestured at his desk. "Shall we sit and discuss rationally?"

Knowing and fearing the answer, I gave him a belligerent glower. "Just say it. What am I?"

"You are much more than we bargained for."

"You're the *thirteenth*, Aria. Deal with it," Ronan shot out, giving his father one of his black-ice looks. "You're the direct descendant of the most powerful sorcerer who ever lived. The master key."

"The descendant of the most evil, manipulative sorcerer that ever walked the earth." Riley grinned maniacally, scrubbing his hands together.

Hearing it spoken aloud changed nothing, except that my legs weakened. "Okay. I'm listening." Poker became my game as I veiled my face.

They both back-stepped toward the twin guest chairs. A strange emotion crossed Ronan's features, but I couldn't decipher it. He was shuttered to me in all ways. Had I only imagined those few moments of bliss at the Rift? Deception was a capital offense where my emotions were concerned now. I'd invoke the penalty phase later.

I marched to Riley's side of the desk. "May I?" I waved at his chair, itching to see if the object on the floor was a gun. In the frenzy, he must've forgotten about it.

"By all means." He threw me another one of his so-like-Ronan charming smiles. However, the viperous charm didn't con me.

I swiveled the burgundy chair around, perched on the edge of the cool leather, and scooted the chair forward. I snuck a peek at the desk leg by my right foot. *Well, hello, precious.* Excitement quickened my heart, and I schooled my face to contain it.

Subtly, I stretched out my right leg, inched the gun sideways. Avoiding the splashes of cooling coffee, I rested my forearms on the desk and began to dog-ear a business magazine to distract my antsy hands.

Riley settled comfortably into a guest chair. "You have two choices, Ms. Walker."

My eyebrows peaked. "Two. How lucky can an evil girl sorcerer get?" The side of my foot nudged the gun, and I finagled the weapon into position to slide it closer.

"In your case, very lucky." As intimate as a kiss, he smiled.

Get real, pinhead. My return smile hurt my face. "How can I help you?" *Now that you've pulled my plug and stolen my paddles.*

Riley moved the envelope to his side of the desk. I gave Ronan a glare that would deflate the ego of a hyena. He had the unmitigated gall to look ashamed. My anger spiraled my power into a twisted sword. It lurked, leaking past the room's barriers.

"You can voluntarily work with us as a team. I'll give you all the considerable information I have about your true identity, family, your heritage, how to work your magic." Riley paused for effect, spreading out his hands in a gesture I found maddening. "Or I will force your cooperation."

"I want some freedom."

"In due time." Riley's rueful look mocked me. "When I can trust you."

User door number one, or loser door number two? I toyed with an expensive gold and marble pen, sliding it up and down between my fingers. "What if I reject your choices?"

Riley drummed his fingers on the arm of his chair. "You have no other option. What do you think will happen to you on the street? You'll be on the run for the rest of your life either from me or the government. If you don't learn to contain and control your emerging power, there's no telling what will happen to you or those around you. Or to the other Forbidden." He paused for effect. "Your best friend will be dead within the week."

I sucked in my middle and dropped the pen with a clunk on his pristine wood desk. Even though I knew the threat to Zoe hovered over my head, I couldn't mask the blood draining from my face. Should I have warned her earlier? Was she safe now? I had to play out my hand.

I toed the gun within arm's reach. A diversion was in order. "That's a beautiful rug you have. I'd hate to spoil it by tossing my cookies all over it." Two strangled coughs erupted out of me and I clutched my stomach. Spurts of power actually rumbled disconcertingly against my hand, as if I was preparing to hatch fairies.

Ronan leapt up. I held up a forestalling hand. "Keep your distance. I'll use the trashcan." Bent over double, I captured the gun in one hand, and reached for the can. A few more fake gags gave me the opportunity to hide the weapon on my lap. The bottom of my sweatshirt covered the gun in the folds of my oversized pants. It was the real deal, not a stun gun. Ronan's stare drilled into me.

Straightening, I grimaced and smacked my lips a few times for good measure. "False alarm, I guess." Energy shot holes in the shroud of deadeners around me. I drizzled a targeted charge of energy onto Riley and his twitchy hand aped an addict tumbling off the wagon.

He appeared as if he was sinking into an apoplectic fit, mottled face explosion and all. Either he cared more for the rug or me. Who knew?

"You should rest. We'll resume talks later." Riley's arrow-straight back trembled his eagerness against his chair.

I moved the gun into position beneath the desk. "No. I rather adore the idea of cracking your shriveled nuts across your expensive wool rug." I cocked the hammer, the sound excruciatingly audible in the swampy tension.

The man-squirming began. Riley's eyes bulged. Ronan instinctively cupped his package, raising the dart gun at the same time. *Yeah, like that'd stop a bullet.* I barely had time to shower them with a sleepy-time spell. My head thumped in agony, but the magic machines spewed out more happy dust inside me. Not enough to send them to the realm of nightmares, though.

"Drop it." I stood and hoisted the handgun into view. The dart gun fell out of Ronan's relaxed grasp onto the floor.

"Slide it away."

As if he'd been sucking down muscle relaxants, he kicked the gun a few feet with the side of his boot, maxing out the three strikes law to do it. A shimmer of pure electricity sparked in the air between us. *Whoa, Nelly, reel in a hint.* Ronan didn't give any indication he'd felt it.

I skirted the desk and kicked Ronan's gun behind me. Riley drooped in his chair, and I almost needed toothpicks to prop open his eyes.

"What'll it be?" My award-winning smile pained my pinched cheeks.

"Calm down, Aria." Ronan languidly extended a placating hand. Crimson suffused his face, proving his internal struggles against my telekinesis. "There's no need for violence."

I clung to his words, using them as an anchor for my sanity. "Shut it. I ought to bang you down with the tranq gun. See how you dig it."

His mouth remained tight despite the paralysis.

"That's right. I have the upper hand now," I cooed. "So here are *your* choices." I pasted on an indifferent smile. "I want a cell and car, and I don't give a rat's puny ass if you've embedded them with tracking devices. Or my personal favorite, I bury you both where you squat."

"You're not a cold-hearted murderer," Ronan slurred

with quiet emphasis. Not a muscle stirred in his pitiful body.

"Don't bet the fairy dust on it. I learned from the master." I landed an arctic glower on him. "And aren't I the most evil sorcerer imaginable?" *As if. Ants don't even fear me.*

"If you kill me, you won't clear the building." A lock of Riley's impeccably styled hair fell over his forehead. "Nor will you ever learn who you are and what happened to your father. You'll never get your hands on my *Illuminaria*."

Unsuppressed rage stiffened my finger on the trigger. Mention of my father was a verbal F-up. Damn it, I couldn't take down the whole building. I needed more time for my new Catwoman powers to blast apart the barriers. I needed to rescue Kiera and Katrina. Ideas simmered to the top of my head. Scrambler Guard had energy I could borrow and use to leverage him to help me. Whatever drug Riley had him on must be suppressing his energy. It was wearing off, and I think the guy knew it from touching me. At the moment, a game of Russian roulette was in order. A game I was no newbie at besting.

"Then you have only one choice." I lowered the gun and spun the cylinder, listening for the clicks, engaging my mind in their placement. Anticipation spread the warmth of adrenaline, and I stroked the barrel of the gun.

"What if I refuse?" Riley's fingers curled and uncurled around the chair arms. Ceiling lights twinkled on the diamond studded Claddagh ring on his right hand, a ring that looked suspiciously like one my father had worn.

I released the gun's hammer, opened the cylinder, and glimpsed the one bullet. Slowly, I slipped the cylinder in place and spun it. I plucked the figurative ace out of my sleeve and lifted the gun to my head. "Then I'll kill myself, now. Deader than a twice-dead vampire. What'll you have besides a bunch of sorcerers with no master? What if you need to close the Rift? What good will the Forbidden do you if you can't control them? If they don't destroy the world first? I bet dead blood is useless in your dumb alchemy spells."

Riley's eyes darkened as if he'd lost his godhood and his offshore bank account to boot. Pain and guilt swept across Ronan's face. He extended his hand toward me, the ditches around his eyes digging into his skull.

A hard kernel of his magic slammed into my gut. My wellspring opened for him with a welcome-to-the-neighborhood gush of energy. Unable to control my shocked gasp, my legs quaked. Light winked in Ronan's soulless eyes and he blinked swiftly in acknowledgment. *Damn it.*

"Aria, please," he pleaded. "Put the gun down."

I invoked another smattering of intangible muscle relaxants, sliding Riley to the floor in a blithering crumple. Ronan's eyes widened. Shrugging his shoulders back, he leapt toward the desk.

Seconds before my finger engaged the trigger, I used my telekinesis to force the gun away from my head and to aim it at Riley not yet passed out on the floor. The gun went off.

The recoil knocked my hip against the desk. The bullet shattered the genie bottle and breaking glass pinged the room. The blast thundered through my soul, rendered me deaf and speechless.

Despite Ronan's liquid limbs, he dove across the desk. Unintelligible words spilled from his mouth as he knocked my head against the chair. The ecstatic pooling of Ronan's spring-fresh magic within me accompanied the haze of midnight sucking me under.

TWENTY-THREE

S played on the floor, I resurfaced seconds later on the receiving end of a hammering, blinding headache. Both Riley and Ronan were conked out, victims of my sleepy-time magic. Ronan slumped across the desk, and I almost swept the hair out of his eyes, so wanting to return to yesterday.

Magic whipped the air, and dense clouds of it pressed on me. It wasn't the barrier of a deadener, but the mass of fae and sorcerer magic surrounding my core of power. Silvery, golden energy dissolved into my every cell. Untainted, precious magic waited for me to rev the engines. The shock of the gunshot blasted away my shields and opened the floodgates. *Holy doppelgängers, what had we wrought by opening the Rift?*

"Game. Set. Match," I muttered to the silent room.

What happened? The chamber of the gun should've been empty. I'd spun the cylinder and modified the spin with telekinesis, listening for the appropriate sequence of clicks that supposedly emptied the firing chamber. All was in place, but something had gone ass-end wrong. Something inside me deflected the bullet-that-shouldn't-have-been away from Riley. Not even my subconscious would allow me to become a cold-blonde murderer.

I squeezed my eyes closed. From the moment I plunged through the vent, I knew deadeners lined the office. Yet I'd gained control of my magic and busted apart the blocks. It was the reason I managed to shift the gun's cylinder to an empty chamber, or so I believed. Holy crap, the bullet almost marbled the sage walls with my brain.

Strangest of all, Ronan's unsullied magic reinvigorated our bond, solid and irrevocable. Joy streamed through me before I became the virtual victim of an Aria drive-by. When he'd dived for me, he never even touched me before I pulled the trigger. Either bad luck thirteen had struck again or something unfathomable had taken root within me. If what Riley said was true, then denial and I were hooking up. The gun earned my nastiest glare.

I'd done the cylinder movement thing before. At eighteen, Zoe and I had found the key to her stepfather's gun safe. Recently dumped by losers, insanely plastered, we were as depressed as tortillas. It was late and Russian roulette with one blank signaled stupid therapy. I shot at my foot, firing on the empty chamber. Only it wasn't empty, and my telekinesis redirected and slowed the bullet before I shot off my big toe.

The next day, I'd swiped my mom's old revolver out of her trunk and learned to spin the cylinder with my mind, listening for the clinks. A useless trick that only worked on a weapon with a cylinder. Don't ask why I felt the need to play with guns. I wasn't suicidal or anything, maybe arrogant and dumb occasionally.

My first life-threatening episode happened when I was twelve, shaping my warped ideas of invincibility. A car had backed into me as I cycled down the sidewalk. It should've flattened me into a speed bump. At the last second, the driver had hit the brakes. She'd reported never touching the brakes, and I pedaled away without a scratch.

The strange incidences hadn't ended there. I never dwelled much upon the wackiness of my life. Just lucky, I guessed. A paradox, if I'd ever heard one.

I poked my ringing ears and sank onto Riley's padded desk chair. He gurgled from the floor and his eyelids fluttered. I shoved the chair away from Ronan who was responding in one-syllable caveman grunts.

Skin pulled taut over the ridge of Ronan's cheekbones. His paleness magnified the tempest of charcoal flecks in his eyes. For an eye blink, his expression softened, then that blasted hard-ass mask descended. He reached to touch me.

"Back off." I brushed him away and swung my noodle legs over the edge of the chair, aiming the gun between Ronan and his father.

Riley listlessly regained his seating and perched on the edge of his chair once again, shaking his head in confusion.

Energy practically ignited off me. I'd need it to get out alive. Riley would not get his slimy hands on the tools he required and craved to rule the world. Nothing mattered but escaping Little Dick's Pokey with my part of the book and my body intact, including every ounce of blood. Rescuing Kiera and Katrina and getting Riley's part of the book would follow, once I escaped and formed a new rebellion. Ronan's betrayal had forced my hand in a different direction.

My aura circled my head in bubbly shades of pink with bits of green and blue converging on the inner rim. Neither of the Rileys appeared to notice, which meant they couldn't see auras. *Score.* If I needed evidence of the triad bond...bingo. Ronan's aura spun sluggishly around him, blue with bits of pink and green. *Wonderful.* Did I want the traitorous fairy-sorcerer connected to me for the rest of my life? If he were to die, what would happen to Adam? If Adam still lived. Heck, what would happen to me if one or both of them kicked off? How connected were we? How connected was I to the other eleven sorcerers and their doppelgängers, if they existed?

Ronan's flinty, dead gaze never faltered from my face. *Stare long enough and I might perform another trick.*

With the puny deadeners in the room, I should've felt his magic more, especially after our fuse at the Rift. Maybe he wore a bio-energy block just for little 'ole me? I couldn't take the chance of finding out. Any iota of trust in him had disappeared with the Seattle sun.

Exhilaration buzzed down my legs, and I fidgeted discretely, crossing my legs tight to wait out the resurgence of my new power. More magic than I'd ever known flooded me, laughing at the deadeners. And it wanted revenge. I was also hell bent on wiping up the floor with Riley's smarmy mouth.

What was a little extra magic careening inside a body if one couldn't exploit its full potential? Before either Ronan or Riley gained their full composure, I tossed out a heavy wave of energy destined to knock out every living being in the building. If it worked, I might become an exterminator in my next life. Ronan did a faceplant on the desk again, and Riley slowly folded over the right arm of his chair.

I scooped up the envelope and stuffed it down the front of my blouse, tucking my hem into my tight jeans to keep it from sliding out. A cell phone poked out of Riley's blazer pocket, and I snagged it, shoved it into my pants pocket.

Exiting stage left, I jetted down the hallway devoid of deadeners. Why would Riley line his office with deadeners, but install none in the hallways or rooms? Too much reliance on his drug-deadener regimen? Or was I too far gone into the land of ancient, illegal magic to even sense deadeners anymore? Nothing penetrated the ecstatic power cocooning me. The energy erupting from me was so intense it should've annihilated every electronic board within a mile. Maybe I *had* decimated all the deadeners.

Magic flooded me with energy and happiness. Free at last, it knew no bounds, using my mind and body as a vessel to control and harbor it. *Prepare for takeoff, flying fairy-monkeys.*

There wasn't a soul in sight until I rounded a bend and spied two guards still kicking it and flanking the double glass doors to the vestibule at the front. Another set of doors barred the outside world from the devil's den. I skidded to a halt, backtracked, and peeked around the corner. A wrought iron gate, lush lawns, and evergreens dominated the front of the complex. Both sets of doors had security pads on them, plus another set of guards—with guns trained on me.

Just as I was about to send the four a dosage of Aria's Slump 'n Snooze, my pinkies kinked. Shrill alarms drowned my pulse roaring in my ears. Commands rose down the hallways and booted footsteps rushed me from behind. Doors banged shut, locking automatically.

As I turned the corner toward the front doors and Riley's office near the reception area, the first two guards drew their guns on me. Darts shot out, aiming for my torso. A wall of solid, invisible air surrounded me, captured the poisonous barbs, whooshing them away in a cyclone.

Growing power pounded in my veins and swelled every cell of my being. Voices chanted in my head, obliterating the tremendous pressure building. It would be fun learning what new magic I could flaunt. *Like this little number.*

A warrior's cry escaped me as I threw up a wall of energy. I concentrated on disabling the four weapons centered on me rather than trying to deflect a barrage of tranq darts. The multi-zone clocks dotting the granite wall on the left struck thirteen after the hour. Without squandering a moment, I spun in a circle and threw up another electrical gust. Hopefully, that time it worked. Lessons on knocking out battalions of people were on tap when I returned home.

The men sported masks of shock, and they drooped to their knees, weapons clattering to the slate floor. Defenseless as dirt, awareness gleamed in eight sets of hazy eyes. I swiped my sweaty palms down my pant legs. Were they dead? I clutched my chest, having to make myself breathe in, breathe out. Damn it, I wasn't a murderer.

Dazed, I dashed up to Riley's office, my gaze landing on Ronan's familiar hulk heaped on the desk. Eyes closed, his chest moved. He coughed and his legs twitched. I very nearly ran to him, dying to wake him and return us to yesterday. Muscles throbbed in my throat, and I imposed an iron control on myself. Until I understood Ronan's game plan, I had to escape alone.

Alarms beeped on the sliding doors to liberty. I sprinted toward them and touched the lock. It fizzled into a thin spiraling stream of smoke, but the door wouldn't open. Stumbling to the nearest guard, I grabbed the security card clipped to his breast pocket. I slid the access card in the reader and pushed open the doors to my new freedom of chaos.

My footsteps pounded down the stamped cement path cutting the lawn in two, jarring in my ears. No one followed my escape from freakshow hell. Had I incapacitated the whole building? I refused to dwell on what I'd done, and forcibly chased off the eight hundred pounds of horror riding my back. Par for the course, the inconceivable tossed another wrench in my escape plan.

Locked twelve-foot high gates blocked my escape hatch. I slid the guard's card key in the reader on the right and the gates hissed open. I resisted the urge to high-five myself.

Willing my heart to quit trying to break through my ribcage, and to stop dying, I dashed through the gates. Glorious power sang inside me, even as realization whapped me, and my stomach sank with it.

Freedom included the price of confusion.

Half the tools I needed to traverse the Twilight Zone remained behind, along with a fractured piece of my heart.

TWENTY-FOUR

Except for an occasional vehicle, the streets remained deserted around the Dominion Research building. I ducked in and out of bushes and behind cars. My elation tested no boundaries, but I refused to allow it to nail me. Worry for Adam, Zoe, Kiera and Katrina undermined it sufficiently. Ronan's fate even chewed away at my self-confidence.

Had Ronan implanted me with a tracker? Had I killed the electronics in the building? Had I killed my own tracker?

Dizzy from my lingering headache and residual drugs in my system, I tripped on a rock in the landscaping surrounding a poop-brown building. A low hedge tempered my tumble onto waterlogged mulch. Groaning, I rolled against the windowless wall and sat on my knees. The stench of moldy mulch filled my nose, gratefully stealing away my vertigo. Away from all the deadeners, the newly open Rift spoon-fed me adrenaline in the guise of powerful ancient magic, like tiny conquerors marching into my every cell.

I breathed in cold, humid air. Halfway calm after counting to twenty, I plucked out Riley's top bling phone.

Fingers crossed, I dialed Zoe's number. It rang twice before she picked up. "Zoe, are you safe?" I hugged my knees to my chest. "I've escaped."

"Aria!" she screeched. "I'm driving around in this kickass car wondering if I should go to the police, but I'm scared. Can you talk?"

Quickly, I relayed the events of the last hour. "Come get me." I looked at the sign on the side of the unmarked building and the address number was thirteen thirteen.

I shrank deeper into the bushes. *Sweet mother of crap.* It had to be a coincidence, right?

Edgy silence lengthened as Zoe sped away from the building. I kept glancing in the rearview mirror, but nobody had followed me. Had I incapacitated the whole circus tent? Were Kiera and Katrina safe? Should we try to rescue them? Apprehension crawled up my spine in a wide trail of ants.

Zoe veered the Mercedes onto a major thoroughfare. "Where to, lady?"

I didn't know what to do. "Just drive." I rested my head on the headrest, the envelope pressing into my breasts. I wasn't ready to share the contents with her. The less she knew, the better for her safety.

The odor of charred burgers hung onto the earthtone interior, causing my belly to rumble against my recharging power. Not good. My stomach never interfered with my telekinesis. I pressed my hand to my middle, nudging down a wispy thread of hysteria. What was inside me now? What had I become?

"How bad do they want you?" Zoe's shaky voice scared

me.

A tear escaped my left eye and I choked up.

"That's twice. You never cry. It's bad, isn't it?"

Composing myself, I slapped the tear off my face, bitch-slapping sense into me. "I think I'm the Holy Grail that just returned abolished magic to the world."

Zoe skimmed the curb and slammed on the brakes in front of a strip mall of lunch crowd eateries and convenience shops. She thrust the gear into park. Her eyeballs would've popped out of her head if they weren't attached. "You? Klutzy Aria?"

"Thanks for the vote." I straightened in my seat. "Get moving." My gaze darted out the windows. "Go." I pushed her hand on the steering wheel.

I needed a plan. Was Adam in on Ronan's backstabbing scheme? I stared at the phone, my forehead scrunched up. I didn't know Adam's number. My head was so screwed up I couldn't even recall his rich family's last name. Brain massage therapy or a lobotomy sounded golden.

The car roared into traffic, suffering Zoe's lead foot. "Riley won't report the car stolen, will he?" Her long, purple fingernails bit into the leather steering wheel.

I swished my hand, half-listening. "He wouldn't risk it. He'd lose me for sure."

"We need to rescue those other girls, right?" She swung the car down another major street.

"Yes. I can't let them stay there. He'll use them as bait to lure me back the same way he dangled you." Breathing evenly, I closed my eyes to regroup my brain cells. "Did you call your mom?" Zoe lived in a studio apartment over the garage at her parents' house, and her mother had a bead on her whereabouts most of the time.

"Yeah. She thinks I'm on a work trip." Uncertainty wavered in her voice and I hated it. We glanced at each other for a second, a moment of unspoken understanding.

"Did she suspect anything?"

Zoe emitted a cackling witch snicker. "Are you kidding? She was arguing with my stepjerk. I guess she finally fessed up that she'd enrolled the twin twits in private school. He's having a shit-fit about spending the money." She paused, a pensive silence descending. "Should we call the cops?"

"No. We're illegals." A branch of ideas sprouted in my head. I jabbed on the GPS.

"That could be tracking us." Zoe shoved my hand away from the GPS controls.

"I'll take the chance." I punched in the access menu. "They're probably already tracking the car." If I hadn't killed everyone, that is. That spot on my neck tickled, and I rubbed it, not feeling anything beneath the surface. "I think they implanted me with a tracking device."

"What? That's illegal." Zoe smacked her palm on the steering wheel.

I blinked up a breeze to keep from rolling my threadbare eyes. "Like anything they do is legal. Get a grip, Zoe. This isn't fun and games. These people are murderers, kidnappers, who knows what else. They probably kill animals for paranormal experiments."

"Kill the sick bastards!" She tossed back her hair and gunned the car on a clear stretch.

I squeezed her arm. She made a sharp turn, dislodging my hand in the movement. "Did they hurt you?"

"They were decent. Even that dumbass Ian didn't hurt me."

"I heard him slap you."

"I raked my nails down his neck first."

"Seriously?"

She sucked in her bottom lip. "Do you know if he's okay? Riley's other men shot him when they grabbed me. They wanted you hard."

My mouth flapped in amazement. "Why do you care what happens to that creep?"

Her lips softened in an innocent smile. "He's not so bad. He was forced into that life. You know, like the mob, death's the only way out."

Again, I bribed my eyes from rolling into their sockets. "You picked that up with your empathic skills?"

"He was going to make a deal with you guys before Riley's mug-ugly dogs chewed him up."

"Holy cow." He was planning to flip on Melisande. I chewed on a fingernail, the next course after snacking on my cuticles.

"What are you hiding?" she asked with deceptive calm.

She knew me better than I did sometimes. I told her what had gone down at the mission church. "I need my phone." Plus, I needed a magical recharge from the Rift, to feed my waning reserves after my magic show at Dominion Research. I could barely float my hair. The gut feeling that magic still flowed out of the Rift refused to budge.

"Where is it?"

"Washington Park Arboretum." Punching in recreation sites on the GPS, I set the park as our destination.

"I'm not even gonna ask," she murmured, listening to the female GPS voice spew out its first direction.

TWENTY-FIVE

The police had posted temporary "closed" signs along the park's perimeter fence. Regular police and Paranormal Vice Division officers—as evidenced by wicked purple bands around their shirtsleeves—guarded the visitor center gates.

"Keep driving." I clutched the door handle. "Something's up."

"Ya *think?*"

A news van cut in front of us and stopped. Zoe stomped on the brakes, jolting us in our seats. My seatbelt practically cut my ribcage in half. Another van blocked us from behind. Reporters, police, and bystanders surrounded a suited, gray-haired man preparing to give a briefing in front of the visitor center. "Go see what's up."

Zoe unbuckled her seatbelt, her hands shaking. "Are you also wanted by the police?"

"Not yet." I waved her away. "Hurry, he's speaking."

Magic wavered in the air. My aura spiked trying to pull me in the direction of the stone circle, wanting to party at the Rift. Could I risk getting closer to the wild energy with all these people in the area? What would it do to me, to those around me?

Moments later, Zoe shouldered through the knot of bystanders and slid into the car. "A dead area of the park is spitting out tons of paranormal energy." Excitement bristled off her, leaving her voice singing. "There've been reports of people lured to the site, and their ESP abilities—" Zoe froze, mouth hanging open. "Cue the evil organ music. You did it, didn't you?"

I chewed on a torn fingernail. "What?" I stared at her accusingly, or at least I tried to, but I think it came off as a look of contrition.

"Don't you dare spin it. What's going on?"

"ESP abilities skyrocketing?" I finished her sentence softly. "Are people *turning* into fairies and sorcerers?"

"They didn't exactly say, but the milling people were making wild guesses." She leaned slightly forward as if to force the words on me. "Your eyes are glowing."

"What?" I jerked the visor down.

"Oh. My. God. Aria, you've been affected—"

My gargled screech drowned Zoe out as I examined my face in the lighted mirror. A glow edged my eyes and painted my face with a new luminosity. Copper and gold streaks highlighted my golden hair, at least two inches longer than yesterday.

"Uh no. No." A warning wailed in my brain. "I'm not one of them. I can't be." I didn't look like a fairy! Neither did Adam, much. We had too much human blood. I edged my finger around my ears. Normal. Would we eventually change? Had Riley been telling the truth about our fae-sorcerer origins? The contents of my stomach pitched. In case I needed to toss my cookies, I searched the ground outside the car. I might as well hook disposable barf bags on my wrist if this kept up.

Hordes of curious people surrounded our car trying to

get into the park. The SWAT team had arrived for crowd control. Night sank fast beneath a billowing mantle of soaked clouds. The earthy scent of winter-spent vegetation drifted in with the faint breeze ruffling the bare trees. It whispered across my skin, invaded my senses, became a part of me. "We need to get out of here pronto."

Zoe gauged our access space. "We're in the middle of a jammed parking lot. Try again."

"Then we hoof it. We need to ditch the car anyway."

"What's the plan in case we get separated?" Grooves drew her eyebrows close to unflattering unibrow terrain. She hooked her hair behind her ears, a sure sign of her agitation since she hated exposing her ears.

I had no choice but to confide in Zoe further. I might be endangering her life, and I hated that part the most. I trusted her with my life and secrets, though. It wasn't like I had a stack of best friend applications waiting at home. I loved her too much to replace her.

"If I tell you, I'll have to kill you." She received my wicked eyewink.

"Bite me, fairy wench." She whacked my upper arm. "I'm already into this up to my red roots."

"Seriously." My fingers bit into her arm. "Anyone connected to me is in jeopardy. I may end up on the run for the rest of my life to elude the dirtbags who want me alive and jerkoffs who'll want me dead."

She gave a wonky shrug. "I need a new adventure. You know you can trust me. Besides, we don't know anyone else who has two ESP abilities. I want to know where I fit in this creeptastic world."

"No kidding." I linked my hand with hers.

"Damn straight." She banged our hands down on the center armrest. "So what's the grand plan?"

I squeezed our fingers together, released her hand. "If we get separated, contact Adam...Freshfields." I smacked my forehead, finally remembering his last name. "I'm not a hundred percent certain I can trust him, but if he's still alive, he'll help you." The neckline of my sweatshirt tightened. "Use your empathic talent to scope him out first. Then tell him everything that's happened." I plucked on my sweatshirt, releasing the anxiety threatening to choke me.

"Adam Freshfields? The guy voted the number one hottest catch in Silicon Valley under thirty?" I nodded. Zoe's face transformed into her do-I-have-a-date-prospect-for-you gleam. "Oh, this is getting better by the moment." She dry-washed her hands. "What if I can't find him, or trust him?"

Ideas weren't zinging into my head with my newfound superpowers. "Go to the PVD if you feel threatened." Who else could help her? Ronan Turncoat? Hell to the no. "I can't risk finding my phone. It's in the middle of this shitstorm." I hesitated, stared long and hard at her. "Listen and don't ask." I downloaded the book-cover blurb of everything I'd left out earlier.

"Hot damn." A mischievous grin lit up her face. "You're a direct descendant of the thirteen Forbidden sorcerers?"

"According to Riley and my mom, I am the *thirteenth*. The most powerful of them all." I nearly choked up a hairball at the idea.

"Hmmm... Riley thinks you're the master key to unlocking Forbidden magic?" Gears turned in her mind, almost visible in her brightly widening eyes. "It explains a lot about you."

I swatted her arm. "What's that supposed to mean?"

She nibbled on her bottom lip. "Just that I can't always read you when you're unblocked." My eyes bugged out. "Your thoughts waver in and out with your emotions like you're not all there."

She'd never once said she couldn't read me. That's why I kept my thoughts blocked half the time around her. "That's because I wasn't all there," I muttered half to myself. I twisted in my seat, surveyed the park. The crowd had thickened. "We should blend in now."

Using Zoe's phone, I dialed information and connected to Adam's hotel voicemail. "Call me." It was the only message I felt remotely safe leaving.

I reached to jab the door button, but Zoe's grip on my arm stopped me. "You really do have fairy blood in you, you know?"

"Thanks for rubbing it in." The wry twist of my mouth hurt my new perfection. "According to Riley, I have all kinds of funky blood in me."

"They said the Rift energy is reacting to those affected—"

"I know." I mashed my fist against the door. "I sensed it miles ago."

The lines between her eyes became gullies. "I heard a cop yak to a PVD agent that he had orders to arrest any paranormals, and to use *deadly* force on anyone who resists."

"Then I won't resist." I shoved my hair behind my ears, the new length bothering me. "Let's hit it. We're sitting fairies in this car. Riley's men probably aren't far behind, and the police are the lesser of the two hells."

We met at the front bumper. A blast of wintry air shivered down the length of me. My sweatshirt didn't work past sundown. At least Zoe had a leopard wrapped around her.

To our left, a group of college kids milled about in the shadows of twilight. We joined them, skirting the fringes of the crowd. Zoe strode in front of me to run interference. I dipped my head to hide my glowing eyes. A racket of excited and scared voices bounced in my ears, my dread swelling to rocket launching levels. The bitterness of damp asphalt clogged my nose, sending my tail spinning into the stratosphere. A narrow froth of clouds scuttled overhead. Dusk's first stars littered the indigo sky and freed the suffocating hold on my heart. They were the first stars I'd seen since landing in Rainy Town.

Despite my natural skewed sense of direction, the Rift enticed me to the right. I could find it blindfolded. The Japanese Gardens loomed ahead, and the circle of stones nestled beyond it in the out of bounds section of the park.

Zoe's phone vibrated against my waist, and I skipped a step in alarm. The unfamiliar shoes didn't help my natural unluck much, and I stepped into a slurping, oozing mud puddle. *Beep, beep, bad luck coming.* "Hold on." I whipped out the phone, not recognizing the local number. "Hello?"

"Blondie?" Adam's voice splintered. "Where are you?"

Relief untied a knot in the back of my neck. "I'm not at DR if that's what you're asking." Ice filled my voice, which wasn't difficult to achieve since I was freezing my butt off. The night had shot my awakening ability to trust straight to the tar pits. Until Adam gave me something concrete to chew on, I had to nibble. "Have you heard from...Ronan...in the last hour?" I had a hard time dredging his name from the cobwebs in my brain. My heart throbbed in my ears, overriding the din of fearful excitement in the air.

"Yes. He said you and Zoe escaped. You could have killed him, Aria."

More relief trickled warmth through the ice in my veins. What if I had succeeded? I didn't want Ronan dead. "Anyone else?"

"Two guards are sleeping it off at the hospital. They'll live."

A freezing sweat washed that trickle of relief away. Numb, I couldn't speak.

"Aria? You okay?" The agony in Adam's voice radiated through the phone.

"He betrayed me." I choked up. Blindly, I followed Zoe into the shadows of an overhanging evergreen, distancing us from chattering co-eds converging on our space.

"No, not true." Nothing he said dulled my misery. "I'm coming for you. Where are you?"

"How do I know I can trust you? Ronan's working for

his father. He set us up at—" I shut my trap lest I stuck my muddy foot in it. "You weren't there to see him cater to his father." I spat the words out like gravel between my teeth. A gust blew a damp, frigid wind over us, and I cast a nervous glance at the ever-changing sky. "How do I know *you* didn't go Benedict Arnold too?"

Three of the college kids, two women and one man, gathered close. One reached past Zoe and tried to grab my arm.

"She's one of us," the shimmery guy exclaimed.

I caught myself staring at the pale blond guy, noticing the wimpy auras around the trio. I lowered my head, hiding my face. Their energy flirted with mine meekly. Fear surpassed my anger at the invasion of my space, and my gaze darted around suspiciously. "Come get me," I snapped into the phone.

"Where?"

"Washington Park. Near—"

"Damn it. Do you know what's going on there?"

"Thanks for the 411," I whisper-yelled. Wheeling in a circle, I tried to shun the hands reaching to touch the slightest bit of my exposed skin.

Zoe slapped at their arms. "Give us some air here, people."

"Twenty minutes," Adam said. "Can you get to the Rift?"

Mr. Blond tried to grab the phone. I jerked back, tromping on Zoe's toes, slick mud sliding me backward. She clasped my arm to keep my ass from kissing the ground and took a powder on her own butt. "I don't know." I mouthed "sorry," and helped her up. I slicked mud off her behind, leaving a nasty residue on my hand.

"Try. Use the energy to defend yourself. It's off limits to all but the scientists. The energy's raw, so be careful. Stay out of the stones and erect a blocking shield. That'll keep you invisible until I get there."

"How do I do that?" I brushed against the brunette girl. She landed the most beautiful smile of devotion on me. I mean, her teeth practically glowed in the overhead lights. Her waist-length hair feathered my side, several locks twining loosely around me. All of them plucked on my aura, a natural magnetism, rather than an energy suck. Electrical heat radiated off me and they slurped it up. I had become their ray of sunlight. *All hail Aria the Queen of Fae.* As if.

"Aria! You listening to me?" Adam shouted.

His voice lugged me out of my baffled unicorn land. "What? Repeat."

He explained how to erect the fae aural shield. "I owe you my life, Blondie. I'll never do anything to lose your trust." He let out a stilted laugh as though he had a hard time admitting an awkward truth. "I don't know what Ronan did, but we'll straighten it out."

My heart thawed. I clutched the phone so tight my fingers grew numb. Of course, the ice age wind chill factor didn't help. "Just get here, please."

"Move along, folks. Playtime's over." A cop advanced on a group surrounding our gang of fae.

"Let's go." I grabbed Zoe's hand and shoved through the trio. "Excuse us."

"Where to?" the short girl asked.

"You're not—" Could I abandon them here to a fate worse than death, if not death? After all, they *were* dead fae walking. Hell, I was the greatest felon of them all. I always wanted to be *somebody*, but I guess I should've been more specific.

I handed the phone to Zoe, the text message champion. "Give up your phone numbers. Then skedaddle before you're arrested. Don't tell anyone what's happening. I'll be in touch."

Their auras wavered in relief and harmony. They rattled off numbers, and Zoe's thumbs blurred on the screen.

A man shouted "hold up" behind us.

"Over there!"

A beam spotlighted us, and a crew of news people rushed over. They'd spotted us, sitting fairies on a log, and our niche of the park lit up like Christmas tree town. *Let the games begin.*

I pushed Zoe from behind. We bulldozed through the crowd, the three fairies scattering in the opposite direction. Someone tugged my sweatshirt, then my mud slick shoes slid, and I fell forward. A large mass bashed me onto the soggy grass. I stuck out my arms to take the brunt of the hit and to keep grass stains off my face, but the force blasted the air out of my lungs. The brute rolled off me, and I sucked in air.

Scores of people talked excitedly. Zoe screamed street gang slurs at a PVD officer. A cop grabbed my wrists and wrenched my arms behind me. Fire licked my shoulders.

"Get up." The cop with a New York accent heaved me to my feet as though I were a toothpick. I wished I was a unicorn so I could stab my horn up his ass.

Someone slapped deadener cuffs around my wrists. A spark of my energy snapped to attention and laughed at the rinky-dink technology. I spat out a blade of grass stuck on my lip. It tasted faintly of dew. Why did I know how dew tasted? It wasn't something that'd ever been in my diet.

The three paranormals—fae, sorcerers, whatevers— huddled together, an overzealous cop training a gun on them. A pair of PVD officers drove up in an unmarked van, squealing tires as they braked to an abrupt stop. Zoe disappeared into the heaving crowd.

The New York brute prodded my shoulder from behind. "Walk toward the van."

I frantically scanned for Zoe, but the sea of people had devoured her. Camera flashes exploded in blinding light, and I hid my face in my shoulder.

The Rift's magic invigorated me, waltzed across my skin, recharged my batteries. My ninja Catwoman powers increased with every passing moment. Dubiously, I followed the mental instructions for the shielding spell Adam taught me. Where he learned it was beyond my comprehension. The air wavered, thick, shimmery. Each time I shifted a limb, air solidified around me and a thin veil shielded me. Digging deep, my magic shorted out the electronic wrist cuffs. Invoking the final words of the invisibility spell, I scampered for an opening in the crowd. A strange mix of energy coursed through me, sweet, pure, earthy. It was more robust, more recognizable than before.

"Son of a bitch," my cop brute yelled. "Where'd the fairy freak go?"

"Asshole, go gargle some bleach." I backed into an open space and waved my arms, jumped up and down, but caught no one's attention.

The three fae stood shaking in fear and anger at the rear of the van. I dashed toward them and brushed against the short girl, sensed acceptance in her touch. Amazement wiped the fright from her eyes.

"Shhh. I'm not here," I murmured, enjoying the airy sensation of invisibility.

The other two averted their faces as the detaining PVD officer opened the van doors. Like lightning, I touched each of their cuffs. The deadeners popped and smoked but no one noticed in the darkness encroaching on the winds of trouble.

"Run when you can," I said in the girl's ear before zooming away.

Diversion time. I shouted, "Hey, fuzz balls." Careful not to bump into anyone, I dashed around the area. I touched a couple of dimwit cops, feathering my fingers over their hands. They reached for me, missed, pointed their guns at nothing, yelled and cursed as I baited them.

Pandemonium broke out, and the sharp smell of anxiety and testosterone clouded the air. I was having way too much fun by the time I realized the three fairies had disappeared.

"See ya, bozos." Light as a leaf on a lick of wind, I jogged into the dark park. Shimmering ghost trees hid me as I searched for Zoe's distinctive red hair and leopard jacket.

Night settled on the area, a moist mantle bogging down the air, but headlights, beams, and camera flashes set the darkness back into the early gloom of twilight. Tree limbs rustled and snapped. Wind swirled dead leaves into the air, shifting into a whirlwind of nervous mauve above my head.

"Where are you, Zoe?" The tired trees of winter absorbed my whisper. Maybe they'd arrested her for smacking a cop, something she'd do in a heartbeat. I wandered closer to the crowds and searched. Nothing.

I counted to ten, calmed my breathing, praying she was okay. Time wasn't spinning backward. Adam and I would have to return to hunt her down. I had no idea what to do about the three fairies or the others that undoubtedly had materialized in the midst of the awakening fae-sorcery from the Void. One crisis at a time.

I rushed toward the stone circle. No GPS required. Magic chased over my skin in a long, slow possession. It tugged on me like the mother ship towing a spacepod, even as I vacuumed the vapor trails of magic inside my center of power.

Who was doing the possession? The Rift or me?

TWENTY-SIX

Magic flooded me with the most enchanting serenity, a sense of belonging inside myself and in my life. I felt immortal, old as the universe, young as a newborn baby. Lazy spring afternoons, summers abloom with reckless abandon, air freshened with sultry promises, melting, sugary. I wanted to lap it up, bottle it, and take it home. Also my new tattoo sizzled in answer to a bizarre silent plea.

I ached for Ronan, the man who'd saved me in my apartment, the man who'd opened up a world I never knew existed, a world I fit into for the first time in my life. The sorcerer of my heart. Half of the two beings I loved so very much, each in different ways. Ways I still hadn't reconciled within myself, a fairy and a sorcerer who made up the whole of the doppelgänger. The realization left me reeling, and pain became an ember in the core of my heart. I had to force my mind off him and his potential betrayal. We may never go back to yesterday. The future was my true path, wherever it carried me into this dangerous and exciting world of the Forbidden.

Canary crime tape roped off a broad area around the Rift. Biohazard and no trespassing signs hung every twenty feet. An electronic fence emitted an electrical hum that vibrated in my ears. Floodlights illuminated each quadrant.

Several people wandered inside the marked zone, holding electronic gadgets, taking notes and readings. I remained outside the invisible fence and strode closer to a short, thin man scrutinizing the screen on a handheld device. A tall, chunky redheaded woman approached him, peering into her tablet, searching for her own cluestick. How much did these people know about the banished magic and the Forbidden?

I shifted to the left and stumbled over a rock that I swear wasn't there a second ago. I swung my arms to catch my balance.

The two scientists whirled in an excited fluster. "Who's there?" the man's voice squeaked. A series of blips and red lights flashed wildly on his electronic device.

Mindful of the face-busting terrain, I rushed into a planter of winter dormant bushes. They dashed behind me until their gadgets fell silent. The man beckoned to a second pair of scientists and the four consulted notes. I bet it took more than four scientists and lots of toys to figure out the speed of dark too.

Tiny lights bobbed in the air and streaked toward them. The swarm of large fireflies buzzed over their heads, zipped into their faces, zoomed away only to charge them again. The four swatted at the bizarre insects, and I slapped a hand over my grin, stifling a giggle. The glowing buggers wouldn't stop long enough to give me a chance to see if they were bitty fairies. Who knew what had spewed out of the Rift. The Void may have been an incubation farm for all the former magical creatures that ever existed for hundreds of years.

Carefully, I walked into the cordoned off area toward

the stones. Electricity pinched me as my passing killed the ineffective deadener block. *Woe is me.*

"Fairy King, come out, come out, wherever you are." A breeze carried my whisper away.

Hands grabbed my hips from behind, tugging me into a familiar hard body. Air whooshed out of me in a moment of panic before Adam's clean, enticing aura circled me. Wow, he felt awesome, so alive, and real.

"Right here, Blondie," he whispered in my ear, then spun me in his arms.

I melted against him. "Can you see me?" I asked in a low voice. "Are we still invisible?"

"Yes and yes." Adam took my hand in his, raking his gaze from my tousled hair to my muddy shoes. "God, you feel incredible. Your magic's in my blood now."

What else was new? I was a new creature of the magical night. I defied definition. The Twilight Zone was now the Aria Zone.

"What exactly do you feel? Can you use my powers? Are you telekinetic?" Curiosity didn't kill the awe streaking up my back.

"I feel your aura in mine. Your magic enhances my new powers, but I can't draw from you and do what you can. Ronan and I are sharing each other's energy. I don't know how it works." He moved so close we became one, with a huge empty pocket. Ronan, I presumed. Was that how we'd feel with all thirteen sorcerers? What would happen when the others found their doppelgängers? I shut the gate on that mental path and inched backward to view what our magic had created.

Seeing Adam for the first time since we'd restored life to his magnificent body, I couldn't resist giving him the once and twice over. The lord of fae appearance had replaced his death-warmed-over exterior. Even in the glare of spotlights, I saw that his skin tone had deepened into the color of honey. A slight glint radiated from his vibrant, blue-violet eyes. Two beautiful fully formed, but subtle, pointed ears peeked through his thick, silky hair. Did I say magnificent? There must be a better word, but I was firing blanks.

"So, I'm a god now?" I joked, defraying my awe, letting the intangible sunlight wafting off him bathe me in its warmth.

"A goddess." Roses and lightning floated in his eyes. Rays of sunlight burned them away, leaving a rainbow in their wake.

Twilight Zone to Aria: we welcome you to your new loony bin. I clutched his arms to keep my spinning head in the air and my watery knees solid.

"Park's off limits until ten o'clock." A PVD officer's loud dismissal sent my heart skipping. Yellow light washed over us and highlighted the last few people the magic and darkness hadn't chased away.

"He can't see us," Adam murmured close to my ear. "Stand still, he'll pass."

The last three people exited the unarmed gate. I hugged Adam tighter. I couldn't describe the attraction between us, the internal tug on everything good inside me, beyond the realm of normal or human. So different from the hot and cold wrenching confusion Ronan caused. Adam still felt as if he was part of Ronan—his lighter half—so pure and energized. On the flipside, I sensed his individual self apart from Ronan. And I had a feeling his unruly fairy glamour created much of the attraction between us. My head whirled with the array of mystifying feelings.

One thing I knew for certain, my head trusted Adam implicitly. No pinkie twitch warning me away. How far I'd come in the trust department over the last few days. It scared the bejeezus out of me. It also offered me hope that I could leave my insecurities and phobia of forming attachments at the Rift. With Adam—and Ronan—I didn't have to hide my true nature or the bad luck, klutzy Aria.

Two officers swept lights over the area. As the beams hit the landscape, I checked out the miracles our magic had wrought. Formerly yellowed grass had transformed the ground into an emerald carpet. Dead tree limbs glistened lively, dotted with early spring buds. Life had reclaimed old mottled brown trees and bushes. Owls hooted in the tallest trees and small animals scurried among the bushes. The whole site radiated life to both the natural world and the paranormal unknown, a treasure trove of unfathomable magical artifacts.

I grinned up at Adam, who hadn't taken his eyes off me. The lights shut down, painting the air with midnight ink, until a natural faint shimmer rose up from the stone circle. Radiant magic sparkled like multi-hued jewels on the trees and flora. "It's beautiful."

"You did this." His smooth, lilting voice was a slow caress down my body.

"Not without help." I hugged him tight. My heart dove into my stomach. "Zoe!" I clamped onto Adam's arm. "I lost her by the visitor center. Three...fairies were almost captured."

Adam called Jax and instructed him to track down Zoe and to look for any paranormals. After he hung up, we walked away from the energy inviting us closer to Mini-Stonehenge. "Was there a reason you came to the park?"

My teeth chattered and I shoved my hands up my sleeves. Adam shrugged off his leather jacket and wrapped it around my shoulders.

"Thanks." I snuggled into its warmth, inhaling his familiar scent, along with a whiff of sunshine and moonlight. More elemental scents invaded my new world. "I thought the hotel might be watched. I wanted to slurp up some of the energy here while I snagged my phone." I scanned the area. "It's in Ronan's backpack." I nearly strangled on his name. "Hey, what happened to you? I don't think Riley saw you. Did you invoke this invisibility glamour?"

Adam snuck his finger across my lips. "The magic must have naturally shielded me. I hung behind to grab the backpack and cover our tracks."

I shook my fist in his face. "The memo fairy hadn't given me Ronan's plan. He nailed us to the wall. Did you know about his scheme?" The words tasted like dirt in my mouth. I grimaced and swished my tongue over my gums. These strange elemental scents and tastes were becoming irksome. I needed elemental chocolate.

He shook my shoulders, his fingers digging into the leather. "Riley found us through luck. Ronan didn't set us up."

"You're a lap behind the field if you think that." My heel caught on a tangle of vines. A clump of limp leaves cushioned my fall to the ground. I looked at my watch. Seven thirteen. Figures. I scooted off the plant onto the moist grass and crossed my legs.

Adam crouched down. "You seriously think Ronan set us up?"

"Too many coincidences. Why did he really go to Melisande's hotel and hide it from us? Calling his father alone from San Jose? His nasty attitude at the Rift?" I wiped my damp hands on my sweatpants. "That's just the icing on the cake of crap."

"He's not exactly the most open person." He held out his hand. "Let's go."

"Where?"

"To the hotel."

"No." A dead flower received the impact of my fisted anger.

He sighed in frustration. "Why not?"

"It's not safe." I clenched my knees before I permanently deadheaded another flower.

"Do you trust me?" He stroked the back of my hand.

His touch fired tendrils of reassurance through my

heart. I jerked my hand away. "Stop playing fairy tricks on me." In the span of seconds, my instincts and trust began sparring. No romance going on there.

Adam searched my face, his eyes glowing around the rims as if embers smoldered behind them. "No games, Aria." He rose to his full height, towering over me. "I'll never betray you, nor lie to you. Nor have I ever. We clear on that?" His tone brooked no trash talk. "What did Ronan do that's got you all fired up?"

My neck smarted. I jumped up, rubbing the spot, dying to rub out Riley's life as easily. I knew I'd disabled the tracking device inside me when I blasted Riley's campus. Why else hadn't his apemen found me by now? Just in case, I wanted double assurances. "Can the energy here deaden a tracking device?"

Adam's nostrils flared as his face went all Ronan scowly. His hair curled and uncurled like an angry fist.

I tugged his hand but the mountain of fairy testosterone didn't budge. "Let's go."

"It's probably a crap-shoot here, but I bet Riley stuck one in you. Ronan assured me his father wouldn't use the trackers because your innate magic made them useless. A lie, but that's how he convinced his father he still had his implanted after he removed it."

We set off toward a thicket of mist-shrouded trees, ghostly silhouettes in the dim park.

"Ronan implanted the tracking device in my neck." I slipped on a patch of soggy grass. "I'm pretty sure I already disabled it." I touched the puncture, zinging it with a ripple of a brain wave, and felt nothing to indicate it was still live.

"What?" Adam stopped abruptly, holding my arm steady. I guess he'd gotten used to my natural bad luck and wasn't taking any chances of my ass kissing the ground.

Birds took flight, squawking, wings flapping. Although I hadn't noticed anything unusual in the gloom, apprehension prickled across my shoulders. "Keep moving."

We continued trudging toward the trees.

"Was Ronan acting for his father?" Adam steered me to the left into a border of bushes along the trail.

"Who else? I awoke and he was sticking a gun thing in my neck. He flat out told me it was a tracker and don't try to run." A small animal scurried across our path, rustling into the bushes. I hugged Adam's arm closer. "I thought I'd dreamed it until my neck just now burned."

"Was Riley in the room?" We halted within the veil of trees. Branches clicked and creaked above our heads, resembling old bones in a hangman's graveyard.

"Ronan was alone, but the room was audio and video bugged." The faint glow from my glowering eyes extended a few inches beyond my face. "I told you he's playing games. This isn't how this was supposed to go down." My right pinkie twinged. My shoulders tightened. *Stop the world, so I can escape.*

A clatter arose in the brush to our right and we spun toward it. A crunch followed in the same spot, and I peered into the deepening black night. The thickening cloud cover had stolen the last of our starlight.

"Are we still invisible?" I'd released my glamour by the Rift.

"No. I can't hold the glamour for long. My magic really isn't mine, you know. It's mostly Ronan's. You might, but wait until we need it."

"Will mine shield you?" Several pairs of footsteps slogged through the wild park area. A spur of familiarity added a new knot of dread in my gut.

"Don't worry about me."

I stood on my toes and raised my lips to Adam's ear. "It's Ronan."

Did he believe me about Ronan? Did I believe me? My heart twinged and my head ached, battling each other. I squeezed Adam's hand so hard, he flexed his fingers, shaking me off. I dug my shoes into the wet ground to keep from running toward Benedict Ronan.

"Hold it together." He rubbed my back underneath the leather jacket. Electricity tingled along the edges of my tattoo at his touch. "I feel him too. There's more to the picture than meets the eye."

"He was negotiating his freedom with my part of the *Illuminaria*." The envelope helped keep the chill off my midriff. Would I ever see the whole book?

Adam rasped his fingers over his chin. "Invoke the glamour and return to the Rift. We'll use the energy there." We skirted a brick planter filled with stinky, moldy compost.

"I read more of the pages than I shared with you two. I wanted something to believe in that didn't come out of your mouth or Ronan's," I explained as if I was sitting on the witness stand.

"I get it."

"I guess Ronan thinks I betrayed him by holding out. I needed to understand how crucial it was to keep them from Riley's hands. You're right about your magic belonging to Ronan. The doppelgängers alone don't have much innate magic...at least not yet. They pull from their linked sorcerers. It's all in the lost pages."

"Ronan and I figured that out. We never thought opening the Rift would change that aspect of our nature."

I needed to tell him another crucial fact I'd learned from those pages that bothered me to the depths of my soul. "The more magic Ronan uses, the more it will hurt you. It's the cost the sorcerers pay to wield their magic. Eventually, he'll kill you if he uses too much magic."

Adam sucked in a breath. I took his hand in mine, tried to peer into his faintly glowing eyes, but he averted his face. Emotion leaked into his death grip on my hand. "If he dies, you die too. If you die, he loses magic. You two balance each other out in that respect."

Adam scrubbed a hand over his face. "God, what a

mess. What would've happened if we'd closed the Rift, even if it was possible?"

"I don't know. I skimmed the pages, but didn't get a chance to read them all."

A branch snapped in the nearby trees. Adam tugged on my hand.

Stealthily, we made our way to the Rift, trudging away from the thin air of malice nipping at our heels. I only tripped once on my thirteenth step. My aura riled up with my new infusion of magic. I tried to restrain it, but Ronan's lure was too strong and a sliver slipped out, opening a fissure, waving a welcome to the Aria Zone sign. Ronan's power yanked harder. Obviously, the connection between us transcended all things human and earthly. If only I could trust it once again. At that moment, my heart let my head take charge.

"She's here," Ronan said, unmistakably loud and clear, and oh so very near. Was he baiting me, or warning me?

"Concentrate," Adam nearly snarled. "I can't help you with magic until I figure out what I'm doing. You can do it. You're stronger than he is."

"I'm trying," I said under my breath. Tug of war ensued between Ronan and me, weakening my tired defenses. Obviously, he'd regained his magical strength. Strong, recharged, an invisible rope of energy built between us, braided with threads of each other and Adam. Wrestling against Ronan's power, I lost control of my glamour.

The light of two flashlights illuminated me. "There's our wayward master sorcerer." Riley's chuckle grated along my last nerve. "Stun her."

I released Adam's hand so as not to disclose his presence under his faltering cloaking spell. I tore off, bobbing and weaving, distracting their attention. The direction of their voices stemmed from the stone circle so I ran in the opposite direction, away from the card-carrying members of the Buzz Kill Club.

Gopher holes created a tricky path, and I feared busting my butt on any misstep. I leapt behind a cedar to calm my racing heart. Peeking around the trunk, I couldn't make out Ronan or Riley, but Ronan's aura glommed onto me, stroking me from head to toe, melting my insides into wanton syrup. I readied a knockout spell and threw the mental blast at one of the two bodies waving the flashlights. A grunt and heavy thump on the ground tailed my targeted knockout. With all my recent practice, it was much easier to direct my brain waves. I couldn't contain an excited grin. *Take that, you sorry saps.*

My second blast shot forward. An infinitesimal whizzing confirmed the mind toss, but I didn't hear a second grunt and thump. Instead, the energy swerved and boomeranged toward my sheltering tree. I lunged behind the trunk, but the deluge caught me and threw me toward the tree. I thrashed my forehead into the rough bark. Blinding white light exploded in my skull. The electrical wave of magic drove me backward in a gust of prickly wind. My legs flew out from under me and I fell, the back of my head smashing into a decrepit, crumbling log.

TWENTY-SEVEN

In muffled tones, I heard my name in two distinct arias that created a whole song, Ronan and Adam's voices merging as one. Riley stood four or five feet to Ronan's left. Stars gathered in my eyes, but they didn't stop me from blasting a targeted dose of an ass-kicking snooze at Riley. He crumpled to the ground in a quiet thump. The Rift magic was already filling me up, slowly but surely.

I was one giant ache from thudding head to searing footpads. On the flipside, Ronan and Adam's magic mated with mine, a sweet intoxicating joining. Soul deep, heart bound. Warmth and sunlight flooded me, and I had the sense of Ronan and Adam's souls dipping into mine, becoming one with all that we had been, all we were destined to be. Complete again, but at what cost? Who'd spin the hard drive that clunked against my skull? My vision swam in and out of focus. I gripped my head to stop it from careening away.

Ronan knelt beside his father and checked his pulse. "She all right?"

"Don't worry, sweetheart." Adam gathered me in his arms. "Where does it hurt?"

"Where...doesn't it hurt?"

"Can you be serious for once?" Ronan's curt voice snipped my last nerve.

"Go suck on a grenade, Ronan." Whether I felt it or not in my battered body, I managed to instill a dose of animosity in my tone. "How dare you throw my magic back at me? I thought you and Dickard wanted me alive?" I spat the words out, along with a leaf that'd snuck its way into my mouth. The faint taste of azaleas coated my tongue. *Ugh.* I was sick to death of kissing the ground and slurping on nature's bounty.

"You did that?" Adam lashed out, his arm hardening on my neck. His fae magic rose, but mine wasn't receptive. In fact, I wasn't sure I could throw another knockback spell at an ant, unless lucky thirteen decided to kick in.

A sharp stick dug into my knee, giving me the encouragement I needed to stand. I approached Ronan and his father, lying prone on the carpet of woodsy debris. I pulled the gun I'd filched from Riley's office out of my back waistband and pointed it at Ronan. "Move away from him."

Sparing a frown, Ronan stood, held up his hands, and backed away. "I'm on your side, Aria."

My anger refused to be caged. "If I throw a stick, will you leave?"

Adam joined us and removed Riley's weapons, which included a nasty-ass dart gun probably filled with Riley's exclusive magic killing elixir. He tossed me a flashlight, then tied an air band around Riley's wrists and ankles, leaving me suitably impressed with his newfound abilities. Before Adam had a chance to back away, Riley was already coming to. I was also suitably impressed with my newfound control, and glad that I hadn't zapped him to heaven, or in his case, hell.

"Well, well, well." Riley sputtered out the words,

struggling against the invisible bindings on his wrists. "Finally, our fae doppelgänger has arisen." Excitement trembled in his recovering voice. "You did well, Ronan, exactly what I'd hoped for."

"You used me to flesh him out?" Stunned rage thickened Ronan's voice, and he slammed a fist against a tree trunk.

The flashlight beam lit up our little Come to Jesus session. "What are you, the pied piper of magic?" I said, my mouth raring to go off on Dickwad. Ronan deserved his chance, so I bit my tongue hard.

"I suspected you had found your other half after we screwed with the Rift. His identity was a mystery until tonight. His pull on your magic had been too strong over the years. Your abilities were hampered by him, his absence. He's the missing element in my alchemic potions using your blood. So much magic had returned to Earth after the Earthquake Cluster event, the shakeup of the ley lines...so much no one knew about or could even begin to fathom. The return of the sorcerer-fae magic, and the return of the magic of the original twelve doppelgängers, latching onto the DNA of humans with an iota of ancient magic in their bloodlines. Neither one of you would have been born without the other to balance you. Now that you've bonded and opened the Rift, you'll reach your full potential. And you'll live now. So you see, in essence, I saved your lives by coercing you to open the Rift properly."

"Not that you'll be around to see it." I smirked and toed Riley's leg.

"Oh, I will, I will." Riley barked out a smug laugh. "Do you really think you can handle the purest form of magic now saturating the world without me? Like you said earlier, I have your instruction manual, and so much more."

"Please." Sarcasm drew out the word. "The bullshit gauge is going to explode. You think I'm gonna waltz into your Club Lockup and bow to your will?"

"No one has access to the *Illuminaria* or my extensive research except me. Anyone tries and it's all set to self-destruct." Riley's smugness defied his bonds. "I have your mother's blood. Who do you think was the second sorcerer to help Ronan open the Rift the first time?" My mouth hung open and he laughed. "Oh, yes. Your mother, father, and I made quite the team in our university days."

"Fat lot of good it did since you couldn't open the Rift."

"Because she wasn't strong enough. She wasn't the true *thirteenth*."

"Shut it." I stamped my foot on a pile of decaying branches, sending splinters flying into the air. "You're not all that."

"You and Ronan are just like your fathers. Idiots who didn't know any better. You need me to teach you the ways of the Forbidden."

I'd have frozen from shock if I weren't already an iceberg. Adam brushed against me, and a tiny spark of electricity radiated up my arm to my shoulder.

Anger and frustration contorted Ronan's features. "What did you say?"

"You're not my son," Riley said in a conspiratorial tone as if he'd waited to drop that tasty morsel for eons. "You never anticipated that one, did you? As smart as you thought you were, Ronan."

"You...are...not," Ronan toiled to speak through his stunned confusion, "my father?"

"Sorry to disappoint, but your mother wasn't my great love." Huskiness broke Riley's steady voice. "Don't get me wrong, your mother gave me everything I wanted. She gave me you, Ronan, from the blood of the last sorcerers on Earth. Fortunately," he chuckled, "she was pregnant with you before we met."

"Who's my father?" Ronan asked, his voice weak and unsure.

"Maggie refused to tell me, only that he was a

descendant of the Forbidden Thirteen and he walked away from her. The idiot had no clue how valuable you and Maggie were to the world. She later told me he'd died, and she'd burned every last shred of evidence of his identity. There were a lot of things Maggie did against my wishes."

Ronan shook his head. "No. I got my blood from her. She was one of the Thirteen descendants."

"Not so. She was a pathetic half-assed seer and nothing more. Maggie destroyed the evidence she'd collected about the Thirteen families so I couldn't readily locate them. I've spent years trying to find Ms. Walker's identity. Too many wasted years because of that bitch's treachery."

"No doubt because she learned of your plans," Adam spit out.

"I only planned to right the wrongs of an ignorant world. The three of you together will lure the others to me. I can help them attain their abilities. It's all spelled out in the *Illuminaria*. Without the *Illuminaria*, you'll all kill each other. With the Rift open now, there's no stopping the magic from returning to this world. It can't be contained in the Void." Riley continued spilling his secrets as if he chewed on a bargaining chip. "The Thirteen will rule this world. What's wrong with that? How can that be a bad thing?"

"What about my doppelgänger." Once again, I held my breath, waiting to hear what we'd suspected.

Riley chuckled. "Your ancestor ruled the Thirteen alone. She created and invoked the sorcery to destroy the world's magic. She created twelve doppelgängers from the original Forbidden Thirteen."

Fascination zoomed through me like asteroids hurtling toward Earth, fiercer than the fear eating my stomach lining. I couldn't imagine whether Riley told the truth or not. A horrible mix of emotions clamped my mouth tight. Riley was willing to spill, so I zipped it. Then I'd hex his luck for eternity.

Pure hatred toward his father contorted Ronan's face into a dark mask of murder. I knew then that his feelings for Riley had never changed. Had he been playing his father since the moment Riley captured us? No longer one hundred percent convinced he'd betrayed me, I wanted to torture and kill Riley for Ronan's sake.

"You're a piece of work," Ronan ground out. "Do you honestly think we'll go along with your mission now, *Dad?*"

Riley clicked his tongue, his OCD as consistent as the Seattle rains. "Are you going to kill me? You going to call the cops or PVD? You won't have a choice. I've got your blood, Aria's blood. I've still got Kiera and Katrina. I've perfected advanced bio-drugs to keep you in line. The second I'm released, it'll take one keystroke on my cell and you'll be incapacitated. It's worked so far, hasn't it, *son?*"

Had he drugged or controlled Ronan all along? Hope perked up my foggy brain. Rift magic seeped into me, nudging out my headache and lethargy.

"What are you thinking?" Riley asked, remaining immobile as though patiently waiting for our magic to wear off. *Au contraire.*

"Absorbing your fairytale." Sarcasm sparked the bitter edge of my fury when I didn't want to provoke him further. Sue my mouth for being a rule breaker.

"Clever words." His eyes shone brightly in the glow of the flashlight. "It's a shame your parents didn't live to see you grow into your birthright." His gaze swerved to Ronan. "Same with yours, Ronan." He laughed in that smooth, scornful way I found beyond irritating.

Rage and loathing shattered my last nerve. "You scum sucking prick!" Satan would get his asswipe back tonight.

Riley curled up and swung out his legs, knocking me off balance. Arms and legs still bound, he lunged to my left away from us and fell back to the ground on his side. A thick cushion of air stopped my tumble and pushed me away from him. Adam's eyes glowed lavender for a second until he shut down his magic.

"I'll stick a deadener gun up your ass and turn you into a lollipop if you try that again," I said. "Thanks, Adam." I erected an aura shield around the three of us.

During that few seconds of our preoccupation, Ronan had extracted a weapon from his jacket and aimed it at Riley. Simultaneously, Riley pointed a gun at Ronan. His wrists were bound, but his fingers still moved.

"You wouldn't dare." Riley's hand shook slightly. "Your doppelgänger and your *master* Thirteen won't let you. I have the information you need to live. It will die with me, and then you'll have nothing."

"I'll have Aria and Adam," Ronan said, quietly lethal and ominous. "That's enough."

I aimed a surge of magic at Riley, a second late and a credit short.

In surreal horror, Ronan and Riley pulled their triggers. Despite the silencers on both guns, the muted shots boomed in my head. The blasts split a hole in our aura meld, splintering it on the damp breeze, diamond flecks scattering onto an ebony canvas.

A dark stain blossomed on Riley's white shirt below his heart. Slack-jawed, he slumped to his knees.

I spun toward Ronan. Through the dim light, I couldn't see where the bullet made contact. Ronan's face betrayed no pain, but out of the corner of my eye, I'd seen him jerk. Terror skewered me and my mind leapfrogged onward.

Riley thumped on his stomach, his mouth working in his last moments of life. "I...loved you...like a son."

"Yeah, well, fathers don't murder their *sons'* mothers."

"I didn't—"

"I was there, you stupid ass. I saw the whole scene from the closet. I have it all on video," Ronan screamed, waving his fist at his pseudo-father. He advanced on Riley, and I thought he might stomp the bastard's smarmy face into the ground.

My shock knew no bounds. Why would Riley try to kill Ronan? Or had he just meant to hurt or scare him? Too bad stupidity wasn't painful. I wanted to hug Ronan, but I held on to Adam's hand, giving him my strength, curling my other fist against my stomach. Ronan needed to kill his demons his way.

The stain on Riley's chest swelled. Blood dribbled down his chin. "She...threatened...to expose me and you to...authorities." He coughed and spit. "She betrayed us. She deserved to die." He laughed a wet, gloppy sound.

Ronan's rage shot a surge of toxicity inside me. Chaos battled as both sympathy and betrayal clouded the bond that should have been springtime fresh and summertime warm. Instead, I felt autumn's wane and winter's cold.

All of a sudden, someone plunged into the scene, a dark wraith from out of storybooks charging from behind us. My watch beeped its hourly chime, a lonely sound in the hostile park, thirteen after the hour. My left pinkie twitched. *Ah, criminy.* Toe tag time.

"And you deserve this," the hooded man said, cool as dry ice. He stepped forward and shot the Dick Tator point-blank between the eyes.

TWENTY-EIGHT

Ronan sank to his knees, his fist clutched to his chest. I screamed and crawled toward him, clawing the wet grass. Woozy and unsteady, I felt like I was lapping up a river of tar until I had my arms around him. I cradled his shoulders on my lap, wanting to give him all the new life inside me. Adam shoved aside the bullet-shredded jacket, revealing a crimson stain darkening the front of Ronan's gray Seahawks T-shirt. Blood drained out of my face, and I wanted to crawl inside Ronan and give him my life's blood. After all this, I refused to let him die on my watch. Not when I was so close to figuring out which side of the light and dark I would choose. *No. Idiot. Wake the hell up.* I already knew I *was* falling head-over-hard-heels for Ronan, even after he'd shattered my heart when I believed he'd betrayed me.

"Don't die, Ronan," I whispered. *Mom believed in you. I believe in you. I believe in us! Oh, God, there's no us without you.*

The mysterious intruder turned on our huddle, pushing

his hood off. It was too dark to make out his features, but his eyes glommed onto my face and he smiled. "This has been a long time in coming." His voice choked on the words.

The barest Scottish accent served up another side order of crap. Was he another of Riley's bounty hunters from the pool of Celtic diversity?

"Who the hell are you?" Ronan ground out. "You kill me and you got nothing. No bounty. It's over."

"I'm Alexander Caliburn. There won't be any more killing tonight." The vaguely familiar man tucked his gun into his shoulder holster. He crouched next to me and gently applied pressure to Ronan's wound.

Adam grabbed the gun out of the man's holster and trained it on Alexander's chest.

Ronan's throat bobbed. "Aria?" He throttled my name.

Without giving the standoff a second thought, I swept tangled hair off Ronan's forehead. My tears dripped onto his cheek as I bunched his jacket over his wound, applying pressure to stem the bleeding.

"You crying over me? Don't—" A hacking cough nixed his words.

"Shhh…" I caressed his clammy cheek.

"Is he dead?"

"I think so."

His eyes closed, eyelashes a fringe of black against his polar-white complexion. "You're safe now…from him."

"Stop talking, will ya." Bands squeezed my heart.

He opened his eyes. "It's not fatal…I'll live." He tried to move his left hand to feel for the injury, but I took his damp hand in mine, keeping him from moving.

"You're all safe from me." The man turned to me, his hand straying to my cheek. I jerked back to avoid his touch. "I'm not here to hurt you. It was never my intent."

"Then what do you want from us?" I demanded.

Two of Riley's guards rushed us. The moment they took in the scene and the gun in Adam's hands, their weapons hit the ground and hands lifted in the air.

"Get Ronan in the back seat of the SUV. Then we'll take Riley's body to his compound before the cops make their rounds." Adam's authoritative voice belied the anguish emanating off him.

"You don't recognize me?" the familiar stranger asked, emotion heavy in his voice.

"I can't even see you in the dark." I helped lift Ronan to his feet. "All I know is you're the man who fired the killing bullet on Dickhead Riley. You've probably been chasing me all over the freaking West Coast. The bounty's cancelled. Now get out of my way." I pushed at him and it was like pushing a boulder.

"Aria Elle." He held my arm, his grip warm, with something familiar in the way he said my name. Like R.L., like Dad used to so many years ago.

My knees sagged. Dad's dead. I shook my head. "No. You betrayed me. You're dead," I whispered.

"It's not true. It's really me," he said as Adam came between us. The guards hefted Ronan under their arms, blocking my view of him.

"Screw you and the asshole you rode in on." I left him standing alone and ran to catch up to Ronan, Adam on my tail. I blinked back the tears threatening to unseat my tenuous new foundation.

We took Ronan to Dominion Research. A skeleton crew was on night duty, and we managed to skirt around them and avoid their questions. I had no clue what they did with Riley's body. The mysterious Alexander took care of everything. The comfort that act brought me reminded me of my childhood, and I gave in to the security he granted me that night.

Surprise, surprise, Riley's Scrambler guard, the one I

kept sensing the ebb and tide of his magic, Carlos Sorentino, was also a doctor. Unable to trust anyone, Riley wanted his prized biochemist close at hand, guarding him. Doctor Carlos kicked into high gear to patch Ronan up. The bullet hadn't hit anything crucial, and Ronan would only have a short stint of physical therapy to return his arm to peak gun-slinging shape.

Blood and gore didn't bother me, but I grew dizzy at the sight of needles sewing flesh. Reluctantly, I left Ronan in Dr. Scrambler's expert hands to hunt down Zoe. Jax and Jon had found her outside the park where the police had forced her out.

I fell into her hug on the couch in Riley's office. "Did the fairies get away?"

"Did you think I'd abandon them?"

"What'd you do, promise to email the PVD team nude photos of yourself?"

Zoe knocked a finger at the side of her head. "Damn, I could've used that one." She grinned wickedly. "No, I just promised a couple of hot, single PVD officers a night on the town with a redfire frenzy and a blonde-streak bombshell."

"No way!" I tugged on her hair.

"It's not like we have to keep the date. Don't get your thong stuck up your crack." She gripped my arm. "Tell me what happened."

While we waited for Adam, I gave her the peapod version of my escapades.

"O-M-G. Your father's alive?" Tears welled in her eyes and she hugged me tight. "Is it over?" She wiped her face on the shoulder of my borrowed sweatshirt.

"Eew. Stop it." I rolled away and sagged on the couch in a comfortable recline, rubbing my shoulder against the back cushion. "For now."

She hugged her knees to her chest. "It's just the beginning, isn't it?"

The door suddenly swung open. Saved by the proverbial

bell. Adam sauntered in, closed the door behind him with a quiet click. A seductive smile lit up Zoe's face, erasing her unease and fatigue. I think she might have drooled on her hand too.

She listed sideways and whispered, "If you're passing on him, he's mine."

Jealousy pricked my heart before we giggled it off. Certain now that it was Ronan in my blood, holding my heart, usurping that part of Adam's magic, I didn't know how I felt about Zoe and Adam together. First, a bone deep exhaustion anchored me, and I needed to go lick my wounds.

The droopy eyes of fatigue hardly detracted from Adam's return to hotness. He was radiant, perfect, and his eyes twinkled brilliantly. Scenes of flowers, meadows, the sun, moon, and stars flickered in his irises. It almost hurt to look at him, but I couldn't tear my gaze away. A lank of tawny-gold hair lay casually on his forehead. Long, silky tendrils framed his honeyed face. His minty aura swirled above him, and if I peered just right, I saw chinks of pink and blue with a fuse of all three colors on the edges. Life bloomed from him like a field of new springtime wildflowers. Even in his exhausted state, he exuded cheerfulness, and his charm wound around me in a silken shroud of euphoria.

He perched on the arm of the overstuffed chair across from the couch. "We're heading back to the hotel." He yawned broadly.

I sat up. Concern creased the tree bark scrapes on my forehead, stinging my skin. "I want to stay with Ronan."

Adam rubbed the stubble sprouting anew on his chin. "He doesn't want to see you right now."

Hurt and guilt curved around my heart. *Oh.* "Okay."

"It's the drugs, Aria."

I narrowed my eyes. What drugs? Ronan had refused a sedative and almost refused a local anesthesia while the doctor dug out the bullet and sewed him up. Then it dawned on me: Riley's advanced bio-chemicals, advanced enough to eclipse a person's will. Ronan had me so convinced of his betrayal, I couldn't see beyond it. I still wasn't one hundred percent sure of his agenda. I tried to blow the cobwebs from my brain, but the eight legs of emotions spun faster and thicker.

Adam interrupted my near short circuit. "He'll stay and shut the place down and destroy the blood Richard collected from you, your mother, Ronan, and the girls. We already sent Kiera and Katrina home before their families called in the PVD and FBI."

A red, raw cuticle earned my attention. "Is he safe here?" I studied my crusty sneakers, loathing the sight of them. Would life ever be safe again?

"Jax will stay. Jon will return with us."

"Riley's body?"

Adam stood up and held his hands out to Zoe and me. "Everything's taken care of." He paused for a long moment. "Alexander—your father—wants to see you."

"He's not my father," I slung back.

As if on cue, the door slid open and the rat bastard sauntered into the room. There was no mistaking that the man who shot Riley was an older version of the father I remembered, the man formerly known as Patrick Walker, a name as fake as my own. Salt sprinkled his thick brown hair. His slightly flared nose and the rare blue-green eyes matched mine. The telling evidence was the round scar on the back of his right hand and the emerald and diamond Claddagh ring he always wore. He had burned himself working on his car a year before abandoning his family.

The fit and trim man had taken off his hooded jacket, exposing expensive slacks and a button-down shirt underneath. I think his Rolex probably cost more than my car. Had he lived a life of luxury while Mom, Granny, and I had scraped by?

"Can we talk alone?" he asked, his gaze sweeping past me to Adam and Zoe.

"They can stay." Zoe and Adam surrounded me, my wingmen in a burgeoning sea of the unknown.

He gestured at a lone chair next to the couch before taking a squat. "Sit."

My gang and I sat rigidly on the couch. Not that I was obeying him, my knees were about to turn to mush. My anger had become a limp noodle instead of a steel rod.

"Spill it. You left. I heard you were dead. Now you turn up as Alexander Caliburn. What gives?" I lashed out.

He scrubbed his hand over his face, plucked on the familiar goatee. He looked young for his age, despite the shallow lines fanning his eyes. "Your mother and I agreed this was for the best. She knew I was leaving. I'm sorry I had to do it that way. We thought it best that you hated me so you didn't try to track me down. Your grandmother wasn't so keen on the idea and had written me off."

"Yeah, no kidding." I snorted. "She freaking hated you till the day she died. Who does that to her own son without a valid reason?"

"Preaching to the preacher." His eyes never strayed from my face. "I stayed away to protect you, to draw others away from you, to throw them off. I was there at significant events, at your graduations, even at some of your public birthday parties. I killed the couple who abducted you from the mall in Las Vegas when you were ten."

"What? I didn't do that?" My mind shot back to that day. The man in the park had cupped his hand over my mouth so hard I thought I was going to die. Then they gagged me and wrapped tape across my mouth. I'd lost control of my telekinesis and thought I'd caused their car to veer off the road to slam into a tree. I'd walked away without a scratch while they hunched over in the front seats conked out.

"That's why your mother moved you to the Bay Area.

Riley had located you in Vegas. The couple worked for him. Even back then, he was looking for anyone with magic. He didn't know who you were, though. He was just hunting anyone with extreme ESP, hoping they were one of the Forbidden Thirteen."

I remembered the incident that triggered our move vividly. I was at the mall for my friend Laura's birthday party. Some boys were taunting us. They started harassing Laura, calling her fat names, making rude oinking sounds. I shut three of them up with simultaneous threads of telekinesis to their brains.

Growing warm under my father's scrutiny, I swallowed hard and waved my hand at him to continue.

"A few years ago, Melisande Aguirre infiltrated my team and stole the half of the *Illuminaria* we'd managed to piece together, which we kept in a separate location. She handed it over to Riley for a king's ransom and her loyalty." He held up his hand to forestall our shocked responses. "The entire *Illuminaria* belonged to your mother. It was supposed to remain in the possession of the thirteenth. That was your mother." He paused for elaboration. "Now it's you."

I rocked forward, my face in my hands. "Screw me now," I whispered. "Mom was trying to fly under the radar by shunning anything to do with the paranormal. She feared the laws and so much more. After what'd happened to the couple in the park, I feared them too." *I feared me.*

"I played cat and mouse with Riley for years to keep him off you and your mother's trail. I drew his people all over the world with false leads, never able to lay my eyes on him as he remained underground. I formed a team to protect you and the others. The team has been in place since the Rift first shifted the year of your births. Once Riley got his hands on the book, everything spiraled out of control. I found out he had your mother's blood on ice, taken during our college days in Ireland. He used it with Ronan's magic to screw up the Rift. I set up the deal where he supposedly paid me off, to get access to his compound. He killed one of my best men, who sacrificed himself for the task by taking my place in a ruse to get inside the compound. He's the father of Matt Barlow, one of the Thirteen. Matt's safely living in our new secure compound in the Santa Cruz Mountains, not far from Adam's house." Adam and I traded shocked stares. "His father knew what was at stake for all the kids if Riley got even one of them under his control outside of Ronan. Especially you. You have the potential to call them all to you. We had to stop him at all costs." He scrubbed his face. "Unfortunately, Ronan's mother was collateral damage."

"What about my mother?" My voice sounded small and squeaky. "Granny Elle?"

"Accidents as far as we know, honey." His face blanched, and his voice grew croaky. "I'm so sorry. Your mother's accident happened before Riley discovered you were in the Bay Area, before we beefed up our security."

"But your man Barlow gave up Aria's identity and whereabouts." Adam shoved his long, thick golden hair over his shoulder as if it bothered him.

"He must have broken under Riley's torture. We'll never know. He was a good man who went to any length to save his son...and Aria." His voice softened. "We gave Riley false leads. It was just a matter of time he'd find Aria through her magic. It's too strong to hide under his detectors. He had his people and electronic detectors stationed around the world. All Aria had to do was walk down a street near a detector and bam. We're still learning the full extent of his reach."

My stomach gurgled, and I sucked in a few deep breaths to still the blooming ache. "Why didn't you just come forward once Riley sicced his dogs on me?" I demanded, having a hard time feeling out his motives.

My so-called father rose and began pacing the room. He

toed aside pieces of the broken genie bottle that'd exploded during my earlier escape. "Riley had you tailed, bugged, you name it. If he even suspected I was alive, it would have blown my cover. I couldn't protect you or the others if that occurred. Your security has been my number one goal since before you were born. I refuse to jeopardize that."

Confusion reigned supreme inside me. I rubbed my temples until a knock on the door served up a side order of reality.

An unfamiliar man entered, carrying a silk-wrapped package the size of a large book. "We got it out of the safe without incident." Alexander accepted the package and dismissed the man.

My father stepped toward me. Adam tensed and I patted his knee. He'd remained silent for the newest tale to join the fairytale tome, and I appreciated his protectiveness.

"This belongs to you." My father set the package on the coffee table. "It's the original *Illuminaria* with the English translation."

Wide-eyed, I ogled the wrapped book. "Except for the missing pages."

"Except for the pages your mother kept separated. We knew the Rift had fractured and either she or you would need them to control it one day."

"How did you get it out of Riley's safe?" Adam touched his fingertips to the cloth. "He said he had a self-destruct device on it if anyone but him tried to open it."

"Only if his fingerprints weren't used to open the safe." Alexander's implication sent a cold crawl of detached body parts up my spine.

Reverently, I peeled back a corner of the smooth cloth and unearthed the illuminated manuscript cover. It was as old as Earth, the edges slightly worn, oils fading the colors of the cover and dirtying edges of the pages. It was beautiful and full of life. I rewrapped the silk around it again and hugging it to my chest, I rose off the couch.

More of the upside down world insanity sank into my bones and I shuddered. Zoe stood and took Adam's hand. They waited, staring at me as I fixated on the multifaceted amethyst, sapphire, and emerald genie bottle pieces twinkling beneath the overhead lights.

Finally, I leveraged my tired and sore butt forward. I picked up a piece of the rainbow glass the color of Ronan's eyes. Thankfully, no one said a word. I was hardly able to explain the unearthly attraction to the genie bottle myself, so why spend my last brain cells to decode it for them. I clasped Adam's comforting hand.

In the corridor, the tug on my aura fought the huge part of my heart that belonged with Ronan. The other part of my heart let Adam lead me away. I think Adam's doppelgänger bond to Ronan would always be a part of me. I'd eventually learn to deal with it. At that moment, all my thoughts centered on Ronan, and *his* magic dominated our triad.

Silent, my father trailed us out of the building, his guards in tow. I was grateful for the chance to dwell on all I had learned that night without him pressuring me for something I couldn't give yet. In time, I think I'll rekindle my love for him.

The king-sized hotel bed was as close to heaven as I'd seen in days. After a quick bath, I donned one of Ronan's extra-large T-shirts and spritzed on his cologne, taking a deep breath of him. I cranked up the heat and snuggled into the sumptuous pillowtop mattress. Zoe began squawking a song in the shower. I stuffed a plump pillow over my head and groaned. *Add to shopping list: duct tape.*

The door swished open, Fin dashed into the room, leapt onto the bed, plastering her furry body against my side.

Adam followed the pooch's path to my heaven. He'd

showered and donned a pair of sweatpants and a white T-shirt, smelling fresh and crisp of soap and shampoo, which enhanced his various underlying scents of the fresh outdoors. He perched on the edge of the bed, resting his hand on my leg.

"I missed you, Finny." I scratched the preening pup's head.

Adam patted Fin's haunches. "Maybe someday we'll find out her story."

"Maybe now she'll start growing." I tweaked the pup's ear, wallowing in her happiness.

The shower door opened and Zoe's rendition of new alternative rock thankfully trickled down the drain. Birds were safe again from the off-key screeching.

Adam leaned forward, his face close to mine. "Sleep tight." He gave me a chaste kiss on the forehead. "See you in the morning."

Yawning, I slipped beneath the covers again. "More like evening." I grabbed his wrist before he moved away. "You're okay now?"

"Would you let me sleep with you if I told you I hurt like hell?" He grinned.

I squeezed his hand and let go. "You couldn't handle the two of us." His laughter followed him into the lonely depths of the other bedroom.

Zoe swept out of the bathroom in a cloud of steam and jasmine. "Can I stick my jewelry in your safe?" she asked much too loudly. "Oops, sorry. You asleep?"

Exit sandman. "Not *now*."

"How can you sleep with that delicious fairy next door?"

"Watch me." I shoved the pillow over my face.

"You're no fun." She fake-pouted. "What's the combo?"

The question gave me pause to think, so hard it hurt. Ronan had broken into the safe, not that my choice of combination was much of a secret to someone who knew me the way he did. Had it been an act on Ronan's part? Or had he seriously tried to bargain for his freedom at my expense? Or was it his father's drugs? My baffled mind refused to ignite and I pushed out a weary breath. Reality would return with the sun...er...clouds tomorrow. "If it's not already open, it's thirteen, thirty-one."

"Well, that's sure original."

"You'd never have thought of it yesterday."

Zoe proceeded to keep the dead awake as she rustled in the closet. The lock clicked open. Fin growled, and I absently pet her.

"You know you have things in here," Zoe's oh-so-intruding voice called. "Hmm, now this is interesting." Curiosity never killed Zoe. Papers crinkled.

"What the—" I thrust the covers off, buried Fin beneath the heavy jacquard, and jumped out of bed. Zoe rushed toward me with a large padded envelope dangling from her hands. We butted heads.

"Oww." We groused in unison, rubbing our heads, giggling.

My pulse revved up. I snatched the envelope out of her hands, stared at the pages inside. Holding them to my chest, I sprinted toward the familiar envelope I'd taken from Riley's office and tossed on the desk after we'd arrived in the suite. I peeked inside to find it stuffed with photocopies of Riley's *Illuminaria* pages copied from Melisande's tablet. Ronan had faked out his father with his own book. "Oh. My. God."

All my doubts fled. My decision became even more final. Would Ronan feel the same after all that had happened?

TWENTY-NINE

Magic, murder, and mayhem were hell on the body. I believe I'd connected all the dots of my bruises possible to connect. Twelve hours after we'd arrived at the hotel, I left the bed better than I'd felt in forever. Zoe and Adam were talking and laughing up a riot in the living room. I wasn't jealous. Well, maybe a tiny part of me wanted to bitch slap her to San Jose. I think they were totally into each other, and if I couldn't have Adam, then I wanted Zoe to have him.

Honestly, I was glad Adam was taking everything so well. What long-term bond and head-trips would the doppelgänger hunks suffer? At some point, I too would have to deal with my own familial issues. Adam told me my father planned to remain incognito until I was ready to deal with him on my terms. More of my animosity toward him slipped away.

I strolled into the bathroom, stripped off Ronan's T-shirt, and gazed at my luminous skin. The bruises, scrapes, and cuts that had colored me like a rainbow were a distant nightmare. Fae magic had healed me faster than a snake shedding its skin. Had I also gained fae immortality? Were the fae really immortal? The nagging thoughts drifted away. I twisted my torso, scrutinized the vine growing up my back. One ebony thorn sprouted out of the bottom right of the vine above my butt crack. A reddish purple flower bloomed on a stem shooting toward my kidney. It had thirteen petals. "Weird, I tell you, weird."

An hour later, I joined Zoe and Adam eating ice cream in the living room.

They clapped.

"Ha ha."

"Ice cream?" Adam held out his freshly scooped bowl.

I pursed my mouth at the pink, brown, and white glob. "No, thanks. I don't eat ice cream."

"Who doesn't like ice cream?" He shoved the bowl closer.

I hadn't eaten ice cream since my father promised me a hot fudge sundae. "Who said I didn't like it?" Nudging him aside, I veered to the left toward the closet. I plucked out my jacket and wound my purple ombre scarf around my neck.

"Where are you going?" Adam approached, his eyes going all alpha male dark on me. I swear they mirrored a black hole.

I rose on my toes and kissed his cheek. "Running an errand. Is Jon or Jax up for a spin?"

Wariness radiated off Adam in waves of exotic spice cologne and slightly singed roses. "I'll take you. Where?"

"No. Just me and Fin."

His aura prickled around mine, his displeasure an odd sensation I'd have to learn to live with among all his other emotions. Along with Ronan's, I supposed. *Allow me to introduce my selves.*

I stroked his sun-kissed cheek, loving the feel of stubbly life grazing my fingers. "Trust me." He was like the sun, a force that had awakened me. Magic shimmered between us, sprinkled me in happy fairy dust.

He growled low in his throat, borrowing a cue from his darker doppelgänger. "Okay. Just tell me where."

I glided my hand down his chest. Electricity popped warm pleasure in my veins, and I drew away before the allure sucked me in. "To the Rift."

His expression clouded. "It's not safe."

"I'll shield myself."

"Why on earth would you want to go there?" Zoe piped up, clanging her bowl on the coffee table.

"Chill, you guys."

Fin ran circles around me, tail whipping up a whirlwind. I zipped around Adam, grabbed my purse, and called out to the brothers. Knuckles rapped on the door, and Jon didn't bother waiting for an invite.

"Come on, Finny." I blew Adam and Zoe a kiss, grabbed Jon's arm and wheeled him around to the door. "See you later. Have fun," I threw over my shoulder. "Don't do anything you'd feel guilty about later. Love you both." I rushed Jon out and hooked Fin's leash on her collar.

"Two hours, Aria." I turned to see Adam give Jon a knowing look. "If you're not back, I'm coming for you."

Jon fidgeted in his boxers. "Um…she's not gonna knock me out and steal my car, is she?"

I slapped his arm. "Don't be a wuss. Let's go."

I had dreamed during my long sleep and awakened with visions of fairies fluttering in my head. Some had wings in all colors of the spectrum, with or without pointy ears, long hair, or short hair. They had glowing eyes and normal eyes. Short, tiny, tall, human size, bug size. Beautiful, mystical, magical. I was their goddess, little humdrum Aria Elle Walker. Forbidden sorcerer extraordinaire. The big, bad thirteenth.

Jon rolled up the privacy window. Funny guy. He could blast me with his wicked gun, yet he was leery of me. Fin hopped from seat-to-seat as if fleas had landed for a party.

Jamming my fists into my coat pockets, my right hand butted against something small wrapped in a velvet pouch. I plucked out the pouch and a chain fell out. Unwinding it, I discovered a gold, floral-engraved heart locket on a heavy chain, along with my lucky charm focusizer. The note read: *I hope you like. Love, Adam.* Adam had stuck in a tiny picture of Ronan. My heart melted as my eyes teared up. He'd known all along, probably before I even figured it out.

I strung the sparkly box chain around my neck. The gold hung warm against my skin, and I loved the tinkling jingle my pendant made against the locket.

Twenty minutes later, we reached the park. Jon parked behind the familiar copse of ghost trees. Brushstrokes of purple and indigo painted the twilight sky. Rain was a recent memory. I grabbed the flashlight and stuck my phone in my pocket.

The door opened and Fin dashed away. "Fin. Wait!" I scrambled out of the car, grabbing hold of Jon's hand. "Hang tight, please. It might take a while."

"No way." He dug in his heels. "I can't let you go off alone."

I tugged my hand away. "I'll zip it if you do." I tried to sneak past his hulking body, but he pressed me against the limo door. "Please. I'll owe you one," I cajoled. "I swear I won't do anything to get you in trouble. You know I can handle myself."

His expression shifted faster than a professional liar on the witness stand. Scowling, he stepped back and flicked his hand. "Go."

I thumbed on the flashlight and ran toward the Rift. Currently closed 24/7, a few guards made regular rounds. I invoked the wicked cool cloaking spell, just in case. Who knew sorcerers and fairies had such fun magic? No wonder it was illegal.

A moist wind blew through my jacket and my teeth rattled. I reached the stone circle without planting my face into a tuft of grass or a crusty pine.

"Fin, where are you?" I swished the flashlight beam at the ground. A snuffle and snort resonated in the center of the stones. Rift energy wavered at my proximity, and the magically charged air swept my chills away. I slid between the two smallest jagged stone pillars and stood in the center.

Fin jumped against my knees, jiggling on her hind legs.

I laughed. "Give me a minute." I killed the beam and stuck the flashlight in my pocket. "Stand in the center with me, Miss Infinity."

Her small body vibrated against me. I closed my eyes and focused on the energy of the stones, calling on the magic that seemed to belong only to me. The ancient magic hummed in my veins. It filled me with ecstasy, encircled me in glittery sparkles. Arms held upward as if reaching for the stars, I danced and lost myself for minutes, days it seemed.

Awash in tingling electricity, I emerged from my trance. The energy dissipated and floated away in a spray of rainbow fireworks. The ritual was instinctive, something I'd never have thought up in a gazillion years before we'd opened the Rift. I grinned and spun in a circle. "Fin?" No response.

I dug out the flashlight and shined it around. "Where are you?" Dread nudged out a slice of my exhilaration. I heard a slight fluttering behind me, the swish of birds' wings, and flashed the light at the ground.

"Did you ever wonder why I lifted my leg to pee?" a bitty exasperated voice said near my left ear. The tiny buzz saw of wings whooshed close to my head.

"Fin?" I backed up a step and saw...her...naked body

fluttering in a flare of light. Gold spots sprinkled the bitty fairy's gossamer wings of iridescent lavender and pink. She was Barbie-sized and imitated one too. Long, golden hair framed a stunning oval-shaped face, flowing down her perfectly proportioned body. I unwound my scarf and spread it open. She flew into the folds, stood on my open palm, and I gently twined the scarf loosely about her tiny body.

Fin was a shifter-fairy? *Infinity...*

"Thank the Goddess. I thought you were going to freeze me to death now that I've finally shifted out of that Goddess-awful canine body." Her voice held a beautiful, lilting Irish accent. "My name is not Fin. Or Finny. Goddess, do you know what identity issues I've suffered from? It was bad enough I shifted into a bloody puppy, having to lift my leg to keep myself clean. I'll never live it down."

Foolishly, I grinned at her, my excitement banging my heart against my chest. "What...what's your name?"

She straightened to her full height and replied with all the stature her ten-inch frame could muster, "Lorelei Wildwood, Queen of the Wildwood Clan, at your command."

At my command? I held out my index finger and she pumped it up and down. "Nice to...er...meet you."

"I'm very glad to meet you, Aria Elle Walker, Goddess of the Forbidden. I've been waiting for this day since I was a wee child."

For little ole me? I gulped and tilted my head. "How old are you?"

"What year is it?" She laughed a tiny, tinkling sound. "I was twenty-nine when the Rift closed. I believe I'll be twenty-nine forever." She looked all of eighteen.

Carefully, I sat on the warm ground in the middle of Mini-Stonehenge and positioned her on my knee. "What happened back then?"

Lorelei plonked down, dangling her legs off my knee.

"All the fae and sorcerers were summoned and locked into the Void, as you well know. The Rift wasn't here, though." She glanced around and sniffed with no small amount of disdain. "Ireland is far more beautiful than this dreary stink-hole."

"Ireland." Despite the warmth of the circle, I shivered. "How'd you end up here? Of all the crap-ass places, why'd they put a Rift in Seattle? I mean, the sun *never* shines here."

Her wings vibrated through the scarf, and a glow shimmered, then winked out as she took a moment to recall. "They didn't *put* a Rift here. These magical stones have been here since before humans inhabited the earth. Once the scared witless humans and your early ancestral sorcerers began culling the Forbidden toward extinction, some fairy clans tried to hide, knowing the end was coming. Most migrated to this part of the world to live in peace. Mountains were plentiful with uninhabited woodlands. Humans would not suspect fairies to journey to a place so foreign and far away from our origins."

"They knew fairies were here if they were summoned to the Void, right?"

A red glow suffused Lorelei. "Possibly." She gripped my knuckle. "You must understand that other magical beings were in this area. The summoning magic the sorcerers used extended to all beings with magic. Fairies just outlived them all and were the last to go."

I swallowed hard. "What other races?"

She released her grip on my finger. "I don't know specifically, since I was not among those fairy clans that migrated here. They're all gone now. Very little of their magic remained in the Void. Few fae were left even though our magic was dominant."

"Plus the doppelgängers?" Cool air replaced the warmth in the circle.

"Yes, them too." Lorelei shuddered. "Half-fairy, half-sorcerer. The residual magic from the dead is drifting out of the Rift. Eventually, it will dissipate or be absorbed by humans or the Thirteen and their doppelgängers." Her hands fluttered up and down.

Whoa, Nelly. I shrugged the matter to the back of my mind. My brain was going to send me a bounced check charge soon. "Why is Adam so human looking without wings, and you're so tiny—"

"Goodness, I see I have my work cut out for me." She rolled her neck, and I think her hands went to her hips beneath the scarf. "The fae come in many varieties. As for Adam..." she sniffed as if I'd stepped in a smelly, brown pile, "...he's a doppelgänger, born of leftover sorcery. Besides, his blood is too watered with humans and sorcerers." Her shoulders lifted and I adjusted the scarf.

"So how did you and Fin shift? How is that possible?"

"Not much to tell there." Her sweet lilt perked up. "When the original Thirteen were closing the final Rift after sending the doppelgängers into the Void, I shape-shifted for the first time ever into a puppy." Embarrassment suffused her face in a cotton candy glow. "I was a little late to the summoning," she said in a whisper that I strained to hear. "I got locked in the fuzzball's body in stasis, where I've been ever since. I think the sorcerers did it on purpose. Those ancestors of yours weren't exactly the nicest beings on the planet."

"So I guessed. I'm sorry for everything they did to you. I plan to make it right. The Forbidden Thirteen will be a better, moral race of sorcerers than ever before."

"There may be more of my kind hiding in the world. I want to find them." The anguished look on her face stopped my pending inquisition. In due time, we'd hunt down her kind, if any remained or had escaped the Void.

"Can you shift back to Fin?" I asked instead. Nothing escaped the realm of reality anymore.

She placed her hands on her hips and rolled her tiny

luminescent eyes. "Goddess, I suppose. Couldn't those damn sorcerers create their shifters from tigers instead?" She smoothed her hands over her arms, tightening her wings around her miniature body. "I'd rather not test the theory at the moment. I very much like my old self and would rather remain a fairy for another eternity."

I laughed agreeably. "No kidding. But I'll miss Fin."

"Posh." She fluttered her hand at me. "You'll like *me* better." She gave me a beauty contestant smile, eerily similar to my own. Hmmm...I seriously doubt this world was ready for two of us. And I'd have to sound a world alert if I had a doppelgänger hanging around the stargate. She slapped my hand, her teeny palm stinging like a snapped rubber band. "You're not a dog fan, are you?"

Heat rose up my face and I picked at a dormant bedding plant. "Well, I am a cat person."

A papery scraping of leaves in the trees by the babbling brook reminded me of the time. "We have to go before the doppel-wardens send the Starfleet posse after me." I gently lifted her in my hand and rose off the warm ground.

"Put me on your shoulder," she suggested. The perfect idea freed my hands.

Another nearby crinkling and snapping alerted me to a looming presence. A tingle inside my core and the surrounding energy identified the intruder. More relief than I cared to admit to gushed through me.

"Ronan?" I whipped out my flashlight and illuminated him at the outer edge of the stones. "How'd you know I was here?"

"Adam." He held his left arm in a sling against his chest.

Lorelei tugged on my ear teasingly. "The fairy and the barbarian. What's a girl to do?" She giggled and pinched my lobe. I tapped her knee and gave her a sideways evil eye.

"How much did you see?" I asked.

He smiled at Lorelei. "Enough to know *Fin's* still

around." He laughed so carefree and happy, and I fell in love with his laugh...and him all over again. "I'll drive you back. I sent Jon away." He extended his good hand.

Without a thought, I took it, his fingers sliding over mine, entwining and electric. Something inside me melted, and that single gesture vanquished the tension between us. The rich scent of his amber spice cologne mingling with the earthy scents of the Rift area curled through the air, aroused my senses, booted out the last of the dust on my hormones. Everything felt right in the world. My head and heart had quit warring with one another. The convoluted impact of the doppelgänger bond waned with every day as I fell more in love with Ronan.

The cuff on his wrist brushed against me. I lifted our hands and inspected the deadener. "Why the deadener? Aren't you done with your father's legacy BS?"

"For Adam." He stopped walking and peered down into my face. His unfathomable stare drilled down to my southern hemisphere in spikes of heated blood. "When I use magic, it kills a little something inside Adam." I sucked in my stomach. "When he pulls from me, it drains me. We thought it best not to use any magic until we figure it out."

"Oh. I read about that...in the book." I fingered my trembling bottom lip. "I'm sorry."

He shrugged. "Everything comes with a price. Magic's going to cost us big time. At least we have the *Illuminaria* now. It's bound to hold answers."

We began a careful trek to the grove. Needless to say, unlucky thirteen still loved me. I tripped in a hole on my thirteenth step and slapped—almost squashed—poor Lorelei against my shoulder to keep her from kissing the ground with me. Maybe wrapping her in the scarf wasn't such a grand idea. Ronan circled his arm around my waist, snuggled me against his side.

After assuring Lorelei was okay and listening to her high-pitched voice ream me a new one, I turned into him.

"Is your telekinesis back?"

"And more." His voice was a velvet murmur. "More magic than I've ever felt. You don't negate my magic any longer. How about you?"

"Same. More magic than ever." Electricity arced around us and my thoughts fragmented. I jumped with a rush of electricity and tried fighting the dance of magic, the spiral of desire. Despite the deadener, our auras still partied together. Thank the Rift. I think I would die if that part of Ronan and Adam didn't dance with such a vital part of me. "How's your arm?"

"Sore. It's not gonna kill me."

He sported a bandage on the right side of his neck in the exact opposite spot where he'd cut out the tracking device on the left. My mind flinched in anxiety. "What happened to your neck?" I rubbed the spot where my dead tracker was buried.

"I had the second tracking device cut out. That's how my—Richard—kept tabs on us."

"Oh." Another piece of the puzzle slipped into place. "Alex...my dad said Richard had been hunting us all over Seattle, everywhere really."

"He's a good guy, Aria. He did what he thought best to protect you and your mom. He even tried to help my mom escape Richard. They had all known each other in college."

I leaned my head on his arm. "I know. We'll get past all this. I want to know him."

Silence fell like a growing slant of sunlight warming a wintry day. Air sighed around me as real as if it touched my face with warm fingers of life and hope.

"Aren't you going to introduce me to your new friend?" His deep voice broke into the coziness of our companionship.

"How much did you really see?"

"Everything." He angled his head, appraising me slowly. "How did you know to do that?"

I tapped my index finger against my temple. "I'm psychic, remember?" He scowled then grinned, and I about swooned for real, holding onto his arm to keep my knees from buckling. That trickle of desire tormenting me expanded into a rushing river. "Actually, it came to me in a dream last night."

"Hey! Don't mind me. Studmuffin and I go way back." Lorelei laughed, the scarf tickling my neck as she twittered and bounced.

"I guess we do." Ronan snorted. "You peed on my shoe once or twice."

Lorelei glowed pink in embarrassment. "You probably deserved it."

As he'd learned to ignore my barbs, he smiled at Lorelei and let her dig slide. I formally introduced the fairy-shifter to the fairy-sorcerer.

"So why did you come here?" Hope shifted my heart into park.

His arm tightened around my waist. "I had to play the part...with my father, and I didn't get a chance to discuss it with you after we were captured. You were drugged. I was drugged—"

I squeezed his waist. "I know." I touched the piece of the genie bottle in my pants pocket, that little part of him in the gift from his beloved mother. "No need to explain." Relief glided down his side. "I'm sorry I mistrusted you."

"I needed him alive to find the *Illuminaria*. You saw how lethal it is."

"I'm glad we have it safe and sound. My dad wants to take us to his compound. It's actually near Adam's house in the hills." I didn't even want to contemplate how our life would play out next. Goodbye to the lonely days of humdrum. How would the new magic affect my luck?

The welcome to purgatory bells continued to ring for me. We had a whole new set of problems to contend with: legal, moral, and magical. Hunting down the other sorcerers and their doppelgängers. Discovering what magic may have seeped into the world since the ley line explosion and since we'd opened the Rift. Do we blab to the world? Do I hide my head in dreams of Ronan? Alas, the world couldn't banish the Forbidden or the magic any longer. Just let them try.

Ronan stopped and looked down at me, flicking curious eyes at Lorelei. She'd fallen asleep curled against my neck, snoring softly. He cupped my face. "I got what I wanted." His voice faded, losing its steely edge.

His warmth pushed against mine and I snuggled into him. "Which is?"

The yearning for my place in this life slipped away and I leaned into him. He brushed his lips over mine once, eased closer for a deeper kiss. His kiss possessed me, owned me, and my lips quivered in unspoken passion. I'd died and slipped into hunky kisser's paradise. I pressed against him, and sudden white-hot desire spiked my dormant girlie parts. Magic slipped out of me and showered us in sparks. I basked in the sensation of my power flowing into him and reversing course, my gaze riveted onto his storm-tossed eyes. He jerked against me in surprise or shock. As long as he didn't stop kissing and touching me, jerk away. Our kiss was fierce, passionate, and hotter than hell. I wanted every piece of him, body and soul, tainted power and pure, right there on the spot. With that one hot-as-molten-lava kiss, he possessed me. And I let him. Desire and satisfaction smothered my lingering doubts.

He groaned deep in his throat, his good arm pulling me to where air didn't exist between us. My heart gave my head a high-five. Breathless, we drew away, a tiny line of confusion marring his forehead.

I smoothed the line out with my finger and said the words he needed to hear. The words in my heart. "I know who I am and I have this amazing magic inside me. But it's nothing without your magic within me. Nothing without you."

"What about Adam?" His right hand slid into my hair, cupped my neck.

"He'll always be a part of me as long as you are. I'm so lucky to have the both of you in my life. But he'll always only be my friend." I kissed him to seal the deal.

I'd found my purpose and my heart.

"Hey!" Lorelei began sliding down my upper arm. I wrenched away from Ronan and caught her on my palm before she tumbled to the ground, twisted in the scarf. She plunked down in an indignant heap, the scarf tying her wings to her sides. The tiny fairy glanced from me to Ronan, her eyes glimmering brighter. "Got any of those chocolate peanuts? No skimping on the chocolate either."

"In the car." A disconcerted twitch of Ronan's lips revealed a flash of white teeth.

She rolled on her side, propped her head on her hand, and tweaked the cuff buckle on my jacket. "Did I tell you I have thirteen *good* luck gold spots on my wings?"

Well, thirteen was my number.

DID YOU ENJOY
FORBIDDEN THIRTEEN?

Reviews are gold to authors! If you've enjoyed this book, would you consider rating and reviewing it at your favorite online retailer or review site? Your review is greatly appreciated!

To stay up to date on Erin Richards' latest happenings, including new releases, sales, special announcements, exclusive excerpts and giveaways, subscribe to her newsletter at: **www.erinrichards.com/connect.htm**.

CHASING SHADOWS
Psychic Justice Book 1

One kiss, one touch, one night.
It's all she wants to last her forever.

Psychic Juliana Westwood returns home after twelve years and foresees a young girl's abduction. Not only does she risk her life delving into the mind of a dangerous kidnapper, she risks her heart assisting the lead detective and child's uncle...the man she was forced to leave behind. Juliana knows Alex doesn't trust her, but can she endure another twelve years without him?

He deadened his heart against loss.
Her return changed everything.

Alex MacKenzie's wary of reconnecting with the woman who broke his heart, but he knows Juliana can save his niece. As they race against time chasing clues, Alex realizes he'll fight to give Juliana a lifetime of forevers...if the kidnapper doesn't destroy her first.

PRAISE FOR
CHASING SHADOWS

"I loved this book and it never faltered from its action and suspense. The story line not only kept my attention but each chapter was suspenseful trying to find out what the kidnapper was going to do and how Juliana would deal with it." ~*Night Owl Reviews* (NOR 5-Star Top Pick)

"This story was masterfully written and illustrates just what a frightfully good imagination the author has to work with." ~*Fallen Angel Reviews* (5-Star Recommended Read)

"A whirlwind of emotions, twists, turns and rediscovered love will keep you breathless!" ~*Fresh Fiction*

"The suspense will keep you turning the pages... The characters are complex and well-developed and there is never a dull moment in the story. If you love your romance with suspense, this is one book you need to read! 5 stars all the way!" ~*The Romance Reviews*

"This book has so many twists and plot turns that a seatbelt should be required. One of the best romantic suspenses that I have read this year and I heartily recommend to any fans of this genre. This book is just incredible." ~*Love Romances & More*

"This author has done an incredible job of writing a suspense story that is hard to put down....The characters are very complex....The plot is very exciting....This story kept me riveted from the first page until the last." ~*The Romance Studio*

ABOUT THE AUTHOR

Erin Richards lives in sunny Northern California. She writes young adult fiction and adult romance, where you'll typically find her characters in peril, whether based in reality or a contemporary fantasy setting. Magic, murder and mayhem are all in a days' work! In her spare time, she enjoys reading, photography, and re-landscaping her backyard, even though she hates digging holes...unless she's burying fictional bodies! Erin also confesses to a fascination with American muscle cars...and reality TV shows.

Please visit Erin Richards online at:
www.erinrichards.com